THE SHADOW PORTRAIT

BOOKS BY GILBERT MORRIS

THE HOUSE OF WINSLOW SERIES

1. The Honorable Imposter
2. The Captive Bride
3. The Indentured Heart
4. The Gentle Rebel
5. The Saintly Buccaneer
6. The Holy Warrior
7. The Reluctant Bridegroom
8. The Last Confederate
9. The Dixie Widow
10. The Wounded Yankee
11. The Union Belle
12. The Final Adversary
13. The Crossed Sabres
14. The Valiant Gunman
15. The Gallant Outlaw
16. The Jeweled Spur
17. The Yukon Queen
18. The Rough Rider
19. The Iron Lady
20. The Silver Star
21. Shadow Portrait

THE LIBERTY BELL

1. Sound the Trumpet
2. Song in a Strange Land
3. Tread Upon the Lion
4. Arrow of the Almighty

CHENEY DUVALL, M.D.
(with Lynn Morris)

1. The Stars for a Light
2. Shadow of the Mountains
3. A City Not Forsaken
4. Toward the Sunrising
5. Secret Place of Thunder
6. In the Twilight, in the Evening

THE SPIRIT OF APPALACHIA
(with Aaron McCarver)

1. Over the Misty Mountains
2. Beyond the Quiet Hills

TIME NAVIGATORS
(for Young Teens)

1. Dangerous Voyage
2. Vanishing Clues
3. Race Against Time

9803

THE SHADOW PORTRAIT

GILBERT MORRIS

BETHANY HOUSE PUBLISHERS
MINNEAPOLIS, MINNESOTA 55438

Published by Bethany House Publishers
A Ministry of Bethany Fellowship International
11300 Hampshire Avenue South
Minneapolis, Minnesota 55438

Printed in the United States of America by
Bethany Press International, Minneapolis, Minnesota 55438

Library of Congress Cataloging-in-Publication Data

Morris, Gilbert.
    The shadow portrait / by Gilbert Morris.
       p. cm. — (House of Winslow ; 21)
    ISBN 1–55661–689–9 (pbk.)
    I. Title. II. Series: Morris, Gilbert. House of Winslow ; bk. 21.
PS3563.O8742S485   1998
813'.54—dc21   97–45452
                                           CIP

To Leon and Joanne Case

When I think of the faithful servants of God I have known—
you two always come to my mind.
I remember so vividly how in the early days you oft refreshed
Johnnie and me—
and helped us along the way.

GILBERT MORRIS spent ten years as a pastor before becoming Professor of English at Ouachita Baptist University in Arkansas and earning a Ph.D. at the University of Arkansas. During the summers of 1984 and 1985, he did postgraduate work at the University of London. A prolific writer, he has had over 25 scholarly articles and 200 poems published in various periodicals, and over the past years has had more than 70 novels published. His family includes three grown children, and he and his wife live in Texas.

CONTENTS

PART FOUR
OPEN DOORS

HOUSE OF WINSLOW

★　★　★　★

THE HOUSE OF WINSLOW

★ ★ ★ ★

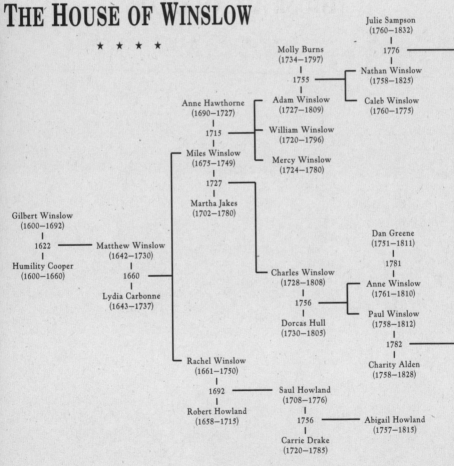

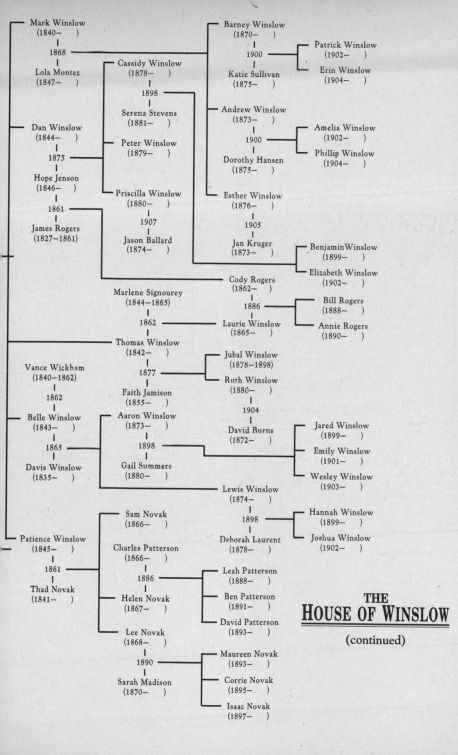

THE
HOUSE OF WINSLOW

(continued)

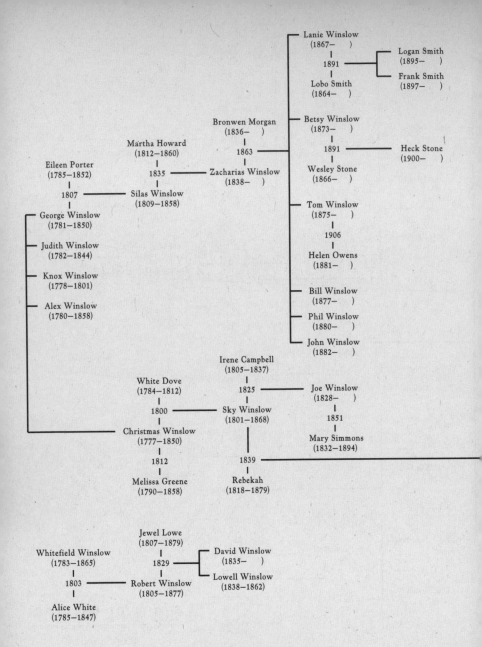

PART ONE

REFLECTIONS OF LIFE

★ ★ ★ ★

CHAPTER ONE

A GLASS OF ALE

★   ★   ★   ★

Cara Lanier, her long, rich brown hair pulled back with a ribbon, the sleeves of her pale blue dressing gown rolled up to her elbows, leaned forward, intent on the canvas before her. Carefully she made one more stroke with her brush, then leaned back to examine her work.

Her small movement was enough to wake the tiny spaniel lying at her feet. He had been stretched out on his side, enjoying the morning sunshine pouring through the tall, mullioned window behind them, his creamy white-and-chestnut coat glistening warmly in the light. Now, however, he thought he saw an opportunity for some attention and leaped into Cara's lap, pushing his way up to lick her face.

"Charley, stop that! You're going to get paint on both of us!"

As Cara's arm moved to protect her paint and the canvas before her, Charley hopped down, but the furry companion was not the least bit repentant. He bent down and gave a sharp bark, begging to play. Then he bounced forward, rump wagging as quickly as it could, dark eyes soulfully pleading.

Cara laughed. "Oh, poor Charley! You get as tired as I do being cooped up in this room, don't you? I just wish I could take you for a walk."

Cara gazed around the room that had become her prison. It was indeed beautiful. At the second-floor front of her family's impressive nineteenth-century townhouse, it was large and high-ceilinged and decorated for lightness and femininity. Two large windows draped in lace-trimmed chintz flooded the room with sunshine on days like today. Cheerful landscapes were placed strategically about the cream-colored walls, and colorful area rugs decorated the highly polished oak floor. A thoughtful hominess was provided by the hand-crocheted spread her mother had made for her four-poster bed and the family pictures, framed in silver, arranged on her dressing table and the fireplace mantel.

This room had once been a place of joy and pleasant retreat. Now, however, after ten years as an invalid, she felt something close to despair as she thought about yet another day within these walls. Her large gray-green eyes filled momentarily with tears. "Oh yes, Charley, I *do* wish I could take you outdoors." Brushing away a tear and giving a deep sigh, Cara scooped Charley back up to snuggle him against her and turned to the window.

The scene she gazed upon was a cheerful one. The spring of 1907 had come suddenly, bringing with it warm breezes. Outside her window she could see children playing in the street. She heard their cries and their laughter and watched for a while, wondering if they were children from the neighborhood. She had lived in New York all of her life in this same house, which had been built in a sparsely populated suburb years ago. Now, however, because of expansion, it was a part of the city itself.

Cara was glad the house had been set back from the road, which now was a busy thoroughfare. She took great pleasure in the small front yard beneath her window. Carefully planned and tended by Henry, the gardener, it offered a season-long treat for the eye—and living models for her paintings. On this bright day, drifts of white, lavender, and purple were accented with bright splashes of yellow and red as tulips, English daisies, and pansies turned their gentle faces to the spring sunshine. Cara glanced back at her painting to see if she had caught this springtime palette of color correctly. She delighted in painting the flowers, although she loved the flowers themselves better than her paintings of them.

Now she watched as a delivery van passed by, a neighbor lady set out in her carriage, and various neighbors strolled down the sidewalk, some walking their dogs. From time to time a passerby would look up and wave at her. She was a familiar fixture in the window, and as the iceman pulled his wagon up to the curb, he called out, "Good morning, Miss Cara! How are you today?"

Cara did not try to answer. She simply smiled and waved

back. Her voice was far too weak to carry out to the street. She watched until he had gone around to the back of his wagon, used his heavy hook to hoist a block of ice to his shoulder, and walked back toward the side entrance, bent beneath the weight of the ice. She could hear their cook, Retta, greeting him at the kitchen door.

Then hearing a tap at her bedroom door, she turned quickly, nudging Charley off her lap. "Come in," she said and was not surprised to see Dr. Geoffrey McKenzie enter. She knew the doctor had stopped in the downstairs parlor first for his usual visit with her father—and to enjoy a cup of coffee and one of Retta's fresh-baked cinnamon rolls before beginning his morning rounds.

"Good morning, Doctor," Cara said and advanced to shake hands with him.

"Weel now, you're looking a little tired today," McKenzie said without preamble. He was a short, thin man with the burr of old Scotland in his speech. Not more than thirty-five, he had a full thatch of rich chestnut hair, and the color was repeated in his short beard and mustache. He looked like a terrier with his busy eyebrows beetling out over his bright gray eyes. Still holding her hand, he took her wrist with his other and grew still while he listened to the pulse. "Not so bad," he murmured, "but you look tired, Cara. How long have you been up?"

"Not too long," Cara said defensively.

"Come now. Tell me how long."

"Well, I did wake up early this morning. I wanted to finish this painting while the morning light was still bright." She reclaimed her hand, then waved it at the canvas. "Do you like it?" she asked eagerly.

McKenzie moved over to the canvas and stood in front of it. He clawed his beard thoughtfully and turned his head to one side for a moment, then nodded. "I don't see how you do it," he said. "It's vurry gud indeed! I think a gift like that has to be born in a person." He sighed and shook his head woefully. "I tried to paint once. It was the awfullest mess you ever saw! But every man to his trade. Now then, let's see how you're doing."

His examination was quickly performed, for Dr. McKenzie had been Cara Lanier's personal physician for the last ten years. He had come from the old country as a young man, and she had grown fond of him, though she was tediously sick of all the medicines and treatments she had endured under his care. Finally when he stepped back and stroked his beard again, giving her a thoughtful stare, she asked, "Well, am I going to live, Doctor Mac?"

"Don't be so frivolous," McKenzie frowned. "No man knows the day nor hour of his death—nor no woman, either."

"Well, if you're right," Cara said, a gleam of humor in her eyes, "it's already settled, so it doesn't matter much. I'll die whether I take your medicines or not." She enjoyed teasing the physician about his strict Calvinist theology. She knew there was not a more thoughtful physician in New York City, and since she saw so few people, apart from her own family, it was always a treat when he stopped in to see her.

"Weel, someday I'll get your theology all straightened out, but for now I'm going to get your body in gud shape."

A cloud passed over Cara's face, and she dropped her head for a moment. "I don't think you'll ever do that, Doctor. Sometimes I think I'll never get out of this room again."

"Now, now, don't talk like that!" McKenzie said quickly. He was very fond of Cara and spent a few moments trying to encourage her. Finally he asked, "Have you been drinking the German ale your father suggested?"

"No, I hate the taste of the stuff!" she said, grimacing.

"I think you should take it. It's going to do you gud."

"How can anything that tastes so awful be good? And whatever you put in it makes it even worse, I think."

McKenzie was taken aback, surprised that Cara had so quickly figured out he was adding medicine to the ale her father had imported from Germany especially for her. *She's a bright woman. Too sharp for any man, I think*, he thought, then defended himself by saying, "We'll try it for another month. Weel you do that, Cara?"

"No, I won't drink another drop of it! It's foul stuff, and it's not going to help me anyway!"

Her voice was flat and determined, and her attitude surprised McKenzie, who was accustomed to a more docile Cara.

"Why, I'm ashamed to hear you talk like that!"

"Did you ever taste that awful ale, Doctor Mac?" She saw his face as he struggled to find an answer. She knew he would not lie, and she also surmised that he *had* tasted it and found it as horrible as she did. "There, you see! You couldn't drink it yourself!"

"I wud if I wanted to get well!" McKenzie replied sharply. Then a wave of sympathy came over him for this woman. From the first time he had seen her, he was baffled by her case. She had

been a vibrant, beautiful young woman. Then, when she was
twenty, she had suffered a serious illness. He had been called onto
the case by an older physician who was a close friend of the family. Both of them had feared Cara would die. To their amazement
she had survived, but then it also became apparent to everyone
that she had lost the bloom of youth and her strength. For the past
ten years she had been confined, for the most part, to this room,
venturing out only on rare occasions. It angered McKenzie that
with all his fine training he could not help her more. From time
to time, he suspected that her illness lay in her heart or in her
mind, not in her body. He examined her carefully with his clear
gray eyes. He wanted to say something comforting but didn't
know what he could say. He knew how much she hated being
penned up in this house, as fine as it was, with every modern convenience. He had heard her talk often of how she used to go for
walks in the parks and the fields in the spring. Even in the fall and
winter, she loved the out-of-doors. As he looked at her, he could
sense her desperate longing to be well and escape the drudgery
of her lengthy confinement.

"I wish you'd at least try it. Your father's set on it."

"I know he is, and I hate to disappoint him, but I will not take
it anymore!"

McKenzie was too wise to argue with her at the moment. He
was convinced she would eventually take the ale. He himself was
not certain of its medicinal value, but Oliver Lanier was a man
accustomed to having his own way. Somehow her father had
heard that the ale was good for patients recovering from long ill-
nesses and had it imported in kegs all the way from Germany. No
one could drink it except Cara, but Henry, the gardener, sampled
it from time to time. McKenzie refused to press the point and patted her shoulder. "Weel now, we'll talk about it later." He looked
at the painting again and said with encouragement in his voice,
"You do so well with your painting. Have you sold any more?"

"Oh yes," Cara nodded, but the success of selling some of her
work seemed not to interest her. "My agent sold four of my paintings at a show in Philadelphia last week."

"Well, I know you must be very proud, Cara. Not many people
can call themselves professional painters."

"I wish I could go out into the garden with the real flowers
instead of only my paintings of them," Cara said.

McKenzie heard the almost desperate note in the woman's

voice, and a sadness rose in him. "I wish I could take you out," he said. "Maybe next week. The weather's turning so nice lately. We'll see."

"Thank you, Doctor Mac. That would be lovely." Cara's voice was flat and without much hope, but she forced a slight smile. "Maybe I'll paint a picture of you." She reached down suddenly and picked up Charley and thrust him at the physician. "Here, let's see how you two look together."

McKenzie did not like dogs, and Charley could easily sense the doctor's displeasure. The two of them looked very uncomfortable. Charley was squirming and growling in his chest, and McKenzie was attempting to keep as far as possible from the animal.

"No, I don't think that would be exactly right," Cara laughed, and her eyes brightened. Reaching out, she took the dog and said, "I'm afraid you and Charley will never be the best of friends."

"I prefer felines myself. I have a cat named Socrates."

"Well, bring him over and let him play with Charley."

"Play with that animal? I should think not! Socrates has too much dignity! He doesn't play!"

The words caught at Cara, and she grew very still. A thought crossed her mind, and then she spoke it aloud. "I don't play either, Doctor. I . . . I wish I could." Then she shook off the thought and smiled faintly. "Come to see me again. Maybe I *will* paint your portrait."

As soon as the doctor had left, Cara sat down on the edge of the bed. Charley hopped up and plumped himself down in her lap. He lay still, content simply to be there, and Cara stroked his silken coat for a long time. Her face grew somber, and from time to time she glanced at the painting, but she had no inclination to return to her work. Finally she lay down on the bed and stared at the ceiling for half an hour. A loud knock on the door startled Cara, and she sat up at once, saying, "Come in," as Charley cleared the bed and ran to the door barking ecstatically.

The door opened and immediately Cara's younger brothers and sisters piled into the room. Six-year-old Bobby ran to Cara and hugged her affectionately, crying out, "Cara, I'm going to the circus!" The boy had fine blond hair and large blue eyes that reflected an underlying rebelliousness. Now he began talking about elephants and lions and tigers, but he was quickly shoved aside by Elizabeth, his twelve-year-old sister, whom everyone called Bess.

"Get away, Bobby!" she said. "I want to tell Cara about my new dress!" With flaming red hair and dark blue eyes, Bess was blossoming into a young woman with promise of great beauty. But she hated her red hair and everything about her appearance, and her emotions were always just beneath the surface, ready to bubble over and explode either in ecstasy or despair. When Bobby tried to shove her away, she immediately began to wrestle with him, the two siblings yelling at each other loudly.

Benjamin Lanier, age eighteen, stepped forward and picked up both children, one in each arm. He laughed over their heads as they protested, saying, "Cara, do you want me to throw these two out the window?"

"No, Benji, let them stand here by me." She smiled up at Benjamin, admiring his auburn hair, blue eyes, and trim figure. He was not all that handsome but had pleasant features and cordial manners. "How can you ever hope to become a minister if you throw children out the window?" she scolded him.

Benjamin gave her an odd look. His mouth drew into a tight line and his good humor fled instantly. "I'm not going to be a minister! I'm going to be a stockbroker!"

Cara smiled wistfully at her brother, who had grown so quickly into the tall young man standing before her. She knew he was only parroting their father's wishes that he become a businessman. Benjamin had been converted at the early age of six and had never wanted to do anything but become a preacher. He especially admired missionaries, and nothing would have pleased him more than the thought of sailing off to China or Africa to preach the gospel. His dream had been a source of continual stress between him and his father, for Oliver Lanier had already ordained that Benjamin would follow in his footsteps and go into business. Now that he was in his first year of study at the New York City College of Business, Benjamin's features, pleasant as they were, revealed a restlessness.

Cara shifted her gaze to her sister Mary Ann, who had come to stand beside her. Mary Ann was a beautiful young woman of twenty-five, with the same blond hair and blue eyes as their youngest brother, Robert, and there was a playfulness in her that came out as she sat down on the bed and hugged Cara tightly.

"I'm going to a party! Millie Langley is getting engaged, and it's going to be a bash!"

"What's a bash?" Cara asked, smiling at her sister's excitement. She loved Mary Ann, who had all of the health and strength and energy she once had. Now, as she held her sister's hand, she said, "I've never heard of such a thing."

"Why, I'm surprised you don't know that! It means a real big party," said Clinton Lanier. At five ten, Clinton was slightly shorter than Benjamin, but he, too, was trim and well built, with rich auburn hair and very light blue eyes. He had an aristocratic face, including a straight English nose and neat features. His sideburns were a little long, but he was clean-shaven. The oldest of the Lanier sons, Clinton had worked with his father since graduating from college and rarely complained, though he did not like the work. Now he grinned down and stroked Cara's shoulder affectionately. "You and I are going to have to go to a bash ourselves one of these days."

"Yes, I'd like that very much," Cara said eagerly. "You find one and get Father's permission, and we'll go." At the mention of their father, Cara saw Clinton tense as if he had been shocked by a jolt of electricity. She had noticed this reaction before. In fact, every one of Oliver Lanier's children feared him except her. Now she said quickly, "Tell me what's going on. I want to hear it all."

Cara enjoyed the next forty-five minutes tremendously. Her cheeks grew flushed and her eyes sparkled as her brothers and sisters drew up chairs, or walked around, or stood over her and talked. Her room had become a sanctuary for them, and despite her father's warnings that they excited her too much, she experienced a joy and a freedom that dispelled the gloom and darkness which had settled on her since she had awakened early at dawn.

Bess nudged Bobby out of the way, saying, "I know what I'm going to be when I grow up, Cara."

"What are you going to be, now? Tell me about it."

Bess's eyes were bright, and she gestured excitedly with her hands. "I'm going to be a typewriter."

"A typewriter?" Cara gasped.

"You don't know that?" Bess cried. "Why, it's a woman who works a typing machine."

"And what kind of a machine is that?"

Clinton stepped in to explain. "You haven't heard of Remington's typewriter, Cara? It's been around for about thirty years, but they've improved on them recently and have made them portable so that more and more businesses are starting to put them to use. It has metal keys on it, and as the keys are struck, it prints a letter in type on the paper held by a roller in front of it. I think it's a great invention."

"Do you have one at the office?" Mary Ann asked.

"No. Father says they'll never last, but I think they will. There are a lot of young women now who operate them in offices all over the country. I told Father we ought to get a typewriter of our own, but you know him. He would really like to go back to the goose quill pen." A sour expression touched Clinton's fine blue eyes, and then he grew quiet.

Cara felt a touch of sympathy for her brother, knowing that he was probably thinking about his frustrations over working with his father at the office.

"Oh, I've got a present for you!" Bobby shouted. "Wait right here!" The six-year-old seemed to have only one pitch for speaking, which was yelling at the top of his lungs. His loud behavior was very irritating to most people, especially his father. Bobby dashed out of the room and soon was back with an object wrapped in brown paper. "Here, Cara. It's for your birthday!"

"But my birthday was two months ago."

"I know, but I only got it this week. I saved my money and Clinton bought it for me. I picked it out, though."

"Oh, it's so nice getting a late birthday present!" Cara exclaimed. "Come here and sit down by me, Bobby, while I see what it is." Cara was surprised and pleased at her younger brother's thoughtfulness. He was a rowdy young boy, but he loved her dearly and was always bringing her some sort of present. Now she opened it and said, "Oh, it's . . . it's beautiful!"

"It's a teddy bear!" Bobby said. "It cost five dollars and twenty-five cents! I saved it up all by myself."

"Oh, you shouldn't have spent so much of your money on me, Bobby."

"But I wanted to. Look, see his eyes?"

It was indeed an endearing stuffed bear with beady eyes and fuzzy fur. Cara stroked it, exclaiming, "Why do you call it a teddy bear?"

"You don't know about that either, Cara?" Clinton asked with surprise. "You've certainly been in this room too long. I thought everybody knew about teddy bears."

"No. Tell me about them."

"Well, President Roosevelt was down in Mississippi and he went bear hunting. His hosts gave him an easy shot at a cub, but he refused to take down the little beast. A fellow named Morris Michtom down in Brooklyn read the story, and he and his wife cut out a cloth bear and stuffed it, giving it moveable arms and legs, and those button eyes you see. They put it out in the window with a sign saying, 'Teddy's Bear.' It sold and they made another one, and Morris wrote to Roosevelt, asking if he could use his name." Clinton smiled and shrugged. "You know Teddy. He said it was okay. So Michtom started making bears, and a couple of years ago they got really popular. Well, there's your teddy bear."

"I love it, Bobby," Cara said. "I'll keep it right here on my bed with me."

"Do you really like it?" Bobby asked.

"I'll always keep it. Thank you very much."

Bess, who was always jealous of any attention that Bobby got, said, "I've got something to show you, Cara."

"I bet it won't be as nice as the teddy bear!" Bobby yelled.

"It will too!" She came over beside Cara's bed and said, "I'm going to show you a turkey trot."

Cara could not imagine what such a thing might be. "What's that, Bess?"

"It's a new dance. Retta showed it to me. She goes out and learns all the newest dances, and then she teaches them to me. Here's the way it goes. . . ."

Bess began to scuff her toes backward against the floor and said, "This is the chicken scratch—and this is the buzzard loop!" She held her arms extended and ran around the room making a noise as much like a turkey as she could. "And this is the turkey trot!" She bounced up and down on the balls of her feet and began craning her neck as gobblers sometimes do. She was so energetic and comical that they all began to laugh.

Cara had long known that Bess was able to mimic almost anything. At first she smiled, then laughed aloud at the antics of the youngster. The room filled with laughter, everyone teasing Bess, who relished being the center of attention.

"What is going on here?"

Instantly Bess stood still and her face went pale. Her eyes fell to the floor and her voice was barely audible as she answered her father. "I was just showing Cara the new dance step . . . the turkey trot, Papa."

Oliver Lanier had opened the door and stepped inside. He was six feet tall and of a massive build with heavy arms and legs that bespoke the strength of a stevedore. His iron gray hair had a slight curl to it, but his beard was almost pure brown. He had stern, cold blue eyes set in a square face, muttonchop whiskers, and now he stared around the room, his eyes settling on each one of his children. They all seemed to wilt before him. "Do you have no consideration at all for your sister's health? I'm disappointed and shocked by your behavior."

"It's all right, Father," Cara said. "I enjoy having them."

"You're not the best judge of that, Cara. You're not well, and you don't need to have this kind of excitement." Lanier's eyes came to meet those of Clinton. "As an older son, I would expect you to have better judgment, Clinton."

"I'm sorry, Father. I just thought—"

"No, you didn't think! You never do! And you, Benjamin—if you conduct yourself at college as you do in your fool ways here at home, I doubt you will ever graduate."

Benjamin's eyes dropped, but he made no reply.

Mary Ann took one step forward and said as defiantly as she could, "Father, Cara gets lonesome in here. We just come to cheer her up."

"You, Mary Ann, would do better to consider ways to make life easier for your sister, not harder. I'll speak to you later!" He glared at her fiercely, then added, "And what's more, young lady, I think it would be entirely inappropriate for you to attend that party you mentioned."

"But, Father—"

"That's my final word!"

Mary Ann's eyes filled with angry tears. She swallowed hard, then looked at Cara before running out of the room, leaving the silence behind her.

Oliver Lanier was not yet finished. He said, "Elizabeth, you and Robert leave at once. I'll have something to say to you later. You need instructions on how to behave around an invalid."

Bobby pulled himself up to his full height and said, "I brought Cara a teddy bear, Papa. It was a birthday present."

"Where did you get the money?" he demanded.

"I saved it up by myself."

Oliver studied his youngest son and shook his head. "You've got to learn the value of a dollar, Robert. Now, all of you leave."

Cara sadly watched as her brothers and sisters left one by one. It disturbed her greatly to see how that familiar look of fear had come into the expressions of each when confronted with their father's sternness. Benjamin gave Cara a parting shrug as he exited last, and after he'd quietly closed the door behind him, Cara turned and said, "I wish you hadn't done that, Father. They were having such a good time."

"You're too tenderhearted for your own good, Cara." Something softened in Oliver's iron expression whenever he spoke with his oldest child. He came over and sat down on the bed beside Cara and put his hand on her shoulder and squeezed it. "You've got to learn to take better care of yourself, Cara. Wild parties such as I just witnessed will not do you any good. If anything, they will bring on a setback."

Cara had been over this before with her father, but no matter what she said, he never changed. A hopelessness settled on her as she shrugged her shoulders and silently leaned back against the pillows.

"Dr. McKenzie tells me there's some improvement in your condition."

"I suppose so. It's hard to tell." Looking out the window, she sighed, then said, "If only I could get outside and breathe some fresh air and get in the sunshine!"

"That will come, my dear Cara. You must be patient."

Oliver's business associates would have been surprised if they had seen the gentleness in his expression just now. Indeed, this was the only time such an emotion ever showed. He had doted on this oldest child of his, and her sickness had been a terrible disaster to him. He had had great plans for her—a proper marriage, children—but her lingering illness had pushed all those dreams aside. For the past ten years he had treated her as gently as his nature would allow.

"The doctor said you're refusing to take the ale I've gotten for you."

"I hate it, Father! It tastes so awful!"

"We all have to bear our difficulties, Cara," Oliver said. His voice grew a trifle more definite, and he added, "I want you to take it before you go to bed. I'll bring it in myself."

"I'm sorry, Father. I just can't drink it anymore. It makes me sick!"

Something about a challenge always stirred Oliver. He had grown up a poor young man and had risen to be a wealthy one. The struggle had been brutal, and he had fought his way to the top. Along the way he had acquired an indomitable habit of sternness. Now he rose and said, "I'll go get the ale right now." Before she could protest, he left the room. A few minutes later he returned carrying a tall glass of the thick brown ale. "Now, I want you to drink all of this, Cara."

"I'm sorry, Father. I just can't," she insisted, shaking her head.

The struggle that went on for the next few minutes was hateful to Cara. She could not remember a time when she had ever defied her father like this, and her reluctance to obey without question stirred something within him. She saw the determined light in his eyes that his enemies often saw and knew that she would never have any peace until she obeyed him.

"Oh, all right! I'll drink it. Just leave it on the table."

"No, I would like to see you drink it now."

Cara understood that he would never accept anything that went against his will. Without another word she took the glass and, her shoulders shaking slightly, drained it dry. Setting the glass down, she settled back on the pillows and lay there silently.

Leaning over his daughter, Oliver kissed her forehead and said with satisfaction, "There, that's my good girl. It will make you better. I'm sure of it."

"Father, can I go out for a walk later today?"

"Not today, my dear. Maybe tomorrow. I'll talk with Dr. McKenzie about it. Now, you rest for the remainder of the day, and I'll come back and read to you tonight."

"Thank you, Father."

As the door closed firmly behind her father, Cara lay there quietly, still enduring the awful taste of the ale. Her eyes went over to the painting, and for a moment she considered getting up and painting some more, but she was exhausted and could not force herself to do it. Finally getting out of bed, she moved over to the window, sat down in the plush chair, and stared out at the bright sunny day and the flowers and the blue skies with puffy white clouds dreamily scudding by. Outside everything seemed bright and cheery, but a dark shroud of sadness wrapped itself around Cara. Though she suffered no lack of anything, she felt more than ever like a prisoner in her own room, and without meaning to, she suddenly began to weep. Tears rolled down her face as she sat there. Finally, she rose and left the window, falling across her bed facedown. Charley leaped up on the bed next to her and began to nuzzle her ear, whining softly. She reached out and hugged him and cried, "Oh, Charley, what am I going to do? What am I going to do. . . ?"

CHAPTER TWO

THE HILLS OF HOME

★ ★ ★ ★

Phil Winslow sat loosely in the wagon seat, relaxing and letting his eyes run over the landscape that stretched out before him. It was a familiar sight, for he had spent the first twenty-four years of his life roaming these hills and exploring the far reaches of the plains that surrounded them. Montana was all he had known until three years ago, when he had abruptly departed for Europe.

As he glanced around, he was impressed with the large expanse of the ranch he called home. After the crowded cities of London and Paris, the skies seemed bigger and bluer, and the open prairie seemed enormous. Now the pale sunshine streamed through the clouds and touched the trees that sloped gently down into the valley where he had been born. Far off, the sharp, pointed mountains pierced the skies, while cottony clouds floated across high above. He thought of the times he had spent in those mountains when the snow was almost waist-deep and he had nearly frozen to death.

Thinking back on his years in this wild land, a smile touched his broad lips. He reached up and fingered his dark brown hair that came down over his collar. *The first thing Pa will say is, "Get a haircut, son!"* He laughed and stroked his face, clean-shaven for the first time in three years. He looked down at his clothes—the same outfit he had donned to make the trip across the Atlantic— a pair of loose-fitting brown trousers, a worn shirt with large sleeves, and an emerald green silk neckerchief tied around his throat. It was not the typical garb for a man from Montana, and he wondered how his parents would react when they saw him. *They'll probably think I'm still trying to dress like some crazy artist*, he thought.

On the wagon seat beside him, the driver began to hum a song. Phil turned to look at him. The tall, lanky man with huge, sunburned and callused hands holding the lines smiled back at Phil and sang the tune out loud—"Wait Till the Sun Shines, Nellie." He had a clear tenor voice, and when he finished the song he turned his shrewd brown eyes back on Winslow, saying, "Guess you don't mind a little serenade?"

"No, sounds good to me. Wish I could sing that well."

"You like that song?"

"Don't think I know it."

The driver, whose name was Nate Fuller, looked at the young man with surprise. He had picked him up walking along the dusty highways and had been struck by the young man's silence. There was something foreign looking about him, and now he asked, "You ain't from around here, are ya?"

"Used to be. I've been gone for a while."

Fuller looked at Winslow's unusual clothing and said, "I could see you wasn't no regular hand round here. You been out of the country?"

"Yes," Winslow nodded. He had been grateful for the ride and now realized he had not paid his "fare" by indulging the driver in the conversation he so obviously desired. "Been over the big water in England and in France for a while."

Fuller grinned and dug his elbow into Phil's ribs. "Hey, how 'bout that? Did you meet any of them French steppers? I hear they're pretty fast."

A smile creased Phil Winslow's lips, and his eyes closed so that they were barely visible. "I guess I saw a few," he said, "which I shouldn't have."

"Man's gotta have his fun when he's young," Fuller protested. "Tell me about 'em."

"Not much to tell. Most of them are pretty homely. Not nearly as good-looking as Montana girls."

"You tell me that?" Fuller was surprised. "I don't know where, but I got the idea that they was some pumpkins."

"Most of them are hard as horseshoe nails. The ones I met, anyway."

Fuller considered the young man's comments for a time, slapped the lines on the backs of the matched bays, and then asked, "What was you doin' over there, if you don't mind me askin'?"

"Don't mind at all," Phil said cheerfully. He turned to cast his eyes around the horizon, then lifted his arm. "Right over that ridge is where I was born."

"Why, that's where Zach Winslow lives."

"That's right. I'm Phil Winslow, his son."

Suddenly Fuller's eyes opened wide in recognition, and he turned to face the man beside him. "Why, shore, I remember you! You used to come to the dances in Grove City, you and your brothers. I heard tell you left. Never did know why, though. Your pa's got a big ranch there, and lots of young fellows would like to step into a situation like that."

"They'd be right, too. My pa has built a fine ranch, and I was a fool for ever leaving it." He hesitated saying any more, then shrugged. After all, the man had kindly given him a ride. The least he could do was to be friendly in return. "I had this idea for a long time that I'd like to be a painter."

"Painter? You mean like paint houses?"

"No," Winslow smiled. "I mean paint pictures. Been making smears ever since I was just a kid. It wasn't that I hated ranching and nursing cows so much," he added thoughtfully, "but somehow this thing was in me, and I just wanted to do it all my life. Most people called me a fool for throwing this all away to go off to Europe to study—probably for nothing."

Nate Fuller shrugged his thin shoulders. "I wouldn't go so far as to say that, Winslow. Now, me, when I was a young feller, I always had a dream somehow of bein' a sailor. Just somethin' about ships that always fascinated me, so I made up my mind to go to sea." He grew silent and his hands were still on his knees. Finally he said regretfully, "Well, look around you. Does this look anything like an ocean? I woke up a few years ago nearly an old man and said to myself, 'One thing I always promised myself was I wouldn't stay here and farm,' and by crackies, I gone and did it!" His eyes were sad as he turned to meet Phil's, and he shook his head. "You're young enough to take a stab at it. You probably won't never regret it. Did you learn how to paint good?"

Phil laughed. "Well, a little bit. Paintings aren't like cows. You *know* you're going to sell a cow, but a fellow could work for a year on a painting and then have everybody walk right by it like it was a street sign."

"You don't say? Well, I'd sure like to see some of those paintings of yours."

"I had 'em shipped over. If you'll stop by my folks' house, you can see some of them hanging on the walls."

"Why, I'll do that."

The two men fell silent, Phil thinking of his homecoming, and Nate Fuller, no doubt, regretting his lost career at sea. Wistfully, Nate began singing his song again. Being a man who never stayed quiet for long, he said, "Guess if you'd been here, Winslow, you'd have heard this song. A couple of years ago it was the biggest thing goin'. I even remember the fella who wrote it—man by the name of Tilser. Think he wrote it for barbershop quartets. It's about clear weather that follows a storm. Then when the big earthquake hit San Francisco last year, he changed it to 'Wait Till the Sun Shines, Frisco.' I guess they was needin' some kind of encouragement after that big quake. Anyhow, he must've made a bunch of money off of that one song. Everybody in the country was singin' it, I reckon."

"I guess I've missed out on a lot in three years. Don't know any of the songs, any of the books that are out, and even less about politics."

"The only politics you need to know is Teddy Roosevelt."

"Do you think he'll run for another term?"

"Can't! Promised he wouldn't! But he's already making noises about who he wants in his place. A fellow named Taft. Don't know nothin' about him, but he won't be no Teddy Roosevelt!" Fuller continued to talk politics until finally the wagon crested a hill. He pointed with his big hand and said, "Yep, there she is. Your pa sure made a nice spread out of it."

It was a beautiful sight to Phil. Many times he had grown lonely for his old home. He took in the long, low ranch house painted a glistening white with its shake roof, bunkhouse, and cook shack. Smoke rose out of the chimney, curling up in a leisurely fashion into the blue sky. The corrals held horses, and his keen eyes picked up a spirited paint prancing around that he longed to ride at the first possible opportunity. It was a fine ranch, and fond memories came flooding back to him. A sense of futility accompanied this, for the three years he had spent in Europe at times seemed wasted. But even so, he knew it was something he had had to do.

A strong streak of stubbornness had shaped Phil Winslow and had gotten him into trouble more than once. As prosperous and challenging and welcoming as the ranch looked, he knew even now he would not be staying there long. He sat quietly on the wagon seat, taking in all the improvements that had been made since he was gone. When Fuller pulled up in front of the gate, Phil said, "I'll walk in from here, Fuller. I want to look things over."

"Why, shore. I reckon they'll be right glad to see ya."

Plucking his suitcase out of the bed of the wagon, Winslow reached up and took the enormous hand of the driver. "Stop in a little later. I'll show you some of those paintings you wanted to see." He grinned and said, "You'll probably say I should have kept on herdin' cows."

"Wouldn't be too quick to say that," Fuller grinned. "I'll take you up on it. Get on in, now, and let your folks have a look at ya. I reckon they're sure gonna be surprised to see ya."

"I hope so. Thanks for the ride."

As Winslow walked along the dusty road that led from the gate to the house, he felt strange, almost like a foreigner. The crowded cities of London and Paris were far away from this place he had called home for so many years. When he first arrived in London, he had walked the streets for days and days, entranced by the famous buildings he had only read about. The history of places such as Westminster Abbey, St. Paul's Cathedral, and the Tower of London had captivated his interest. And then a frenzy to paint had come upon him and he'd spent weeks painting them all.

Taking a deep breath, he suddenly realized how much he had missed his home during those three years. Now, however, as he looked out across the land, the crisp air and the azure sky that seemed to stretch out to infinity brought a sense of completion to him.

"Hey, what in the world do I see here?"

In his concentration, Phil had not heard the sound of a horse approaching. He turned and saw Lobo Smith, his brother-in-law, mounted on a fine chestnut gelding. Lobo was not his real name, but he despised his given name so much that he refused to be called by it. He swung off the saddle and put his hand out. He was not a tall man, not over five ten, and weighing no more than one hundred sixty pounds, but there was a solid roundness to his arms, revealed by the light tan shirt he wore. He had a muscular chest, and there was an aura of strength about him. Shoving his narrow-brimmed hat back, he exposed a wealth of curly brown hair and one bright eye the color of indigo. The other was covered by a black patch, but the one indigo eye gleamed with excitement.

"Well, the prodigal has finally come home," Lobo murmured, his grip hard on Phil's hand.

"Hello, Lobo. Yeah, I reckon that about sums it up."

"Folks know you're comin'? They didn't say nothin'."

"No. I didn't know myself when I'd get here, but I guess they'll let me in the front door."

"I guess they will." Lobo had married Lanie Winslow, one of Phil's sisters, and the two men had become very close friends. Lobo had never understood the force that drove Phil to leave his home and sail to Europe to become a painter, but he had said often, "A man needs to do what's inside of him, Phil."

Now Lobo said with a grin, "Give me that old suitcase. Guess if you've carried it across the big water, I can tote it the rest of the way."

Phil surrendered the well-worn bag, and holding the lines of his chestnut with his left hand and the bag with his right, Lobo asked, "You home for good, Phil?"

For a moment Winslow hesitated. He had no real plans, except he knew he had learned all he could in Europe. He had not liked the Continent and just two months earlier had decided to come home. He arrived with empty pockets and nothing more than the clothes on his back, but he had learned something about painting.

"I'm not sure. I don't think so, Lobo."

"Still got that paintin' in your head, I reckon."

"I guess so," Phil said absently, looking around. "The place looks good," he went on. "How are the folks?"

"Finer than frog hair. They're gonna eat you alive, Phil, and them boys of mine, Logan and Frank, need an uncle for a while."

When Phil stepped up onto the porch, the door swung open with a bang, and his mother, Bronwen, came flying out. He saw that her hair was the same brilliant auburn it had always been, with touches of white only adding to its sheen, and her sparkling green eyes seemed to laugh as she threw her arms around him.

She hugged him close and whispered, "Well now, it's fine to see you."

A trace of her old Welsh lilt was still in her speech, and as she clung to him, Phil felt the loneliness he had tried to ignore, for she had been a mother such as one only reads about. Over her shoulder another voice came, this one louder and more boisterous.

"Well, look what the wind blew in!"

Releasing his mother, Phil took his father's handshake and then felt himself gripped by the strong arms that went around him. Zach Winslow had always been a powerful man, and now as he stepped back, Phil saw that his father had hardly aged in the time he had been gone. At sixty-nine, his brown hair had only just begun to be streaked with gray, and when he lifted his hand, Phil noted the forefinger that had been shot off by a Confederate sharpshooter.

"You couldn't give us a little warning? That would have been too hard for you, I guess!" Zach scolded, but his eyes were laughing as he grabbed Phil's arm. "Come in the house. We're going to kill a fatted calf. Lobo, you think you can find one?"

"Reckon we got a few stringy critters. I'll pick out the worst of 'em."

Phil grinned at Lobo, then walked arm in arm into the house with his parents. The feeling of loneliness that had plagued him for the past few months faded, and he knew that, at least for a time, he was home.

★ ★ ★ ★

When Zach Winslow had designed the ranch house that would provide a permanent home for him and his family, he had told the builder, "I want a dining room big enough for my family, all the kinfolk, and all the neighbors who want to crowd in. I'll pay for it, and you do it."

The builder had done well, creating a room that reflected the great western plains in its light and airy spaciousness. Three enormous windows along one wall opened onto a spectacular view of the distant mountains. The high-beamed ceiling made the twenty-by-forty-foot room seem even larger than it was, and two wagon-wheel chandeliers hung from the lofty beams on heavy chains. The polished hardwood floor and the honey-colored pinewood paneling gave the room an informal homeyness that put visitors instantly at ease.

Zach had filled the walls with the spoils of his hunting adventures—huge racks of deer and elk antlers—while on decorative shelves he had arranged small stuffed birds and game. Pictures of the Winslow ranch in rustic wood frames encircled the room. Bronwen had added her own touches to the decor: she had made curtains of heavily starched cotton in rich earth tones and had created tiebacks out of old horseshoes nailed into the wall. A large rag rug that she had spent many years making now lay beneath the heavy knotty-pine dining table. The table, which of all the furniture in the room most exemplified the character of the Winslow family—strong and stately—was surrounded by high-backed chairs, upholstered in a woven fabric of Cheyenne design. Silver candlesticks sat on a matching runner on the table. The Indian motif was further complemented by a wool blanket, woven in the natural colors of the plains, that hung above the massive stone fireplace.

Bronwen had also added a certain elegance to the western decor by including family heirlooms along the wall opposite the windows—a delicate maple china cabinet and two larger mahogany buffets, displaying an assortment of fine cut-glass pieces, china plates and platters, as well as silver trays, a coffee set, and candleholders. On the wall above the two buffets, she had proudly displayed some of Phil's paintings that he had recently shipped home from Europe.

When Phil came down to breakfast in the morning and entered the dining room, he was surprised to find his entire family sitting at the table waiting for him. He had slept like a log all night, and the clanging of the dinner bell on the front porch had startled him from a peaceful slumber. He was no longer in the habit of rising at dawn. Now as he sat down at the table and greeted his family, a lump rose in his throat at seeing again those who loved him. At one end sat his parents, flanked by Lobo and Lanie, and across from Phil sat his two nephews, Logan and Frank, ages twelve and ten.

He grinned at them, for they were exact replicas of their father, Lobo Smith. They even had the same indigo eyes. To his left was his brother Tom and his wife, Helen. Phil grinned and nodded at Tom. "I can't get used to having a lawman sitting in the house. Why aren't you out catching criminals or something?"

Tom Winslow wore a sheriff's star on his shirt. He leaned back and studied Phil carefully, a lazy grin on his lips. He was sunburned, and his hands showed the mark of his trade, which had been herding cows until he had been elected sheriff the previous year. "I might start right here in this room. No tellin' how many laws you broke over in Paris and London—and right here in Montana for that matter."

"Oh, don't be foolish, Tom!" Helen said. Tom's wife was a petite woman with a pair of brilliant blue eyes and an attractive face. They had been married for only six months and the aura of being newlyweds was still on them. She reached over and squeezed his arm. "You be nice, you hear me, Tom?"

"Nice? I'm always nice, except with criminals. This brother of mine may need to be locked up. We could take some of the meanness out of him down at the county jail."

"Why, that's utter nonsense, Tom!" Bronwen snapped as she brought in a huge platter of scrambled eggs balanced on one arm and a basket piled high with buttermilk biscuits in the other. No sooner had she set down the basket than Tom reached for a biscuit. She soundly whacked his knuckles and chided her son for his bad manners. "Wait until after the blessing! You got no more religion than a Gila monster!"

Helen got up to help carry in the rest of the food, and the table was soon brimming with steaming dishes of crisp bacon and sausage, huge stacks of pancakes, and heaping bowls of fried potatoes. Freshly squeezed orange juice and milk had already been poured into large glasses, and heavy mugs awaited the hot, steaming coffee that Bronwen placed on the table in two ornate silver coffeepots.

Zach leaned forward, his elbows on the table, and shook his head. "Well, I don't guess the tribulation age has begun yet. You think this will keep you until noon, Phil?"

"I reckon so, Pa." He looked over the steaming mountains of food and said, "It looks like we ought to invite half the county in. Mom, how do you expect me to eat all this?"

"You're too thin! I'm going to fatten you up!" she said, smiling.

They all looked toward Zach, and when he bowed his head, they followed suit.

"Heavenly Father, I'm thankful for this food and for this house. I thank you for this son of ours who's been brought back safely. We acknowledge that you've done it all. So we ask you to put your hand on him and on all of us and help us to please you in all our ways. In the name of Jesus. Amen." Then without losing a breath, he reached out, stabbed some pancakes, and said, "Tell us what all you been doin' over there in Europe."

"No, you tell me first what you've been doing here. How're Betsy and Wesley?"

"Fine," Zach said as he lathered butter on his stack of pancakes, then reached for the hot maple syrup.

Betsy was Phil's other sister, a few years younger than Lanie, and she lived in Chicago with her husband.

"They got a fine boy. Named him Heck after Heck Thomas."

"That's a good name," Phil said, biting down on a piece of bacon. "It's a wonder he didn't arrest you, Lobo."

Phil referred to the time when Lobo had been very close to stepping over into the outlaw life in Oklahoma Territory. It was there he had met the Winslows and fallen in love with Lanie, the oldest girl.

Lobo's one eye glittered, and he said, "You're right about that. If Lanie hadn't taken to reformin' me, I reckon I'd have been hanged by Judge Parker."

Lanie reached over and tapped Lobo playfully on the arm. She was one of the most beautiful women Phil had ever seen. Her figure was stately, and even at the age of forty, she still had most of her youthful grace. Her rich auburn hair and brilliant green eyes came from her mother, as did the high coloring of her cheeks. "Phil, have you heard from your brother John?" Lanie asked. "He's doing well at Yale with his law studies. I expect he'll eventually become a politician."

"That would be bad," Zach glowered. "A lawyer *and* a politician in the family at the same time. Don't know how it could be much worse."

"You stop that foolishness right now, Pa!" Lanie frowned at him. "Your youngest just might be President someday. I'm right proud of my little brother."

"Uncle Phil," Logan piped up, his bright eyes sparkling, "tell us all about what it's like over where you went to."

They all wanted to hear about his travels, but Phil was reluctant to say too much. He ate slowly, savoring his mother's home-cooked food, and waved his fork around as he described some of his adventures. "I came back on a ship called the *Lancaster*," he murmured. "We sailed from Cobh, Ireland, to New York in five days and forty-five minutes."

"My, that's something!" his mother said. "When I came over

in steerage, it took a month and a half. I thought we'd never get here."

"Neither did I! I was waitin' for ya." Zach winked at her.

Bronwen sniffed at this. "Waiting! I had to run you down and *make* you propose! I felt sorry for you!"

Everyone laughed, then suddenly Logan jumped from his chair and ran across the room, despite the warnings from his mother. Coming back, he held the paper up and said, "Look at this, Uncle Phil! I bet they ain't got nothin' like *this* in Paris or London."

Taking the paper, Phil saw that it was a copy of the *San Francisco Chronicle*. "What's in here you like so much?"

"Look here," Logan said eagerly as he helped Phil turn the pages. "Look at this. It's pictures and a story."

"Why, sure it is! I never saw anything like this in a paper."

"They call it a *comic strip*, I think," Logan said. "This one's called *Mr. A. Mutt*. My cousin Cass sends it to me every week. After you finish eatin' I'll show 'em all to ya."

"Now, don't bother your uncle," Bronwen scolded. "He's had a long trip and is all tired out. He doesn't want to read any silly things like that!"

"I guess I do, Ma," Phil grinned. "It makes more sense than most of the things in the paper." He studied the comic strip and shook his head. "What will they think of next?"

Suddenly Lanie spoke up. "I saw Lois Gardner last Thursday." She tried to appear nonchalant, making the idle remark.

Instantly alarms went off in Phil's head, for he and Lois Gardner had been seeing each other before he had left for Europe. He had fancied himself in love with her for a time, but she had not felt the same way toward him. "Is she married?" he asked.

"No," Lanie said quickly. "She always asks about you every time I see her, though."

"She had her chance at Phil," Bronwen said firmly. She had never liked Lois Gardner, seeing nothing in her to admire, and now she said, "You stay away from that woman. She's just out to snare a man, Phil."

"I doubt if her father would want her to marry an impoverished artist with no future," Phil laughed.

"Don't say that," Lobo spoke up. He was buttering a biscuit and bit off half of it before he nodded. "Some of them artist fellows make lots of money, I understand. Might as well be you."

"That's kind of you to say, Lobo," Phil shrugged, "but there are about a hundred thousand starving artists all over Europe who can't sell a thing they paint. I don't think it will be much better in the States."

After breakfast Phil spent the morning with his two young nephews. He took them out on horseback on some of the trails he had ridden as a youth. As he watched them carefully, he thought once, *It's good to be home again. Why can't I have sense enough just to stay here and marry Lois Gardner? We could have ten kids, and with her old man's money, he would set me up even if Pa wouldn't—which, of course, he would.* The thought played around in his mind. He was an imaginative man who spent a great deal of time daydreaming, but there was a hard core of realism in him and he finally said to himself, "Lois wouldn't care for starving in an attic in some big city, which is what I'll be doing soon enough."

★ ★ ★ ★

The days passed pleasantly as Phil Winslow reacquainted himself with his homeland. Every day he rode the hills and the plains, helped Lobo with the cattle, and made short trips into town with his mother to do some shopping. It was a relaxing and easy time, but as the days went by, he grew more and more restless.

His mother was the first to notice. She had a keen sense of discernment, and finally one day after supper, as they sat together on the front porch looking out toward the golden sun sinking behind the mountains, she said, "Tell me, now, Phil. What is it that's in your heart?"

Phil was jolted out of his reverie, for in truth, his mind had wandered far away from the beautiful sunset before him. He leaned over and squeezed her arm. "You know me best, Ma. I never could figure out how you knew exactly what I was thinking."

"Well, devil fly off! It's not hard. You're so preoccupied, I'm surprised you don't run into a tree. What is it? More painting, I think."

Phil shifted uncomfortably. "I've been telling myself what a fool I'd be to leave this place again. Everything I could ever want is right here. Why, I even thought about proposing marriage to Lois Gardner." He smiled and saw his mother's face tense. "Don't worry," he said. "I'm not going to."

"I know." Bronwen turned and her face softened. "You'll be leaving soon, won't you, Phil?"

"I'm afraid so, Ma."

"I knew it. I told your father two days after you got here that you would never stay."

They sat there talking, and soon Zach came out and joined them. A quietness had settled over the land, and the stars began to twinkle like diamonds in the ebony sky. Finally Phil said softly, "I know you're disappointed in me, Pa. I'm not the kind of son you'd like to have had."

"Don't you believe it," Zach said quickly. "I don't know much about painting, but you've been given something special that's not in most men. The only thing I want, son, is for you to do this painting business for the glory of God. That's what the Scriptures say. Whether you eat or drink or paint, do it all to the glory of God."

"I never read that last part, Zach!" Bronwen scolded him. "But I know what you mean," she added. "Do you think you can be an artist for the glory of God, son?"

Many times, all alone in his room in London, Phil had thought of his parents. He remembered the hours upon hours that his father and mother had read the Scriptures to him when he was a child. They were the best Christians he knew, and he had come to accept the Lord himself at an early age. Though Paris and London had their share of grave temptations, he had found a good church in London and had kept his faith intact. Now, however, he was somewhat confused, and he said, "Back in the Middle Ages everyone painted for the glory of God. If you painted at all, you painted the Holy Family, Jesus, Mary, and Joseph, or one of the saints. Things have changed a little bit since then. I've wondered a lot how I could serve God as a painter."

"If that's what you want, why, you'll find it. God will help you," Bronwen said.

"I'll be leaving right away."

"Your mother told me she thought you would," Zach said. "Where will you be going?"

"New York, I think."

"Will you be in an art school?"

"Yes, I think so. I've learned a lot of techniques over in Europe, but now I need to get the feel of America again. I guess I can find some interesting things to paint in a city as big as New York."

"Well, you've got kinfolk there. Several of them. Mark Winslow is getting on in years like I am, but he's still a mighty important man. If you need any help, you could go to him."

"I don't think I'll trouble him. I want to make it on my own. You were good, Pa, to help me through this trip. I know I couldn't have made it if it hadn't been for your help, and I appreciate it."

"There's plenty more where that came from. Whatever I can do. Just let me know."

Phil hesitated. "Thanks, Pa. I'll remember that. Maybe I will let you help me financially. It doesn't make any sense to go to New York and work all day just to stay alive when I'm going to learn how to paint."

Zach Winslow was a thoughtful man. "I'll tell you what. I'll send you some money every month. If it's not enough, you write and let me know. You turn your head to this painting business. Learn how to do it and serve God. That's what I want to see. Never think I'm disappointed in you. Your mother and I are very proud of you. When I look at those paintings on the wall, I'm just glad God gave us a son with such a gift. I know it's going to work out for you, son."

Once again Phil Winslow thought how blessed he was to have such caring and supportive parents. He thanked them quietly, then went over and hugged his mother, kissed her, then slapped his father on the shoulder. "I'll be leaving soon, but I won't forget it."

That night he went to bed knowing he'd only have a few days left to enjoy his home, and he offered up a prayer to God. "I don't know how I can make a painting to glorify you, Lord, but I'm sure going to try. Keep me from wrongdoing in that big city and let me serve you with all my heart. In the name of Jesus I ask it." He closed his eyes and for a long time lay there thinking about what the future held for him. He had no plans except to pursue his goal of serving God with all of his heart through his greatest passion—painting.

CHAPTER THREE

BIG CITY ENCOUNTERS

★ ★ ★ ★

The city of New York hit Phil Winslow with a tremendous impact. He was not unacquainted with large cities, having wandered the streets of London and Paris, but something about the bustling, raucous streets and the raw culture that had exploded on the island of Manhattan struck him with the force of a sledgehammer.

It all began when he alit from his sleeping car at the Grand Central Terminal and was immediately engulfed in a confused mass of people streaming everywhere. His ear was filled with a polyglot babble, and as he stood there for a moment, he exclaimed to himself in amazement, "Why, I never heard such a thing!" He had known, of course, that New York had been flooded by the Irish and Germans, but he also heard languages he was pretty sure came from other countries—he guessed Italy, Poland, and Russia.

The tracks stretched out endlessly, with trains lined up one after the other. Some of them were sending boiling clouds of steam and smoke high into the air, and others were releasing hissing jets of steam from underneath that threatened to engulf the other trains. Shaking his head, Phil wandered around in the mass of people that were arriving and disembarking. Finally, he made his way to a broad street outside the Grand Central Terminal. He wanted to find a room close to the art institute, so he walked across the street to a cabby who was leaning against his horse-drawn vehicle carefully peeling an apple and asked, "Say, buddy, can you tell me where the American Institute of Art is?"

"Sure. It's not far off Fifth Avenue, down near Madison Square. Need a lift?"

"How much would it cost?"

The driver was a lanky man with narrow brown eyes and a mouth full of enormous teeth. He chomped into the apple, chewing on it thoughtfully, and then nodded. "One buck. Welcome to the big city."

Grinning, Winslow tossed his suitcase into the carriage and said, "You're on!"

A garrulous individual, the driver informed Winslow that his name was Harry Grebb. After Winslow had introduced himself, Harry asked, "Where you comin' from, Phil?"

"Montana. But I've been across the water for a while studying art."

"That so? Now you've come to the big city."

"I guess so."

"Gonna be a painter, are you?"

Phil shrugged, saying noncommittally, "I'm going to study anyway."

"I knowed a painter once. Nuttiest fellow I ever met! Didn't stay sober a day in his life that I know of. He was doing some painting down the street from me. Just paintin' the streets. That street I live on ain't nothin' to write home about. He got so drunk I had to hold him up while he painted."

"Were his paintings any good?"

Grebb made a grimace, then bit into the apple again. Chewing thoughtfully like a cow munching on her cud, he said, "Well, like I said, Phil, the street I live on ain't never gonna be on no postcard. I told him I'd take him over to Fifth Avenue where he could paint some of those fancy houses, but he never would do it. Said he wanted to paint life like it really was."

"I bet I know what you told him. You probably said that Fifth Avenue is life like it is for the Vanderbilts and the Astors."

Grebb laughed aloud. "You're pretty sharp, Phil! That's exactly what I told him! Come on now, hoss! We'll show Phil here some real fancy places."

As they proceeded down the busy streets, Harry Grebb gave Phil a brief history lesson. Harry knew a surprising amount of history about New York, since he had lived there all of his life, as had his parents. He improved Phil's knowledge of the place with many interesting details. "Fifth Avenue," he said, waving with his whip, "was just a dirt avenue once. That was back when my great-grandfather had a farm not far from here. He was Dutch. Fifth Avenue got started when a Dutch family decided to build a mansion on the place. They called it the "Brevoort." They built it right over there, facing onto Fifth. You see it? And then they built a hotel, and pretty soon churches started buildin' all over the place. The mayor moved in there, then all the rich folks took a likin' to it. I guess they all wanted the name Fifth Avenue on their address."

Phil stretched his neck as they passed by one of the Vanderbilt mansions and was informed by Grebb that the Vanderbilt family had spent fifteen million on four mansions along Fifth Avenue. "Those Vanderbilts have built a lot of fancy buildings here in New York, including the Grand Central Terminal you arrived at." They passed the Waldorf-Astoria Hotel, which was one of the most impressive buildings Phil had ever seen. A little farther down, Grebb said, "See that place?" He waved at a square building that was heavily ornamented. "That's Madame Restell's place." Grebb gave Phil a sly look and said, "She helps girls that have gotten into trouble."

"An abortionist?"

"I reckon. That ain't what it's called around here, so much, but that's what she does."

Finally they passed Delmonico's Restaurant, and Grebb said, "It'd take your war pension to eat in that place, but they sure got some fine grub. We turn up there—off on Broadway." They made an oblique turn where Broadway angled off of Madison Square, and two blocks away Grebb said, "There it is. That's the art institute."

Phil looked eagerly toward the building, which was not as impressive, of course, as the massive homes and churches on Fifth Avenue. It was, however, to his knowledge, the best art school in New York. He said quickly, "I guess I'll get out here and try to find a room close by."

"Anything round here is going to be pretty pricey," Grebb advised him. "I can take you to some cheaper parts of town if you like."

For a moment Phil hesitated, then he said, "I guess that might be a good idea."

"I could take you over to the Seventh Ward down on the East

River. It ain't fancy, but I make out there," Grebb said.

"I think that'll suit me fine."

The next hour was a revelation to Phil. He had seen poverty in Europe, but what he saw in the deteriorated tenement house section of the Seventh Ward was frightening. He listened as Grebb informed him of how the tenements were built.

"The fronts of these houses, you see, were pretty nice at one time, but the rich folks moved away. Families comin' in from Italy and Germany had to have some place, so they took these big, fancy houses and divided them up into little apartments—lots of apartments. And then behind them, where the yards were, they added other buildings, so that the people in the back don't have no yard or nothin'. Sometimes just an air shaft between buildings. So many people crowded in here that the whole place got run down real fast. It's pretty rough, Phil."

Phil cringed at the thought of families living in such cramped, squalid conditions. Finally, after they'd driven around some more, Phil found a neighborhood he thought looked more inviting down on Nassau Street. He figured it was at least two miles back north to the art institute, but he was healthy and strong and knew the exercise would do him good. Getting out of the cab, he handed Grebb one dollar and added two bits, saying, "You've been a big help, Harry. Thanks a lot."

"Watch out for these city slickers! They can skin a frog, and he won't even know he's been skinned."

Grinning at the tall man, Phil waved, then turned and began walking up the street, looking for "Room to Let" signs. Finally spotting a brownstone that looked more promising than some of the others, he climbed the steps and rang the doorbell. The landlady who opened the door was short and dumpy, with iron gray hair and a pair of sharp, dark eyes that took him in carefully and with obvious suspicion. But when he offered to pay in advance she grew more cheerful.

"I'm Mrs. Brown," she said. "I have to be a little bit careful. Not everybody who comes here is upright and honest. You never know who you can trust."

"I'll try to behave myself, Mrs. Brown."

"Are you a Christian man, Mr. Winslow?"

"Yes, I am."

"Well, that's all right, then. I'd like to invite you to our church, Calvary Baptist. It's very close."

"I'd be glad to come and visit," Phil said at once. He followed her to the second floor, where she showed him the available space. It was actually a tiny apartment, with a sitting room and a bedroom. Both rooms were small, and only the sitting room had a window, covered with a dingy curtain. All the walls were a dirty light green, and the dull wood floor was covered with dark spots, as if it had not been cleaned for years. The furnishings were, Phil thought, *basic*: a broken-down brown couch, two high-backed chairs upholstered in a tattered chintz, a single heavy table holding an old brass lamp, a small pine bed, a bedside table whose marble top was cracked down the middle, and a tall chest of drawers with knobs missing.

"The bath is right down the hall, Mr. Winslow. You'll have to furnish your own towels, you understand."

"Yes, of course. Thank you, Mrs. Brown."

After the landlady had left, Phil opened his suitcase, unpacked his few belongings into the chest of drawers, and hung the one nice suit he had brought on a peg on the wall. He had shipped his art supplies, and they would not arrive for several days. He was not all that anxious to begin, anyway. He sat down on the bed and stared at his dingy surroundings. *Well, here I am in New York. I wonder if I will fare any better here than in London or Paris.* Pulling off his shoes, he stretched out, closed his eyes, and went to sleep fully dressed.

★   ★   ★   ★

To Phil's surprise his painting supplies arrived shortly after he had settled into his rooms. He had spent the time until then wandering the streets of New York and had already decided on what his first painting would be. The most spectacular building in the city was a "skyscraper," the term having first been applied to tall buildings a few years earlier. It was the elevator that made such buildings possible, and of all the New York skyscrapers, the Flatiron Building was the most striking. Its jutting wedge shape rose twenty stories straight up into the sky without a break, except for the symmetrically arranged windows on each floor. Something about the structure fascinated Phil, as it did the whole nation. Perhaps it was because all the buildings he had ever seen were square, and this wedge-shaped skyscraper reminded him of slices of pie stacked one upon another.

Early on the day after his supplies arrived, he set out with his palette, box of paints and brushes, and his folding easel and chair. Seating himself firmly in front of the wedge, as far back as he could get, he quickly sketched out the building. Soon a small crowd had gathered around him. It amused him, for in Paris painters were so common that people paid them no more attention than if they were a mailbox or a signpost. Now he was constantly bombarded with opinions such as, "I think you ain't makin' it tall enough, mister," or, "Look, you ain't got enough windows in it. You want me to count the stories for you?"

Phil answered all their questions, rather enjoying the novel experience. It was a refreshing thing to be admired, and obviously those who gathered around felt he was doing something worthwhile.

One young man, no more than seventeen, stayed for a long time. Finally, Phil turned and smiled at him. "You ever do any painting?"

"Me? Oh, I used to try a little, but I never done stuff like that."

"Here." Phil handed him the brush. "Why don't you give me a hand?"

The young man, who had large innocent blue eyes and a thatch of tow-colored hair, was astonished. "Why, I'd mess it up!"

"No you won't. Just have a try at it."

Phil stood back and watched, and the small gathering of onlookers egged the young man on until finally he stepped forward and began adding some of the pigment that formed the windows on one side of the wedge. "Why, you're doing just fine," Phil said as he watched the young man. "You've got a real touch for it."

"Do you really think so, mister?"

"Sure. You ought to keep up with your painting."

"I will! That's just exactly what I'll do!"

After his morning's work, Phil picked up his supplies and headed back to his rooms, feeling he had been an encouragement to somebody. As he made his way through the crowds, he thought, *Maybe I didn't do that young fellow any favor. Most artists never make a dime off of what they do.*

He slept well that night, and the next day he rose and dressed, his mind on the art institute. He wore a pair of Levi's, faded through many washings and with the cuffs a little ragged, and a pale blue cotton shirt, also limp and loose fitting. He looked at himself in the mirror and grinned. "I don't know if I look eccentric enough for an artist." But then, maybe artists in New York City were more uppercrust, he thought. He wondered if he should be wearing a top hat and tails instead. He had written a letter to the institute and had been invited to come for a "visit"—which Phil understood to mean that they would refuse to admit him if he had no talent.

He took four of his smaller paintings, wrapped them in brown paper, and tied a string around them. The sun was shining, but he felt some apprehension, despite the beautiful morning. When he arrived at the art institute, he stood for a moment outside and took a deep breath. *Well*, he thought, *I can always punch cows if this doesn't work out.* He had felt exactly this way when he had arrived in London, but his determination had brought him through that, he reminded himself. So, squaring his shoulders, he moved ahead and entered the building. He stood and looked around at what was obviously a reception area. A heavyset man with rosy cheeks and hazel eyes was sitting behind a desk reading a book.

"My name's Winslow," Phil said to the man. "I'd like to see Mr. William Crumpler."

"Right over there. Second floor. Take the stairs," the man said, barely lifting his eyes.

"I don't know Mr. Crumpler."

"You see a man that looks like a bulldog, that's him."

Grinning at the brief and amusing description, Phil ascended the stairs to a large studio filled with students sitting at their easels. After scanning the room, he had no trouble identifying Mr. Crumpler. His face indeed resembled that of a bulldog, with broad jowls that drooped, an undershot jaw, and a flushed complexion. The portly man was standing over a young woman seated at her canvas. He was gesticulating wildly, and his voice carried clearly across the room, where at least a dozen other students were busy working on their canvases.

"I've told you a hundred times, Miss Warwick. If you don't practice, you'll never become a painter!"

As Phil approached and stood to one side waiting, he heard the woman's clear reply. "Why, Bill, I don't care whether I ever make any money painting or not. I just do it because I like to irritate you."

Crumpler glared at her, then shook his head. "You're wasting your time here. Why don't you go somewhere else? You can afford to."

The woman was wearing a white smock and turned to examine the newcomer instead of answering her instructor. She had long blond hair tied up on her head with a green band, which matched her green eyes. She was quite stunning to look at, despite the austere whiteness of her smock, and she smiled at Phil in a pouting way that suggested an easy familiarity with men.

"Hello," she said. "You're new."

Taken aback by her attention, Phil stammered, "Why, yes . . . yes, I am. I didn't mean to interrupt." Turning toward the man standing beside her, he inquired, "Are you Mr. Crumpler?"

"I'm Crumpler. What's your name?"

"Phil Winslow. I wrote some time ago and—"

"Yes. I have your letter. What makes you think you're an artist?"

Phil was startled by the suddenness of Crumpler's attack, but he met the man's steady gaze and answered this time without hesitation. "The pictures I paint, sir."

"Let me see them."

"You mean here? Now?"

"You want a private audience? Maybe they're no better than Miss Warwick's pictures, but then you probably don't have as much money as she does. I don't need any more loafers here. I've seen too many come through here as it is. A waste of my time, they are. Just let me see the pictures!" he snapped.

Feeling intimidated by the man's bluntness and the stares from the other students, Phil untied the string and lifted the first painting out.

"Put it on that easel right there!" Crumpler commanded.

When Phil had done so, Crumpler came and stood right in front of it. He stared at it as if it were an enemy, and Phil remained silent. He did turn to face the woman once, who winked merrily at him, and her lips curled upward in a smile.

The painting was of a fisherman on the docks of London. He was an old man with his face seamed and weather-beaten by years of toil at sea. He was sitting on a stool making repairs on his net, his eyes cast down. Phil had wanted to catch the impression of fading strength that comes to men who work hard for years. The strength was still there—at least he thought so—but he had been unhappy with the background.

"You think this is good?"

"It's better than some I've done," Phil answered.

"It's adequate," Crumpler said. "Let me see the rest."

One by one Crumpler studied the pictures. One was a landscape, another a scene of an impoverished street in London's East End. Phil had been appalled by the poverty he had seen there and had made the focal point of the painting some ragged children who were skinny and vacant eyed with hunger.

"Who do you think would buy a painting like this?" Crumpler demanded.

"I never thought about it. I saw something that intrigued me and I just wanted to paint it."

"Oh, I assume you've got plenty of money, then! You're not thinking of making a living. That's good because you probably won't."

"I don't have plenty of money, but I've got enough to pay the fees," Phil said coolly.

Crumpler stared at Phil for a long moment, then grunted. "You can stay a week. After that we'll see. Set up over there and start working."

"Yes, sir," Phil said, but as he turned his head, he winked at the blond woman, who giggled.

"I can give you some help," she offered flirtatiously. "I know how to get next to *all* the instructors . . . especially Mr. Bill Crumpler here."

"Why don't you go do something worthwhile!" Crumpler snarled. "You're wasting your time here, Miss Warwick! You'll never be an artist!"

"Is he always like that?" Phil asked as Crumpler walked over to observe the work of another student on the other side of the room.

"Always."

Phil went to the side of the room with a window, set up his easel and the fresh canvas he had brought along, and began painting. As always, when he painted, he closed out the whole world and concentrated only on the canvas in front of him. He was painting a scene from memory—one that he had tucked away in his mind some time ago. It was of a street cafe in Paris where he had spent many hours talking with other aspiring young artists. He lost himself in bringing out the details as he put them onto the canvas. He could never understand the magic, or the miracle, as he thought of it, that occurred when he began to paint. Somehow out of his mind a memory would begin to take on a life of its own.

It would go down his arm, and the brush in his hand would come alive, and soon the image he saw in his mind would begin to take shape on the canvas. It was not totally automatic, for he had to think and lay the strokes on according to the rules he had learned from the skilled painters with whom he had studied in Europe. It was the hardest work he had ever done yet at the same time an experience of sheer joy.

"I've been to that cafe. It's on the Rue de la Pais."

Startled, Phil turned around and saw Miss Warwick examining his work.

"That's right. You've actually been there, Miss Warwick?"

"Sure. I spent two summers in Paris. When were you there?"

"I just got back from Europe," Phil said. "I was in London for two years and Paris for a year."

"Well then, we might have sat right next to each other at that little cafe." Her eyes sparkling suggestively, she sighed an exaggerated sigh. "Too bad we didn't run into each other, Mr. Winslow. We might have had a good time. You may call me Avis, if you like."

"And you can call me Phil. Have you been studying here long?"

"Depends on what you mean. I've been dropping in for a couple of years, but I don't stay with it. Come on. You've had enough work for one day. Let's go have a drink."

Phil stared at the woman. Her brashness startled him, and yet he had met many women, especially in Paris, with that same sensuous look about them. She was about thirty, he guessed, and apparently had seen as much of the world as he had—or more!

"I don't drink, but I'll buy you supper," Phil offered.

"You don't drink? Now, that'll be a switch. Come on, then."

They left the art institute, and she led him to a cafe two blocks away. "This is a good place," she said. "Not much to look at, but the food's good." As soon as they had ordered their meal, Avis began interrogating him. She sat back, observing him carefully, then finally said, "So you're a cowboy fresh in from Montana? A good-looking fellow like you won't have any trouble getting all the girls he wants."

"I guess I've come to paint—not to chase girls."

"Is that right?" The statement seemed to be a challenge to Avis, and she smiled slowly. "Well, we'll see about that."

* * * *

In the week that followed, Phil found himself spending more and more time with Avis Warwick. It didn't take long to see that she possessed only a very minor talent for art and that painting was not a serious matter with her. Some days she did not come to the institute at all. One time she came in and stayed all day but threw away the canvas she had worked on with a curse. She was outspoken and drank freely—not at all the kind of woman Phil Winslow needed or wanted in his life at that moment. Yet, despite his better judgment, he found himself going out with her after each day's work for a meal together. He could not understand why she seemed so fascinated by him. Once she told him, "I've never met anybody like you, Phil. You don't smoke, you don't drink, you don't run around with women. I thought cowboys were different."

"Plenty of them are," Phil shrugged. "I guess if it hadn't been for my parents' good upbringing, I would have been that way, too."

Avis watched him for a moment, then asked, "You ever fall for a woman?"

"Once or twice."

Avis reached over and put her hand on his, squeezing it. "Maybe you've been saving yourself for a real woman. We'll find out about that, won't we?"

Phil smiled at her but pulled back from her touch. "I don't need any complications with women, Avis. If I'm going to be an artist, it'll take everything I've got," he murmured as he left her that evening.

The next morning was Saturday, and he decided to look up his cousin Peter Winslow. He had received a letter from Cass Winslow, who was an expert in the genealogy of the Winslow family. Cass evidently kept track of all of them, and the letter had read, "I don't know if you've ever met my brother Peter Winslow, but he's in New York. He wants to be a race car driver. We Winslows need to stick together, so go over and meet him, Phil. You're about the same age, and all young fellows in a big city need a friend."

Phil *was* feeling somewhat lonely and decided he would take Cass's advice. He had no trouble finding the address. When the cabby stopped in front of a row of buildings, Phil walked up the steps to the brownstone and found the name *Peter Winslow* on one of the slips of paper under the mailboxes. Stepping inside the building, he found room number three and knocked on the door.

When no one answered he turned to leave, but a young woman stepped out of a room across the hall and studied him carefully. She was an attractive woman with enormous eyes, black hair, and a European look about her. He noticed a sizable scar on her left cheek that ran from her temple down to the corner of her lips.

"Are you looking for Peter Winslow?" she asked.

"Why, yes I am."

"He's out in the backyard working on a car. I'm going out that way."

"Thanks," he said. "I'm Phil Winslow."

"Oh, you're a relative of Peter's?"

"A distant one."

"I'm Jolie Devorak. Come along. He'll be glad to see you."

"Well, we've never met before."

"That's strange. You're in the same family, but you've never met?"

"I guess there're lots of Winslows."

The two went out the back door at the end of the hall, and Phil saw two men working on a car painted a red so brilliant it almost hurt his eyes. On the side of it in fancy lettering was the name *Jolie Blonde*.

"Peter, a relative of yours is here to see you."

Peter Winslow had been half under the car. He came out, wiping his hands on a greasy rag, and gave Phil a curious look. "Family, you say?"

"I'm Phil Winslow. My father's Zach Winslow. Your brother Cass, out in California, gave me your name and address. Said we Winslows ought to stick together."

"Oh, sure! Cass knows every Winslow in the United States, I guess." The two men shook hands. Peter was a very tall man, at least six two, about Phil's age. He had hazel eyes, auburn hair, and a friendly grin. "This is Easy Devlin." He gestured to an undersized man standing nearby with a wrench in his hand. He had a pale, thin face, sandy hair, and brown eyes.

"Glad to meet you, Phil," Easy said. "Even if you *are* from the same family as this galoot!"

Jolie interrupted the introductions. "It's time to go get something to eat. If we're going to catch that auto show, we've got to go."

"We're all going to the National Auto Show at Madison Square Garden, Phil. Do you like cars?" Peter asked.

"Don't know much about them, but I'd like to go. What's the show all about?"

"Well, the automobile makers want to show off their new models in hopes of selling their cars. Other people just like to look around out of curiosity. There'll be all kinds of makes," Peter said. "Come on. I think it'll be fun for you."

Phil Winslow enjoyed the show thoroughly. He had never seen so many cars in all of his life, and Peter Winslow seemed to know everything about every one of them. "This is a Winton, Phil. It's got a gasoline-powered engine—seems to be the wave of the future. They can go a lot faster than the steamers and electric cars. The Winton's giving that Oldsmobile over there a run for its money."

"What about Henry Ford? I heard he was up to something new."

"He certainly is. He's in a big legal battle now over patents to the gasoline engine, but he's talking about building a good basic car at a price that common folks can afford. If he succeeds, it may be something that outsells all these others. Say, look! That's Mr. Ford standing right over there!"

Startled, Phil stared at the tall man wearing the plain black suit. Ford was a sharp-featured man with a sober expression, and suddenly Ford looked up and saw the three.

"Why, Peter!" Ford smiled slightly and came over to extend his hand. "I've been wondering about you."

"Hello, Mr. Ford. Good to see you again. These are my friends Jolie Devorak, Easy Devlin, and Phil Winslow."

Ford spoke to the three, then said, "I've expected you to come back asking for a job, Peter."

"Well, I thought about it, and I may yet. I'd sure like to work for you again, Mr. Ford. I'm really excited about your plans, but you know me. I'm working on a race car."

"Still at it, are you? Well, you've got the head for it and the hands. I hope you do well, Peter. If you want a job, I've always got one for you." Nodding, Ford turned and walked away, speaking to those he passed.

"So that's Henry Ford," Phil said. "I've heard a lot about him, and he wants you to work for him."

"I did once," Peter said. "I punched the foreman out and got fired." He grinned rashly and winked at Jolie. "That's when I hit the rails and ran into Jolie and Easy here. We were all hobos together, weren't we?"

Jolie smiled and said to Phil, "You wouldn't believe what happened. I shot a man who was trying to throw Peter and Easy out of the boxcar."

Startled, Phil stared at the young woman who was beautiful despite the scar on her face. "Well, I'll have to be careful and mind my manners if you tote a gun."

"Oh, I don't do that anymore," Jolie said. "We're all going to get rich with the *Jolie Blonde* here." She laid her hand fondly on Peter Winslow's arm, and he grinned down at her.

They wandered for some time through the vast selection of cars on display. They were speaking together about race cars when a young man standing close by evidently overheard their conversation.

"Excuse me. Are you in the racing-car business?"

"Trying to be," Peter said. He gave the man his name and said, "We're in a race next Saturday. Do you race?"

"No. I wish I did, though. My name's Clinton Lanier."

After introductions were made, Peter asked, "What do you do, Clinton?"

"Why, I work in my father's brokerage house."

"Oh, a stockbroker! That sounds like a good life!" Jolie exclaimed.

"Good? It's terrible! I go to the same old office every day."

Jolie studied the young man, who was not over five ten but trim and well built. There was an air of money about him, something she had learned to discern long ago. "Why don't you buy a race car and get into the swim yourself?" she asked.

"I'd like to, Miss Devorak, but my father—well, he doesn't quite see things my way."

"Well, that may be, but if you'd like to see the car that's going to beat them all, you'll have to drop in at the race next Saturday. It's going to be a good one. People are coming from all over, but I think we can win. Don't you reckon, Easy?"

Easy Devlin was rather gloomy as he replied, "I don't know, Peter. It's going to be hard—some stiff competition out there."

Clinton was intrigued by his new acquaintances. He walked

around with them at their invitation and fell into conversation with Phil. He found it fascinating that Phil was a cowboy and was going to be an artist.

"I guess I admire you a lot, Phil—giving up your family business to do what you really want to do."

"Sometimes I think I'm the world's biggest fool," Phil shrugged. "But I've got to give it a try, or I'll never forgive myself when I get old."

Phil's answer seemed to trouble Clinton, and he said little for a while. When it was time to leave, he said, "Can I give you a lift, Phil?"

"Why, sure." They said good-bye to the others, and Phil got into Clinton's horse-drawn buggy parked a block from Madison Square Garden. "I figured you'd have an automobile," he said.

"Father thinks they're a fad. He's wrong about that."

Phil gave directions to his boardinghouse and listened as Clinton spoke with great enthusiasm about cars. Finally, Phil said, "You know a great deal about cars. Did you ever have one?"

"No. Father wouldn't stand for that, but I have a friend who has one. We've taken it apart a dozen times. It's about the only hobby I have, and I can't say anything at home about it. Father would burst a blood vessel."

It was dark when they reached the old brownstone on Nassau Street, and Clinton halted the horse and pulled the buggy to a stop.

They got out and walked toward the steps, still speaking eagerly about automobiles. Both men were startled when out of the shadows a rough voice broke into their conversation.

"Hold it right there, you two! Let's have your money and there'll be no trouble!"

Phil turned cold and wheeled to face the three men who seemed to have appeared from nowhere. Their faces were invisible in the gloom, but he saw at once that two of them carried knives, and one had a stout club about two feet long in his hand.

The leader, the largest of the trio, held out his knife, then put out his free hand. "Just put your money in there, and you gents can go on. No trouble now, is it?"

Clinton said at once, "Do as he says, Phil. We don't need to get killed over money."

Clinton had no qualms about forking over what money he carried to avoid trouble, for he had plenty more. But Phil's entire bankroll was in his pocket, and he had no intention of giving it up to some roughnecks. He planted his legs firmly and held his hands slightly out from his sides, saying, "You fellows move along. You won't get a dime from us."

A laugh came from the three as they made a half circle around the two men. One of them, a tall man with a derby pulled down over his face, waved his club in the air and said, "I'll bust your face in! What would that get you?"

Phil did not like to fight, but now he saw there was no way out. Without warning he suddenly moved forward, twisting his body to one side, and his right leg came up with a tremendous kick that caught the bulkiest of the men right in the face. It drove him backward, and he dropped his knife.

Clinton could scarcely believe what he had just seen. In the darkness Phil had moved swiftly and then the man with the knife had been suddenly driven back. Clinton had no time to think more because the thin man with the club suddenly leaped forward and brought it down with a thud on his head. Clinton tried to get his hands up and catch the first blow, but the second struck him on the side of the skull and knocked him to the ground, unconscious.

Phil turned to face the other two, who advanced toward him, and once again his foot lashed out and caught the man with the club in the lower part of his stomach. The man fell to the ground and curled up and screamed, holding himself in a fetal position.

The third man, shocked and astonished by seeing his two friends so easily overcome, still held the knife in his hand. Phil advanced toward him and threatened, "I'll break your neck if you don't get out of here! Which will it be?"

For one moment Phil thought the man might try to attack him, but the hooligan took one look at his two friends, then swirled and scurried away into the darkness. Phil retrieved the knife that lay on the ground from the first assailant, folded it, and stuck it into his pocket. Taking the club, he jerked the thin man to his feet and said, "Do you want the police to lock you up or do you want to run?" He shoved him backward, and this man, too, disappeared. The large man scrambled to his feet, a bewildered look on his face, as if he could not understand what had happened, and then he also turned and lumbered away.

Phil tossed the club down and knelt beside Clinton. "Are you all right, Clinton?" he asked with concern. He pulled the young man up and saw that his eyes were fluttering. "Come on. I'll get you to a doctor." He half picked up Clinton and got him in the buggy, and when Phil climbed into the driver's seat, the injured man slumped over against him.

"What's your address, your home?" Phil asked.

"Two . . . twenty . . . Essex Street . . . that way," Clinton pointed with difficulty.

Phil drove the buggy at a fast clip, wondering if he should go first to a hospital, but he did not know where one was. Besides, the young man's family needed to know. He had to ask directions from Clinton twice more, but finally he pulled up in front of an imposing and elegant townhouse. He wrapped the lines carefully, jumped out, then ran over to pull Clinton out of the buggy. The young man was unconscious again, so Phil slung him over his shoulder and walked up the steps. He rang the door and stood there fidgeting impatiently until finally a woman in a maid's uniform opened the door. Recognizing Clinton, she uttered a short scream.

"He's been hurt," Phil said. "I need to put him in bed."

The young woman scurried about frantically, then ordered, "Come this way, please!"

Phil followed the maid to a room on the second floor. By the time he had laid the young man down, the room had filled with people. There was another young man called Benjamin, a young woman called Mary Ann, and an older couple, who Phil soon learned were Clinton's parents, Oliver and Alice Lanier. He quickly introduced himself and explained what had happened.

Oliver looked at Phil suspiciously, then demanded, "What was he doing in that part of town?"

"Mr. Lanier, I expect you'll have to let him tell you when he comes around."

Fifty-year-old Alice Lanier, wrapped in a soft gray robe, stood by the side of the bed where Phil had laid Clinton. Her mild blue eyes were troubled, but she did turn to Phil and say, "Thank you so much for taking care of Clinton."

Oliver said briskly, "I'll send for a doctor at once."

Phil would have left, but he was detained by Benjamin, who drew him to one side. "My sister Cara would like to know about this. Do you have time to see her?"

"I suppose so."

He followed young Lanier into another bedroom farther down

the hall, where he found a woman about his own age standing in the middle of the floor. She was wearing a light blue dress with black lace trim that buttoned from the high waist seam to the hem with a narrow flared skirt.

A look of anxiety crossed her face as she listened to her brother describe what was happening. Her voice was warm as she said, "We're very much in your debt, sir."

"Well, I did what I could. If he hadn't given me a lift home, it would never have happened."

"I'm going back to see how he is," Benjamin said and left the two of them alone.

"Please sit down," Cara said. "I want to hear all about it." She sat down herself and listened as Phil explained. When he was finished relating the details of the attack, she said, "Please, Mr. Winslow, we can't thank you properly tonight. Could I have your address?"

"It's not really necessary." He gave it, however, and studied the woman carefully. There was something strange about her. He found her attractive, but he thought, *She looks like she's been ill. I'll have to ask Clinton about her later.* He stood up then and said, "I'll be going, but I think Clinton will be all right. It's just a nasty bump on the head."

Cara came forward and put her hand out. It was unusual for her, for she did not usually offer her hand to men she had only just met. Now she whispered again, "God bless you, Mr. Winslow. I thank the Lord that you were there."

Phil held her hand, which was warm and softer than he would have expected for someone so thin. He hesitated a moment, then nodded and said, "I hope your brother's feeling better soon. Good night, Miss Lanier."

After he left, Cara went and sat down on the bed. Her heart was beating fast, and she was worried about Clinton. Something about the whole event had stirred her and she wondered what the young man who had brought her brother home was really like.

CHAPTER FOUR

"DON'T BE AFRAID OF LIFE...."

★　★　★　★

By the middle of May, Peter and Easy had put in many long hours working on the *Jolie Blonde*. Always striving to find some way to coax another mile-per-hour out of the machine, the two rose early and worked sometimes until after dark. They interrupted themselves only to roam the city looking at other automobiles for new innovations, and twice they attended races to check out the competition. Neither of them had much money, so they cut expenses in every way possible, which meant living in a rather dilapidated boardinghouse and eating bologna sandwiches until the very sight of bologna sickened them both.

Late one Thursday afternoon the two were finishing a hard day's work when Jolie came out, her face alight with an excited smile. Her enormous powder blue eyes sparkled, and she came up and grabbed Peter and gave him a hug, then did the same to Easy. "Guess what?" she said. "I've got a job!"

"What kind of a job?" Peter asked, smiling down at her fondly from his lanky height. "That looks like a job-hunting outfit you've got on." Jolie smiled and struck a pose, showing off her high-collared white bodice and slightly flared moss green skirt with a matching jacket, cinched in with a dark green velvet belt.

"Do you like it?" Jolie turned and gave the skirt a spin, always pleased when Peter had a compliment for her.

"Shore we like it," Easy said. "You're prettier than a spotted hound pup trottin' under a wagon."

Jolie laughed aloud. Happy and excited to tell her good friends her news, she began to speak rapidly. "I had no idea what kind of a job I was looking for, but I went down to Broadway and looked at all of the theaters, and it just came to me that maybe my experience helping to make movies might open up something. So I just decided to start in asking for work."

"I guess that makes sense," Peter said, wiping his hands on an oily rag. "You might even have gotten a recommendation from some of the people back at the studios."

"I did that." Jolie grinned triumphantly. "Before we left I got them all to write letters of recommendation. I didn't know what good they might do, but look how it all worked out. I landed myself a fine job."

"Which one of the shows did you get hired on with?" Peter asked.

"It's a play called *The Warrens of Virginia*. It's all about the Civil War. I've got to tell you all about it."

"Well, you can't tell us here. Come on. I'll buy you both a hamburger," Peter offered.

"Not this time!" Jolie exclaimed. "We're going to eat out at a fancy restaurant. My treat!"

"We can't spend your money like that!" Easy protested.

"Yes we can! I'll be making a good salary, and we deserve a celebration. Remember, we're the Three Musketeers."

Despite their protests, Jolie pestered them until they finally agreed. They went inside the house, washed, and put on their best clothes, which didn't amount to a great deal. As soon as they were all ready, the three of them left to go to a restaurant to hear about Jolie's new job.

"Where are we going?" Easy demanded. "I'm right particular about what I eat." He grinned wryly. "Bein' in Sing Sing for five years sorta whetted my appetite for good eatin'." Whenever Easy mentioned his time spent in prison, a gloomy cloud seemed to darken his otherwise cheery outlook.

"I'm hungry for seafood," Jolie stated. "We're going to an oyster house."

Jolie had done her homework in picking out a place to eat, for she took them to the fanciest of oyster houses—the grandiose Grand Terminal. It was set underground at the Grand Central Terminal. When they arrived, they were somewhat intimidated by the graceful art ceilings decorated in an elegant herringbone pattern. When Jolie saw the doubtful looks on the faces of her companions, she said, "Come on! We've got the money, and we're as good as anybody else!"

The maitre d' approached them with a rather suspicious look, but Jolie said boldly, "We'll have the best table in the house."

Something about the young woman's confidence seemed to pacify the maitre d'. "Yes, madam. Please follow me."

The three followed him and were soon seated at a table, menus in hand. A sparkling tile ceiling arched overhead, and all the tables were covered with immaculate white linen and set with shining silverware, glittering crystal glasses, and snowy linen napkins folded in elaborate shapes. A six-piece orchestra played softly in the background.

Easy looked around and muttered, "There wasn't anything like this in Sing Sing!"

"There isn't anything like this anywhere!" Jolie added as she stared at the beautiful table.

The three studied the menu, trying to choose from the many tempting offerings, including several varieties of seafood, game, salads, and every sort of wine, brandy, and ale.

"I'm going to have a lobster," Jolie announced to her friends.

"I never could figure out how to eat those things," Peter complained.

"I'll show you how, but you get what you want," Jolie said.

When a waiter came to fill their water glasses and take their orders, Easy determined to eat a lobster for once in his life. While they waited, Easy looked around the restaurant and said, "Jolie, this sure is some fancy place. We're gonna have to win a race with the *Jolie Blonde* to pay you back."

"Don't worry about it, Easy. It's my treat. Besides, I've got a decent job now," she said as she laid her napkin across her lap.

When the waiter returned with their dinners, Easy stared at the large lobster set in front of him, then up at the waiter. "Why, it looks like a big bug!"

The waiter attempted to conceal a grin, then said, "It tastes a little better than that, sir. I assure you."

Peter said, "Do we dare ask a blessing over that bug?"

"Sure. Go right ahead. If God made it, I guess I can eat it," Easy replied.

The three bowed their heads, and Peter offered a quick prayer of thanks, then they began at once. The food was delicious, although Easy had much difficulty with his.

"How do you get at this thing?" he asked.

"I think you crack it with those pliers. The claws, anyway," Peter offered.

Easy struggled gamely with his lobster's claw, finally cracking it. "I must've been crazy to order something you had to get out of a suit of armor to eat. What's this?"

"I think that's drawn butter. You dip the meat in it before you eat it," Jolie said. She had learned this by watching the group at the next table. As Easy tasted it, she asked, "Do you like it?"

"Well, not as good as barbecued goat, but it ain't bad. Don't reckon it will hurt me none if I can keep it down."

Jolie and Peter laughed at Easy's predicament, and the three friends sat there enjoying their meal. While the musicians continued to play, Jolie began explaining how she had gotten her job. "I went inside this theater and asked to see the manager. Well, I got the manager of the theater, but he didn't help me any—he said I'd have to talk to the producer. When I tried to find him, I couldn't. But I did meet one of the actors. He was the nicest man. His name was Cecil B. DeMille. He told me the producer was out of the country and asked if he could help. I told him all about working in the movie business out west and that I was in New York and needed a job. He seemed to think that I wanted to be an actress, but I told him that I could help with the costumes and with the prompting and things like that."

"What sort of a fellow was he? Was he like the movie actors we met?"

"He had real sharp eyes and was beginning to lose his hair, but he was so nice, Peter. He took me to the director, Mr. Dunn, and made a special plea for me. Well, it must've been God's doing because Mr. Dunn said, 'You know, we've been needing help with the prompting, and Ethel, our costume lady, is going to have to leave. Her daughter is sick.' Anyway, I got the job."

"Well, congratulations. You're still in show biz." Peter smiled. "Now you can support us all in style."

"They're going to pay me thirty dollars a week. That'll buy lots of parts for the *Jolie Blonde*, won't it, Peter?"

"It'll sure help." Peter's brow furrowed. "We've got to get that thing running right, or we're never going to get her in a race." He looked down at his hand and said, "Burned my hand on the engine yesterday. I hope it doesn't give me any trouble."

Easy suddenly looked up and said, "You don't have to worry about that, Peter. I'll take care of it."

Peter, who had refused to go to the doctor because of the cost, suddenly grinned. "I forgot you were the expert on all these kinds of things. What's the Easy Devlin method for curing a burn?"

"Why, there's not much to it," Easy shrugged. "First you take a gill of chicken fat, and you take six eggs and roast 'em on the live embers until they're hard, and then you take out the yolks. The next thing, you mix 'em all together and cook 'em in the fat till they're black, then you add some rue and take it out and strain it through a towel. When it's all ready, you gotta cool it with a gill of olive oil."

"Sounds complicated to me. Are you sure it'll work?" Peter winked at Jolie, for the two enjoyed hearing Easy's folk doctoring and superstitions.

"Work? Does a bear sleep in the woods? I should say it works! Of course," he said, shrugging his thin shoulders, "Jolie will have to be the one to make it."

"Why will I have to make it?" Jolie demanded.

"Because it will only work when a man makes it for a burn that's on a woman, or a woman has to make it for a burn that's on a man."

"Oh, I should have understood that!" Jolie said, repressing a smile. "I'll remember that the next time." She held out her hand. "I've got this small wart started on my thumb here. I've forgotten what you've said to take warts off." It was not really a wart, but Jolie liked to tease Easy about his unusual remedies.

Glancing at it casually, Easy scratched his head. "Well, the best way would be to bathe it in the water in which a blacksmith has cooled his irons. Of course, you have to do it when he ain't lookin' at ya."

"I don't think we're going to find many blacksmiths around here," Peter said.

"Well, the next best thing is to take a string and tie as many knots in it as you got warts, then go bury the string." Easy looked at them suddenly with a supercilious scowl. "I know you two don't put no stock in this kind of thing, but that's because you ain't educated!"

"I'll tie a string tonight and go out and bury it," Jolie promised. She knew she would do it, for she was very fond of Easy and didn't want to hurt his feelings.

As the three walked home after their meal, the stars overhead began to sparkle in the darkening sky, appearing like diamonds on a great blue velvet dome. The streetlights of the city did not shine as brightly, it seemed, as those millions of stars. When they reached the apartment building, Easy went to bed at once, but Peter said, "I'm going to sit out on the steps in the backyard."

"I'll sit with you. I'm not sleepy," Jolie said.

They went outside and sat down. Peter looked at the shadowy figure of the *Jolie Blonde* and said, "It was nice of the landlady to let us keep the car out here. I don't know what we would have done in a city like this."

"Do you really think you'll win a race in the *Jolie Blonde*, Peter?" Jolie asked.

She turned to him and the soft silvery light of the moon silhouetted her face. Her lips turned up slightly at the corners, and her voice grew soft as she spoke to Peter. The fragrance of lilac from her hair suddenly came to him, sliding through the armor of his self-sufficiency. She had a way of smiling that was very attractive when her chin tilted up and her lips curved in pretty lines. A serenity had come into her features that he loved. He thought about the terrible life she had led and was suddenly pleased that their paths had crossed. For a moment he studied her beautifully fashioned face, thinking, as he often did, *If only she'd get that ugly scar removed.* Yet whenever he would mention it to her, she refused to hear of it, saying that such an operation would be too expensive, and there were no guarantees it would even work.

"Sure we will. We'll win a lot of races, and then," he said quietly, "we're going to take you to a doctor and see about getting that scar fixed."

Quickly Jolie turned her head. She was embarrassed about it and had spent most of her life turning her face away from the world—ever since her stepfather had inflicted the scar. "I don't think about that," she said.

"I think you do. You're always honest, Jolie. I don't know why you turn away every time I try to talk to you about this."

He saw the oval of her face with the dark streak lying like a velvet strip across the left side of her face. As he studied her, he remembered when he had first met her. She had been little more than a leggy kid, built more like a boy than a girl, and full of fire. She now possessed all the fullness and grace of a mature young woman but had lost none of her spirit. It seemed very important to him that she get her scar removed and find a husband. He wanted good things for her and wanted to tell her some of his thoughts. But now that she had become such an impressive-looking woman, he somehow found it more difficult to express himself to her.

An owl suddenly sailed across the sky, casting a shadow on the ground in front of them. They both looked up, and Peter shook his head. "I guess they must feed on rats. That's about the only game there is in the big city."

Jolie watched the owl disappear silently into the darkness, then asked again, "What about the car, Peter? When are you going to enter it in a race?"

Peter shook his head. "It's all a matter of money, I guess. I'll be racing against men who have plenty of it, and we have to make do with what we've got."

"I hate thinking about money," Jolie said abruptly. "Life is so short, and grubbing after money is the last thing I want to spend my life doing."

"I feel the same way, but it takes money to buy the parts we need," Peter said as he looked at the *Jolie Blonde*. "I don't know how to explain it, Jolie, but I've got to do this thing."

"All right. I'll help you with what I earn from my new job. We'll take every penny we can find, and we'll get the *Jolie Blonde* put together as well as we can. Don't be discouraged, Peter," she said, suddenly putting her hand on his arm and squeezing it. When he turned to her, she was smiling. "We can win. I know we can."

Peter reached out, put his arm around her, and hugged her. "That's what I like to hear. You're good for me, Jolie."

Jolie was silent, for the touch of his arm and the pressure of his body against hers made her heart begin to race. She had known since she had left her adolescence behind that Peter Winslow, who had been kinder to her than anyone she had ever met, was very special to her. Now as she felt his heart beating, she whispered, "I want to help you all I can, Peter."

★　★　★　★

When the butler opened the door and greeted him, Phil Winslow had a sudden impulse to turn and walk away. He had received the invitation in the mail to have dinner with the Lanier family and had debated about accepting. He had not been favorably impressed by Oliver Lanier on his last visit. Still, he had been anxious to learn more about the young man, Clinton, and was more curious, perhaps, about Cara Lanier. Since the night the thugs had jumped them, he had thought of the woman often. His brief encounter with her that night had caught his attention. Now, shaking aside his thoughts, he spoke to the butler, who was waiting for his response.

"I'm Phil Winslow."

"Ah yes, Mr. Winslow. Please come in." The butler was an older man with silver in his brown hair and cautious brown eyes. He stepped back to allow Phil to enter, closed the door, and said, "The family will be down to dinner shortly. Perhaps you'd care to wait in the drawing room."

"Yes, that's fine."

Phil looked around in awe as he followed the butler. The opulent foyer was larger than many people's living rooms. Tall, dark walnut doors were framed with leaded-glass side panels. Ornately carved moldings framed the towering ceiling from which hung a long cut-glass chandelier. A deeply textured silk wall covering framed an ornamental walnut fireplace and a stately grandfather clock chimed the quarter hour as he walked past. A wide staircase curved majestically toward the upper floor, and standing beneath it was a gleaming, marble-topped cherrywood table holding a crystal vase of fresh-cut flowers and flanked by two velvet-upholstered occasional chairs. Beneath Phil's feet, a dark inlaid wood floor gleamed in the soft light, its finish polished to perfection.

As the butler showed him through the drawing room door and stepped aside, Phil looked around the even larger and more opulent room—almost overwhelming in its richness of pattern, color, and ornamentation. At first he thought there was no one there. Then he heard his name called and, looking toward the fireplace, saw Clinton Lanier rise and stride across the room, extending his hand in welcome.

"Phil, I'm so glad you could come."

"Hello, Clinton. How's your head?"

Clinton grinned and touched his head, which now had a faint, shadowy blue mark. "After I finally woke up, I was a little addle-pated for a while, but I think I've still got what few brains I was born with." Clinton laughed. "One thing, though—since I was in no shape to talk that night—I do want to thank you very much for what you did for me."

"What I did for you was take you down to a rough part of town and get you beat over the skull. No thanks needed for that."

"No, that's not how I see it," Clinton said. "I don't see yet how you got us out of that mess. All I remember is getting hit over the head with a club. But I did see you kick that first man. How in the world did you do that?"

Phil grinned, held out his hands, and said, "An artist has to have his hands, otherwise he's out of business. When I was in Paris, there was a new sort of self-defense called kick boxing. It was really pretty impressive. Where I grew up men used their fists to fight, but there's a lot more strength in a man's leg than there is in his arm. The idea is that you kick people instead of hitting them, so I picked up a little of that."

"You must've picked up more than a little," Clinton insisted. His eyes gleamed with admiration. "I wish you could teach me some of that."

"Well, you won't be needing it, Clinton, if you stay out of dark alleys and the kind of neighborhoods I live in. I think—"

"The family is waiting, sir," the butler interrupted. "Dinner is on the table."

"Come along, Phil," Clinton urged, taking his new friend by the shoulder. "The family's dying to hear about our adventure, and since I was out of it, you'll have to tell them all about it."

Phil had little inclination to relate the incident, but he walked with Clinton through gilt-stenciled doors into the long formal dining room. As an artist he couldn't help being caught up by the soaring frescoed ceiling from which hung a brass and crystal chandelier with beautifully etched globes. *This is almost like a small museum*, he thought as he took in the many gold-framed paintings displayed on the walls, some portraits, others landscapes.

The family was gathered and waiting before yet another elegant fireplace, this one framed in imported tiles, a crackling fire radiating warmth into the room. The long dining table, draped in damask and lace, was set with handsome gold-trimmed china, ornate silverware, and delicate crystal, which sparkled by the light of the tall white tapers in silver candelabra framing a bountiful arrangement of spring flowers and ferns.

Seeing the young men enter, Oliver Lanier strode toward them to offer his hand.

"Welcome to our home, Mr. Winslow."

"Thank you for the invitation, Mr. Lanier."

"Have you met everyone?"

"I think so, but," Phil nodded, running his eyes around the family, "things were a little hectic the last time I was here, so I might not get everyone's name right."

"I don't doubt it, sir," Oliver said, drawing Phil toward the family group. "Well, let me name them again. Cara, Mary Ann, Benjamin, Elizabeth, and Robert. Now, let us all sit down, and we'll hear what you have to say about the great adventure you and Clinton had." Lanier stepped over to hold out his wife's chair while the young men assisted their sisters.

Phil took his place at the table and watched appreciatively as the first course, a delicate carrot soup, was carried in by neatly dressed servants. The main course soon followed—roasted beef tenderloin, mashed potatoes, fresh green beans, and corn oysters, and following the main course, a French salad, then imported cheeses and fresh fruit. Finally, a special treat—ice cream snowballs. Phil ate hungrily, but only as he was able while telling the story of how the ruffians had tried to rob them and answering the family's questions. Through it all, he made little of his own part.

"That's the worst storytelling I ever heard!" Clinton exclaimed. "Here you demolished three thugs with your bare hands, or your feet I might say, and you act as if it were nothing."

"I've already spoken to Clinton," Oliver said, leaning forward and placing his large hands on the table, "about his part in it. He showed very bad judgment going down to that part of town after dark."

"Well, I live there, so I don't have much choice," Phil shrugged.

"Ah," Oliver said. "And just what is it you do for a living?"

"I'm an artist, sir."

Cara had said almost nothing and was as pale as always, but she was truly enjoying herself. The family rarely had dinner guests, and even more rarely did she attend. Her father usually had her meals served in her room. For this special occasion, she had worn a burgundy velvet with a high-necked, loose-fitting bodice trimmed with gold braid and a narrow flared skirt decorated around the bottom with an undulating pattern of matching braid resembling the waves of the ocean.

Now Cara's eyes lighted up. "How exciting to have a real artist in our house!" she said eagerly.

"Are you successful, sir?" Oliver asked pointedly.

Phil suddenly grinned. "You mean, have I sold a lot of paintings? No, sir. I suppose you might say I'm just a student. I've been studying in Europe for the past three years. And now I'm a student at the American Institute of Art."

"Oh, I'd love to hear all about it! Did you go to Paris?" Cara asked.

"Yes. I spent a year there. Most of the time in the Louvre. It's a little bit discouraging, Miss Cara. You see all the great paintings by the great artists, and you feel like you're doing nothing but dabbling."

"Tell me a little bit about the paintings you saw."

"My daughter," Oliver interrupted, "is an accomplished artist herself. She has sold quite a few of her paintings."

Phil did not miss the note of pride in Lanier's voice, nor how his large, square face changed as he looked at Cara. *She must be his pet*, Phil thought. *He doesn't look that way at any of his other children.*

"It must not be very difficult to sell paintings if my daughter can do it from her sickbed."

Phil was quiet. He sensed Oliver Lanier's displeasure and could tell that the big man thought little of a grown person who spent his time dabbling with paints. Oliver was a man of practical impulses, the kind Phil had often met, and the idea of making a living, or even of being an artist, was repugnant to him. Now Phil shrugged, saying, "I suppose that may be true, Mr. Lanier. Most painters never make a living." A flash of contempt leaped into Oliver's eyes then, and at that moment, Phil knew there was no hope that this successful businessman would ever stoop to include a lowly artist in his social circle. He thought it strange as he glanced at Cara, whose delicate features and sensitive attitude were so different. There was something different also, he decided, in Clinton, and even in all the rest of the Lanier sons and daughters. *They must get their gentleness from their mother. They certainly didn't get it from their father.*

The meal finally ended with a tense but controlled altercation between Clinton and his father. Phil had mentioned the *Jolie Blonde* and his cousin Peter Winslow, who intended to be a race car driver, and at once Oliver's face had flushed.

"Nonsense! All nonsense!" he growled.

"You mean racing, Mr. Lanier?" Phil inquired.

"I mean the whole nonsense of automobiles! They'll never amount to anything!"

"I'm afraid I'll have to disagree with you about that, Mr. Lanier," Phil said easily. "I admit they're an innovation, and I grew up with nothing but horses, but when you look around now, you can see that they're the coming thing."

"They're loud and they stink up the air!"

"I'll admit that's true. Still, many new inventions aren't particularly pleasant at first."

"Can you imagine what will happen," Lanier stated flatly, "if they ever go as fast as the prophets say they will? Why, they'd kill more people than all the wars in history." At that point Clinton tried to make a defense, but his father gave him a harsh look and a stern rebuke. "Clinton, we've discussed this before, and here's my final word! Automobiles will have no part in your life! You have plenty to do to learn the business without wasting your time on all this newfangled nonsense!"

An embarrassed silence fell over the room, and Phil felt very bad for Clinton, whose face had grown red, his lips tightly closed. Shifting his glance, Phil saw that Cara, too, was humiliated and angered by her father's harshness. She lifted her eyes to her father and seemed to plead with him to have some understanding.

"I'd like to see some of your paintings, Miss Cara," Phil spoke up suddenly, hoping to alleviate the unbearable tension.

Relieved, Cara stood to her feet. "If you all will excuse us, I will show Mr. Winslow some of the things I've done."

"You take him right along," Alice said. "Bring him back down to the drawing room afterward."

"That will be too much for her to do, Alice. She's had too much excitement already. See how pale her cheeks are?" Oliver rose and came over to his daughter. He stood towering over her and looked down. "You may show our guest a few of your paintings, and then I want you to drink your ale, take all your medicines, and go straight to bed."

"But I feel fine, Father."

Oliver shook his head. "I'm afraid I must insist, my dear. Go along now." Turning to Phil, he issued one final warning. "I trust you will not overtire my daughter, sir."

Recognizing the warning, Phil nodded. "Of course. I won't be long."

The two left the dining room, and Cara led Phil along the hallway to the stairs. Holding on to the railing, she ascended slowly. Phil modified his steps to stay with her.

She turned to him and said, "I'm sure it must be annoying for you to have to put up with an invalid, Mr. Winslow."

"Not at all, and I wish you'd call me Phil."

Color flushed in Cara's cheeks, and she said, "That would be nice, and please call me Cara."

When they reached the top of the stairs, Phil said, "I don't want to be impertinent, but you're not really an invalid, are you?"

"I had a severe illness ten years ago. I've never really recovered from it, and the doctors are quite mystified." Then, as if shutting the door on the subject, she lifted her head and said, "Come, I'll show you what I've done. But I warn you, they're not like what you've seen in Europe."

"Some of it was pretty bad," Phil said. "I don't know how some of them ever got into the museums."

When they stepped inside the room, he swept it with a quick glance. Instantly he recognized that this was the tower in which Cara Lanier hid herself from the world. He took in all of the treasures of her childhood and the pictures of the family. The furniture itself was comfortable, and the room was large and spacious—but a prison, he quickly grasped, all the same.

"Now that I'm here," Cara said, turning around, "I . . . I don't think I want you to see my work."

"Why not?"

"It's not—well, I've never had anyone except my agent look at it."

"You never go to the shows where your pieces are shown?"

"Oh, never! Father would never permit it!"

"That's a shame, but please allow me to see them. I insist."

He smiled at her, and at that moment Cara thought he looked very masculine and that he exuded health. She studied the tanned planes of his face, then said quietly, "All right. If you insist."

Moving across the room, she opened a large wardrobe that obviously had been made to hold her paintings. She took out two of them, set them on a table, leaning them against the wall, then removed two more and placed them beside the others. "There," she said and stepped back to watch his reaction.

Phil instantly made a judgment. He was disappointed in her work, but it was not that they were bad. Rather, they were . . . bland. All four paintings were flower arrangements of roses, tulips, marigolds, and daisies. The technical aspects of them were good indeed, and it was on this quality that he began to speak. "I admire your brushwork in this one," he said. "It must've been very hard to do the centers of these daisies as exactly as you have." It looked almost like a photograph, except for the colors.

"It is slow, but then . . ." Cara smiled, "I have plenty of time."

As Phil studied the paintings, commenting on the various artistic techniques she had used, he found himself more and more intrigued by this woman. He had found out from Clinton that she was thirty years old. By that age most women were married and raising families. The story of her sickness and of her poor health, of course, could account for her not marrying. But there was something about her that puzzled him. The paleness of her skin could be accounted for simply by being indoors, but he had no sense of the weakness that one usually associates with an invalid. He had the impression that beneath all of the trappings of illness was a strong, vigorous woman. He had no reason for believing this, but he had learned long ago to trust his impressions.

Her paintings all lacked that spark of inspiration one looks for in true art. It was as if she had painted only from the surface of her mind and talent. Nevertheless, her work did have some special qualities. Somehow, especially in the painting of the daisies, she had managed to capture a picture of vibrant health and strength. The vivid colors seemed to leap off the canvas. It was obviously a scene from the front yard, as were the other three, but she had caught the blue sky, and the sun was magnificent.

"When I was in Holland, I saw a great deal of the Flemish masters," he said finally. He stepped closer and peered at the picture of the daisies. "They are most famous for the way they are able to capture sunlight. It's amazing. You feel like you can almost touch it and your hand would grow warm. Miss Cara," he said, "you've got something of that in this painting here called *Daisies in the Morning*. I don't think I've ever seen light treated any better."

Cara's face flushed at his compliment and her eyes grew warm. "How kind of you to say that."

"I don't think it's kind. I could make some comments that aren't quite as amiable." Phil smiled rather crookedly. "But I'm a guest in your house, so I'd better withhold them."

Cara was nonplussed. She stared at him, for she had been guarded from adverse comments. She had no life, except with her family and her painting, and now this tall man had suddenly said there were things wrong with them. She straightened up, and her eyes lost their warmth. "What do you mean, not quite as amiable?" she demanded.

"Oh, nothing about the technical aspects." Phil recognized that Cara was not accustomed to bold critiques of her paintings, but he wanted to stir her up to see what lay beneath the fine veneer of manners and careful composure that she showed the world. "Technically these are fine. The brushwork, the proportion, the symmetry, and especially the colors. You have a real flair for that."

"Well, what else is there?" she asked coolly.

Phil hesitated, then shrugged. "There's more to life than flowers, Cara."

"I'm well aware of that!" she answered rather defensively.

Well, I touched her that time, Phil thought. He considered changing the subject, but he was interested in the woman. She did not have the life and the vitality that he admired in most women, but still, without any evidence, he believed it lay somewhere deep inside, longing to burst forth. He felt about her as he did about a painting that he was just starting. Somewhere in the paint and in the canvas was a masterpiece. He felt all he had to do was make it come together. Of course, as an artist, he could bring paint to the canvas. But how does one stir up a woman who is wealthy and has never known life except as a carefully protected individual, almost as if she were sealed in a cocoon?

Cara saw his hesitation. "Of course there's more than flowers, but someone has to paint flowers."

"No argument there. Some of the finest paintings I've seen in Europe, and in this country too, are of flowers. But my theory of art is that an artist should put things on a canvas that move people, that stir them, that make them angry even. A painting should at least make some sort of statement about the world in which we live."

"But . . . these flowers are a part of our world."

Phil had a flash of intuition. "Let me see some of your paintings that aren't of flowers," he said and watched her face. He saw it change and knew he had hit a nerve.

"I . . . I don't have any."

"You see? You love flowers, which is very commendable, but as I said, life is a lot more than flowers."

Cara stared at him and felt intimidated by the health and zest for life that radiated from him. She saw a strength in him that she admired. It was not like the strength of her father, for his was no more than indomitable control and harshness. No, this man standing before her was strong, but his strength lay under an amiable exterior, even a fine-looking one. She had had a few sweethearts before her illness, but that had been years ago. Long, long ago she had given up any hope of romance and courtship and marriage. But now, as she looked at Phil Winslow, something stirred within her heart. It was so faint that she was not even fully conscious of it. All she knew was that he was a man who had brought something into her castle that had not been there before. She had been content and satisfied about her painting, confident that it was good, and that she had one small accomplishment to smile about in her confined world. Now this man had come in and challenged the one possession she had. Anger flared up in her, and she said, "I don't think it behooves you, an artist who has never sold a painting, to bring charges against me!"

"I'm sorry I've angered you," Phil said quietly. "I didn't mean to. I think you have great talent, maybe greater than you realize. I believe you're capable of painting more than a daisy."

"I don't want to hear any more of this!" Cara said, raising her voice.

"Very well. Once again, I'm sorry we disagree. I didn't mean to be offensive." He paused for one moment, then looked into her eyes and said, "Don't be afraid of life, Cara."

A silence fell over the room. Cara could hear only the ticking of the mantel clock. His words seemed to find a lodging somewhere deep inside her. They had a prophetic sound, and very rarely in her life had anything struck her so hard and so sharply. *Don't be afraid of life.* The words seemed to echo, like a tolling bell deep within her. Suddenly unable to listen any longer, she said abruptly, "Good-bye, Mr. Winslow."

"It's Phil . . . and good night, Cara." He turned and left the room, unaware of the devastating effect his visit and his words had made upon her.

As the door closed, Cara realized that her hands were trembling. She held them together and turned quickly and looked at the pictures of the flowers that she had labored on for so long. She had been so proud of them, and now with one visit, with one phrase, this man she hardly even knew had managed to destroy the foundations of her happiness.

Don't be afraid of life.

The words came to her again and again, and even after she went to bed she could not sleep, mulling over in her mind what he had said. *There's more to life than flowers.* A wave of resentment flooded her. "What does *he* know?" she said aloud. "He's strong and healthy, and I'm confined to this room and can do nothing! What is there for me in life besides my painting? Now he's taken the pleasure of even that away from me."

Cara lay there thinking of the evening and knew she would not be able to put it out of her mind. She had been impressed by Phil Winslow in a powerful way. True enough, she did not meet many men such as he appeared to be. Her father, she knew, despised him as a worthless trifler in art. It mattered not that Clinton warmly admired him, and she herself had been so grateful to him for the assistance he had offered to Clinton. Now, however, as she lay there, her hands clenched into fists, she whispered, "What do I care what he thinks? He's just a penniless artist! Father's right about him!"

Her sudden agreement with her father did not help the swirl of troubling emotions she felt inside. To her shock and amazement, she found tears running down the sides of her face. She wiped them away quickly and said, "I won't let him make me cry! He's wrong. He has to be wrong. . . !"

CHAPTER FIVE

A TIME TO LIVE

★ ★ ★ ★

Life at the art institute was entertaining but at the same time rather depressing for Phil Winslow. Day after day he would go early, after a sparse breakfast, then paint for hours. One day, however, he had stopped painting. He was sitting and staring out the window when Crumpler, the instructor, came by. "Why aren't you painting, Winslow?" he demanded.

"No more canvases."

"Buy some."

"No money."

Crumpler stared at Phil, then shrugged. "Come along." He took him to a storeroom where hundreds of old canvases, abandoned by former students, were stacked up to the ceiling. "Grab some of those," he said. "You can use them again." A look of contempt curled his thick lips. "The world won't be losing much. Most of it's junk anyway."

Phil grinned. "How do you know I won't put more junk on it?"

Crumpler was as sparing with his compliments as Ebenezer Scrooge had been of his money, but now he finally said grudgingly, "You've got something in you, Winslow. I'd like to see it come out."

As bleak as the words were, they spurred Phil to do more. He now had an unlimited supply of canvases and only had to buy paints and a brush from time to time. He threw himself into the work in a zealous frenzy, irritating the other students, who looked down upon him.

One of the things about Winslow's paintings that puzzled Crumpler and annoyed the other students was his choice of subjects. Most of them were painting still lifes, landscapes, or portraits, for that was where the money was. Phil had become almost obsessed in depicting various settings from the streets of New York. He roamed the poor immigrant district near his boarding-house, and once painted a picture of a German family who had agreed to pose for him. He had managed to make friends with this family by bringing them sweets. He chose their front room as his setting, allowing the dilapidated furniture and a stove with stacked bricks replacing a missing leg to bring out the hard poverty the Schultzes lived in day to day. He depicted honestly the ugly, ill-fitting clothes the children wore, and the way they stared at him with large eyes. He spent a great deal of time on the faces of the father and mother, both lined by poverty, hard work, and disease.

He had brought the painting to the institute and placed it on the easel, intending to fill in some of the final details. As he started to apply some finishing touches, he noticed that the other students curled their lips up and then passed right on by.

When Crumpler stopped, he stared at the painting for a long time. Phil sat there waiting for the acid comment that was sure to come.

"Why did you want to paint this?"

"I guess because I get tired of daisies and apples and fruit bowls."

"No one would ever buy a picture like this."

"I didn't think they would."

"Why paint, then, if you can't sell a picture?"

"I guess I'm just the artistic type. I'll probably wind up starving in an attic somewhere."

Crumpler was not satisfied with Phil's flippant response. He continued to study the picture and said, "Have you ever heard of the Ashcan School?"

"Ashcan School? No, what's that?"

Crumpler shrugged his beefy shoulders. "A group of painters who paint stuff like this. I guess they picked the name all right. They like to paint pictures of the backyards of tenements. All pretty grim stuff."

"Who are they? What're their names?"

"Don't know most of them. One of them's named John Sloan. He was a student here for a while a long time ago. Some of his paintings are in the window of an art shop. I don't know why. They'll never sell."

"I'd like to see them."

"It's over on Eighteenth Street. Place called Maxim's."

Phil left at once to find Maxim's. There he saw paintings in the window such as he had never seen before. They were not "nice," but instantly he realized that this man Sloan had absorbed the poor of New York into his bloodstream, and now they somehow vividly came to life on his canvas. He stood before one painting of three women out on a rooftop drying their hair. Two of them, a brunette and a blonde, sat on the ledge. All wore clumsy-looking shoes, obviously marking them as lower class, and soot-blackened tenement houses rose up into the smoky air behind them. To one side, a clothesline full of underwear and work clothes flapped in the breeze. The main figure, wearing a white chemise, was pulling her blond hair forward over her shoulder, allowing the sun— what there was of it—to dry her hair.

Another painting, obviously by a different artist, portrayed two young girls dancing in the street. It was a dark portrait, except for the light that illuminated the faces of the girls. The face of the one on the right glowed, and her hair spun as she danced around. Her expression of joy spoke loudly and contrasted vividly with the poverty shown in her heavy shoes and worn clothing.

Going inside, Phil wandered around and found himself more impressed than he had been by the paintings in the art museums of Europe. *These are real*, he thought. *They show how life really is*. He paused before a portrait of two wrestlers. They were on the mat struggling, one man with his head braced against the mat straining to keep his shoulders from being pinned. Every muscle stood out on the two men, the terrible strain captured in paint. The pink flesh of the central wrestler about to be pinned was the most life-like thing Phil had ever seen.

"You like that?"

Phil twirled to see a man standing beside him, a small man with a bushy red mustache and a pair of alert blue eyes.

"My name is George Maxim—but everyone just calls me Maxim. You like the painting?"

"I've never seen anything like it."

"A man named George Luks did it. You can almost smell the sweat on those fellows, can't you?"

"Yes. How much is it?"

"How much have you got?" Maxim smiled.

Phil laughed. "Not enough to buy it, I suppose. Do you sell many?"

"No, not too many," Maxim said. He cocked his head to one side, and his lips turned up in a smile. He fingered his mustache and said, "You're a painter, I take it?"

"Trying to be."

"Most painters don't like these fellows, Luk and Sloan. They call them the Ashcan School."

"Is it a large group?"

"They're called 'The Eight.'" He named them off and said, "I take it you'd like to be number nine."

"I like what they're doing. Look at this one. Who did it?"

"Everett Schin." Maxim studied Phil and said quietly, with interest, "You think that's good?"

"Well, look at it."

It was a portrait of the backyard of a tenement. All across the back of the painting a run-down building rose up, cluttered with junk, with clothes flapping on a drooping clothesline. At the bottom a woman was hanging out clothes, and piled against a nearby fence were broken boxes and scraps of metal. To one side was the inevitable outhouse with an open door. It was a world he had seen often, and Phil said, "I think it's great."

"That's too bad."

Phil looked at the man in surprise. "Why is it too bad?"

"Because they're all going to starve to death, and you as well! I advise you to paint flowers. That's what people want."

Immediately Phil thought of Cara Lanier, with her paintings of immaculate, neatly done daisies in white porcelain pots. "I'd rather do this," he said and shrugged.

Maxim laughed. "Come back and bring some of your work. I'll put one in my window. Maybe somebody will buy it."

"Why, thanks. That'll be fine. I'll do it."

The visit was repeated many times and, indeed, Phil did take several of his paintings to George Maxim, who took them on commission. None of them sold, but Phil and the art dealer became fast friends.

Another friend was Avis Warwick. She was evidently in one

of her working moods, for she came to the studio every day during a period of a week and a half.

"You work too hard, Phil," she said at the end of the first week. "I think I'm working too hard, too." She laughed at herself. "No one else ever accuses me of that." Then abruptly she said, "You can take me out tonight—or I'll take you. Whichever way you want to look at it."

"All right, Avis," Phil said. He was tired, and he agreed to meet her that night in front of the institute. He had no idea where she lived. She never mentioned her life away from the world of art. It was a bit of a mystery about her, but she apparently had plenty of money.

That night when they met, she said, "Tonight's on me, Phil. I know you're broke."

"I don't care much for a woman paying my way."

"Is your male pride hurt?" she asked, a coy smile turning her full lips upward.

"I guess it is a little bit. I'm used to paying my own way and for my dates."

"It won't hurt you to break a rule now and then. I break a lot of them." She winked at him lewdly and grinned. "I'll tell you all about my rule breaking. Maybe we can find one to break together."

Something about Avis Warwick seemed to relax Phil. He laughed suddenly. "All right. Where are you going to take me?"

"I've been wanting to see that fellow Harry Houdini perform," Avis said. "They say no locks can hold him. I've always been one to try to break free from any kind of chains, so I might pick up a few tips. Come on."

They bought tickets with Avis's money for the front row and enjoyed the show immensely. Houdini, the famous escape artist, proved to be an entertaining fellow. He was a fine-looking man with black curly hair and direct light blue eyes and had a winsome personality. He also had a body that most men could only dream about. When he threw off his robe and stood clad only in a pair of trunks, Avis reached over and grabbed Phil's arm. "Look at those muscles! I believe he could break those chains just by flexing his arms!"

Houdini was indeed a muscular man. He was not heavy, but every muscle seemed delineated. He allowed himself to be chained hand and foot. As he carried on a clever monologue with his audience, spiced with jokes, he slipped out of the chains as easily as a man takes off his coat.

"Look at that," Avis said. "You need to take lessons from Harry."

"How's that, Avis?"

"Why, you're all bound up, Phil. Bad upbringing. I bet your parents made you go to church and keep the Golden Rule."

"I'm afraid so. I'm a pretty respectable fellow." Avis leaned against him, and he felt her body pressing against his arm. When he looked at her, there was a strange light in her eyes.

"I'll help you get out of some of that if you stay around long enough."

After the show they went to a restaurant. This time it was Delmonico's, and Phil enjoyed the ostentatious interior, saying, "After hamburgers and corned beef, this is pretty fancy fare."

Avis was enjoying herself. She had dressed carefully for the occasion, which was unusual for her. Her dress was made of dark rose-colored silk and had a tight bodice decorated with lace above the bosom and down the sleeves. Neck and waist were trimmed with a darker burgundy silk, and she wore gloves to match. In addition, the flared skirt sported a large embroidered design in the same color all around the bottom. Avis was a very attractive woman, and all eyes seemed to turn toward her wherever she went. She was accustomed to the attention, though, and said, "Do you ever expect to be rich, Phil?"

"No, not likely."

"I've never been poor. It must be awful."

"Well, I've never been poor either. My family's got a big ranch in Montana. I could go there if I wanted to and punch cattle for a living."

"Too tame for you?" she asked, smiling across the table.

Phil grinned recklessly. "I guess so. I'll probably starve to death as a poor obscure artist."

The band began playing and Avis straightened up. "Come along. Dance with me."

"I'm not much of a dancer," Phil said.

"Well, I am," Avis smiled. "I'll show you."

They moved out on the dance floor, and Phil looked around at the other couples. "What in the world kind of a dance is this?"

"It's called the Grizzly Bear," Avis said. "You don't know it?"

"No, and I don't think I want to either. Look at that!"

All around them men were simply putting their arms around women, and the women responded in like fashion. They were joggling around the floor hugging and laughing.

Seeing the look on Phil's face, Avis laughed. "You look like a Puritan. Come on. Put your arms around me." She did not wait but grabbed him in a hug, pressing her body against his, and Phil was almost forced to put his arms around her in return. "Well, we can't just stand here hugging. Let's dance."

The Grizzly Bear was quite an ordeal for Phil. It appeared to him to be little more than an excuse for men to hug women and vice versa. Avis enjoyed it, but Phil was glad when they got off the dance floor.

Later on when they left, she said, "I don't think I've ever met anybody like you." They were in a carriage headed down toward Phil's boardinghouse. When they got there, she asked, "Would you like me to come in?"

Knowing exactly what was in Avis's mind, Phil felt strongly tempted. However, he quickly said, "I don't think so, Avis. Not my kind of thing."

Avis Warwick was fascinated. "I can't read you, Phil," she said. "Most men would beat my door down to spend a little time with me."

"I can understand that. Nothing personal," he said.

Avis leaned back in the carriage and asked, "Is it religion?"

"Yes. That's it."

"You're one of those Christians, I take it."

"Not a very good one." Phil felt he was getting in over his head. "I guess God's not through with me yet. Are your feelings hurt?"

"Sure they are, but it's not over." She smiled, leaned over, and pulled his head down. Her lips were soft under his and she moved against him. Her hands were locked behind his head, and he could not move. Suddenly she released him and laughed. "Go on in. I won't attack you tonight. There's always tomorrow."

Phil stepped out of the carriage and glanced at the driver, who had turned to watch, a grin on his face. "Good night, Avis," Phil said. "I'll see you Monday."

The next morning Phil awoke early, ate breakfast, and went to church. It was, perhaps, appropriate that the minister preached on Joseph's temptation with the wife of Potiphar. He was a fine minister and was quite adept at setting forth the account with well-chosen words. He described vividly Potiphar's attractive wife as she tried to seduce the youthful Joseph. As the preaching went on, Phil was suddenly very glad that he had been able to pull himself away from Avis Warwick.

After the service he wandered the streets for a while, then decided to pay a visit to Peter Winslow and his companions. He arrived to find them out in the backyard working on the car. He was surprised to see Clinton Lanier there as well. Clinton, dressed in what appeared to be some of Peter's castoffs, was bent over peering into the car's inner works, but as Phil approached, Clinton straightened.

"Why, Phil," Clinton said, "glad to see you!"

"Hello, Clinton. What are you doing here?" Phil asked, shaking the man's hand.

"Peter's letting me help with the car a little bit." He grinned and suddenly looked much younger than his twenty-seven years. "These three act like I'm going to wreck it or something."

Jolie Devorak was also wearing an old set of mechanic's coveralls. She had a spot of grease on her cheek, and her black hair shone in the afternoon sunlight. "We're going to make him our mechanic. He can do all the dirty work."

Easy grunted. "He's going to have to learn more than he knows now." Easy was very jealous of the *Jolie Blonde*, but he really liked young Lanier. "He's learning, though. I'm giving him lessons."

"Doesn't look like you need any more help here, Peter," Phil said.

Peter shook his head and returned the grin. "Never had so many volunteers."

"I'll just watch. I don't know much about cars."

It was a pleasant afternoon for Phil. He had developed a real liking for Clinton and also for Peter. They took a midafternoon break and sat around drinking the lemonade that Jolie had brought out. She had gotten ice and chipped it with an ice pick, filling their glasses. As they drank it, Peter mentioned that Cassidy had written him.

"He knows more about the Winslows than anybody I ever heard."

"He sure does," Phil agreed. "You know much about our family tree?"

"Not as much as I should," Peter said. "My father does,

though. He keeps up with it. He's always talking about Christmas Winslow. Now there was a man for you."

"Who was that?" Jolie asked.

"Why, he was a mountain man. He trapped beavers and married a woman who was half Indian. I think her name was White Dove," Phil said. "My favorite, I think, was a man called Gilbert Winslow. He came over on the *Mayflower*."

The two men talked about their family history, and Clinton said, "I think it's great that you know all about your family all the way back to the days of the *Mayflower*. I don't know anybody past my grandfather on my mother's side."

"Well, maybe you'll be the start of a dynasty, Clinton," Phil said.

Jolie had been listening, fascinated as always with the Winslow lineage. Now she said, "I guess you two are the real aristocrats. The rest of us are just pups."

Clinton laughed with her. "I think you're right, Jolie."

"Well, you're a rich pup, anyway," Jolie teased him.

"That's my father. He controls all the money."

"You'll take over though one day, won't you?" Jolie asked. She was curious about this man, for he was strangely shy for the son of a wealthy stockbroker. The two of them drew off to one side, and as the others were talking about the engine of the car, she asked, "Don't you like being a stockbroker?"

"Not much. If I had my way, I'd be a tinker or a mechanic."

"Can't you do that as a hobby?"

"Do you know you've got grease on your face?"

Startled, Jolie reached up to touch her cheek.

"No, over on this side." Clinton whipped out his handkerchief and reached out, but the grease was on the side by Jolie's scar and she turned away. He said, "I was just going to wipe it off."

Jolie grew quiet and seemed to have lost her liveliness. She stood there for a moment, then shrugged. "All right." She turned her face and stood there watching him as he removed the grease. She watched for some sign of revulsion in his eyes but saw none.

"That's a bad scar. How'd you get it?" he asked casually.

"It looks awful, doesn't it?"

"Why, no!" Clinton said. "Of course, no scars are particularly nice, I suppose. Why don't you get it fixed?"

"It costs a lot of money."

The abruptness of her reply startled Clinton. Money was not

one of his problems, and suddenly he was confronted with a young woman whose dark eyes were bitter. "I'm sorry," he said. "I forget about money. I don't care much about it myself."

"You know, I don't think you do. And you really don't seem to mind this scar either, but I do. I think about it every day. I try to find ways to let my hair cover it, but that doesn't work."

"You're very pretty, Jolie, and more than that, you're a fine young woman. I enjoy being around you."

Jolie flushed and said, "Why . . . thank you, Clinton. That's nice of you to say."

"Not hard to say at all."

"Why haven't you ever married?" she asked abruptly. "Most men your age are at least thinking about it."

"Because if I did, I'd have to bring her into our house, and I wouldn't bring any young woman there."

Surprised, Jolie arched her eyebrows. "Why, that's a fine house you live in, isn't it?"

"Oh yes. The house is fine. It's just that—well, sometimes it gets a little tense inside."

Jolie waited for him to go on but saw that he was embarrassed. "I didn't have a very good family life myself," she said. "It was my stepfather who gave me this."

"Sometimes," Clinton said slowly, his eyes filled with gloom, "I wish my father would hit me with something. It would be better than all the other things he does that bother me. Well, I don't want to complain," he said, not wanting to burden this young woman with his troubles, "but I do want to talk to Peter about the car." He turned and the two approached the trio who were bent over the engine. "Peter, I've got to go," he said, "but I want to help with the car. I know I'm not enough of a mechanic for the actual work, but I can help with the money." Reaching into his pocket, he pulled out an envelope and said, "I've squirreled this away, and I want you to use it to fix up the *Jolie Blonde*."

Peter stared at Clinton with astonishment. "Why, I couldn't let you do that, Clinton!"

"Why not?"

"Well, you'll never get it back, for one thing."

"Doesn't matter. I'd just like to be a part of what's going on."

Peter Winslow stared at the young man and then smiled. "All right. You're on." He took the money and handed it to Easy. "There you go, Easy."

The small man opened it and stared at the cash on the inside. "Wow!" he said, thumbing through it. "Let me add it up. Tomorrow morning the *Jolie Blonde* gets a new shot of life."

Jolie smiled at Clinton. "Peter and Easy and I have called ourselves the Three Musketeers. I guess it'll have to be the Four Musketeers now."

"Well, actually," Phil said, "there *were* four musketeers."

"There were?" Jolie asked with surprise. "I thought there were only three."

"There were three at first, but then they were joined by a young fellow named D'Artagnan," Phil said. "It was one of my favorite books. Still is. D'Artagnan was quite a fellow." He reached over and slapped Clinton on the shoulder. "You'll have to work hard to keep up with him. You've read the book?"

"Yes. I always admired D'Artagnan but never saw myself as a hero."

Jolie reached over and took his hand and shook it. "You're our hero if you can help us win the races."

Very much aware of four pairs of eyes fastened on him, Clinton suddenly felt warmly accepted. With these friends he felt he was part of something exciting. "That's great. I'll do what I can, but don't tell my father about this. He'd have a stroke."

"We won't be likely to see him," Phil said.

"Well, you might. Cara asked me to give you an invitation. She gets real lonely, Phil. She doesn't have any visitors at all—just the family. You're the first one she's invited to come visit in who knows how long. I'd like for you to do it, if you would."

Phil actually had thought of going by to see Cara, but his last visit had been rather disastrous. Nevertheless, he said quickly, "Why, I'd be glad to, Clinton. Did she name a time?"

"Later this afternoon, if you can make it."

"I'll be there."

★　★　★　★

"Why, Mr. Winslow, come in."

Phil stepped inside the door of the Lanier home, greeted by Mary Ann Lanier. He was not wearing a hat or a coat, so he couldn't offer either of them to her. Instead, he smiled, saying, "How are you, Miss Mary Ann?"

"Fine. I'm so glad to see you."

Mary Ann was a very attractive young woman, her blond hair and blue eyes nicely complemented today by her green tailored day dress. There was a lightness about her spirit that was pleasing—except when her father was present. Then she, like all the rest of the family, grew sober and even gloomy.

"Won't you come into the library? I have someone I'd like for you to meet."

Wondering who it could be, Phil said, "Of course." He followed her into the library, and a young man who was looking out the window turned and stood there expectantly.

"This is my friend, George Camrose. He's the assistant pastor of the Calvary Baptist Church in Brooklyn. Reverend Camrose, this is the gentleman I spoke to you about, Mr. Phil Winslow."

The two men shook hands, and Phil felt immediate approval for the young pastor, who was no more than twenty-five years of age, he guessed. He had dark hair and steady gray eyes.

"I'm glad to know you. Miss Mary Ann has told me all about your adventure with Clinton. It was quite fortunate you happened to be there."

"Well, Pastor, I don't suppose you heard all the story. It was my fault that Clinton got attacked in the first place. I live in a rather seedy neighborhood over on the Lower East Side, and he had offered me a ride home. We came out of it fairly well, though."

"Clinton told me you used a rather startling method of attack. Kick boxing he called it." He lifted his eyebrow and shook his head. "I used to do some boxing myself when I was younger. Never heard of kick boxing."

"It's an effective means of self-defense. I'm not too good at it, but those who are can beat up a man pretty well. So you did some boxing yourself?"

"Oh, just on an amateur basis," Camrose shrugged. "I gave it up, of course, when I entered the ministry. Pugilism is a disreputable world."

"You're going to have to visit the church and hear George preach," Mary Ann said. Her eyes were bright and she made an attractive picture as she stood there looking with pride at the young man. "George is going to be a missionary in Africa someday."

"Really? That's most commendable. I would certainly enjoy visiting your church. What time do your services start?"

"Ten o'clock. We'd be most happy to have you. It's just a small church, of course. As a matter of fact, it's meeting in a storefront right now. We hope for better things."

"They will be better. You'll see," Mary Ann said.

"I suppose you go there, Miss Mary Ann?" Phil asked.

"Why, no. Our family goes to a downtown church." Her eyes went again to the young minister. "I'd like to go hear George, but Father won't hear of it."

"We could use your voice and any musical ability you might have." Camrose grinned faintly. "We don't have a piano player, and I'm the world's worst." He looked hopefully at Winslow. "I don't suppose you can sing and play a piano?"

"No, sorry. I'm a follower as far as hymns are concerned, but I'll be there Sunday morning to do what I can."

"Fine! I'll look forward to seeing you."

The three stood there speaking of the church, and Mary Ann said, "Well, Cara's anxious to see you. I'll take you to her room."

"Oh, I think I can find it. I was there once before. You stay here and entertain the preacher." He put his hand out, saying, "See you Sunday morning."

He left the room, very much aware of Mary Ann's obvious interest in the young minister. "Going to Africa as a missionary," he mused out loud. "*That* won't sit too well with her father." When he reached the door of Cara's room, he knocked gently and at once heard her say, "Come in." Opening the door, he stepped inside and found her sitting in a chair by the window.

She rose, saying, "I saw you come. Did you get detained downstairs?"

Phil moved over and bowed slightly. "I stopped to meet Mary Ann's friend, Reverend Camrose."

"Oh yes, George! What a fine fellow he is!"

"Going to be a missionary in Africa, she tells me. That's quite a dangerous undertaking. I have some relatives who are over there, both Winslows, Barney and his brother, Andrew. I wonder if Reverend Camrose will be in their area."

"Oh, that's so interesting! Did you mention it to him?"

"No, I didn't."

"You should. He's fascinated to hear anything about Africa."

"Well, I'll be visiting the church Sunday morning. If we have time, I'd be glad to tell him and give him their addresses, too." He grinned broadly. "They're always trying to recruit new help for their mission work over there." He thought for a moment, then turned his head to one side as he asked, "Would your father approve of a thing like that?"

Cara remained silent for a moment. "No, I'm afraid not. As a matter of fact, he doesn't even approve of George."

"Not enough money and position?"

Cara's pale face grew slightly pink. "I'm afraid that's part of it. He and Father really aren't the same kind of man."

"No, I don't think they are. Still, some men marry their daughters off to fellows who are different from themselves. You don't think your father would ever give in, or has the young man made an offer?"

"Yes, he proposed, but when Mary Ann mentioned it, Father went into—" She started to say something, then changed her mind. "He became quite displeased."

Phil could imagine what "quite displeased" meant—probably a towering rage. He could picture the bull-like Oliver Lanier striding the floor and pounding his massive fists into his meaty palms, shouting, "My daughter marry a penniless preacher? Never in a thousand years." Phil shook the image out of his head and steered the conversation away from the Lanier family. "I brought you a present," he said and took the flat, rectangular package wrapped in brown paper from under his arm. He handed it to her with a slight smile. "I don't think you'll like it."

"What a thing to say," Cara said. "It's one of your paintings. I can tell."

"Yes it is. Take a look and see what you think."

As she unwrapped the package, Phil thought suddenly that it was a rash thing to give her such a painting. It was, he knew, not the kind of picture Cara Lanier would appreciate—or possibly even understand. Still, he had thought long about it and considered that it might be helpful in some way to break through her veneer of undisturbed gentility.

The painting was of a young girl Phil had seen. She was no more than ten or eleven and was standing outside the tenement building in which she lived. She had on oversized men's shoes and black stockings. The huge shoes gave her a grotesque appearance, which was not helped by the faded brown dress, also a hand-me-down from some woman. It was patched and bulky, gathered around her waist by a string. She was looking down. Her hair would have been blond had it been clean. As it was, the smoky air and the grime of her environment had dulled it to a murky, dirty brown. It was unkempt, unwashed, and had not had a comb or brush pulled through it for some time.

Her face, however, was angelic. Though dirt marred it, beneath the grime and the filth was a pretty girl. Had she been born in high society, Phil thought, she could have been anything. She was holding a torn and battered doll in her hands, and he was close enough to see that her hands were red and swollen. He had studied her carefully, and the image seemed to have transplanted itself into his mind. When he got back to his room, he immediately sketched the child and found he could call up the scene with complete clarity without any difficulty. He had entitled it *A Twelve-Year-Old Worker*, for he assumed she worked in one of the sweatshops or factories where children of no more than eight or nine put in twelve-hour days, sometimes working seven days a week. He had been proud of this painting because it had captured something of the poignancy he had seen in her face and in her eyes, but he did not have the faintest idea how Cara would feel about it.

Laying the paper aside, Cara held the picture up to the light and immediately stood stock-still. She was so still that only the breeze coming through the open window stirred her rich brown hair. It added a touch of red, which Phil had not noticed before, giving it a most attractive tint. Her eyes grew wide and her lips parted, but she said nothing for a long time. Finally she moved over, put the picture on an easel, then stepped back and kept her eyes fixed on it.

Phil remained silent, determined not to ask her opinion. After what seemed forever, she turned and said, "I know why you brought this picture. I mean this particular one."

"Do you?"

"Yes." Cara stood before him, her hands at her sides, and there was tension in her still features. She had very smooth skin of a satiny texture, and her gray-green eyes were steady as she studied him. When he did not speak, she said, "You wanted to shock me, didn't you?"

"Not exactly that," Phil said, disturbed by her intense scrutiny. "I only wanted to show you that there are other kinds of painting in the world."

"I always knew that."

"Certainly, but perhaps I wanted to show you the difference between us."

"I know what you think of me. 'Don't be afraid of life.' That's what you said."

Phil was startled at the anger he saw in her eyes and how rigid her back was. She had evidently dressed carefully for this visit in a flattering, light blue-green dress, but now she was visibly upset. "I didn't mean for it to sound like that."

"I think you did, Phil." She had forgotten to call him Mr. Winslow, for the painting had brought back all of the pain and disturbance that his remark had caused her. Every day she had thought about it, and now she said, "You think I'm afraid of life—that I'm wrapped up in cotton bunting here in this room. Well, you're right, but what else can I do? What kind of life could I have except the one I have now?"

"You could put life into your paintings," Phil said. He had prepared this speech very carefully, not expecting to have the opportunity to make it. "I know that you're not in good health, but you have the talent to paint things besides still life. What does this picture mean to you?"

"It's rough. I don't mean the style, but that, too. Your painting is much rougher than most men's. You use broad strokes and put the paint on so heavily that it strikes you almost like a blow. But it's not the style. It's the material, isn't it? You're hoping that people will look at this painting and see a poor, wretched girl, half-starved and mistreated, and it will make them want to do something about it."

"You make me sound like a missionary."

"It's true, isn't it?" she asked. She put her hands behind her and stepped forward. "Isn't it so? You do want to change the world."

Phil was somewhat taken aback. "I never thought of it like that, Cara," he said. "I would like to help people. There's nothing I'd like better than to take this young girl and give her a chance to be somebody, to buy her nice clothes, to give her an education, but I can't do that. I don't have the money, and even a millionaire couldn't do it for all the poor. But somehow with this painting, people could look at it and see something that needs changing. There are a lot of people that don't even know that this kind of poverty exists."

"You mean my family?"

"No, I didn't mean your family exactly, but it's true enough, isn't it? Most of you never come in contact with this kind of poverty."

Cara suddenly felt vulnerable. She turned and walked to the window and looked outside, staring blindly at the flower beds that had given her so much pleasure. Now she wondered if she would ever be able to go back and paint again as she always had.

Without turning around, she said, "Tell me about England and France. Have you ever been to Italy?"

"One time," he said, "I took a freighter and then hitchhiked." He came over to stand beside her and began to speak of the hills of Rome and the countryside. "I went down to the grape-growing country and did a lot of painting there. The skies seemed bluer somehow, and the people had rich olive complexions, and a lot of them sang with gusto. Of course I didn't understand a word of it, but it was fun painting such happy people."

"I'd give anything if I could travel and visit some of those far-away places," Cara said.

"Well, I think you might go. Is your health really that bad, Cara? Do you ever get outside?"

"Sometimes when the weather's very nice, Clinton or Benji will take me down to the park. They treat me as if I were going to drop dead any minute."

The bitterness with which she said this caused Phil to lift his eyebrows. He had not heard her speak so harshly about her condition before. "I don't understand. It seems to me that fresh air and sunshine and exercise would be exactly what you need."

"That's what I keep telling Dr. McKenzie, but—" She broke off suddenly and gave him a startled look. She had almost said, *My father won't permit it*, but somehow she knew the reception such a confession would find with her outspoken friend. She shrugged, saying, "I've given up on ever living a normal life."

"Cara, you shouldn't say that!"

"Phil, I've been in this room now for ten years. It's like . . . it's like a grave to me, even with this pleasant furniture, these pictures, and all of the wealth you see here. I'd give it all up for a room with a single bed, a chair, and a table in the country, just to be close to flowers and butterflies and birds."

Sensing how despondent she felt, Phil Winslow reached out and put his hand on her shoulder. She was not a large woman, and her face suddenly seemed childlike in spite of her thirty years.

"I'd like to see that happen for you, Cara," he said. "Isn't there any hope?"

"I don't think so. Father would never permit it."

Phil wanted to rap out an answer about fathers who didn't know what was good for their children, but he realized that such a statement would only hurt Cara and would do her no good. Determining to talk more about this later, he said, "I'll tell you what. Why don't you start painting more rougher subjects?"

"Like what?"

Phil grinned boyishly. "Well, like me. Why don't you dash off a painting of me? You couldn't hurt my looks. Here I am a ratty, poor artist." He was, indeed, wearing old clothes. It was all he had, except for one good suit he saved for special occasions. "Here, I'll sit over in the sun, and you can paint me. Then you can paint a park bench around me." He looked down and grinned, then picked up Charley. "You can put Charley beside me. Well, make him look sort of ugly a little bit. Put some fleas on him and paint him with his fur all matted and clogged up with dirt. You can call it a tramp artist and his dog."

Cara laughed. "I'll do it," she said. "Move that chair over in the sun and sit down while I get a canvas." She moved quickly to the wardrobe with a sprightliness in her step that surprised her. Pulling out a fresh canvas, she set it on the easel, got her paint box, selected a brush, and pulled some charcoal out to do a pre-liminary sketch. "Now while I paint you, tell me some more about England and France. . . ."

★   ★   ★   ★

After Phil's visit, Cara felt livelier than she had for days. She did not, however, mention the painting to anyone. Rather, once it was dry, she wrapped it carefully and concealed it behind several others. She had made a good beginning with it, she thought, but would not allow Phil to see it until it was all finished. He came back twice, always in the afternoon, and the painting progressed. Each time she grew more and more pleased, for the painting had released something in her she had not known was there. Phil wore the same clothes each time, and she had caught some of his lean, muscular strength. She had taken special care with his dark brown hair, which he still wore over his collar, and had carefully delineated his tapered face and his cleft chin. She wanted to capture the rough masculinity, the strength, and the vigor in his face and also in his figure. She could not remember ever painting anything that had caused her to wake in the morning thinking about the work she could do. It had become a joy to her she could hardly explain.

When he came back the following week for the third visit, she said, "I'm going to finish today. I've worked on it ever since you left. Now sit down!"

"Yes, ma'am," Phil said with mock subservience. He picked up Charley, ruffled his fur, and said, "That mistress of yours is getting to be quite the bossy woman."

He sat still, stroking Charley's fur, looking out the window, occasionally glancing toward Cara. Her face was serious and intense, and he thought, not for the first time, *If she'd just get some color, and get her hair fixed, she'd be a beautiful young woman.* He continued to speak for a time about his travels abroad, amusing her with his anecdotes, and finally she stepped back.

"All right. You can look now," she said rather nervously.

Phil put Charley on the floor, then walked around and stood in front of the canvas. He studied it carefully, aware that her eyes were fixed on his face.

Finally she said, "Well, don't just stand there. *Say* something!"

Phil turned and said, "Cara, you've got more talent than I thought. That's a great portrait. Look at Charley," he said. "You've caught him exactly. You made him come alive on the canvas. Look at the glint of light in his eyes, and you've captured the wiggle he makes before he jumps."

Cara expelled a gust of air with relief. "Never mind Charley. What about *you*?"

"Well, I think I'm better looking than that."

"Why you egotistical—!"

Phil laughed and in his excitement reached over and took her hand and kissed it without thinking. "Miss Cara, you've done a great job on a very unworthy subject." He held her hand and saw her face grow pink, and then realizing that he may have embarrassed her, he dropped her hand. "I didn't mean to get so carried away," he said, "but the painting is great."

Cara was upset by the sudden touch he had given her. It was the first caress from a man she had felt for ten years. Her head seemed to swim for a moment, and her hand had the sensation of burning. She turned away slightly so he would not see her confusion, then whispered, "Do you really like it, Phil?"

"More than like. It's outstanding! You're a better artist than I am."

"Oh no, not really!"

"Oh yes. Really." He reached out, took her shoulder, and turned her around. "I'm glad I met you," he said simply. "I . . . I haven't ever been able to tell you this, but I like you very much, Cara."

Cara dropped her head, unable to face his penetrating eyes. She was very conscious of his hands on her shoulders. It made her feel strange indeed, and then she managed to tell him, "What a nice thing to say, Phil. You've been a breath of fresh air to me."

Phil laughed and said, "Well, that's the first step on the emancipation of Cara Lanier."

Startled, Cara looked up at him. "What do you mean by that?"

"I mean, now that you're not condemned to painting one daisy after another, we'll have to find new ways to spend some time together. For example, why don't we go out in the garden and take a little walk?"

"Oh, I couldn't!"

"See there? You're not emancipated yet. Come on, Cara," he urged. "I'm your guest. There's nothing wrong with going for a little walk. You need to show me all your beautiful flowers that you've been painting."

Cara knew that Dr. McKenzie would object and her father, if he discovered it, which he probably would, would be angry. In fact, he might even forbid any more visitors. Nevertheless, it was too tempting. "All right, Phil," she said, "let me get a coat."

Phil waited until she pulled a light off-white jacket out of the chifferobe, then he helped her put it around her shoulders. Moving ahead, he opened the door for her. When they walked downstairs, they encountered Mary Ann and George Camrose, who were still in the parlor.

Mary Ann jumped up from the couch, saying, "Why, Cara, what are you doing?"

"I'm only going out to walk around the garden and to show Phil the flowers," Cara said quickly. She hesitated, then said, "I'll be all right, Mary Ann. Please don't tell Father."

When the two stepped outside, Mary Ann turned to Camrose and her face filled with astonishment. "If Father finds out she's gone outside, he'll have a fit."

Camrose understood Mary Ann's concern completely. He had already felt enough of Oliver Lanier's displeasure to understand what the man was like. "Then don't tell him," he smiled. "And tell the servants not to tell him. It'll be our little conspiracy."

"I thought preachers weren't supposed to do things like that."

"It will give Cara a little happiness and some freedom. That's not wrong," he said simply.

Mary Ann was touched by his obvious consideration for Cara. She touched his chest and said, "How sweet of you."

"Then I'll have a reward for being so sweet." Camrose leaned over and kissed her on the lips, then leaned back. "That's another thing preachers get criticized for. Kissing pretty girls. I don't think it's such a sin though, not when the girl is you." He smiled broadly at her expression. "Sit down again. I'll tell you some more about Africa."

Outside in the garden, Cara walked slowly on the cobblestones and saw the shock on the gardener's face as he looked up from where he was digging in the rich brown soil. "Hello, Henry," she said. "The snapdragons are magnificent. You've done so well."

"Why, thank you, Miss Cara." He stood to his feet, dirt on his knees, the look of astonishment obvious on his face. "You're lookin' better. Glad to see you outside, and good day to you, sir."

"This is Henry. He's the best gardener in America, or anywhere else for that matter," Cara said, smiling.

"I believe it, looking at these flowers. You've done a great job, Henry. I commend you on it."

"Why, thank you, sir." The gardener watched as the two walked on down the rows of red and gold and yellow flowers and muttered, "Well, I'll be a monkey's uncle."

Cara enjoyed the fresh air and stroll for thirty minutes, but it seemed like only a few seconds to her. Finally she turned and said, "I must be going in now. Thank you so much for coming by. It was thoughtful of you."

"Do I get the picture?"

"No," she said. "I want to keep it for myself." A humorous light touched her eyes, and she smiled. "I like the job I've done on Charley."

"What a put-down," Phil groaned. Then he took her hand and said, "I'll be going then, but I'll get even with you."

"Why, what do you mean by that, Phil?"

"It's my turn to do a painting of you now. I'll come next Tuesday and you can sit for me."

"All right. That would be nice."

He walked her to the door, and when she stepped inside, he said, "Good-bye. I'll see you when I come by for your first sitting."

"Good-bye, Phil."

Cara shut the door and walked slowly down the hall. Her heart was beating fast, and when she passed the sitting room, Mary Ann came flying out. "Oh, how nice that you two are able to talk! He is nice, isn't he, George?"

"Fine fellow. He's coming to church Sunday," Camrose said.

"Yes. He has relatives who are missionaries in Africa."

"Does he, indeed!" Camrose exclaimed. "I'll have to ask him about that. They might be of some assistance when I arrive there."

Mary Ann reached out and took her sister's hand. She whispered, "Do you like him, Cara?"

"Yes. I do indeed, Mary Ann. I like him very much!"

CHAPTER SIX

A FAMILY AFFAIR

★   ★   ★   ★

June 15 was a target day for the Four Musketeers. The big race on Long Island was set to begin at one o'clock that afternoon. Clinton was more excited than any of the others. He had made excuses to be out of the house at night and had even managed to slip away from the office during the day several times to come and check on the progress of the car. He had been permitted to drive the *Jolie Blonde* on a test run, and when he had come back, he jumped out and threw his arms around Jolie unselfconsciously. "There's nothing like it!" he shouted, spinning her around, his eyes blazing with excitement.

Jolie was crushed to his chest and laughed. "Put me down! You're going to break my ribs!"

Embarrassed, Clinton quickly set her on her feet and apologized. Over the weeks they had become close friends as they worked on the race car. He liked to take her out for coffee and talk about racing, and she enjoyed listening to him.

On the fourteenth, they finished tuning the car up in the backyard, and when Peter and Easy decided to go out early to Long Island and sleep there, waiting for the events of the next day, Clinton said enviously, "I wish I could go."

"So do I. Let me go with you, Peter," Jolie pleaded.

"Oh, that's no place for a woman, sleeping out under the stars," Peter said firmly.

Jolie begged, but Peter was firm, and finally Clinton said,

"Let's you and I go out and get something to eat. I've got to be in fairly early, but I'm starving."

"That sounds like fun."

The two of them went to an Italian restaurant named Mama Mia, a small place Jolie had discovered one day when she was out for a stroll. It was a family-run business, and Mama herself came to take their order.

"I'll have manicotti a la romana with ricotta, and bring me some of that eggplant parmigiana."

"I didn't know you spoke Italian," Clinton said with astonishment.

"I don't, except to know the names of some food. What will you have, Clinton?"

"The same, I guess." He grinned at the large woman with the black eyes. "Bring me twice as much as you bring her."

While they waited for their orders to come, Clinton talked excitedly about the upcoming race. In the meanwhile, they ate huge chunks of freshly baked bread layered with butter.

After Mama had returned with their food, Clinton ate with enthusiasm. "This is great," he said. "I don't know why, but I just never tried Italian food before. I didn't know what I was missing."

"Well, it's cheap and filling. I guess rich people don't have to worry about that," Jolie said wryly.

Clinton's face flushed. "I wish you wouldn't call me rich," he protested.

"Well, you are rich, aren't you?"

Squirming uncomfortably, Clinton picked up the bread, broke off a piece, and buttered it. After he had nibbled at it, he said, "I guess so, but it sounds like a bad disease the way you say it."

"Why, I don't have anything against being rich," Jolie said with surprise.

She underscored her protest with a sweet smile and indeed made a charming picture. Her coal black hair formed a halo of thick curls, and with it her light gray dress, trimmed with lace and pearl buttons made a perfect frame for her expressive face. As she continued to speak, he admired her enormous blue eyes and mobile mouth, which could subtly tease as well as express her delightful moments of gaiety. Clinton found her most provocative, a beautiful picture of a woman like no woman he had ever known before, and he felt the things that a man feels when he looks upon beauty and knows it will never be for him.

"Clinton," she asked abruptly, "do you intend to spend the rest of your life doing exactly what your father tells you to do? Don't you ever hope to have any life of your own?"

Her question cut Clinton Lanier deeply, for it was something he had been struggling with for some time. He was a clever young man, with a fair share of business acumen. Yet, despite his seeming success, he was not at peace with himself. At the office, he spent a great deal of time gazing out the window and daydreaming of what it would be like to be free in exactly the way Jolie suggested, but there always was the shadow of his father looming over him. He had often wondered if other fathers ruled as absolutely as Oliver Lanier did in his own house. Long ago, Clinton had determined that if he ever had a family, he would have none of his father's autocratic ways. Now he twisted in his seat and lifted his hand to rub it along his jaw line, a certain sign that he was nervous. "I hope not, Jolie. I have dreams of my own," he said finally.

They left the restaurant then, and he took her back to the rooming house. When they reached the front door, he said, "I enjoyed our time together, Jolie."

"It was fun," she said. She hesitated, then put out her hand. "I'll see you tomorrow at the race."

Taking her hand, he held it for a moment and nodded. An impulse came to him, and he studied her face, which seemed soft and glowing in the silver moonlight. The streets were vacant, and a strange silence hung over the neighborhood. "I promised my mother something once, but I'm going to break that promise."

"Why, you shouldn't break a promise to your mother," Jolie exclaimed. "I'm sure she's a nice woman!"

"Yes, she is, but I'm going to break this one." He hesitated for a moment, then said, "I promised her I would never kiss a girl on the first date, but I'm going to."

Leaning forward, he kissed Jolie on the lips, then straightened up. It was a quick caress, but he savored the warmth of her lips and smelled the fragrance of her hair. "You're looking very pretty tonight, Jolie. Good night."

Turning, he walked quickly away, got into the carriage, and drove off. Jolie stood watching him. She slowly reached up and touched her lips, then shook her head in wonder. "Well, what am I supposed to think about that, Mr. Clinton Lanier?" She was not shocked, for she had been kissed before, and yet there was something touching about this man. A dissatisfaction came to her then, and she said, "Clinton Lanier, you're going to have to declare your independence someday," then she turned and walked into the rooming house.

* * * *

"I'd like for all of you to meet a good friend of mine," Phil said. "This is Avis Warwick. She's studying at the art institute—and she's never seen an automobile race." As he introduced his friends, he watched their faces nervously, never knowing when Avis would drop some outlandish remark that might shock them.

"I didn't know automobile drivers were so handsome." Avis greeted Peter with a gleam in her eyes. "If someone had told me, I'd have taken up racing myself instead of art."

Peter was stunned, and a quick glance at Jolie told him that she was not pleased with Avis's comment. Clearing his throat, he managed a grin, saying, "Oh, all of us drivers are good-looking— it's a requirement."

"Well now, you must show me this car of yours." Avis took Peter's arm possessively and led him away. She was looking up at him, smiling and giving him her full attention.

"Quite a lady friend you've got there, Phil," Easy spoke up, a calculating look in his eyes. "Don't take her long to decide if she likes a fellow or not."

"She's pretty outlandish," Phil admitted, watching the two. He turned to Jolie and said, "Better keep your eye on Peter. I think she's decided that a racing driver is a better catch than a starving artist."

"He's acting like a silly schoolboy," Jolie practically spat out. "Can't he see what she is?" By the time the call came for the drivers to man their cars, Avis had captivated Peter with her charms.

"Never met a woman quite like Avis," Peter remarked as he walked toward the car beside Easy.

"No? Well, I've met a few in my day," Easy shouted over the roar of the engine. "Better watch your step, buddy!"

Just before the race was about to begin, Peter climbed into the driver's seat with Easy right beside him. Peter looked over and grinned. "I don't know why two men have to be in these cars all cramped up. What are you going to do if we have engine trouble? Get out and fix it while we're going ninety miles an hour?"

"Ninety miles an hour?" Easy laughed. "Don't you wish it was so? What do you think? Have we got a chance, Peter?"

"I don't know. All I plan on doing is to step on the gas and keep it there until we win, or run off the track, or hit somebody."

"The competition looks pretty stiff," Easy said.

Peter looked around with a worried expression. "I think that fellow Lancia driving the Fiat is the one to beat."

"Yeah, I heard about him. He's the son of a soap manufacturer. That's some machine he's driving. I heard he won the race up in Boston last week. The rest of the drivers didn't see anything but dust."

He looked around at all the cars lined up, their engines roaring, waiting for the starting signal. "We're going to have to go some to beat these fellas. That fellow Charles Row—you see him in that horrible-looking yellow Wolseley? He won the Gordon Bennett cup in that last year, so when you see yellow try to go by it."

As soon as Easy spoke, the gun sounded, and Peter yelled, "Here we go, Easy!"

The air was filled with a thunderous explosion as fourteen powerful cars started at once, roaring as they took off down the speedway. Since there was no grandstand, the crowd stood on both sides of the dirt track, quickly surrounded by the rising cloud of dust.

As they made the first turn, Peter shouted, "Well, we're in the middle of the pack, Easy. All we got to do now is beat the other half."

"Watch where you're goin'! That guy in the Bugatti is going to close in on you and cut you off!" Easy hollered.

It was a demanding race, for some of the best drivers in America and a few from overseas had come to race for the prized trophy. The cars, all of them two-seaters, roared and jockeyed for position. Peter frequently wiped his goggles with a quick swipe of his arm, but before long they were again coated with dust. At times he was driving by little more than sheer instinct. One car rammed into the side of the *Jolie Blonde*, knocking it sideways, and Easy half rose and shook his fist, shouting at the driver, who grinned back at them and held one thumb up in the air.

"Knock him off the road, Peter!" Easy yelled.

"No time for that. We can fight after the race is over."

Clinton and Phil stood along the side of the track with Jolie and Avis, watching the race. Jolie had been very cool to Avis but now forgot about her in the excitement. They watched as the cars spun around the track, all trying to move into a better position. Halfway through, one of them caught the wheel of the car in front and threw both cars into a spin. The others swerved, but another car, coming up from behind them plowed into the spinning cars.

"Look out, Peter!" Jolie cried. Only by expert driving did Peter manage to steer his way around the tangle.

Avis Warwick watched calmly for a while, then she, too, grew excited. She had a strong competitive streak in her, and now her eyes lit up as she saw that Peter had a chance to win.

The last lap became a duel between Peter and a big green Bugatti that roared like a banshee. They fought for first place, but when the checkered flag went down, it was the Bugatti that won.

"They lost!" Avis cried. "They came so close."

"They did well to come in second in that field," Clinton said. "Come on. Let's go and congratulate them."

They shouldered their way through the crowd and watched as the driver of the Bugatti took the cup and the prize, but then Peter was awarded a smaller cup and an envelope with cash in it.

Avis ran up and hugged Peter. "You did marvelous." She suddenly reached up, pulled his head down, and kissed him.

Peter was taken aback, and glancing around, he saw Jolie staring at them with displeasure. "Time to go out and eat and celebrate. We didn't win, but we came close."

Phil begged off on the dinner that followed. Avis insisted on taking them to a French restaurant. As soon as they went in, all of her guests were immediately aware that this woman was no tourist. The head waiter came up and bowed as soon as he saw her.

"Ah, Madame Warwick, your usual table?"

"Yes, and you'll have to treat us nice tonight. This is the famous racing driver, Mr. Peter Winslow."

"Ah, Mr. Winslow, it is a pleasure. Please come this way."

They were seated at a table over to one side of the glass-walled dining room, and at once Avis said, "Let me order the food. If you don't like one dish, you'll have another." Immediately, she began to order in French. When the food arrived, it was constantly being whisked away and replaced with a new dish before they had finished.

"I don't get enough of anything to eat," Easy protested as the waiter removed his plate and put another one in front of him.

Avis laughed at him. "There's plenty more to come. Peter, you're going to dance with me. Clinton, why don't you ask Jolie to dance?"

Clinton rose at once. "Why, of course."

Easy sat back and watched the two couples move out on the floor. When the waiter came by, Easy grabbed him by the arm and said, "Hey, buddy."

"Yes, monsieur?"

"Who is this woman, Avis Warwick?"

"You do not know her? You are her guest, are you not?"

"Yeah, but I don't know much about her."

The waiter leaned forward and lowered his voice. "She is the widow of Charles Warwick, who was one of the wealthiest manufacturers in the state. He was an old man when he married. When he died, he left all of his fortune to his widow. She is a very wealthy woman."

"Well, glad to hear it. Maybe I can have some more of them snails you been bringin' in here."

Avis was dancing with Peter and smiling up at him, saying, "Are you proud of what you won or sorry that you didn't win first place?"

"We were lucky," Peter shrugged. "We shouldn't have even finished in the first five. Their cars were built a lot better and much faster."

"Why don't you get a bigger, faster car?"

"It takes a lot of money, Avis."

Avis considered him awhile, then said, "Maybe I can help."

"Help in racing? You don't know anything about it, do you?"

"No, but I could help with the money. I've got plenty of that."

"I couldn't take money from a woman," Peter objected.

Avis Warwick was pleased with his reply, but she laughed. "You *are* a dinosaur. There are no more left like you. Come on, let's go get something to drink. Oh, I forgot, you don't drink. Well, let's go get *me* something to drink," she said as she hooked her arm in his and led him back to the table where Easy was enjoying another dish of snails.

The party went on for quite a while, and when they finally left, Avis packed them all into cabs that were waiting. She held on to Peter's arm and said, "I'll take care of this one. Good night to the rest of you."

Jolie sat between Clinton and Easy in the cab, fuming. "Who does she think she is?"

"She thinks she's a rich woman," Easy said wryly and told Jolie what he had heard about her wealth from the waiter.

"Well, I don't care if she is rich. I don't like her."

"Now I remember reading something about her," Clinton said. "She's kind of an outlaw—always getting into some kind of jam. I just didn't remember it before."

When they arrived at the boardinghouse, where Easy and Jolie got out, Clinton got out with them and said, "Congratulations, Easy. That's a wonderful car you and Peter have built."

"Couldn't have done it without your help, Clinton," Easy said. He looked at the two and said abruptly, "Good night," then walked quickly into the building.

"I've got to get home," Clinton said.

Jolie was still angry. "I can't stand that woman! You can tell she's no good!"

"How can you tell that?" asked Clinton, surprised at Jolie's outburst.

"I've seen enough no-goods to know one. Haven't you?"

"Well, I guess not really." Clinton had not seen a great deal of the world, and now he asked uncertainly, "Will I see you again, Jolie, getting ready for the next race?"

"Yes, I expect so, Clinton. Good night." Jolie turned and stalked into the building.

For a moment, Clinton stood there and watched, then he climbed back into the cab and gave the driver directions to his house.

Jolie went to her own room and paced angrily, clenching her fists. "That Avis woman! You can tell what she's like. She's after men, and she doesn't care how she gets them. Peter's got to be warned. Don't guess she has to care, with her money. Surely Peter's got better sense—" She stopped, then said, "She's beautiful and rich." Slowly her hand reached up and she touched the scar that traced her cheek in a long line. She grew silent then and tried to shake the thoughts out of her head.

★ ★ ★ ★

When Clinton got out of the cab, he paid the driver and walked inside. He had barely closed the door when his father strode out of the study and came rapidly down the hall, his face cloudy. "Where have you been, Clinton?" he demanded.

Clinton considered lying for one moment, but something stirred within him. "I've been out with some friends."

"Out where?"

Again Clinton tried to evade the issue, but his father pressed for an answer. "Where have you been that you're so ashamed of it?"

"I'm not ashamed of it! I've been to an automobile race with the Winslows. Phil was there and his cousin Peter was in the race. I told you about them. Fine young men, both of them."

"I told you I didn't want you to go to those races! Besides, it's late. They weren't racing this time of the night."

Now half angry, Clinton said, "We went out for supper."

"Alone? Just you men?"

"No, Avis Warwick invited us to a fine restaurant and a young woman named Jolie Devorak went along, too. I don't really want to talk about this now, Father."

"We'll talk about it all right! Don't you have any idea who Avis Warwick is? Why, she's nothing but a hussy! Everyone in New York knows she's nothing but an adulterous woman! I'm ashamed of you, Clinton! And this other young woman, she's probably no better!"

For the first time in his life, Clinton looked at his father and said with a timbre of defiance in his voice, "You don't even know anything about her. She's a fine young woman! There's nothing wrong with Miss Devorak!"

"Who is she?" Oliver Lanier's face was flushed and his eyes were squeezed together. He hated for any situation involving his family to be out of his control. He listened impatiently as Clinton tried to explain Jolie Devorak. "It sounds to me," Oliver said, "like she's living with those two men. I forbid you to have anything to do with them!"

"Father, I'm twenty-seven years old. I'm able to choose my own friends."

"I don't care how old you are! You're still not able to make the right decisions. I'm warning you, Clinton. We've been through this before. I'm tired of this foolishness, and you'll have to make your choice. Either go out and try your crazy idea of racing cars or become a useful member of the firm! You can't do both. Now which will it be?"

For one moment Clinton came very close to saying, *I'll see whom I please when I please*, but somehow the thought of being penniless frightened him, and instead he replied, "You're not being fair, Father."

"You've heard my terms. Now which will it be?"

Clinton stood there for a moment, and then a feeling of hopelessness seemed to engulf him. "All right," he said. "I won't see them anymore."

"Now you're talking like a man with sense."

Clinton went upstairs to his bedroom feeling dejected for not having stood up to his father. He went over to his desk and slowly pulled out a sheet of paper. Sitting down, he sighed and began to write, for he did not want to face Jolie or Easy or Peter again. He simply thanked them for their company and said that he would not be seeing them again. Slipping the note into an envelope, he addressed it and put it down, then slowly began to undress. A great bitterness settled on him. He realized he had failed himself and would never again feel any pride in himself as a man apart from his father.

★ ★ ★ ★

Two days after the race, Phil Winslow stopped by to see Peter and noticed Jolie was upset about something. While Peter was helping Easy with the *Jolie Blonde*, he turned to her and said, "You seem awfully quiet today. Something the matter?"

Reaching into her pocket, she pulled out an envelope and handed it to Phil. She waited until he had finished reading it, then said bitterly, "His father probably found out about his going to the races and then going out to dinner with us and forbade Clinton to see us anymore!"

"That's bad. The man needs to stand up for himself."

"I think he's forgotten how. You met Mr. Lanier. What's he like?"

"He's brutal—a strong man who's used to having his own way. But I thought better of Clinton than this. After all, he's old enough to be his own man."

Clinton's decision to stop seeing his friends preyed on Phil's mind the rest of the day. When he went to the Lanier house the next day for his appointment with Cara, instead of continuing with the portrait he was doing of her, he said, "Tell me about Clinton."

Cara, of course, had heard all about her father's tirade and her brother's acquiescence to his unreasonable demands. It was impossible to keep a secret in this house. She had tried to talk to Clinton, but he had been so despondent that he could do no more than say, "Father forbade it, and there's nothing else to say." She had stood there for a moment, then had said, "I'm sorry for your friends."

"I'm sorry for Clinton," Phil said, after hearing the story from Cara. "What kind of a man is your father, anyhow?"

"He's a good man," Cara said defensively. "You just don't know what it's like living—" She broke off abruptly, then said, "You just don't understand Clinton's position."

"No, I don't. I don't understand Mary Ann either. She's in love with a preacher who's a good man, but she can't have him. You want to go out and walk in the park and lead a normal life, but you can't do it. Now Clinton wants to make friends outside of his office and try something on his own, and he can't do it. Tell me some more about your father. I don't think I've ever heard of a crueler man in my whole life."

"Don't say that!" Cara pleaded. Tears sprang to her eyes, and she said, "Father had a very hard life. He didn't have a penny, and you don't understand how hard he had to work."

"And that makes it all right for him to enslave his own children? You'll never be a painter or anything else until you are able to stand up to him, Cara. And Clinton will never be a man, and Mary Ann will never be happy and free to marry the man she loves. All of you are living like slaves under your father's roof."

Cara listened and grew more miserable. Finally she whispered, "I'll have to ask you to leave."

"Cara, listen to me—"

"I'm not feeling well. Please leave, Phil."

Phil stared at her, then said, "All right, if that's the way you feel."

As soon as he was gone, Cara went over and fell across the bed and began weeping. She slept hardly at all that night, and the next day when Dr. McKenzie came to check on her, he was very concerned. Her father came in, and McKenzie said, "I'm thinking she's had a setback. Too much company, I'm afraid."

"It's that artist fellow. He's kept her stirred up. He's a bad influence on the whole family. I'll not have him in the house again!"

Oliver Lanier was as good as his word, for the next day Phil was handed a note that read, "Your attentions to my daughter are unwelcome. You have been a bad influence on her, and upon my son, and upon my family in general. From this day forward you are not welcome in my house." It was signed, "Oliver Lanier."

Phil took the note, tore it up, and threw it down. A cold anger washed through him, and then it passed. Instead he felt a great pity. "Those poor people," he whispered to himself. "Work slaves in the tenements are freer than they are. God help them all!"

PART TWO

TROUBLED WATERS

★ ★ ★ ★

CHAPTER SEVEN

"LOVE DON'T ALWAYS ADD UP, JOLIE...!"

★ ★ ★ ★

Americans looked back on the year 1907 with mingled admiration and apprehension. As always, the year had produced tragedy and turmoil, as well as triumph and victory.

The Chicago Cubs won the World Series with Tinker, Evers, and Chance in the infield, defeating the Detroit Tigers 4–0. But the big news in baseball was yet to come, for Walter Johnson, age nineteen, signed with the Washington Senators. The Big Train, as he was called, would become the greatest fast-ball pitcher ever.

Barnum and Bailey Circus, created in 1881, became the Ringling Brothers Barnum and Bailey Circus and toured the country triumphantly, drawing huge crowds wherever it set up its tents.

Jack London continued to dominate in literature, but the poetry of Robert Service, set in the Yukon and including his poems *The Cremation of Sam McGee* and *The Shooting of Dan McGrew*, swept the country.

Horse-drawn vehicles in New York were giving way to motor buses and electric trolleys. American motorcar production reached forty-three thousand, and, even though automobiles were more expensive than horses, businessmen slowly began to accept the motorcar as a part of American life. The big news of 1907 was the financial disaster that struck the nation. A stock market crash rocked the country, and one man single-handedly averted the financial panic that followed. On October 23 a rush by depositors to withdraw their money from New York's Knickerbocker Trust was stopped by financier J.P. Morgan. Morgan obtained a pledge of ten million dollars from John D. Rockefeller, and ten million from the Bank of England, which arrived in the British steamship *Lancaster* on her maiden voyage.

And so as January 1908 came, bringing with it cold blasts that froze the streets of New York, that city and others sighed with relief and looked forward with the optimism so inherent in the American character to a New Utopia.

★ ★ ★ ★

The feel of snow was in the air as Peter and Avis walked down Broadway. The two of them had taken a half holiday. Avis had stopped by and practically pulled Peter away from his car, saying, "Come along. You've got to go shopping with me."

Peter had protested but actually had been glad to leave the *Jolie Blonde*. He had closed the hood, shot a quick glance at Easy Devlin, who scowled, then grinned. "Okay, let's make our getaway."

"You don't be gone all day, you hear," Easy had called out as Peter walked away. "We still have lots of work to do on this here car if we plan to have her ready for the race coming up."

Now as they moved along the crowded streets, Avis took a deep breath and lifted her face to the gray skies above. "I love cold weather. I hope it snows."

"You haven't had to ride in cold trains like I have," Peter returned as he pulled his collar up around his neck. He brushed against her arm and thought of how close they had become in the time since they had first met. They walked together until finally she led him into A.T. Stuart's enormous store. Stuart's dominated the retail dry-goods trade in New York. It was the largest importer in the nation, and today all five stories were filled with people. Avis promptly led Peter through the crowds to the elevator, for a ride to the fourth-floor ladies' wear department.

Stepping out of the elevator as soon as the operator had brought the floor level, Peter glanced around at the fashions, some of them displayed on dressmaker's dummies. "What an amazing sight!" he exclaimed. "This is like Sunday afternoon in Peacock Alley, only more so."

Avis laughed. "There's something for nearly everyone here. But I like Stuart's because they've got the latest fashions, not just something your mother would wear." She stopped before a dress with a trailing skirt. "That's a pretty fabric, but that style is on its way out. Every time I wear one, I think how absolutely stupid it is to wear a dress that drags through trash and spittle and germs from the sidewalk!" She stepped into the next display area and turned back to Peter, beckoning him over. "Now this is more what I like."

"That?" exclaimed Peter, joining her and examining the object of her interest. "That looks like something a woman would wear in the privacy of her bedroom!"

He couldn't help staring. The mannequin before them was modeling a sheath gown that had just arrived from Paris and was quickly becoming all the rage with style-conscious American women. As far as he could tell, this model had a skirt that was little more than a cloth tube from hips to shoe tops. "It's got all the charm of a gun barrel, or an umbrella stand," Peter scowled. "How does anybody ever walk in one?"

"You don't—at least not very quickly or very far. It's what's called a hobble skirt," Avis said. "I have to agree that from a practical point of view, it's a crazy idea—though maybe not more than some other styles that have come out of Paris." Despite the evaluation, her eyes sparkled as she looked at the dress, but she gripped Peter's arm possessively and, lowering her voice, confided, "I think it's psychological."

"What? A tight skirt?"

"Yes. Some man invented that," she asserted positively. Her green eyes flashed, and she ruffled her strawberry blond hair with her free hand, saying, "Men always want to keep women tied down, or tied up in some way. So that's why they hobble them."

Peter laughed aloud. "My father hobbles horses out west to keep them from wandering. Maybe it's a good idea."

Avis gave him a direct stare. "No man will ever hobble me," she snapped. "Come along and look at this." She stopped before another displayed garment. "What do you think of this?"

Peter studied the blouse and finally said, "It looks like it's been punched by one of those things that makes holes in paper. It's got holes all in it."

"Of course it has. It's called a peek-a-boo."

"And the material is so thin you can see through it. It seems to me," Peter said, "that women are now wearing in public what they only wore inside their bedrooms at one time."

"That's the idea, to make you men look at us. Come on. I'm going to try on some clothes. You can sit over there."

For the next two hours Peter sat as Avis tried on dress after dress, and he had to admit that no matter what she put on, she made it look good. Some of them were rather daring, and as he frowned, she came over and grabbed him by his hair and pulled his head back. "You're nothing but a Puritan," she whispered. "I need to reform you from all that."

Finally, after she had made her selections, they left the ladies' department burdened down with packages. "I'm glad men's clothes don't change," Peter muttered. "The only change I've seen is that men are wearing derbys instead of high silk hats."

"Here, I've got a present for you," Avis said. She fished into her pocket and came out with a small package. "You can open it in the carriage."

When they were outside and had stored the purchases that Avis had made, Peter settled back, with Avis sitting very close to him. He could smell the perfume she had on, a pleasing fragrance that was always with her. As she leaned against him, he was distracted but continued to open the package. When the paper fell away, he exclaimed, "Why, it's one of those watches you wear on your arm!"

"Yes. See how handy it is? Let me put it on," Avis offered, smiling at him. She fastened the watch by the leather strap and said, "Isn't that nice?"

Peter Winslow stared at the watch, then twisted his shoulders uncomfortably. "You know, there's an idea going around that no true man would wear one of these."

"Why, there's nothing to that! Soon they'll be the in thing for all men. Why, the pocket watch will be in museums in another year."

Peter laughed and reached over and pulled her toward him. She came eagerly, put her arms around his neck, and drew him closer and kissed him. Peter Winslow knew that he really had nothing in common with Avis Warwick. She was a woman completely immersed in the world's values, longing for what the day could offer, never thinking of the future. She craved the things that satisfied the flesh and gave no thought, apparently, to the spirit. Still, as she came back to him and kissed him again, all this was swept away, and he forgot their many differences.

★　★　★　★

The race was exciting and Jolie Devorak cheered herself hoarse as Peter drove the *Jolie Blonde* to victory. Despite the cold weather, an extremely large crowd had gathered in Newark to watch the field of seventeen of the fastest cars in the country duel it out. Peter had driven a smart race, letting some of the drivers batter each other in the sharp curves, and then in the last three laps he had come from behind to win.

Jolie rushed forward to join those who gathered around as Peter and Easy climbed out, but she stopped abruptly. Avis Warwick was suddenly there smiling up at Peter as the photographers snapped photos from every angle.

As Peter answered the questions of a reporter from the *New York Times*, Jolie could not help but remember how *she* had been the one beside Peter before Avis Warwick had come into their lives. Now she could not force herself to go forward. She stood back and watched as Peter and Avis departed arm in arm. She was startled when Easy suddenly said, "Why didn't you come over and get in the picture, Jolie?"

Turning to the undersized mechanic, Jolie stared at him and the bitterness she felt somehow spilled over. "It looked like Peter was pretty busy!"

Instantly Easy's eyes came to meet those of Jolie. He had become very sensitive to this young woman and understood immediately the emotion that was racing through her.

"Well, I guess it's pretty flattering to a feller having a rich woman make over him like that. Most would lose their heads, I reckon."

"I suppose so." Jolie turned to go away, but Easy fell into step beside her. He said casually, "I knew we was gonna win that race because I dreamed of white clouds last night."

"White clouds? What does that have to do with the race?"

"Why, everybody knows if you dream of white clouds it's a good sign. It's just like when you dream of a funeral. A weddin' is gonna follow."

"What if you dream about a wedding?"

Easy shrugged his wiry shoulders eloquently. "Well, that ain't so good, Jolie. Every time you dream about a weddin', there's death a-comin' somewhere down the road."

"I think that's a bunch of foolishness! Dreams don't have anything to do with what happens to us."

"You ought not to talk like that, Jolie," Easy protested. "Why, back once when I was fifteen years old, I dreamed about a black dog three nights runnin'. And it wasn't but six months after that when the cholera epidemic came and just about wiped out the whole town."

Jolie had long since given up on trying to change Easy's strange views. He was tremendously superstitious and spent a great deal of time collecting remedies that he was convinced could fight off disease or cure those already in progress. Now she could not help but smile and say, "Did you get those warts off your hand?"

"No, but that was because I didn't start soon enough." Easy looked down at the back of his left hand and shook his head dolefully. "But I've got a sure-fire cure now that I'm gonna try." Without waiting, he launched into it eagerly. "Never known this one to fail, Jolie. What you do is take a grain of corn, cut the heart out, and cut the wart until it bleeds. Then you take a drop of the blood and put it in the corn, where the heart was taken out, then you throw the grain to a chicken."

"And then the wart goes away?"

"That's right. I just ain't had no fresh green corn, but now I've got it all right."

By this time the two had gotten beyond the crowd, and Easy could tell that Jolie was still angry. Reaching out, he took her arm and said quietly, "You don't want to worry about Peter and Avis. She don't mean nothin' to him."

"I don't care. It's no business of mine."

Easy had known for a long time of Jolie's devotion to Peter Winslow, and now he said gently, "You know, a lot of things can be figured out if a body's smart enough. Some things you can add up, and some things you can't." He dropped his hand and said slowly, "Love don't always add up, Jolie."

Startled, Jolie lifted her eyes. She had enormous eyes of a peculiar powder blue hue set in her squarish face, but they generally did not betray her feelings. She had become skilled at hiding what went on inside her, mostly because of her scarred face. Now, however, Easy had caught her off balance, and she stared at him, unable to speak. Finally she shook her head stubbornly and said, "It's none of my business what he does, Easy."

Easy watched as Jolie wrenched herself away and stalked off, her head held high and her back stiff. There was a stubborn set to her shoulders, and Easy shook his head, muttering sorrowfully, "I sure do hate to see Jolie actin' this way." He had thought many times of Avis Warwick, and now declared, "I wish she'd find someone else to lavish her attention on. Man in love ain't got no sense whatsoever!"

★ ★ ★ ★

Clinton Lanier was in the crowd in New Jersey watching the race. He had been sent by his father on an errand, but had made the trip a long one by stopping by the race track. He had not seen Peter or Jolie since his father had forbidden him, but each day he had become more and more bitter about his father's order to stay away. Now he lost himself in the roar of the machines and felt his heart catch in his throat as Peter barely avoided disaster on a turn. When Peter won, however, Clinton did not go forward to congratulate him; instead he turned to leave without speaking to anyone.

"Hello, Clinton!"

Clinton stopped abruptly, startled at the sound of his name, and when he turned to find Phil Winslow coming toward him, he flushed as if caught in some wicked deed. The first thought that came to him was, *What if he tells Father that I'm at the races?* Then he realized that Phil Winslow was not likely to be seeing his father at all, and he managed a smile, saying, "Hello, Phil."

"Great race, wasn't it?"

"Yes it was. Peter's a good driver."

"You taking a holiday from the office?"

"Not exactly." Clinton struggled for a moment, then shrugged. "I had some business to take care of close by, so I thought I'd come on and take in the race."

Somehow Phil understood that the young man was embarrassed and quickly decided that it had something to do with being at the race track. *His father's got him afraid of his own shadow,* he thought. Aloud he asked, "How's the family?"

"Very well," Clinton said briefly. He hesitated, then added, "Cara misses you a great deal, Phil."

The comment surprised Phil Winslow. "She does? I'm surprised about that."

"Why should you be surprised? You know she doesn't have any life at all."

The bitterness in Clinton's voice startled Phil. He glanced quickly at his friend's profile and saw that embarrassment and anger were mingled on Clinton's aristocratic face. "I wish things were different," Phil said. "I'd like to go see her, but I don't think I'd be welcome."

"You probably wouldn't be, at least by Father, but Cara misses you. None of the rest of us know much about painting, Phil. About all I can say is 'that's a nice picture.' You ought to hear how she talks about you. Her eyes light up and she gets pink in the face."

"That amazes me. We don't agree at all on painting styles."

"Oh, I know that! She told me your idea—to paint things from life."

"Well, I was afraid I might have insulted her."

"No. Nothing like that." Suddenly Clinton was filled with an impulse. "Look here, Phil. It would be good for Cara if you would drop by sometime. I know you think our family's weak—"

"I don't think anything like that!" Phil protested. But at the same time he realized that this was *exactly* what he thought. Still, he could not say that to Clinton. "I just don't want to intrude where I'm not invited. I admire your sister very much. She's got more talent than she even realizes." He saw Clinton's face glow with the compliment and went on to say, "It's a shame that she can't go to Europe. She'd enjoy it."

"Europe? That's about as likely as my going to the moon! Father's dead set against her going anywhere but her room."

Phil did not answer, but a bitter reply leaped to his lips. He bit it off with an effort and shrugged, saying, "I had supposed that was the case."

Suddenly Clinton turned, stopping so abruptly that it caught Phil off guard. "Look here," he said earnestly, his direct blue eyes catching at Phil. "Why don't you just drop by sometime? I know it sounds a little bit, well, sneaky, but you could go during the day. Father's always at the office."

"Doesn't sound right to me. I hate to go sneaking around."

"I know you do, but in a case like this, it would give Cara a great deal of pleasure. She doesn't get many good things in her life. Cara's a sweet woman, and she's had a rough shuffle. I wish you'd do it, Phil."

"All right, Clinton. I will." Phil was surprised at his own agreement, but discovered that he was perfectly willing to be a sneak if that is what it took to encourage Cara. He wanted to believe that rules didn't count where men like Oliver Lanier were concerned, but that was not what he needed to say to Clinton. The two walked on, and before they parted, Phil said, "If your father catches me and turns a shotgun on me, I'll hold you responsible."

Somehow Clinton was relieved by Phil Winslow's attitude. He admired the man tremendously and slapped him on the shoulder. "Don't worry. I'll even sneak around to the servants and let it be known that my father doesn't need to know every visitor that Cara has."

"You're pretty sneaky yourself, Clinton," Phil grinned. "I'll drop by tomorrow if you'll put that word out."

★　★　★　★

"Miss Cara, you got a caller—a *gentleman* caller!"

Cara Lanier looked up from her book, startled. She was sitting in a wicker chair bolstered up by enormous crimson pillows, and Charley began barking with excitement as he danced around Ruth, one of the maids.

"A gentleman caller? What are you talking about?"

"It's that young man, Mr. Winslow. The painter you talked about so much. He's come to see you."

Instantly confusion swept across Cara's face. She had thought a great deal about Phil Winslow but had not dreamed he would come back after all that had happened. She gasped, "I can't see him! Tell him to go away, Ruth!"

"Oh, Miss Cara, I can't tell him that!" Ruth did not add that Winslow had flirted with her audaciously, and that Clinton had warned her he might be coming and had slipped her a dollar to be sure she brought him to see Cara—and kept her mouth shut as far as Oliver Lanier was concerned. Now Ruth came over and patted Cara's shoulder. A young girl of eighteen, she was very fond of Cara. "Please, ma'am. Just let him come up for a while. He's the nicest young man. Any young woman would be glad to see *him*!"

For a moment Cara hesitated. Two impulses struggled within her. One was to let Phil come up, for she had missed his company and his conversation, though her feelings had been bruised by his rather harsh comments about her art. Nevertheless, she had a deep admiration for his work, even though she considered some of the subjects he painted rather peculiar. On the other hand, she knew her father would be furious if he found out she had seen Phil. A small streak of rebelliousness suddenly surfaced in Cara. Though it had been hidden there for a long time, she had carefully subdued it. But now she was bored with herself, bored with her work, and she said abruptly, "All right, Ruth, but help me change clothes."

"Yes, ma'am!"

Ruth helped Cara put on a dark blue day dress with a high collar, long narrow sleeves, and a closely fitted skirt trimmed in black velvet ribbon. Ruth pushed Cara down in a chair and quickly and expertly smoothed her hair and pinned it with an ivory comb, then said, "Now you pretty up your face while I go get Mr. Winslow."

Cara found her hands were trembling, but she pinched her cheeks and bit at her lips to bring out a little pink. Then rising, she discovered her knees were weak and moved only slowly across the room. She could not understand why her heart was racing, but when the door opened and Phil came in, she put her hand out at once, saying, "Phil, I'm so glad you came." His hand closed around hers and his smile was genuine. "Won't you sit down and tell me what you've been doing?"

"You're looking well, Cara," Phil said. He held her hand a moment, squeezed it, and saw the pleasure in her eyes. He knew how lonely she must get, from not only what Clinton had told him, but from his own surmises. Now he moved over and sat down, saying, "That's a pretty dress. Is it new?"

"Why, not very." Cara did not add that it was over a year old and that she had never found occasion to wear it. Cara sat down across from Phil and leaned forward. "I'm a little surprised to see you, Phil."

"Surprised? Why should you be surprised?"

"Well, we came fairly close to a quarrel."

"You call that a quarrel? Let me tell you, when you get in a quarrel with Phil Winslow, you'll know it! My quarrels leave dead bodies in the streets!"

"Oh, don't be foolish!" Cara laughed, but it was like a gust of fresh air had blown open the windows of her stuffy world and filled her room. His face was ruddy with the cold, and he had taken off his outer coat. Beneath the lightweight ivory-colored shirt, she could see the long, lean muscles of his arms and his sturdy neck. Glancing down, she looked at his hands—painter's hands, but his years in the saddle and with rope had left them lean and muscular and sinewy. "Tell me what you've been doing," she said.

Phil leaned back and began to speak. He was surprised at the healthy flush in Cara's cheeks, for always before she had been poised but weak. She seemed stronger now, and this pleased him. He began by telling her about the race that Peter had won. Then he launched into a description of Avis Warwick and related how she had suddenly come into Peter's world and tried to sweep him off his feet.

"She's a pretty fast one, Cara," he shrugged. "I don't know much about her, except she's got enough money to buy the mint, and she's after Peter."

Cara had already heard about Avis's coquettish behavior, some of it from Clinton. "What would she do with him if she got him? Does she want to marry him?"

"I don't think she's the marrying kind. She's the merry widow, Cara. From what I hear, she's kind of like a praying mantis."

"A praying mantis? You mean the insect?"

"Yes. I read a book by a Frenchman called Fabre. Don't know what I was doing reading a book about bugs. I think it was in a line cabin I stayed in one winter. I guess somebody had left it there, though I don't know what kind of a cowboy would read a book about bugs." He grinned at the memory and thought of the fearsome blizzard that had nearly buried the cabin and isolated him in a white and silent world. "I read that book ten times. I think I can quote it from memory."

"What did it say about the praying mantis?"

"Well, the female's a pretty rough customer. She's about twice the size, or more, of the male, and she has the unfortunate habit of eating her husband when she has no more use for him."

"I can't believe that!"

"Well, it does sound unsociable, doesn't it? Anyway, I always think of Avis sort of like that—devouring her men friends. At least so I've heard."

"Have you told Peter this?"

"Well, not in so many words. He wouldn't listen to me anyway. He's decided to make a fool of himself, and when a man makes that decision, he has to go ahead and learn the hard way."

"No, that's not so!" Cara argued. She felt rather strongly about young Peter Winslow, although she had never met him. Now she said, "The Bible says that we are to warn those who are hurting themselves."

"It also says not to rebuke a heretic lest you become like him." Phil was interested in Cara's fascination with Peter and Avis. "It goes on all the time, Cara. That's the way life is." He was instantly sorry, for he saw her drop her head at his remark. He hastened to say, "Oh, he'll be all right! Nothing like a young man getting jilted by a woman to toughen him up!"

Carefully Phil steered the conversation to other things, finally mentioning an article he had read in the paper. "Do you know this fellow, Bradley Martin?"

"I've met him. His wife's very nice."

"What sort of fellow is he?"

"What do you mean?"

"He must be foolish. The article said he spent three hundred and sixty-nine thousand dollars to give a ball at the Waldorf."

"I read about that. It does sound extravagant."

"Extravagant? Can you imagine what could've been done with that money? People are starving to death all over New York, and here he had to transform that grand ballroom into the Palace of Versailles. The story said he had tailors brought in from Paris who worked for weeks on all kinds of costumes made with silks and lace and pearls. Everybody dressed like in the Court of Louis XV. Apparently some fellow even came dressed in a full suit of armor inlaid with gold that cost a fortune. Foolishness, if you ask me!"

"Yes it is. I agree."

"I wish some of that money could go to Mary Ann's friend, George Camrose. He could use it in that little church he's with."

"Mary said you've been going to the church."

"Yes. I go every Sunday. George is a fine minister," Phil nodded, his tone shaded with admiration. "He comes straight at you with the truth. Preaches the gospel red hot and served up with plenty of hot peppers."

Cara laughed aloud. "It sounds like a supper you would have out west."

"Well, he's pretty fiery, but at the same time you know he cares about people, and that makes a difference. I'm willing to take straightforward stuff as long as I know the man preaching it has a real love in his heart for people."

"Mary Ann's very fond of him."

"Yes, I know. I suppose your father has still forbidden her to go to the church. I never see her."

"I'm afraid so."

"What does he have against Camrose? He's a young man who would make a fine son-in-law."

"He's going to Africa. Father knows he'd lose Mary Ann."

Phil wanted to say, *A woman of her age is able to make her own decision, and if God's calling her, she ought to go.* However, it was not time for that, and he knew it would hurt Cara. Instead, he said, "Let me see some of your new paintings."

"Oh no. Not today."

Instantly Phil knew something was wrong. "What's wrong?"

"I haven't been painting lately."

Phil leaned forward, his eyes intent, and asked, "What's the matter, Cara? Are you disturbed about something?"

"I . . . I don't know." Cara could not put into words why she had ceased to paint. A few times she had gotten out her oils and her canvas and had started in on a new picture. But every time she tried to put paint on the canvas, Phil's words kept ringing in her ears. *Art should be like life, not just pretty flowers.* It had angered her at first, and she had struggled through producing one rather miserable example of a still life, then had put her paints away. Now she said, "I don't know, Phil. I just don't feel like it."

"I think you ought to force yourself. I don't believe in inspiration."

Startled, Cara looked at him. "You don't? You don't think artists have to be inspired?"

"I believe more in *perspiration* than inspiration. Sometimes I start on a painting and it just comes from nowhere. The paint," he said, with an intense look in his fine eyes, "just seems to lay itself on the canvas. That's good, and I like it. But there are other times when I can't do anything right. I can't think, my fingers won't work right, and the paint won't go on right. Nothing seems to work right. What am I supposed to do then?"

"Wait until you feel it."

Phil suddenly leaned over, stood up, and paced the floor, finally coming to sit down beside her on the chaise lounge. "Did you ever hear of a plumber saying, 'I don't *feel* like unstopping that drain.'" He made a posture, putting his hand over his heart and looking up to heaven. "I just don't *feel* it," he moaned as if he were in pain.

Cara laughed. "That's ridiculous, Phil!"

"Why's that? A man knows the plumbing's got to be fixed. He doesn't wait until he feels like fixing it. He just gets down and finds out what's the matter, and he keeps working until it's fixed. So, when I start painting, no matter how hard it gets, I just keep on going. You know, some of the best things I've ever done have come when I didn't *feel* it. I struggled, but I kept going until I finished."

Cara sat entranced as Phil Winslow spoke of his art. She realized that he had a great talent and had put his talent to better use than she had. She had no one to talk to about art, and she longed for a friend who shared her love for painting. She had read books about art, but they became dry and dull. But this man before her was exciting and vibrant and alive with a passion for capturing real life in his paintings. His eyes sparkled, and from time to time he got up and paced the floor, throwing his arms about with abandon. It was extremely exciting to her, and her eyes glowed as she sat and listened avidly.

Phil suddenly broke his words off and gave a sharp laugh. "The end of my lecture on inspiration," he said. "You get the idea." He came over and sat down beside her. "I don't mean to overwhelm you with my half-baked ideas, Cara."

"They're not half-baked at all. I see exactly what you mean," Cara said earnestly. "You're saying that most artists use inspiration, or the lack of it, to justify their laziness."

"Why, that's exactly right! You're a smart woman. You think exactly as I do." Phil reached over and picked up her hand and held it. "I'm glad there's at least two of us that feel like that. Most people don't, you know."

Cara was tremendously conscious of the warmth and strength of his hand on hers. He was unconscious of his strength and held her hand so tightly that it ached, but she did not try to withdraw it. Instead, she smiled and said, "Tell me some more about your theories on art."

Phil gladly obliged, and it was only when he looked at the clock on her mantel an hour later that he started, saying, "My word, look at the time! I've been prattling here for over an hour, Cara! Why didn't you shut me up?"

"Please go on, Phil. I find it all so interesting."

"No, I'll come again another time, if I may."

Phil stood to his feet and Cara rose with him. Her eyes were bright, and she said, "I can't tell you how much I've enjoyed your visit."

"Have you really? I wasn't sure whether I ought to come. Our ideas are a little bit different—not about inspiration, perhaps, but about other things."

"I know. I thought a lot about what you said, Phil." She wanted to say more, but at that moment the clock began to chime, and they both glanced at it. "Promise you'll come back," she said.

"All right, I will." He hesitated, then said, "I had Clinton bribe the servants not to tell your father I've been here."

To Phil's surprise, Cara laughed. "I was going to do the same thing myself," she said. "I will anyhow. A double bribe never hurt anything."

Phil was pleased with her levity. "That sounds good to me." He put his hand out, and when she put her hand in his, he held it gently, then bent over and kissed it. It was something he had never done, but the fragility and the obvious difficulty of her circumstances moved him. He looked up to see color spread into her cheeks and said, "I enjoy being with you, Cara. I'll see you again soon."

When the door closed behind Phil, Cara stood absolutely still for a moment. Charley came over and looked up at her quizzically, turning his head to one side. He barked once to get her attention, and leaning over, she scooped him up and buried her face in his fur. "Be still, Charley," she said as he wiggled around and began licking her chin. She carried him over to the lounge and sat down. She remained still for a long time, abstractedly stroking Charley's silky coat. She knew she would remember every word that Phil had said and would go over the scene again and again.

"I hope," she whispered to Charley, "he comes back tomorrow."

CHAPTER EIGHT

TAKING AN OFFERING

★ ★ ★ ★

When Phil Winslow grew discouraged and it seemed no one would ever buy even one of his paintings, he would seek out the older man who had become both a close friend and a valued counselor. Now he walked slowly along the snowy street, so preoccupied with his struggle for recognition that he didn't even notice the children engaged in a ferocious snowball fight around him. Suddenly a hard-packed missile skimmed his cheek, stinging him and making him look up in surprise.

"Hey, watch out there!" He grinned and reached down, scooping up a handful of the loose, wet snow. Quickly molding it into a firm ball, he took careful aim and sent the snowball flying at the grinning, redheaded ragamuffin nearby but missed as the boy agilely dodged out of the way.

"Nah, you couldn't hit nothin'!" the boy yelled with delight, before packing another snowball and firing back at Phil. Phil took it on the shoulder, then threw himself into the fight. Enjoying the contest, he tried to return the boy's well-aimed volleys for a few minutes, but then, throwing his hands up in surrender, he laughed and shook his head. "You're too good for me, bud," he said. "You need to be pitching in professional baseball."

"That's what I'm gonna do," the redhead said, nodding confidently. "You just wait and see. Someday you'll be sayin', 'I got hit with a snowball by Red Pickens back when he was only ten years old.'"

"Red Pickens. I'll remember that name," Phil said, then passed on down the street.

An arctic blast had hit the city the night before, and now the cold cut to the bone. Looking up, he saw the inevitable washing out on lines strung between the buildings and across balconies, frozen, stiff, and hard. Instead of floating in the breeze, long underwear, shifts, shirts, trousers, and dresses swung in unison like a frozen wave as the wind whipped them back and forth. Pulling his overcoat closely about him, Phil blew on his hands, then jammed them into his pockets. He made his way along the streets until he arrived at a three-story red-brick building that had once been a mansion but now was a run-down tenement house. Moving up the steps, careful not to slip on the snow that had packed into slippery ice, he knocked on the door.

Almost at once it was opened by a short man with a shock of dark hair and a walrus mustache. A cigar was clenched between his teeth, sending a spiral of gray smoke upward, and Robert Henri removed it long enough to say, "Come in, cowboy, before you freeze to death."

Henri always called Phil "cowboy" because of his background, and now his brown eyes glinted as he said, "You bring anything for me to look at?"

"Not this time, Robert."

"You're getting lazy," Henri grunted. "Come on in. We're having a lively discussion."

As Phil stepped into the smoke-filled apartment, he saw two other painters, George Luks and John Sloan, sitting at the kitchen table. Their wives were gathered on the sofa, enjoying their own visit. Phil greeted the women, then joined the men at the table. Soon he was sipping strong coffee and enjoying the talk. He glanced at the three men and thought, *There probably are no three better artists in all of America, but nobody knows it.*

His judgment may have been good concerning their abilities, but the three men had received little recognition for their particular type of art. Robert Henri, who was recognized more for his teaching than for his own painting, had one rule. "Forget about art," he would tell his classes, "and paint pictures of what interests you in life." For Henri this meant the city of New York. He had passed on to some of his students his passion for painting the denizens of the Bowery and the Lower East Side, the poorest and most crowded parts of the city. Now his students carried out his concepts with vigor, boldness, and vision.

John Sloan, who sat next to Phil, was a man no one would notice in a crowd. Average in all things, from his nondescript brown hair and mild blue eyes, he preferred unsavory sections of New York like the Tenderloin. He turned out picture after picture of the tawdry, vice-ridden life he found there, preferring to paint ordinary people rather than Mrs. Astor's "Four Hundred" of the social elite. He had run for the state assembly as a Socialist the previous year and readily admitted that he was glad to lose. He was forty years old now and had sold only three paintings, but his biggest success had come when President Theodore Roosevelt had admired one of his paintings—"Three Women on a Roof Drying Their Hair"—but had not purchased it. Sloan felt strongly about art, and sometimes his deep bass voice would rumble until it overwhelmed those who listened to his passionate discourses.

George Luks, who sat next to Henri, was, in Phil Winslow's opinion, the best painter of the group. At least the best portraitist. He had led a fascinating life, studying in Paris and Dusseldorf, and he used broad swatches of color to energize the figures in his paintings. He was a burly man, powerful and thick shouldered, much like the men in his many paintings of bar scenes.

Luks had brought a painting, and Henri had placed it on an easel. Now they all criticized it loudly and enthusiastically. It was a system that was hard on artists, but Henri felt that the only way to improve a man's work was to make him see how he could have done better, starting by showing him where he went wrong.

"George, this painting has a lot to be said for it," Henri observed mildly. The picture was of a crowd of immigrants, the background a row of tenement houses. "You've made it too busy," Henri said, "There are so many people that the viewer can't really concentrate on any one."

"Have you ever been down on Hester Street?" Luks demanded aggressively. "That's what it looks like, Robert!"

"An artist just doesn't paint what something looks like. He's got to cause the viewer to see what he wants him to see."

"I don't agree with that at all," Sloan spoke up. He sipped his coffee thoughtfully, then rumbled, "It's our job to paint what we see. That's what George saw down on Hester Street, and that's what he ought to paint."

Henri, however, only became more emphatic. "That's not the way art is! Art always selects!"

"I don't understand that," Phil said. "What do you mean, 'selects'?"

"Well, suppose someone set out to describe in detail everything that happened to a character in a novel. He could include scenes of all the actions a character might do, but it would make the book terribly slow and boring. The writer carefully selects the scenes he wants his reader to remember. Those that are important to his story." Henri turned to Luks and poked at him with his finger. "And that's what you haven't done in this one, George!"

"I'm not sure I agree." Sloan shook his head. "I think the busyness here is what George was trying to get at, wasn't it, George?"

"Why, of course!" Turning to Henri, George's face grew animated, and he raised his beefy hands to illustrate his point by gesturing and pointing at the fine details of the painting. "I wanted to show what life was like on Hester Street, and that's how busy it is. This fellow right in the front, wearing the white hat and smoking the cigar—I suppose he's the central figure. But suppose I left everybody else out. Why, it wouldn't have been like Hester Street at all—unless it was midnight."

The argument went on with energy, and Phil was amused when Luks grew somewhat antagonistic, but finally Robert Henri smiled. He was a charming man and a great teacher. "I think you're right after all, George, and I do get the sense of tremendous activity from your painting. You were right and I am wrong."

Luks stared at his teacher. He had been prepared to offer a more rousing defense, but now he could not, since Henri had given him such praise. Embarrassed, he turned to Phil and said, "You didn't bring anything?"

"Didn't have anything worth bringing," Phil shrugged. "I thought I might just pick up some hints from you fellows."

"That's no good," Henri said in disgust. "The only thing that teaches a painter anything is to paint! I've been to enough art classes to know that all you learn to do is *talk* about painting."

"That's right," Sloan said quickly. "There's too much talk in art and not enough doing. How many people do I know that started out with some talent, but they wound up talking about what they were doing, and not doing it!"

The companions continued their talk around the table, Sloan and Luks puffing away on their pipes, until their wives shooed them away from the table long enough to set it. Then they all sat down to a plain but nourishing meal of roast beef, cabbage, and fresh-baked biscuits.

When all were finished and the women had cleared the table and started washing up, Phil took a chair back in a corner and mostly just listened to his fellow artists' conversation, contributing only occasionally. It was a time of peace and enjoyment for him, for his visits to Henri's were always encouraging. Finally he rose, however, and promising to bring some of his work to the next meeting, he took his leave.

On his way back down Eighteenth Street, he stopped in at George Maxim's Gallery. Maxim, as usual, was sitting on a high stool behind the counter, reading a German book. His eyes lit up as Phil walked in, and he carefully marked the book with a slip of paper. "Well, good to see you, Phil."

"How are you, Max?"

"Fine . . . just fine." He came around to shake hands with Phil, then said regretfully, "No sales as yet, but you're a young man. Your time will come."

Phil had been encouraged by all the talk at Henri's, but during the walk the enormity of his quest suddenly had come upon him. He knew there were hundreds, or maybe even thousands, of young artists—and old ones, too, in New York—all thinking they were going to be successful painters someday. He was well aware that most of them would never fulfill their dreams. He had begun to wonder if he would be one of those impoverished, unnoticed painters who spent their entire lives pursuing a goal that could never be achieved.

Some of his concern must have shown in his face, or perhaps in the droop of his shoulders, for Maxim quickly led him to a table next to the stove.

"Sit down," Maxim said. "We can have some tea, and I've got a cake from the bakery." Ignoring Phil's protests, he pushed him into a chair, and soon the two men were washing down pieces of a moist and fragrant plum cake with sips of strong China tea.

Maxim waved at the paper, saying, "I see that Oklahoma's just become a new state. How many is that now?"

"Forty-six, I think."

"Wonder how many there'll be. Someday we'll take in Canada and Mexico."

"No, that won't ever happen," Phil said. "Forty-six is about big enough, I think."

Maxim sipped his tea, and his bright blue eyes scanned Phil's face. "Feeling a little bit down, are you, Phil?"

"Just a little, maybe."

"That's the way it goes with us artists, I suppose. We all have our ups and downs, but God's in His heaven. All's going to be well."

"You really believe that, don't you, Max? That everything's going to turn out all right in the end?" Phil's wide mouth tightened grimly, and he shook his head. He stared down into the dainty cup he held, swirling the amber liquid. "With all the wars and the tragedies that occur right here in New York—the killings, the poverty—you still believe everything's going to turn out all right."

George Maxim was a strong Christian and had been a help to Phil before at times like this. "The Bible says that all things work together for good to them that love God," he said firmly. "You love God, and therefore the thing you're going through right now is good."

"Well, it doesn't seem like it." Phil grinned tightly. He leaned back in his chair, soaking up the heat that radiated from the coal stove, and added, "I'm sorry to be such a complainer, Max. Sometimes it gets to me."

"Of course it does, but remember this. God's favorites have gone through the furnace of affliction more often and for longer periods than anyone else. Why, look at Joseph. God intended to make a great man out of him, but look what Joseph had to go through. He was betrayed by his brothers, thrown into a pit, sold into slavery; then he had to go to jail. But God was in all of that, Phil. When Joseph finally came through all those ordeals, he became a great man. It was the difficulties that made him what he was, not the good times."

Phil sat quietly enjoying the wisdom of the dealer, grateful that he had found one friend who had a faithful heart and a firm hold on the Scriptures. Maxim, somehow, reminded him of his own father, although they were dissimilar in so many ways. His father and mother both had this same firm grip on who a man or a woman was in God's sight, and they both felt that God often uses hard circumstances to shape and mold the character of human beings.

"Why, it's all right there in First Peter, Phil. Look here, let me read it for you." Jumping up, Maxim ran across the room, snatched the worn, thick Bible from the desk, then hurried back to his seat. He thumbed through the pages, licking his thumb often, until finally he said, "Ah, here it is! It says here that we have 'an inheritance incorruptible, and undefiled. . . . ' That's what we've got, and not only that, but verse five says we 'are kept by the power of God through faith unto salvation. . . . ' So there! We have a great heritage, and we're kept by God. But look at verses six and seven." Clearing his throat, he read clearly and with obvious pleasure. " 'Wherein ye greatly rejoice, though now for a season, if need be, ye are in heaviness through manifold temptations: That the trial of your faith, being much more precious than of gold that perisheth, though it be tried with fire, might be found unto praise and honour and glory at the appearing of Jesus Christ. . . . ' " Pounding the table, his eyes gleamed. "There it is, Phil. Right in the Word of God. God uses these hard times to purify us. One day you'll look back on it all and thank God for the things he has worked into your life through them."

"Do you think I'll ever be a successful painter, Max?"

"Depends on what you mean. Successful as in 'rich and famous'? Maybe. I believe you have it in you to be a great painter, Phil. But the success God wants for you is to bring you to maturity in Christ—whether or not you ever become known as a painter."

"I guess that's why I come here, Max, to have you encourage me." Phil smiled with affection at his friend. After a bit, as they continued talking, he began wandering around the room, staring at the paintings. Finally he came back and said, "It's been good, Max, but I've got to go to work now." He accepted an invitation to dinner the following night, then headed back to the institute.

It had begun to snow again, blanketing the busy streets in a fresh layer of sparkling white. The bells on the horses' harnesses jingled and made a fine contrast with the muffled roar of an occasional automobile. Phil thought, *I like horses best, but they're on their way out. Ten years from now there won't be a horse on the streets of New York.*

When he entered the institute, he was surprised to see George Camrose talking to Bill Crumpler. The sight amused Phil, for Camrose had been there before, and his attempts to convert Crumpler had been rather volcanic—at least on Crumpler's part. The burly art instructor looked ready to explode right now. He was waving his arms around as if he were sending semaphore signals to a distant receiver. His short black hair was standing on end where he had shoved his fingers through it, and now as Phil approached he could hear the excited rumble of Crumpler's voice. . . .

"And who knows whether the Bible is true or not? We don't have any of the original, do we? There could be all kinds of errors in it, and I think there probably are."

"You don't think that about anything else, Bill," George Camrose said. He was, as always, slightly amused at Crumpler's overheated defense of his agnosticism. "We don't have any copies of the *Iliad* or of Caesar's writings. All we have are copies of copies, but everybody believes those."

"That's different! That's altogether different! None of those claim to be the Word of God."

"That's right. They're not the Word of God. The Bible has stood the test of time and speculation for these many centuries. Men and women, too, have tried to destroy it, but it's still there." Camrose clapped his hands suddenly on Crumpler's shoulders, saying, "One of these days God's going to catch up with you. You're a gone goose, Bill."

"Keep your grubby hands off me, and keep your grubby sermons to yourself!" Crumpler suddenly looked over and saw Phil. At once, he said, "Throw this holy man out for me, Phil! You and I've got work to do!"

"Sorry. I've come to borrow your prized student," Camrose said.

Phil quickly came to stand before Camrose. "What's up, George?"

"I need some help. I've got some needy families that are in pretty bad shape. I need to find some money fast. So you and I are going to go out and take a collection for them." Camrose was wearing a derby hat, and with a mischievous gleam in his eye, he whipped it off and stuck it out in front of Crumpler. "The Widow Williams is about to be thrown out on the street. She's got four kids—none of them over seven. Dig deep, Bill."

Crumpler stared at him. "You got nerve asking for money!"

"Come on, Bill," Phil urged. "She needs it. Be a good fellow."

Crumpler scowled but shoved his hand down in his pocket, came out with some crumpled bills, and tossed them into the hat with an air of defiance. "You two will probably go out and drink it up at a bar," he snorted, then turned and walked away, swinging his arms in an exaggerated fashion.

"Well, that's a good start," Camrose commented. He smoothed

the bills out, put them in his pocket, and stuck the hat back on his head. "What about it?"

"I don't know, George," Phil said. "I've never done anything like this before."

"Well, God values humility, and I don't know anything that gives a man more humility than going around begging. I've got some names here. Too many for me to see. Would you mind going by and letting these folks know? I've given you the easy marks. I'll keep the skinflints and the Scrooges. I'm pretty well accustomed to them and to getting thrown out of places."

Phil grinned suddenly. "Sure, I'll do it, George."

"I don't suppose you've got a rich relative, have you? It'd help to have one millionaire who could do more than all the names I've got."

Phil suddenly looked up, surprise washing across his face. "You know, I do have one rich relative."

"You do? Here in New York?"

"Sure. He's Mark Winslow, Vice President of the Union Pacific."

Camrose's eyes opened with surprise and his jaw dropped slightly. "Mark Winslow's your relative?"

"Well, I don't know if he'll claim it or not, but actually we both go back to a fellow named Gilbert Winslow, who stepped off the *Mayflower*. Different branch but same line, same family."

"Do you know him?"

"I've never met him, but he knows my father, and I've heard lots of stories about him. Interesting fellow."

"Come on," Camrose said, excitement brightening his eyes. "I don't have another millionaire to put the arm on. Mark Winslow, may the Lord prepare you for what you are about to receive."

★ ★ ★ ★

Mark Winslow looked up as his secretary, a slender young man with hazel eyes and a fine head of blond hair parted in the middle, said, "Two gentlemen to see you, sir."

"Who are they, Simpkins?"

"I've never seen them before." Simpkins shrugged slightly and with some distaste. He was accustomed to having to screen Mark Winslow's visitors, for many showed up in the outer office that the vice president had no need or inclination to see. "One of them's a minister of some sort, and the other claims to be a Winslow."

Mark laughed abruptly and straightened up. He shook his head and said, "You're the most suspicious human I ever saw, Simpkins. '*Claims* to be a Winslow.' What makes you think he isn't?"

Simpkins sniffed. "I can't say, sir. Do you want to see them, or shall I send them away?"

"Send them in." Mark Winslow rose and arched his back as he waited for the visitors to come in. At the age of sixty-eight, his once raven hair was now silver, and his lean form had thickened with age. Yet there was still some of the strength of body and certainly of will which had so marked him years earlier, when he was a peacemaker for the Union Pacific. He had been able to break heads or fire forty-four men quicker than any of his enemies could.

When the two visitors entered, he looked at them, puzzled. "Have we met before?"

"No, sir. I'm Zach's son, Phil."

"Why, of course, Phil. It's been a long time since I saw your father," Mark said with pleasure. He stepped across to take the young man's hand. "How is he doing?"

"He and Mother are both doing just fine. This is my friend, Reverend George Camrose, Mr. Winslow."

"How about Mark?" Grinning, he shook the preacher's hand, took his measure, and apparently liked what he saw. "Sit down. I'm glad to meet you, Reverend. Where's your church?"

"Down on the Lower East Side. Just a small church," Camrose said. "I'm planning on going to Africa one of these days. I met your son Andrew when he was here a few years ago." Camrose took a seat, and his eyes grew contemplative. "He told me about all the hardships he had had, but somehow he stirred something in me. I'd like to have his address."

Mark Winslow nodded with enthusiasm. He was intensely proud of both sons who were now serving as missionaries in Africa. "That sounds wonderful, Brother Camrose. I'll do better than that. Give me your address, and I'll have both my sons write to you."

"That would be great." Camrose smiled.

The three men sat there talking, and finally Phil said rather nervously, "You might want to throw us out the window, Mark, when you've found out why we've come."

"Why, I hardly think I would. What is it?"

"It's my fault, Mr. Winslow. We have some hardship cases in our neighborhood, families in terrible predicaments, and I started out to try to raise some help for them. I forced Phil into helping me." He grinned wryly. "I suppose you're used to having a parade of folks come through with their hands out for help."

"Don't put it like that, Brother Camrose," Mark said quickly. "Tell me about these cases. Maybe I can help." He sat there listening, his sharp eyes never leaving the face of George Camrose until George had finished speaking. Only then he responded, "I'll be glad to help. It's hard times for the poor in the winter."

The older man went to his desk, made out a check, then waved it to dry the ink. "Let me know if this isn't enough."

Camrose took the check, stared at it, and his eyes widened. "Why, this is most generous, sir! Most generous! It will do the job very well!"

"What about you, Phil? Are you going to Africa, too?"

"Worse than that. I'm a struggling artist. One of the ten thousand in New York who will probably starve to death in an attic."

Mark laughed aloud. "Well, that's putting it in its worst form. Are you any good?"

The blunt question caught Phil off guard. "I thought I was, but nobody else seems to agree with me—at least the people willing to buy paintings."

"I'd like to see what you've done. Not that I'm any expert," he warned, "but my wife, Lola, is. Got the house filled with her paintings. Why don't you two come out and have supper with us? Bring some of your paintings with you."

The invitation pleased Phil, and George Camrose was delighted at the opportunity to get to know the parents of two missionaries to Africa. They agreed to come out the following Thursday, and left the office feeling elated at how everything had turned out. Phil thought about his friend Maxim, who was always insisting that all things do work out for good for those who love God.

"Mark Winslow is some man, Phil," Camrose said with admiration.

"You ought to hear his stories sometime. He fought in the Civil War and was a Texas gunman after he got out."

"You're kidding me!"

"Not a bit of it, and his wife dealt blackjack in a saloon."

"They been married a long time, then?"

"Oh yes. I guess forty years."

"That's really something. I hope I can say the same someday."

The two were walking along the street and the sun had come out, turning some of the snow to slush. Avoiding the deeper puddles, they stopped in at a restaurant to have a sandwich and a bowl of soup. After it was set before them by a burly waiter—who barely missed digging his finger into Phil's soup—George began to speak of his personal life. Soon he was revealing a desperation that Phil had not suspected.

"I guess you might as well know, Phil. I've got an overwhelming love for Mary Ann Lanier."

"She's a beautiful woman."

"Yes, and from a rich family." Camrose tried a spoonful of the soup and burned his lips. "That's hot!" he exclaimed and began stirring it slowly. His eyes were soft, but there was doubt and some fear in them. "Can you imagine taking a wealthy young woman who's never lacked for anything into the middle of Africa? Reverend Andrew Winslow spoke of some of the hardships: fevers, diseases, wild animals, no comforts at all in most of the outlying districts, which is where I want to go." He lifted his eyes, then shook his head with despair. "I love Mary Ann, but I couldn't ask her to do a thing like that."

"I think you'd better. That's her choice, not yours, George."

"Do you really think so, Phil?" Camrose asked, his eyes brightening. Then he shook his head again. "It wouldn't matter what she wanted. Her father would never agree."

"Have a try, George. You never know what God's going to do. If He's determined to put you two together, then you'll get together."

Camrose grinned briefly. "You sound like a hyper-Calvinist."

"Well, I don't park my buggy on the railroad tracks. I've got better judgment than that, but I do think that God is interested in all that we do. Why wouldn't He be interested in whom we marry? That's the biggest decision we make, isn't it? Aside from salvation itself."

Determination came to George Camrose. "You're right, Phil. I keep forgetting that nothing is impossible with God."

The two men sat there and Phil Winslow thought of the Lanier household. His thoughts had often been on Cara Lanier, and now he saw that George Camrose was hopelessly in love with her younger sister. Within himself a thought arose. *God may have intended these two for each other, but He'll have to knock Oliver Lanier out of the way before it happens!*

CHAPTER NINE

TROUBLE IN PARADISE

★　★　★　★

"Cara, look what I've got here!"

Cara Lanier was propped up in bed, sketchbook on her knees. Looking up, she was amused to see Mary Ann close the door and furtively look around.

"What is that you're hiding? You must be ashamed of it," Cara said, watching curiously.

"I brought you some of the latest songs. You only listen to operas and things like that!" Mary Ann was wearing an attractive light green dress that suited her slender but well-shaped figure, and a gleam of fun shone in her eyes.

"Well, I take it these aren't operas." Cara smiled as Mary Ann dumped several paperclad disks out of a brown paper bag onto the bed. Cara picked up one and read the label. "I Wonder Who's Kissing Her Now." Amusement spread across her face. "Father would have a heart attack if he knew you brought things like this into the house!"

"Oh, he's not here, and you need to hear some of the new music." She took one of the disks from Cara, then moved over and put it on the Victrola. "Now listen to this," she said after winding it up and carefully placing the needle on the disk.

A tinny voice filled the room with rollicking song.

Take me out to the ball game.
Take me out with the crowd;

Buy me some peanuts and crackerjacks
I don't care if I never get back.
So let's root, root, root for the home team;
If they don't win it's a shame,
For it's one, two, three strikes you're out
At the old ball game.

"What kind of a song is that?" Cara asked, staring open-eyed at the large flared horn perched on top of the music box.

"Oh, it's the biggest song on the market. That's what they sing at all the baseball games now. It's become kind of a theme song. But listen to this one." Mary Ann removed the disk and, moving quickly, replaced it with another. This time it was a man's rather fruity voice as he crooned,

I wonder who's kissing her now;
I wonder who's teaching her how;
I wonder if she
Ever tells him of me;
I wonder who's kissing her now?

Mary Ann played the song twice more, each time moving around the room in an imitation dance, holding her arms as if she were embracing a man.

Cara laughed outright as Mary Ann spun around the room. "You're crazy," she said, "and that song is absolutely silly."

"It's not silly at all!" Mary Ann pouted. She stopped and removed the disk, saying, "It's sad. Here's this man who's had a sweetheart once, and now for some reason she's gone, or he's gone, and he's thinking about her. He's wondering if anybody's kissing her."

"Is that all you've got to think about, kissing and hugging?"

"Well, don't you ever think about things like that, Cara?" Mary Ann asked quickly, then her hand flew to her mouth. "I'm sorry. I didn't mean to say that."

Cara put the sketchbook down and folded her hands. The thoughtless question by Mary Ann had touched something in her. She sat there quietly staring at her hands, and Mary Ann came over and sat down beside her, putting her arm around her.

"I'm sorry, Cara. I didn't mean to—"

"It's all right, Mary Ann. Most women do think of things like that, I believe. I should've given it up years ago, thinking about kissing and men."

"Then you do think about them!"

"Yes, who could help that? But it can never come to anything. I'll never get out of this room. I'll die on this bed, I suppose."

Mary Ann flinched at the bitterness in Cara's voice. Her older sister had always been to her such a tower of strength. She never complained and always managed to put the best face on things despite all the disappointments she had faced because of her illness. Mary Ann saw an emptiness in Cara's eyes that shocked her deeply. "You mustn't think that, Cara. God can do wonders. I know it's hard for you, and it's been such a long time. But we mustn't give up. We must keep on praying."

Cara's eyes suddenly filled with tears and she dashed them away, saying, "There, you see, you've got me crying. Now I'll have to drink some of that awful ale that Father insists on. Every time I feel sorry for myself and think of people more fortunate, I think of people who don't have to drink that ale."

"Why don't you just pour it out and let Father think you drink that awful stuff?"

"I couldn't do that."

Mary Ann said defiantly, "*I* could!" Her eyes grew bright, and she added, "I'm not going to stay here always, Cara. I'm going to get out of this place. I'm going to marry George, and I'm going to Africa with him, and we're going to serve God there on the mission field."

Cara sat there listening, and compassion for her younger sister filled her heart. She knew the life and the longing for something different that existed in Mary Ann. She was happy that it had turned toward serving God instead of to the world, but at the same time she knew how unlikely it would be that Mary Ann would ever marry George Camrose.

"I want you to do something for me, Cara," Mary Ann said abruptly. Plumping herself down on the bed, she reached out and took Cara's hands, squeezing them firmly. "I want you to ask Father to let me go to George's church instead of our church."

"Why, he'll never agree to that!"

"He will if you ask him. He loves you better than anybody else. Sometimes I think you're the only one he does love."

"What an awful thing to say!"

"I know it, and I didn't mean it quite that way. But he's got a special feeling for you."

"I know. Sometimes I wish he didn't," Cara said wearily. "It won't do any good for me to ask him. He's got his mind made up, and you know how stubborn he is."

"But will you try?" Mary Ann pleaded. "Just ask him."

"All right, I'll try, but don't get your hopes up."

It was impossible for Mary Ann to be depressed. She had a hopeful spirit, and there was an effervescent quality to her that pleased everyone except, perhaps, her father. He thought it was silliness and did not hesitate to say so. Now, however, she got up and said, "Now, we're going to play some more. This one is fun. It's called, 'The Glow Worm.' "

" 'The Glow Worm?' What an awful title!"

"The salesman told me that it comes from the Germans and everybody's singing it. It goes, 'Glow little glow worm, glimmer, glimmer. . . .' "

★ ★ ★ ★

Oliver Lanier entered Cara's room, walked across the floor, and stood towering over her. "How do you feel today, my dear?"

"Very well, Father. And you?"

"Oh, I'm all right." Pulling a chair up, he sat down and leaned forward. "What have you been doing with yourself all day? Any new paintings?"

"No, I haven't done anything lately."

A frown creased Lanier's forehead. "You haven't painted for several weeks now. What seems to be the trouble?"

Cara wanted to tell him that it was not her health, but her new dissatisfaction with the things that she had always done that troubled her. She had not been able to paint flowers again, for Phil Winslow's admonition, *You have to paint life, Cara—life is more than flowers,* had been ringing in her mind ever since he spoke it. She had defended herself, sometimes almost speaking out loud. *How can I paint life? The only life I have is here in this room that I'm so sick of. You can go out into the streets, and in the fields, and see what life is like. But I'm a prisoner here in this room!* She did not say this aloud, of course, for her father would never understand. "I am just, perhaps, waiting for a good idea for a really good painting."

"I'm sure you'll do well. I'm very proud of you, Cara. I wish the rest of your brothers and sisters had the dedication that you have."

Cara wanted to defend her family, but she knew that it would be useless. She started to speak when her father suddenly pulled a newspaper out of his inner pocket and said, "I wanted to read this to you." Pulling a pair of spectacles out, he settled them on his nose firmly, then began to read. There was a triumph in his voice, an obvious pleasure about the article he was reading.

"*Whoever calls this art?* That's the name of the article," he said. "It was published in the newspaper last Sunday. I don't suppose you read it?"

"No. I didn't see it, Father."

"Well, you've been so taken with this new style of painting that I wanted to let you know what the world thinks about it." He straightened his back and began reading more loudly than necessary. " 'The new group of painters that have emerged from the New York scene has been aptly named. They are called the Ashcan School. Indeed, it would be difficult to find a better title, for the product of all of these men comes from the ashcan school of mind and deserves to be, literally, in the ashcan of the streets.

" 'Led by Robert Henri, the small group of supposed artists have been spawning pictures that are at the same time vulgar, ineffective, and poorly done. They not only are badly executed, but they certainly have the wrong subject matter. George Luks' latest atrocity is a representation of two men, sweaty, muscles straining, and obviously not a fit painting to be hung in a decent and respectable home. Who would want a portrait of two thugs adorning their living room or parlor? Another one of the group, John Sloan, has for his masterpiece a painting of McSorley's Old Ale House over on East Seventh Street. It is a typical saloon with a fixed house rule against women. The picture delineates men getting drunk at a bar and a barkeep in a striped shirt feeding a herd of mangy alley cats. The alley cats, in some ways, have more dignity than the drunks lining the bar.' "

Looking up at Cara, Lanier squinted. "What do you think of that? It goes on. I'll leave it with you. I want you to read it carefully."

"It's very . . . interesting. Have you seen any of the pictures?"

"Certainly not, and I don't intend to! You have the right idea, Cara. There's beauty in this world, and it's the artist's duty to portray it. Art is supposed to uplift. How can anyone be uplifted by a picture of a group of drunks at a Lower East Side bar?"

Cara had long ago learned that trying to argue with her father was like arguing with the Rock of Gibraltar. To her knowledge he had never changed in the least, and now she was certain he would not. "I'll read it," she said. "Thank you for bringing it."

"That's not all. There's a final note. I've marked it."

Cara looked at the article and saw a small paragraph with a circle heavily bordering it. She read aloud, " 'Another one of the Ashcan School is a young man named Phil Winslow. Winslow has real talent, but he is throwing it to the winds by painting slums, scenes of degradation that would be better left in the dark. Wake up, Winslow! The world has no place for the kind of filth that you are putting on canvas.' "

Cara's throat closed, and she looked up to see her father smiling at her triumphantly. "There," he said. "That settles that!"

It did not settle it in Cara's mind, but she determined to change the subject.

"Father, I want to talk to you about Mary Ann."

"Mary Ann? What about her?"

"She very much wants to attend George Camrose's church. I wish you'd give her permission."

"I certainly will not!"

"But why not, Father? He's a most admirable young man. You said so yourself when you first met him."

"I may have said that, but that was before this nonsense about going off to Africa."

"You think taking the gospel to those who don't have it is nonsense? Father, you can't mean that!"

"Well, perhaps not," Lanier said. He unwittingly had backed himself into a corner, for he was not against foreign missions. He had, in fact, given large sums of money, but his own family had not been involved then. "George Camrose has a bright future here. I took pains to talk to some of the leaders in the denomination. They all speak highly of him. With help from some of us who have influence, he could get a fine church right here in New York. Why, he had an offer from Faith Church before he went to that small church—if you can call it that—where he is now."

"He felt the people there needed him more, Father."

"He has talent, and God expects every man to use his talent to the utmost. He could be ministering to hundreds of people, maybe even thousands. It's not unlikely. He has the appearance, he has the delivery, and he's sound theologically. Yes, he is a likable young man. I've told Mary Ann all of this. As a matter of fact," Lanier said, "I've told Camrose himself."

"You told him this?" Cara gasped in shock. "What did he say?"

"He simply said that God had called him to preach the gospel in Africa, and he has not been willing to listen to my more promising proposals." Oliver was not accustomed to being put aside so easily, but after two futile attempts to get Camrose to change his views, he had washed his hands of the affair. Now he shrugged, saying brusquely, "Well, he's not open to sensible suggestions. I've told Mary Ann he's not suitable for her."

"But she loves him."

"Don't be ridiculous. She doesn't know anything about love. She certainly doesn't know anything about living in a dirty hut in Africa. Why, she wouldn't even last a year, Cara! Do you know how many missionaries die on their first missionary trip?"

Cara sat quietly listening as her father went on. She knew it was hopeless to try to dissuade him, and now she had no more to say.

"Now, we'll hear no more about Camrose or about this fellow Winslow. I'll go get your ale for you."

"Father, I believe I'm doing very well without it."

"Now, Cara, let's not have this argument every time. Your improvement is partly because of the ale. I'm certain of it! So be a good girl."

After Lanier had brought Cara's ale and had watched with satisfaction as she drank it down, he kissed her good night and went to his bedroom. He found his wife prepared for bed, brushing her hair out. Alice Lanier had smooth brown hair without a trace of gray at the age of fifty. She was still a very pretty woman and Lanier stopped long enough to put his hands on her shoulders, then he lifted his hand and ran it down her hair. "I always loved your hair," he said. "The first time I saw you, I think it was all I saw. It is still beautiful."

It was a rare compliment, and Alice turned with surprise. "Why, thank you, Oliver," she said. "I always like to hear you say things like that."

As if afraid he had been too complimentary, Oliver turned away, clearing his throat roughly. He was a man who feared to let his emotions show, although he had them. This would have come as a surprise, for in his struggle to achieve wealth he had hardened himself. It was not for him to let his enemies know that he had softness; that was the way to get hurt! Now as he pulled off his coat and began to undress for bed, he said, "I just had a talk with Cara. I think it cleared the air quite a bit about that young Winslow."

"I think she misses him. She had a wonderful time talking about art."

"We'll get somebody else in to talk about art."

Oliver said this as if it were the same as hiring an interior decorator to wallpaper the dining room. To him a need was always met by money. It was a way of life with him, and now as he put his mind to it, Alice knew he would find someone—even if he had to hire them—to come in and talk to Cara by the hour about art.

"I don't think that's possible. We don't make friends like that."

"Friends? What friendship could she have with a penniless artist who's gone off the wrong end?"

"She's still a young woman, and she enjoyed his company, Oliver. I don't think you really grasp what a hard time Cara has—never seeing anybody except the family or Dr. McKenzie. I was excited for her when she got interested in Phil Winslow."

"Excited?" Oliver turned quickly and his eyes narrowed. "What were you excited about? Surely you don't think she could be interested in him as a suitor?"

"Why not? She's only thirty-one. When she gets better she could marry and have a life."

"We've talked about this before. She'll never be better."

Alice was hurt by her husband's brusqueness and the hard edge to his voice. She could not understand it, for she had seen over the years that if Oliver was tender with anyone—other than herself—it was with Cara. Now as she thought about it, she finally decided to say something she had never dared to say. She turned around and took a deep breath, then said, "Oliver, I think you love Cara deeply, but sometimes we can even hurt those we love."

"What does that mean?"

"It means sometimes we want to hold on to people, and by holding on to Cara, I think you've not let her—"

"That's nonsense! Of course I love Cara! I love all my children, but she's special. She's not well, and I'm very protective."

"I think you're too protective of her. I've been meaning to talk to you about this for a long time." Alice stood up and went over to stand directly before Oliver. She was a small woman with mild blue eyes and a round face. She had always been completely dominated by her husband. A loving mother, she had tried to protect her children, but somehow she had become, even from their first days of marriage, so afraid of displeasing Oliver that she had caved in when he had treated the children roughly.

"I think we ought to try something different with Cara."

"Another doctor? We've tried a dozen. McKenzie's the best we've found."

"I don't mean that. I mean we ought to get her out of the house more. Let her get more involved in things like parties and shopping."

"I'd be happy if only she were able, and as she improves—as I certainly hope she will—we will do that." Oliver put his hands on his wife's shoulders. He had not understood a word she said and now added, "Naturally I love Cara. We both do, but we've got to protect her from herself."

"I think sometimes, Oliver, she'd rather go out and have a few good times and die rather than stay secluded in that room for the rest of her life."

Oliver was shocked. "What do you mean by that? That's an awful thing to say!"

"Not awful at all. Which would you rather do? Have a short life where you at least get out and see people and flowers and excitement, or stay in a room for the rest of your life?"

"Not at all to the purpose, Alice! I'm surprised at you! Why, this is foolishness you're talking!"

Ordinarily Alice Lanier would have immediately caved in, but she had become desperate over the past few months watching Cara, and she thought of her other children. "I've never spoken to you about this, but I think you're unfair, especially to Clinton, but also to Mary Ann and Benji."

Astonishment swept across Lanier's face. He ran his hand over his iron gray hair, then shook his head in bewilderment. "What are you talking about? Why, I have provided everything for my children."

"Everything but—"

"Everything but what?" Oliver demanded. "What is it you were going to say?"

"I don't like to say this, Oliver." Alice put her hand on his massive chest and looked up with apprehension in her eyes. "You've provided everything but love. You're too hard on them, Oliver. You always have been. Oh, not on Bess and Bobby. You weren't on the others either when they were small, but as soon as they started to grow up and tried to make lives for themselves, you've ruled them with an iron hand."

Affronted to his heart, Oliver stared at Alice. Throughout their entire marriage, she had never dared challenge him on anything, and he was shocked. "I can't believe you're saying this to me!"

"I don't like saying it, but it's true. Look at Clinton. Here he is twenty-eight years old. You know he doesn't really like the work in your office. He wants to do something else, something with his hands, something with machinery."

"Well, wouldn't that be wonderful! Instead of having a fine career for himself in one of the best brokerage firms in the country, he could be a mechanic, and I suppose you'd like for him to get one little room in a tenement house and starve to death."

"It doesn't have to be like that. If you could just show a little interest in him and go to the races with him. Do something with him, Oliver. As far as I know, you haven't done anything with Clinton since he was a boy."

Her words stung, for they were true. Oliver blinked his eyes and his mouth tightened. "And where have I failed Mary Ann and Benji, now that you've decided to educate me."

At that moment Alice knew that any more talk would be hopeless. He had closed his mind and heart, and she saw the blunt stubbornness on his face. Discouragement swept over her, and she said in almost a whisper, "Oliver, if you don't learn to love your children, to be kinder to them and to enter into their lives—you're going to lose them." She turned away, leaving him staring at her as she walked to the window and stared outside.

Oliver had not been confronted like this for years. And to hear it from his own wife came as a terrible shock. He had taken pride in seeing that all of his children had the finest clothes that could be bought. Their rooms were well furnished, even luxurious, and they had the best medical care that could be provided. But now for the first time a small doubt suddenly touched his blunt spirit. And then a dart of fear pierced his stoic armor of control. It was not much, just a disturbing thought, but the idea of losing his family was the most frightening thing he could think of. For years he had felt that he was protecting them from their own foolishness, but now Alice's words seemed to echo in his mind, and deep inside, something happened. He knew he would not forget this conversation for weeks, or even months, try as he might. Still, he was a man of immense self-confidence. *I've done the right thing for my children*, he thought. *Alice is wrong. I'll have to make her see it.*

He went to bed that night and listened until his wife's breathing revealed that she was asleep. Sleep did not come to him, however, and for what seemed to be hours he lay there holding himself still, thinking of what Alice had said. Finally he got up and went to stand beside the window. The fire had died and it was cold in the room, but he did not notice it. He thought of the time when he had taken Clinton to a circus when the boy was nine years old. He recalled how Clinton's auburn hair had flashed in the sunlight as they approached the tent, his eyes shining with anticipation, and he remembered how Clinton had held on to his hand as he bought the tickets and they entered. He remembered so much of it that it surprised him—the aerialists flashing through the air in their silver costumes, the nine elephants rearing up in unison, and all the time Clinton talking constantly, his face alight with excitement.

Outside, the night was dark and the sky was dotted by a few feeble stars. Oliver stared at them blindly through the window, thinking of that trip to the circus so long ago. Try as he might, he could not remember another time after that when he was ever really close to his son. A heaviness fell upon him and sleep eluded him. Finally he dressed quietly and left the room. Stepping out of the house into the cold night air, he walked the grounds, trying to put aside what Alice had said. But as he thought of Cara lying in bed helpless, Alice's words kept coming repeating in his mind. "I'm not keeping her back!" he muttered. "I want her to be well more than anything else." But then the thought of her leaving came to him almost like the piercing of a sword, and the face of Philip Winslow came before him. Then he remembered how Cara's eyes and face had lighted up when the young artist had been there.

"He's no man for her," Oliver said gruffly, "and that's the end of it!" He turned and walked heavily back into the house, leaving the cold stars to glitter overhead so far away.

CHAPTER TEN

"HAVE YOU EVER WANTED A MAN?"

★ ★ ★ ★

Cara looked up from the paper she was reading, her eyes glowing. Charley had been lying at her feet, eyes closed and apparently asleep, but at her slight movement, he looked up, alertly cocking his ears and then speaking to her with a quick bark.

"Look here, Charley. . . ." Glad to be addressed by his beloved mistress, Charley jumped onto her lap and pushed aside the paper, raising his face close to hers. Cara stroked his silky fur but pushed his head away as he attempted to lick her nose in return. "If you'll stop that long enough, I'll tell you what I'm going to do. Let me read this to you." Charley looked intently at her face, as though trying to understand her speech. When it became apparent to him that at least she was not going anywhere, he lay down on her lap and made himself comfortable.

" 'A show of some of the fledgling artists in the New York area will be held tomorrow, the sixth of March, at the Eighteenth Street gallery of George Maxim. Mr. Maxim has long been a supporter of what has been called, with some derision, the Ashcan School of painters, including such painters as Robert Henri, Everett Shinn, and George Luks. Mr. Maxim invites the public tomorrow to come and view this new movement in modern art. He especially emphasized that paintings by a brand-new artist, one just bursting upon the scene in our city, Mr. Phil Winslow, will be shown, and the artist himself will be present to speak to those interested in his work.' "

"Do you hear that, Charley? Phil's going to have a show!" Sharing her pleasure, she hugged Charley until he struggled free, then again tried to lick her face.

"My face doesn't need washing, Charley, but I believe yours does."

Cara read the article several more times. Then, her excitement stirring, she suddenly stood, spilling Charley onto the floor. Scrambling to his feet, the spaniel gave her a startled glance, then wandered off to find a more secure place in which to continue his rest.

Cara paced around the room, exercising as best she could in the limited space of her bedroom. Her restlessness felt similar to that when the idea for a painting was beginning to take shape, but this was more urgent. An idea was forming, but doubts troubled her. As she paced, she dealt with them one by one, eyes narrowed, until she finally took a deep breath and headed out of her room.

At the end of the hall she knocked on Mary Ann's door.

Mary Ann opened the door, still holding the thick book she had been reading, and exclaimed, "Why, Cara! Is something wrong? Don't you feel well?"

"I feel well," Cara said, stepping into the room, "but I'm having a strange thought. I may be losing my mind."

"Oh, don't be foolish. You're the most sensible one in the whole house!" Mary Ann laughed. Then she saw the seriousness in her sister's expression. "Come and sit down and tell me about it."

"You won't believe me," Cara said slowly. "But I'm thinking of defying Father." She looked up to catch the response from her younger sister and saw, with surprise, a pleased light had come into Mary Ann's bright blue eyes. "You look happy about it. It's not a nice thing to do, to deceive your parents."

"It's about time you broke out of the prison you've built for yourself," Mary Ann said sharply. She was excited and leaned forward to squeeze Cara's arm. "What are you going to do, free yourself by burning down the house? I'll get the matches."

It was Cara's turn to laugh. "Don't be silly. It's just . . . well . . . look at this." She handed Mary Ann the paper, folded open to the article she had just been reading. She watched intently while Mary Ann read it, then continued. "I'm going to that show, Mary Ann, but you'll have to help me."

Mary Ann was willing to help her sister, even in something this hard. She loved her father, but it was a confining sort of love. She felt even more like a prisoner, if possible, than Cara, and now she whispered, as if Oliver Lanier were crouched outside the door with his ear to the keyhole. "What do you plan to do? How are you going to get there?"

"I want you to get Father's permission to take me down to be photographed. He asked me to have a photographic portrait done some time ago, but I just haven't felt like going. I don't like having my picture taken."

"That'll be easy enough. I've heard him say several times he wants to have a large photograph of you. What do we do then?"

"Well, we'll go and do exactly what I said, but after the sitting we'll go see the new paintings."

The two sat there making hurried plans. Both of them grew excited, and Mary Ann was thinking, *This is just the sort of thing Cara needs. She's actually got some color in her cheeks and her eyes are sparkling*. Aloud she said, "What if we get caught?"

"There's really no reason why we should. But if we do, we do." Rising to her feet, she said, "You'll help me, won't you, Mary Ann?"

"Of course I will."

As soon as Cara was out the door, Mary Ann began to walk rapidly back and forth. Her mind hummed with ideas, but she began to devise a plan of her own. Quickly she went over to her writing desk and scratched out a quick note. It simply said, "George, this is a secret, but tell Phil that Cara will be at his show tomorrow. Tell him to look for her and to be very nice. She needs some encouragement." She hesitated for a moment, then wrote with a slight blush, "Love, Mary Ann."

Putting the letter in an envelope, she took it downstairs and found James, the coachman. "James," she said, "I have a very special errand for you, and I want you to take this note to Reverend George Camrose over at his church. Be sure you don't give it to anyone else. Find him and put it right in his hand." She had slipped two dollars around the envelope and smiled winsomely. "This is for you if you do it—and be sure you don't tell anybody."

James had an adventurous spirit, despite his forty years and thickening body. Eyes twinkling, he winked and grinned. "You can count on me, Miss Mary Ann. Nothing I like better than taking love letters between sweethearts."

Mary Ann smiled back, and as James quickly left, she spoke to the empty room, jaw firm. "Now, Father dear, let's see you stop this meeting from taking place."

* ★ ★ ★

Phil looked across the table at Jolie and nodded approvingly. His artist's eye took in the gently tailored soft brown woolen jacket and matching skirt that set off her lovely form. The snowy white lace-trimmed blouse gave her a bright, fresh look. The late-winter sun streaming through the cafe window brought out the highlights of her dark hair and finished the picture perfectly.

"I like that outfit," Phil said. "You make a lovely picture in it."

Jolie flushed. "Thank you, Phil," she said.

As he often did now, Phil had come by to see what progress was being made on the car. Jolie had quickly accepted his invitation to lunch. Now she was eating her chocolate ice cream with great relish and did, indeed, look very well, except for a worried expression about her eyes.

"Something troubling you, Jolie? You seem a little bit . . . well . . . not depressed, but worried. Are you worried a little?"

"I am a little . . . about—" She broke off abruptly and put her spoon down. She shifted in her chair a moment, then said, "Well, it's really about Peter. I'm concerned about him. He spends almost every night with Avis Warwick."

"That's what Easy told me. He doesn't care for her, and I see you don't either."

"Nothing personal, but she could cause Peter a great deal of trouble."

Phil leaned back and studied the young woman carefully. He knew he had to be very cautious with what he said, for Jolie obviously was in love with Peter Winslow, even though she had never said so. Finally he said, "Peter's a levelheaded fellow. He'll be all right."

"No man's levelheaded where women are concerned. He's just as capable of making a fool out of himself as any man."

Phil laughed. "You don't think much of us, do you?"

"Oh, I'm sorry, Phil. I didn't mean to be so snappy." Slowly

Jolie picked up her spoon and took another bite of the ice cream, rolling it over her tongue as she thought about happier days in the past. Things had changed, and not for the better. Before, she had done her work and then rushed home to work on the car with Peter and Easy. They would go out to eat, or eat at the rooming house, after which they would take walks or just relax and talk together. Mostly the talk had been of cars and racing, but Jolie had not cared; it was the feeling of camaraderie she treasured. Now it seemed to be slipping away from her.

"I don't suppose it would do any good for me to talk to him. As a matter of fact, I tried a little bit. But he seemed to have wax in his ears or something." Phil made a grimace and shook his head. "I believe you're right. When a good-looking woman throws herself our way, most of us men are apt to be a little bit dazzled."

He looked at his watch and then exclaimed, "I've got to go! This is the day for my great show—you know, the one when I'm going to sell all those paintings and get rich and famous." He grinned wryly as he stood up. "You care to come along?"

"I'll come by later, Phil. Easy wanted to come, too, so we'll see you at the gallery."

"All right. Wish me luck."

"I'll always do that, Phil."

Phil smiled, reached out, and squeezed the girl's shoulder. He had a fondness for her, and her unhappiness troubled him. Now he hurried out the door and made his way quickly to the gallery. As he rushed in, he found Maxim pacing back and forth with excitement.

"Where have you been?" Maxim demanded. "We've had people coming in for an hour."

"Sell anything yet?"

"Not yet, but lots of lookers." Maxim tried to hide a grin. "I think some of them have come to see what Ashcan painters look like. Come on. I'll introduce you to them."

The time went quickly, and Phil found himself besieged with questions. "How did you learn to paint?" "Why do you paint such dreadful scenes, like the slums?" "Have you ever sold any paintings?" "What's the least you would take for this painting?"

He fielded all the questions but sold no paintings. Maxim kept coffee and hot tea on, for the weather outside was brisk. After about twenty cups of coffee, Phil began to feel as though he was sloshing when he walked. He had started to remark on this when he turned and saw the trio coming through the door—Cara Lanier with Mary Ann and George Camrose.

George's eyes lit up as he spotted Phil. "Well, we're here to salute the conquering hero." After shaking hands with Phil, he winked at the two women. "Would you like to have his autograph?"

"I'd like to see all of your paintings," Mary Ann said. "I demand a lot of attention."

Cara said nothing. She felt intimidated and oddly out of place. She rarely escaped the confines of her room, and now the large number of paintings on the walls and their kaleidoscope of color dazzled her. Maxim had literally covered the walls with pictures, besides stacking others on racks around the shop.

Seeing Phil's friends gathered around him, Maxim came over and let Phil introduce him.

"Let me show you around, Reverend, Miss Lanier."

"All right," George said. "Come on, Mary Ann. Maybe we can buy each other a present."

As soon as they were gone, Phil turned to Cara and said quietly, "It's so good to see you here, Cara."

"I . . . I read about the show in the paper, and I wanted so much to come."

"Does your father know you're here?"

"N-no, not exactly. Actually, he's been insisting that I go have my picture made at the photographic studio. It was just down the street and—" She halted suddenly and said with a disgusted look in her eye, "I don't know why I'm lying to you, Phil. Mary Ann and I decided to break away. Well, I decided, and she's helping me. If Father finds out, he'll probably throw me out of the house."

Phil laughed with delight. "I don't think so. He's very fond of you, Cara."

"Yes, he is." Cara felt uncomfortable with this, for she knew Phil had only seen the hard side of her father. But it was not possible to explain the other side to anyone. She said, "Show me your paintings, Phil."

"All right."

The next two hours were, perhaps, the most delightful in Cara's life, at least in recent memory. Phil was a good host. He took her around, showing her not only his own pictures but those of the other artists. He talked about them with warmth, with intelligence, being highly critical and at the same time pointing out the good things about them.

As for Cara, she was dazed by the vivid colors, the exuberance, the vitality of all the different paintings. They portrayed a side of New York City she had never seen, streets where the poor and downtrodden gathered—and showed them, not always miserable, but sometimes dancing. One painting portrayed the celebration of an election victory, with people dancing in the streets. Another, by Luks, simply showed a young, ragged boy with a broad, hilarious grin and the love of life twinkling in his eyes.

"Now, I like this young man," she said. "I'm sure Mr. Luks must have seen him somewhere. Nobody could dream up a face like that."

"He looks happy in spite of those ragged clothes and his dirty face. I guess it's well to remember that the rich aren't always happy and the poor aren't always miserable." Phil grew serious then and drew close to Cara. She could feel the pressure of his arm against her as he pointed out how excellent the painting was. Finally they got to a picture of a young couple walking down Broadway. They were obviously poor, and also obviously in love with each other. The young woman was wearing a very modest, worn dress, and the young man had a derby tilted over his eye. It was a fine summer afternoon, and they were out enjoying the weather and a leisurely stroll together.

"You can see how much she loves him. How do you ever put that on a piece of canvas?"

"I guess you have to need somebody," Phil said slowly.

"*Need* somebody?" Cara was amazed. "What do you mean?"

"I can't explain it, Cara." Phil turned to look at her. She was pale from her long confinement. Still, there was a half-hidden vibrancy in this woman that he had learned to admire. As he watched her now, he thought, *If she could only get away and have some freedom, she could be a woman any man would be proud of.* He struggled to find the words he needed, and finally only said, "I can't explain it. It's just that when I try to paint, I usually need to do something. I need to say something." He looked at her and asked abruptly, "Have you ever wanted a man, Cara?"

Cara's face suddenly grew pink, and her eyes flew open with astonishment. "Why . . . why, what a thing to ask!"

"Well, have you?" Phil persisted. "I'm not being nosy. It's just obvious that the young woman in the painting needs that young man. There's something in her eyes, in her body language, that says it, and I think artists have to have something inside that's reaching out, needing to be expressed. Sort of swelling up, and then, somehow, through a God-given ability, they can put it on canvas."

Cara was silent. She did not know what to say to such frankness. *Have I ever wanted a man?* she asked herself, and then as she looked up, almost timidly, she whispered, "I could never paint like that."

"You don't need to paint like *that*," Phil said. "That's the way this particular painter puts paint on canvas. It's his vision. But you've got something in you, Cara Lanier. I knew it the first time I met you. You've got more talent in you than any five painters need, but you've kept your heart bottled up and refuse to let the things out." Phil suddenly reached out and took her hands, ignoring the onlookers who were moving about. "There's something in you, Cara," he said quietly, "and someday you're going to let it out."

Intensely aware of his hands holding hers and of his eyes seeming to pierce her spirit, Cara could say nothing. Somehow she recognized the truth but could not respond to the things this tall, strong man was saying. She stood there for one moment, then pulled her hands back and turned away, leaving Phil shaking his head and wondering if anyone or anything could bring out the woman Cara Lanier had never let the world see.

★   ★   ★   ★

Peter and Avis Warwick came to the exhibition that afternoon. Peter informed Phil they were on their way to a race. "Come on and go with us," he said.

"I wish I could, but who knows? Somebody might stop by and buy a picture."

Avis had been looking around at the paintings by herself. She walked back over to where Phil and Peter were talking about the race and said, "I'll buy this one, Phil." She pointed to a small oil nearby.

Phil was surprised. "Aren't you going to ask how much it is?"

"All right. How much is it?"

Phil suddenly grinned. "How much have you got, Avis?"

Avis winked at him. "Come on, now. Name your price, then I'll bargain with you."

Peter went over to the picture and examined it. It was a crowded picture of New York stevedores, strong men straining to move heavy barrels and bales to and from oceangoing ships. There was an obvious poverty about them, yet they exuded life and excitement. "Why would you want this? Just go down to the docks," he grinned, winking at Phil.

"Don't pay any attention to that barbarian," Phil said. "I was thinking of asking fifty dollars for it."

Avis reached into her purse and pulled out several bills. "Sold," she said. "Wrap it up. I'll take it with me."

"My first sale," Phil said, "and probably the last."

As Peter and Avis left the gallery and headed to the track, Avis spoke in her most charming manner. "Peter, I want to ask a favor."

"Ask away." Peter was driving Avis's car, a powerful Maxwell, and enjoying the feel of the wind as it whipped around his goggles. He risked a quick glance at her, then said, "Wait a minute. Maybe I better modify that. No telling what you'd ask for."

"It's not much," Avis wheedled. She pulled herself closer to him and reached up and tucked his hair under his cap. Her own hair was blowing in the wind, and she shook her head to free it still more. "I want you to let me ride with you in the race."

Peter laughed outright. "You know I'm not going to do a crazy thing like that."

"Why not?"

"Because it's too dangerous, and you could get hurt."

"You could get hurt, too!"

"Now, that's different, Avis. It's what I do. Goes with the territory."

They sailed down the highway and Avis continued to beg him, but Peter said, "Not a chance, Avis. I'll do a lot for you, but not that."

Avis almost responded angrily. She was accustomed to having her own way, but there was a set about Peter Winslow's lips that told her she would be wasting her time. She thought, *There are more ways than one for a woman to get her own way.* She smiled and said sweetly, "I'm glad to see you're thinking of me—of my safety, I mean." She pulled his head around and kissed him, and the car swerved wildly.

"Hey! Save your kisses until we get stopped!"

"I'll remember that," Avis said. She smiled, and a look of determination formed on her face. *Sooner or later*, she vowed, *I'll be riding beside him in one of those races!*

CHAPTER ELEVEN

THE CALLING

★ ★ ★ ★

Jolie could not help but let the miserable feelings churning inside her show on her face as she stood backstage at the theater where she worked. Several times Maude Adams, the star of the play, gave Jolie an odd look. After the final curtain had fallen, she came over and asked quietly, "Jolie, what's the matter?"

"Matter, Miss Adams?" Jolie looked up startled and saw a quizzical expression in the beautiful eyes of the actress. "Why . . . why, nothing. Have I done something wrong?"

"No, it isn't that, but I suppose in this business one learns very quickly to read people. When you first came here you were so happy, and for the past week you've been walking around as if you've lost your best friend. Your mind's not on your work."

Jolie bit her lip in embarrassment. "I didn't mean to neglect my work, Miss Adams. I'll do better in the future."

"I didn't say that you did." Maude Adams was not only a lovely woman, but she was probably the best actress on the New York stage. She was also a very compassionate and sympathetic one. Now she said quickly, "Sometimes it helps to talk. I'd be glad to listen."

For one moment Jolie was tempted to pour her heart out, but the story was too long and complicated. "That's very kind of you, Miss Adams, but really, I'll be all right."

"I'm always available if you change your mind."

Jolie watched the actress turn and walk away to her dressing room. For one moment she felt compelled to go after her, to tell her of the problems that had come to complicate her life. Then she sighed and shook her head. "No sense telling it to Miss Adams. She couldn't help anyway."

An hour later Jolie left the theater and made her way to the boardinghouse. All she could think of was that Peter was making a fool of himself over Avis Warwick. As she walked along, the streetlights threw their reflection over the faces of those who passed by, and from time to time someone would turn to look at the young girl who had the scar on her face, but Jolie did not notice. She had not eaten all day, and now as she trudged along, oblivious to the clattering of the horses' hooves on the cobblestone and the talk of people that passed her occasionally, her mind was fluttering like a bird in a cage that could find no way out. Her lips tightened with anger, and she thought, *She's no good for him! Why can't he see that? All he has to do is open his eyes and see that she doesn't have any interest in him. She's an older woman. She's a very worldly woman, and Peter is a Christian. What's the matter with him?*

She finally reached the boardinghouse. When she entered she was startled to see Peter coming out of Easy's room with a grim face. "Peter, what's wrong?"

"It's Easy," Peter replied, shaking his head. "He had an accident."

"You mean . . . a car wreck?"

"Oh no, nothing like that!" Peter assured her. He ran his hand through his hair in obvious frustration. "Of all times for this to happen!"

"Well, what was it?"

"Oh, he was starting the car, turning the crank. It got away from him, spun around, and broke his arm. His right arm, too. He won't be working on any car now for a while."

"But he's all right, isn't he?"

"Oh yes. It just has to heal up."

"Is he in the hospital?"

"No, he's in his room. Come on in and see him, won't you? He's feeling pretty low."

Jolie nodded. "Of course." Easy was lying in his bed, his eyes half closed, but he opened them as Jolie bent over him.

"Hello, Jolie," he whispered. "What a dumb thing to do! I should have had better sense."

Putting her hand on Easy's forehead, she brushed his hair back and said, "It's not your fault. It could happen to anyone."

"As many cars as I've started, I should have remembered to stay out of the way of that crank! Look what a mess I've gotten us into. Who's going to work on the car? Who's going to ride with Peter in the race?"

"Don't worry about that. You just get some rest. Everything will be all right." She stood there the few moments it took for Easy to drop off to sleep, then left the room with Peter.

"That was pretty strong dope the doctor gave him, I guess. It just knocked him out, didn't it?"

"Poor Easy. But it could have been worse, I suppose."

Nodding, Peter said, "Yes, of course, but it puts me in a bind." He stood there silently for a minute, then said abruptly, "I'm going to let Avis ride with me in the race."

Stunned momentarily, Jolie stared at him. "Why, you can't do that!"

"I know. I've given all the arguments against it, but it'll be safe enough, and she's driving me crazy. That woman is as stubborn as can be. I'll let her ride with me this one time and she'll get enough of it."

"Peter, you mustn't do it. It's too dangerous!"

Peter shook his head and tried to summon a grin. "Someone's got to ride with me, and it'll get it out of her system."

That was not the end of the argument, but no matter what Jolie said for the next two days, Peter could not be dissuaded from letting Avis ride with him in the *Jolie Blonde*. He had already promised Avis and said he couldn't go back on his word. Jolie was furious. She wanted to say, *If anyone's going to ride with you, why not me? I've been with you from the beginning*.

Peter was oblivious to Jolie's anger. He had his mind on the race, and now that Easy was out of it, he had to do all of the mechanic work himself. He was also caught up with Avis Warwick, so he did not even notice the hurt that he had brought to Jolie Devorak.

★   ★   ★   ★

George Camrose had a pleased expression on his face when he saw Mary Ann Lanier enter the church. The small storefront room was packed, not a seat left, but he went down at once to greet her. Smiling, he said, "Mary Ann, I didn't expect to see you."

"I almost didn't come. Father's gone out of town, and I just made up my mind I had to hear Barney Winslow."

"Come on. I want you to meet him before the service. Then I'll find you a good seat right up front."

"Oh no! Everyone will see me!"

"Well then, I'll find you a seat over at the side. You're looking so pretty I'd like for everyone to see you."

Mary Ann smiled. She had dressed for this occasion in a chocolate brown skirt and jacket, and a soft white blouse with a lacy jabot hanging down from its high neck. The jacket was a favorite of hers, with large lapels, sleeves narrow at the bottom but very full at the shoulder and trimmed with four rows of dainty ribbon around each wrist.

Her face was rather pale, for it had taken considerable courage for her to leave the house, knowing she was going against her father's wishes. She had said nothing to anyone, but after George had told her of the special service with Barney Winslow, the missionary from Africa who had become more or less an idol to George Camrose, she had finally thrown caution to the winds and come directly to the church. As she walked up the aisle with George, a tall, well-built man stepped forward to meet her.

"Reverend Winslow, this is Miss Mary Ann Lanier."

"Well, I've heard a great deal about you, Miss Lanier." Something about Barney Winslow appealed to Mary Ann. His hand was large and strong, but his grasp was gentle. "You've got this young preacher quite distracted." He smiled at Camrose, saying, "I think we've discussed Miss Lanier at breakfast, lunch, and dinner. All I hear every moment of the day is how lovely Miss Lanier is." He laughed, then seeing Mary Ann's discomfort said, "Don't let me embarrass you. I'm just a rough preacher, Miss Lanier, and it's a pleasure to meet you."

"I'm pleased to meet you, too, Reverend Winslow. Phil has talked so much about you and your work in Africa, and I'm anxious to hear your sermon tonight."

Barney Winslow smiled even more broadly. "A lady told me once, 'Reverend Winslow, every sermon you preach is better than the next one.'" He laughed shortly, saying, "If you unravel that, it means 'your sermons are getting worse all the time.' But I'm glad to have you." He looked at George Camrose and said, "I'm claiming this man for God and His service. God's call is on him, and he'll be in Africa very soon." He looked at Mary Ann and said nothing, but there was a strange light in his steady gaze. He said no more but turned and went back to sit on the platform.

"Come on, Mary Ann, I'll find you a seat."

Mary Ann followed George, and he managed to move some people over so she could have a seat with a good view of the speaker. "Don't you run away after the service," he whispered. "I'm sure there'll be some people coming forward to the altar call, but I'll take you home afterward."

"All right, George."

Mary Ann sat quietly, wondering if she had done the right thing in coming. Something in her said that it was wrong to disobey her parents, and she knew how much it would displease her father. Nevertheless, she felt a certain excitement as she sat there. Something about Barney Winslow and his total commitment to God intrigued her. He was weathered by his years in Africa, but there was a kindness and a steadiness in him that she admired.

The service began when George Camrose went to stand before the pulpit. "We're going to praise God with our voices," he declared. "Some of you, like me, may not have the best voices in the world, but God wants to hear our praises anyway. Let's stand together and let God know that we love Him."

The song service was spirited, and when they sang "The Old Rugged Cross," it seemed as though the Spirit of God swept across the congregation. Mary Ann's heart was moved by the solemnity of the moment. She had always loved the song, and now as she tried to sing it, tears suddenly sprang to her eyes. In a strange way she knew that God was not only in this auditorium in the midst of this congregation, but close in a different way, too. It was rather frightening to her. Such a thing did not happen as a rule. She loved God, but this was so personal, so intense, and awe overcame her at the thought that she was standing in the very presence of God.

Finally the song service ended and Barney Winslow, after being introduced by Reverend Camrose, stood up and began to speak. He was not a thundering preacher calling down fire and brimstone upon sinners—at least not this evening. He simply related his testimony, which was indeed thrilling. He told how he had gone astray as a young man and had become a prizefighter, a *pug*, as he called it. And then he told of when he had gone to Sing Sing Penitentiary and how during his time there God had convicted him of his sins. He related how he had been released by a miracle of God and then had gone on to serve the Lord in Africa.

It was a simple testimony, but Mary Ann was so moved that her handkerchief was soaked from the tears that freely flowed. She was twisting it as Barney continued to speak.

"This is a big world, and the Scripture says, 'The grace of God that bringeth salvation hath appeared to all men.' It is our responsibility as believers to see that every person hears of the grace of God. Not everyone is called to go to Africa, or to China, or even to leave this country. Some of you are called to be the witnesses of Jesus in the neighborhood where you live, in the shop where you work. Wherever you are, your call is to declare the abundant mercy and salvation in our Lord Jesus Christ."

He went on speaking quietly about what it meant to be a witness, and finally his eyes grew bright, and he lifted his hand with a gesture of excitement. "But some God calls to leave their home. Some to cross the seas. Some to go to foreign fields. I strongly feel," he said abruptly and his eyes swept the congregation with his searching gaze, "that some of you sitting out there are being touched by God right now. Some are being invited to become part of the greatest task in all the world, to spread this glorious Gospel of the Lord Jesus Christ wherever men and women and young people are hungering to hear it. . . ."

Mary Ann Lanier suddenly could not keep her head up. Sobs rose to her throat, and she dropped her head and fought to control the turmoil stirring within her. She knew abruptly and without a doubt that she was one of those God was touching. Her first impulse was to whisper within her spirit, *Oh, God, not me!* But as Barney spoke on about proclaiming the riches of Christ, something in her, almost like a whisper, said, *Will you not bear witness for your Savior in Africa?*

Suddenly Mary Ann was aware that people around her were standing, and she heard Barney say, "If you will give your life on the foreign field, come forward and let me pray for you."

The congregation began to sing, and Mary Ann was trembling so much that she could hardly stand. She grasped the chair in front of her, her knuckles grew white, and she was shaking all over. And still the voice came again, and yet not a voice, but more of a whisper in her spirit, *Will you not bear witness for the Lord Jesus in Africa?*

Mary Ann Lanier had led a life of ease, but suddenly she knew all that was over. She knew that if she did not answer this call, somehow life would be over for her. God was inviting her to the greatest adventure of all. With a sob, she stood up and joined the small group that had gone to the front. When she got there, she could do no more than stand, and then she felt hands on her shoulders. She looked up through blurred eyes to see the face of Barney Winslow. He said nothing for a moment, but then he reached over and pulled George Camrose with his free hand. He took both of their hands, and said, "God has told me that you will serve Him together in Africa."

Mary Ann began to sob, and she felt George's body trembling. Looking up, she saw tears rolling down his cheeks, and then Barney said, "Let us all kneel. Let us kneel right here and commit your lives, George and Mary Ann, to Jesus, as He leads you in the path that He has chosen."

The three knelt, and both Mary Ann and George felt the hand of the missionary on their heads. He prayed a marvelous prayer, calling down the blessings of God upon their lives, and finally, when he lifted them up, his own cheeks were wet with tears, but his voice was triumphant. "You are committed to God's work in Africa."

Many of the congregation came to encourage those who had surrendered their lives to God's service, and George Camrose was as happy as he had ever been in his life. Something had changed, and he knew that God had moved in a powerful way during the service. His eyes met those of Mary Ann, and he saw a soft glow of assurance in them that had never been there before.

Finally the last of the worshipers left, and Barney said, "Well, George—quite a miracle, eh?"

"Yes! I know that God was here."

Barney put his hand on the minister's shoulder, his eyes filled with joy. "Let's get home. I want to write about this to my family."

"You go on, Barney, and would you please take Mary Ann home? I . . . I want to stay here and pray for a time."

"Sure. I know how it is. We can talk about it later."

Barney and Mary Ann left and George walked back and forth in front of the pulpit praising God for His mercy. He was so filled with the joy of the Lord that he was startled when a voice broke into his prayer.

"Reverend Camrose. . . ?"

Turning quickly Camrose faced the young woman who stood

before him. "Why . . . Miss Devorak! I thought everyone had left."
He stepped closer, noting at once that her face was pale and she
was twisting a button on her coat nervously. Camrose had been a
pastor long enough to recognize the symptoms of spiritual disturbance and quickly asked, "What's the trouble, Miss Devorak?"

"I . . . I can't—!" Abruptly tears sprang into her large eyes, and
she stood before him unable to speak.

Jolie was not a young woman who wept easily—indeed, she
had prided herself on being able to control her emotions under
difficult circumstances. She had come to the service out of curiosity, for Peter's remarks about Barney Winslow's interesting
background had intrigued her. She had come alone, taken a seat
in the rear of the church, expecting to be "entertained" by a good
testimony from the former boxer. However, as Winslow began
speaking, a vague discomfort began to grow within her. At first
she was merely uncomfortable without knowing why, but as the
sermon went on, a sense of misery and emptiness took the place
of that. Although the missionary spoke little of hell and the pun-
ishment of sin, a sense of guilt began to trouble her. As the speaker
continued, Jolie fell under a weight of conviction.

Memories of past misdeeds long buried seemed to float to the
surface of her thoughts—things she had long forgotten. Desper-
ately she sought to evade them, but nothing seemed to drive them
away. If the church had not been so crowded, she would have
risen and left, but so awful did the guilt in her heart swell that
she feared everyone would see the signs of her past written on
her face.

Clenching her hands until they ached, Jolie had yearned for
the service to end. She had sat through the invitation, and then
afterward as people began filing out, she wanted to leave with
them—but something had held her in her seat. Her plan had been
to wait until everyone had left before slipping out, but then the
pastor had remained, praying as he walked back and forth at the
front of the church. Finally the storm of fear and guilt that swept
though her was too great—she had to talk to someone! Rising
from her seat, her limbs trembling, she moved slowly toward the
front of the church and finally found the courage to call the pastor's name—only to find that she was helpless to say more.

"Come and sit down, Miss Devorak." Camrose took Jolie's arm
and led her to the front row of chairs. She was almost as helpless
as a puppet under his direction, and as soon as they were seated,

he asked quietly, "Have you had bad news about your family?"

"No. I . . . I have no family."

"Are you ill, then?"

Jolie turned her face toward Camrose, and her voice was barely above a whisper. "I don't think so, but I feel so . . . so awful!"

Instantly Camrose discerned that the young woman's trouble was spiritual, and he asked directly, "Are you saved, Miss Devorak?"

The question seemed to strike Jolie with a force that was almost physical. She shook her head, then spoke raggedly. "N-no. I'm not!"

"But I think God must be calling you."

"Calling me?"

"Why, yes, God does call people."

"But I haven't heard Him!"

Slowly Camrose led Jolie into the Scriptures. Pulling a small New Testament from his coat pocket, he began to read to her. She listened to the words with an avidity he had never seen, and after a time she asked, "What do I have to do be saved? Keep the Ten Commandments?"

"No man or woman has ever kept them, Miss Devorak—except the Lord Jesus Christ. The Law was given, according to the book of Romans, chapter seven, to show us what sin is. 'I had not known sin, but by the law: for I had not known lust, except the law had said, Thou shalt not covet.' Earnestly Camrose spoke and was pleased to see that the Scripture was having its way with the young woman. "You see, the Law can only tell us what we *should* do. But we can never keep the Law—none of us. In this same chapter God shows us a picture of an individual who struggled to keep the Law—and utterly failed!"

Jolie listened as Camrose read. " 'For the good that I would I do not, but the evil which I would not, that I do.' "

"Why, that's what happens to me!" she exclaimed.

"Certainly, but don't think you're different, because I think everyone of us tries to get to heaven by keeping the Law. In fact, there are multitudes who are members in good standing of churches who are lost because they are taking this false way."

"But . . . if I can't get to heaven by being good . . . what's left?"

"Jesus is left, my dear Miss Devorak!" Camrose's face glowed and his tone was exultant. "Romans chapter three gives us this glorious word—'But now the righteousness of God *without* the law is manifested, being witnessed by the law and the prophets; even the righteousness of God which is by faith of Jesus Christ unto all and upon all them that believe. . . . ' "

Jolie listened as the young pastor spoke of Jesus, Scriptures rolling from his lips, his eyes alight with love. Finally she asked, "But . . . how does it happen? I mean, what do I have to *do*?"

"In the book of Acts, the sixteenth chapter, a man asked exactly that same question: 'What must I do to be saved?' Now the apostle Paul might have told the poor fellow to keep the Law—or he might have instructed him to join the church and be baptized. But he did not! Here, I want you to read his answer to the man for yourself."

Jolie looked down at the line that Camrose indicated, then read haltingly, " 'Believe on the Lord Jesus Christ, and thou shalt be saved, and thy house.' " Fixing her gaze on the words, she read them silently. Suddenly, a peace she had never known filled her heart. Lifting her face, she whispered, "I believe in Jesus."

"Are you ready to give Him your life? To obey Him as your Lord?"

"Yes!"

"Then we will pray—and as we pray, I want you to ask Jesus to speak to you. I believe that He will—and when He does, you must do exactly what He commands—no matter what it is. Will you do that?"

Jolie didn't answer but slipped to her knees. Her shoulders were shaking and sobs came from deep within. Camrose knelt beside her and began to pray.

When Jolie left the church sometime later, she was radiant with joy. Stepping outside, she looked up at the sky and it seemed much more vibrant with color, and as a songbird poured himself out, the sounds seemed more alive than any she'd ever heard. As she moved along, she could not speak, but in her heart she was saying, "Lord, whatever you ask of me—I will do it!"

CHAPTER TWELVE

SPEED!

★ ★ ★ ★

The following Sunday, as Phil Winslow came out of the store-front church, George Camrose pulled him aside. "If you've got a little time, Phil, I'd like to talk with you."

"Why, of course, George."

"Go back to my study. I'll be there shortly."

"Right."

Waiting in the small study, Phil looked over the books that lined the walls. He had picked out a volume of sermons by Charles Haddon Spurgeon and was reading it with interest when an agitated Camrose came in. "Always liked to read Spurgeon," remarked Phil, replacing the book.

"Probably the greatest preacher of the century," George said, but his mind was not on the merits of Spurgeon. He paced the floor nervously for a moment, then turned to Phil, his face tense. "Did you hear what happened when Barney Winslow spoke at the evening service earlier this week?"

"No. I wish I could have been here. What happened?"

"When Reverend Winslow gave the invitation asking for volunteers for the mission fields, Mary Ann came forward."

Phil stared at his friend and whistled softly. Then he smiled and came over and slapped Camrose on the shoulder. "Why, that's wonderful, George. That makes things much simpler now."

"Simpler?" George Camrose stared at Winslow. "Do you know what her father will say when he hears about it?"

"I can imagine." A wry smile touched Phil's lips. He thought of the bullish force of Oliver Lanier and shook his head. "He'll probably lock her up in her room for the next ten years like he has Cara."

"I wouldn't put it past him! He's a good man, but he doesn't have the right idea about raising his children."

"You're right about that. What are you going to do, George?"

Camrose looked down at the floor as though studying the intricate pattern in the faded carpet. The silence ran on so long that Phil prompted him, "You've got to do something."

"I know it, but what?" When George looked up, anguish filled his gray eyes. He stared at Phil. "What would you do?"

"Run off with her, George."

Phil's abrupt answer startled the minister. "Why, I can't do that!"

"Why can't you do it?"

"Well, because it just won't—" Camrose broke down then and could not seem to finish his sentence. "Well, maybe you could do that, but I don't think I can."

"I don't think advice is much help in a case like this," Phil said thoughtfully. He stuck his hands in his pockets and looked up at the ceiling for a moment, then said, "You believe that God's called you to Africa, don't you?"

"Of course!"

"Do you believe that God's called Mary Ann to go to Africa? Is this call real?"

"I'm convinced that it is. You should have seen her, Phil. The glory of God was in her eyes."

"Well, it seems to me if God's called you, then God will make a way to bring about the fulfillment of that call. I don't know how right now, but I believe that if we'll pray about it, as I know you will, God will open a door."

Camrose was startled by Phil's words. "Well, it seems that you're the pastor and I'm taking your advice." He put his hand out and said, "This is very important to me."

"I know it is. It's a big step, George, and I will pray with you about it. Let's do it right now." The two men bowed their heads and committed the matter to God. When Phil's short prayer was finished, George said huskily, "Thanks, Phil. You're a help."

"Now, maybe you can pray about my problem."

Quick understanding leaped into George's eyes. "About Cara?"

Phil lifted his eyebrows and shook his head. "Is it that obvious?"

"When you speak of her there's something in your voice that gives your thoughts away. In a way," he said, "your problem is worse than mine. She's an invalid, after all."

"I'm not sure but what much of that is a state of mind. She's been told so often that she's an invalid, I think she believes it. There was a lady like that back home. Every time I'd go see her, she would open the door, and say, 'Why, Phil, what's wrong with you? You look sick.' Before I left there, I'd actually *feel* sick."

"I know. The power of suggestion, and Oliver Lanier makes some mighty strong suggestions. But we'll pray for Cara, and God can do any miracle. . . ."

★   ★   ★   ★

"I'm telling you, Peter, you'd better not let her get in that car!"

Easy Devlin waved the cast on his right arm before Peter Winslow's face. He could not work yet with the hand, but he had stayed constantly beside Peter, who had spent hours working on the *Jolie Blonde*, and during most of that time, Easy had doggedly argued against letting Avis Warwick ride in the race.

"Sing another tune, Easy," Peter said impatiently. He was wearing a pair of white coveralls stained with grease and was bending over the engine. "I'm tired of hearing about Avis and this race. She'll be all right."

"That's what you think!" Easy grinned. "You know what happened this morning?"

"I don't know. What?"

"A bird got in the room. Flew right in through my bedroom window." Easy reached down with his left hand and pulled Peter out from under the hood. He was much shorter and had to look up at Peter as he demanded, "So what do you think about that?"

Peter was exhausted and could not think clearly. He rubbed his forehead with his sleeve, looked up at the sun which was very hot, and said wearily, "So a bird got in your room! So what?"

"Of all the ignorant people I ever heard! Don't you know that's the worst luck in the world, for a bird to get in a house? Why, back when I was a kid a bird got into our house, flew right in through the front window, and two days later my oldest brother got trampled by a wild horse. Broke both of his legs. Now, you see?"

"Easy, you are the most superstitious human being I've ever met!" Peter jerked his sleeve away from Devlin's grasp and said, "Why don't you go somewhere and do something else? The car's in as good a shape as it's going to be. We'll win the race, and Avis will give up after one ride. You'll see. The new thrill will wear off, and you'll be all right soon, and it'll all be over."

Easy shook his head. "Well, I didn't intend to tell you this, but now I see I've gotta." Taking a deep breath, he whispered, "Last week I was helping Jolie clean up—and I dropped the broom. And then before I could pick it up, why that girl *stepped right over it*! Now, that tears it, don't it? Even *you* gotta know there ain't nothing to bring bad luck more than doin' a thing like that!"

Peter glared at Easy in disbelief and then shook his head. "Go away, Easy. I'll see you later."

Devlin stared as Peter turned and walked away to the house. He shouted after him, "All right, but you'll see! You'll see!"

★   ★   ★   ★

Avis met Peter as he came out of the house the next morning. She was wearing a dashing new outfit: fawn-colored jodhpurs, black boots that sleekly followed the curves of her calves, a crimson silk blouse, and a dark blue corduroy jacket.

"How do you like my racing outfit, Peter?" she asked demurely. Her eyes were shining with excitement and she turned around once like a model, then waited for his admiration.

Peter stared at her, then grinned. "Well, you'll be the best-looking woman in the race. I'll say that, Avis."

"I'm the *only* one. I guess that's kind of a left-handed compliment." Avis came forward, reached up, and threw her arms around Peter. "It's going to be great! We're going to win! I just know we are!" she whispered. She pulled his head down and kissed him. There was an abandon in her gesture, and she never seemed to care who was watching, for nothing she did ever embarrassed her.

It embarrassed Peter, however, and he pulled back, protesting, "Avis, for crying out loud! Don't be kissing me in the streets!"

"Well, let's go in the bedroom, then. Would that be better?"

Peter's face reddened. He could never tell how serious Avis Warwick was. He did know she was the most forward and free-speaking woman he had ever met. Perhaps this accounted for the fascination he felt for her. "Well, I guess that wouldn't do. Mrs. Mason is very strict about such things. And don't say we can go to your bedroom, because I won't do it."

"My Puritan," Avis smiled. She reached up and touched his cheek, then whispered, "I don't know what I see in you. I've always liked dashing men. You're nothing but a plodder, Peter Winslow."

"You're right about that, but that's what it takes to get a racing car ready."

Avis took his arm and said, "Come along. Let's go for a trial run."

"All right, but you're going to get that pretty outfit dirty."

"That's all right. I'll buy another one." Avis laughed up at him. Her eyes were sparkling, and a vivacious smile lit up her face. "It's going to be fun," she said, "and we're going to win."

Some of her excitement seemed to pass on to Peter, and he grinned. "We'd better. If we don't, I'm out of the racing business, it looks like." He put his arm around her and they walked away, speaking of the upcoming race. Looking down at her, he was thinking, *What an exciting woman she is*. But even as he thought this, he had a quick vision of Jolie's face as she had warned him not to let Avis ride. Quickly he shook off the memory, saying, "It'll just be for this one race. It'll be all right. . . ."

★　★　★　★

The air was filled with the thunder of racing engines, and Avis Warwick, goggles in place, suddenly turned to Peter and shouted, "Beat them all, Peter! Step on the gas and never let off!"

"Right!" Peter grinned back at her, then gripped the wheel, his knuckles white as he waited for the starter's gun. As always in a race, his nerves were strung tight, and now he forgot everything except the stretch of track that lay ahead of him.

He had come early, along with Easy, Jolie, and Avis, to study the competition. He and Easy knew which machines were the ones to beat, and the two had carefully planned their strategy.

Jolie was at the track, too. She had said nothing about Avis, merely, "Good luck, Peter."

"Thanks, Jolie." He reached out and took her hand. "Don't worry. The *Jolie Blonde* will be a winner. Always friends, aren't we?"

"Yes, always friends."

Now as Peter sat there, tense as a coiled spring, waiting for the gun, he saw a look in Jolie's eyes that he could not understand, but there was no time to think of that now. He felt the pressure of Avis's shoulder against him, and then the crack of the starter's pistol sounded out over the engines' roar. He floored the accelerator and felt the *Jolie Blonde* lunge forward with a surge of power. The air was filled with screaming engines and tires keening against the track, and then all was speed and blur and motion!

Peter never could remember very clearly the first three laps of the race. He remembered only that the Dusenburg kept crowding him against the rail. The driver, a big German with a heavy mustache, was laughing, and Peter knew it was because he had a woman riding in his car. There had been much attention paid to Avis before the race, as all the photographers had crowded around the *Jolie Blonde* snapping pictures. Now Peter tried to maneuver ahead of the Dusenburg but had trouble getting by. The driver, Max Mueller, grinned in delight as he continued pushing Peter over to the rail.

Anger surged through Peter, and Avis screamed, "Don't let him get by with that, Peter! Knock him over!"

Peter waited until there was a clear space, then he swung the *Jolie Blonde* to the right. The front of his car caught the back of Mueller's Dusenburg and knocked him almost into a spin.

"That's the way! Give it to him!" Avis screamed. She had pulled her helmet off, and her hair was flying in the wind. Her face was shining with excitement, and Peter knew she did not realize the danger in what they were doing.

Three times they circled the track, and on the next lap, Mueller came up beside them again. His face was scowling now, and suddenly Peter grew wary. He slammed on the brakes to let Mueller pass, but Mueller suddenly swung over and the back of his car snagged the front of the *Jolie Blonde*.

The wheel was wrenched from Peter's hands, and although he grabbed for it wildly, the car fishtailed and went out of control.

As the *Jolie Blonde* went careening down the track, changing and swapping ends, Peter could see nothing as he tried to fight the spin. Then he felt the rear of the car rise up and his heart leaped, for he knew they were going over.

"Avis—" He yelled and reached over to put his arms around her, but even as he did, the car flew up, then came down on its side with a thunderous crash. Peter's grip was torn loose from Avis, and he felt himself spinning and rolling in the dirt. He heard the crash as the *Jolie Blonde* smashed into the railing, but he could not see.

When he finally stopped rolling, he felt blood inside of his mouth. The roaring of the cars sounded like thunder, and he staggered to his feet. One car was weaving madly to avoid him and passed by so close he thought he felt it touch his leg. He did not stop though, for his eyes were riveted on Avis Warwick, whose body lay crumpled against the barricade. Staggering forward, he reached her and fell down beside her. He rolled her over and saw that her eyes were closed and she was limp.

"Avis," he shouted, "are you all right? Can you hear me?" But no answer came. He picked her up and turned, carrying her down the track to where an ambulance he had never thought he would need was waiting.

★　★　★　★

Peter, Easy, and Jolie sat together in the hospital waiting room. A large clock on the wall ticked off the seconds, and for a long time no one said anything. They had been there now for over an hour, and finally Easy jumped up and growled, "Why don't they tell us *something!*"

"Sit down, Easy. They'll let us know as soon as they can." Jolie reached up and pulled Easy down. Her own face was pale, and she turned to study Peter, who had not said a word since they had followed the ambulance in. Peter had ridden with Avis in the ambulance, and now his face was pale as wallpaper paste. His lips were drawn so tightly together they seemed bloodless, and his eyes were in a trancelike stare.

Jolie reached over and took his hand. It was limp and he seemed unaware of her touch. He stared down at the floor, his body stiff and unyielding.

Finally a door opened at the end of the hall, and a doctor wearing a white jacket and a stethoscope came out. All three rose as he approached and introduced himself. "I'm Dr. Wardlow. Are you Mrs. Warwick's family?"

"We're her friends," Peter said hoarsely. "How is she, Doctor?"

"What about her family?"

"I don't . . . think she has any. Not close anyway," Peter said. He was studying the doctor's face, trying to find something hopeful, but he saw nothing. The doctor was a short, muscular man with black hair and equally black eyes. Now he looked Peter over, as though to read his thoughts, and said quietly, "It's not good news."

"Is she alive?" Jolie whispered.

"Yes, but she's very badly injured. I've been waiting until she woke up. She has a serious concussion, as well as being pretty scratched up and bruised." He paused, then added, "She also has some kind of injury to her lower body." He hesitated again, seeming to have difficulty in finding the words. Finally he shrugged and continued. "I'm sorry to tell you, but Mrs. Warwick woke up ten minutes ago, and the truth is, she has no feeling in her lower limbs. She's paralyzed from the waist down."

Peter Winslow reared backward and shut his eyes. He said nothing, and Jolie reached out and took his arm to steady him.

"She'll be all right, though, won't she, Doctor?" Jolie asked.

Dr. Wardlow shook his head. "I'd like to be more positive, but the truth is, we just don't know at this point. She may be all right tomorrow. We're pretty sure her spine's not broken, so that means it's nerve damage, and it's hard to predict just what the end result will be. Whatever the case, she's very upset. I've given her something to quiet her, so she's gone back to sleep. When she wakes up, though, she'll be frightened and need someone beside her."

"I'll be there," Peter Winslow said.

Jolie looked up quickly at his face and thought, *He feels responsible. He feels guilty about what happened.* What this meant she did not know, but she watched as Peter pulled himself from her grasp and walked across the room, following Dr. Wardlow. She knew somehow that life had changed and that Peter Winslow would not be able to shake this thing off. As the door closed, she thought, *He'll never leave her now.* Then she turned and walked slowly out of the hospital. Easy followed her, saying nothing, as they stepped out into the night.

PART THREE

CROSSROADS

★ ★ ★ ★

CHAPTER THIRTEEN

A DARK TUNNEL

★　★　★　★

A heavy silence hung over the waiting room, thick and oppressive as the fog that sometimes invades the seashore, blanketing everything in a deathly stillness. The waiting room itself was as stark and unadorned as an unimaginative architect could make it. The furniture consisted of worn chairs in a kind of leprous puce color. Their corduroy upholstery had been worn smooth, and from several of the cushions, tufts of cotton peeped out of the various tears and split seams. On the wall hung a large painting of sleek, shining thoroughbreds leaping fences with an exuberance that contrasted bizarrely with the dingy gray paint that peeled off in one corner by the single window. The window was open, and the feeble light of a gibbous moon filtered through it, supplemented only by a single lamp perched precariously on an end table. The coffee table was off balance and rickety, and the magazines were six months old or older. All of this produced a somber and gloomy atmosphere capable of depressing anyone forced to sit there.

Earlier in the day the room had been crowded with people jockeying for seats, some men smoking incessantly and filling the air with blue, acrid smoke. Now, however, it had only three occupants. Peter Winslow slumped in one of the worn chairs, staring at the painting of horses sailing over fences, but not really seeing it. His auburn hair was mussed from the countless times he had run his hands through it, and his eyes were red-rimmed from lack of sleep. He seemed almost asleep, for his eyes were half closed, almost concealing them. His lips were drawn together into a straight line, then turned down at the edges, and there was a life-lessness about him that was completely out of keeping with his usual cheerfulness.

Easy Devlin sat beside Jolie Devorak at the end of the line of chairs. He was holding a chipped blue coffee mug, which he now lifted to his lips. Sipping its contents, he frowned, then stared into the cup. "If that's coffee, I wish it was tea—and if it's tea, I wish it was coffee." He stuck his finger into the murky liquid, stirred, then examined his fingernail. "It's a pure wonder it didn't eat it off. The coffee in Sing Sing was better!" He looked down the row at Peter. "You reckon he's ever going to say anything, Jolie?"

With a sigh, Jolie shook her head. Fatigue edged her features, and weariness from waiting for hours had brought a slump to her rather square but rounded shoulders. The scar on her left cheek seemed to stand out, for her face was pale. Unthinkingly she shook her head so that her black hair fell forward to cover it. It was a habitual motion, held over from childhood. She spoke softly, her voice barely rising above a whisper. "I don't know, Easy. It would be better if he would talk, but all he does is sit there and stare at that dumb painting."

Easy looked over at the painting and shook his head. "That fellow sure don't know much about horses. Look at the fetlock. It ain't nothin' like a real fetlock. If a fella's goin' to paint horses, he could paint a fetlock right, don't ya think?"

Jolie did not even answer. She let the silence fall over the room again, broken only by Easy as he sipped noisily at his cup of cof-fee. They had all been at the hospital off and on for twenty-four hours without sleep, and now she turned to say, "Easy, why don't you go home? You can't do any good here."

"Neither can you."

"Well, not for Avis anyway." Her eyes went back to Peter, and she added, "I'm going to see if I can get him to go home and try to get some rest."

"Won't do no good. That feller's stubborn as a blue-nosed mule, Jolie. You know that."

Ignoring Easy, Jolie rose and walked toward Peter, her heels making a rhythmic clicking noise on the worn pale gray tiles. She sat down beside Peter, put her hand on his, and said quietly,

"Peter, you need to go home and get some sleep. If there's any change, I'll come and get you."

At the sound of her voice, Peter jerked and his eyes flew wide open. The distant look in his eyes revealed to Jolie that his thoughts had been far away, and there was a certain wildness in his expression for a slight moment. Then he shut his eyes, took a deep breath, and released it in a shuddering sigh. "No," he murmured, "I'll stay here—but you go on, Jolie. No sense you and Easy losing sleep."

Without replying to this remark, Jolie sat there, her hand on his. He had, as she had often thought, the hands of an aristocrat, with long, tapering fingers, strong but flexible. She had often thought he might have been a great musician, a pianist perhaps, but now there was a slight tremble in his hands, something she had never seen before.

"She'll be all right. We can't give up hope," Jolie said.

Peter did not answer. He pulled his hand back and ran it through his hair again, ruffling it, and then suddenly rose and walked over to the single window without speaking. He stared out, and finally Jolie went back to her previous seat and said firmly, "Easy, you go on home."

"What about you?"

"I'll come along pretty soon."

"All right. Maybe I can take the day shift." Easy rose, stretched his back painfully, then tapped the cast on his arm. "If I hadn't broken this wing, this never would have happened."

"It might have. You might have been hurt in the accident. Nobody knows about things like that."

"No, it was just bad luck. I told you, didn't I, about how a bird got into my room a few days ago?"

"Yes, you told me, Easy. Now go on home."

"If that bird hadn't got in, none of this would have happened." He reached down, pulled his cap over his sandy hair, and left without another word.

Turning, Jolie kept her eyes on Peter, who stood immobile at the window, staring down. She was tired of sitting and rose, arched her back and then walked slowly back and forth to get the blood flowing again. The sound of her heels on the tile marked off the passage of time that seemed to creep rather than flow. Finally she went over to stand beside Peter. *If I could just think of something to say to him—something that would help him snap out of it.*

I've never seen him like this. She could not, however, think of anything to say and was startled when Peter turned to her with anguish distorting his expression. His lips were pulled tightly together in a grimace and two lines between his eyebrows were deep furrows of grief. He looked at her, seeming not to recognize her, and once again she knew that his thoughts were in the room with Avis. She reached up and put her hand lightly on his chest and felt the beating of his heart but said nothing.

Looking down at Jolie's hand, Peter leaned over suddenly and grabbed her shoulders. His grip was so strong that it hurt, but Jolie did not let it show in her face. "It was my fault—all my fault, Jolie!"

"Don't say that, Peter. She chose to go of her own free will."

"I . . . I should have stopped her."

Knowing that it would make no difference whatsoever, Jolie said, "It wasn't your fault. These things happen. Everyone who gets in a car and races knows something like this may happen. It could have been you, Peter."

Suddenly Peter's eyes closed and his cheek began to quiver. Jolie saw with astonishment that he was breaking down. Peter was one of the strongest men she knew, but this tragic accident was too much for him. She reached up, pulled his head down, and put her arms around his neck. She felt his whole body trembling, and his cheek on hers was wet with tears. Her lips broadened in a maternal fashion, and she held him as his body shook and he struggled to hold the tears back and to control the sobbing. She murmured inaudible and meaningless phrases, stroking his back, as she might have comforted a small boy who had fallen and hurt himself.

"That's all right, Peter," she whispered. "It's all right to cry. I do it myself sometimes."

The paroxysms that shook Peter Winslow went on for some time, and then finally began to mitigate. He cleared his throat, pulled himself away, and turned to stare out the window. He pulled a handkerchief from his back pocket, wiped his eyes, and blew his nose. Clearing his throat, he said hoarsely, "I . . . I haven't done that in a long time."

"Anyone can do that at times like this."

"Not me. I've never had to go through anything like this," Peter said and shook his head almost violently. "What if she dies, Jolie?"

"She's not going to die. The doctor said she wouldn't."

"What if she's paralyzed and can't walk again? Do you know what that would mean to her?"

"It would be terrible, but we mustn't think of it. We must pray that God will do a healing work."

"She doesn't believe in God."

"But we do. You and I can pray."

Peter did not move. He stood there stiffly, his hands clenched in front of him, and he did not answer. Jolie waited for him to respond, and finally he muttered almost inaudibly, "She's got to walk. I don't know what I'd do if I had to live the rest of my life knowing she was a cripple because of me."

Jolie felt a sudden mixture of anguish, grief—and jealousy. She knew now that she had been jealous of Avis Warwick for a long time. The woman had wealth and had captivated Peter Winslow with her wiles, as she had many men in the past. Jolie had always been possessive of Peter; now she recognized that her feelings for him were not simply those of a young girl with a crush on an older man. They had grown much deeper than that.

Now an anger arose in Jolie over Avis's foolishness in putting herself into such a dangerous situation. She was headstrong and accustomed to having her own way, and it had finally brought her to this place, with a dark shadow hanging over her. Still, Jolie could not speak about any of this to Peter. She laid her hand on his arm, bowed her head, and began to pray silently. It was a difficult prayer for her. She had to force herself to say the words without the emotion that should accompany it. If it had been Easy or Peter or Clinton, or any of her other friends, it would have been simple, but now to pray for this woman who had come like a thief in the night to steal the man she loved required a force of will such as she had never had to exercise before.

And then something came to Jolie—a thought that forced itself into her mind so powerfully she knew it did not rise from her own heart. She heard no voice, yet so vivid was the thought that came to her, it was almost as if it were spoken aloud.

For a few moments Jolie struggled with the impulse, telling herself that it was just a stray thought, but it grew stronger. She remembered one of the things George Camrose had told her was that Jesus spoke to His sheep. Finally she gave up the battle and said, "Peter, I think God wants me to pray for you."

"Why . . . I guess I need all the prayer I can get."

"No, it's more than just that," Jolie said quietly.

She turned her gaze on him and there was a strength in her voice and an assurance in her eyes that he had never seen. Determination was written in the tight line of her lips and in the set of her jaw.

"I think you need more of God in your life."

Peter was startled and his speech was uncertain as he finally nodded. "I think that's right, Jolie. I never told you how I got saved, did I?"

"No, you never did."

"Well, it's not an exciting story. I've always sort of envied those people who have dramatic testimonies—you may have heard some of them."

"You mean seventeen car wrecks and an invitation?"

Peter smiled despite his agitation. "Something like that, I guess. I was only twelve years old and hadn't really been a bad kid. An evangelist came to our church to hold a revival. I was there on the last night of the meeting, but I wasn't paying much attention to the sermon. Can't even remember what it was about. I was thinking about going fishing the next day with my dad. All of a sudden I heard the preacher say, " 'Except ye repent, ye shall all likewise perish.' " Peter looked directly at Jolie, strain on his face. "I was only twelve, but I knew about hell and about being saved. I'd heard it every Sunday of my life!"

Jolie waited for Peter to continue, but he dropped his head and said nothing. Finally she asked, "What happened then, Peter?" Lifting his eyes, Jolie saw that he was weeping again.

"I got saved, Jolie. When the invitation came, I almost ran down the aisle. The pastor met me and sat me down. Then my father came. They were so gentle! They prayed for me and I asked Jesus into my life—and He came!"

"I think that's a marvelous testimony, Peter!"

"Not very dramatic."

"I guess it would have been more dramatic if you'd grown up lost and chased women and become a drunk—and gotten saved when you were sixty and your life was gone!" Jolie's words were stern, but her lips were as soft as the look of understanding in her eyes. "But you didn't have to go through all that. I wish I'd been saved when I was twelve years old."

Peter stared at the young woman, then shook his head. "You're right, Jolie, but I haven't followed the ways of God—not really.

I've been so caught up with cars that I haven't given myself to God as I did back when I was a boy."

"Then it's time for you to begin again," Jolie said firmly. She took his hand and bowed her head, then began to pray, "Lord, I ask you to help Peter be the man that you want him to be. Take him back to the time when he first was saved—and let him begin all over...."

As Jolie prayed, Peter felt very strange. He was miserable about Avis, but even more than that, the conversation had taken him back to the first days of his Christian life, and he realized that he'd lost something along the way. He began to pray silently, then spoke aloud, "Oh, Lord, forgive my wandering! I've lost the love I had for you—but I want to find it again...!"

Neither of them ever knew how long they prayed together, but finally Peter lifted his head, and Jolie saw something in his expression that had not been there earlier. His eyes widened and he grasped her hands firmly.

"Jolie, I . . . don't know what's happened, but I feel like I did that night when I got saved!"

"Oh, Peter! I'm so glad!"

Tears of joy filled Jolie's eyes. And as she stood there, she prayed for herself, *Lord, I know he doesn't love me, but I love him!* Aloud she said, "Now we'll just have to wait and see what God is going to do, won't we, Peter?"

★ ★ ★ ★

Jolie had finally gone home at Peter's insistence. Now as dawn broke, Peter still stood staring out the window. The street outside was beginning to be more visible in the lightening gray of the morning. A single tree, no more than seven or eight feet tall, spread its spindly arms with a few undernourished leaves. No one apparently thought to water it or care for it, and now it seemed almost as though it were praying as it lifted its shriveled leaves high toward the heavens.

"Mr. Winslow—?"

At the sound of his name, Peter wheeled instantly, his senses becoming alert. He saw a doctor standing there, a new one he had not seen before. "Yes, Doctor. How is she?"

"I'm Doctor Smith. I've just been examining Mrs. Warwick."

"Well, how is she?"

"About the same, I think." Smith was a gangling man with traces of Boston in his speech. He had pale blond hair and hazel eyes, wide-set and bulging. His lips were pursed, small and drawn up into a bow, and there was a carefulness in his expression that disturbed Peter.

"She is going to walk again, isn't she? She's not going to be paralyzed?"

"It's too soon to say. It would be good if you could get her family here. Does she have any in the area?"

"I don't think so. Her parents are dead. She has one sister out on the West Coast, somewhere in Oregon, I think. They're not very close."

Dr. Smith teetered back and forth on his toes and weariness drew fine lines in his face. "I'm not happy with her condition. She seems to have absolutely no feeling whatsoever in her lower extremities."

"Well, what kind of treatment is there?"

Dr. Smith seemed angered by the question but only said in his terse manner, "Right now, to be frank, there is no treatment. We'll continue to try to find out what caused the damage—where it lies. Then, perhaps, we can do something. Until then we can only wait . . . and pray," he added almost lamely.

Peter stared at the physician, an angry reply almost leaping to his lips. Somehow, however, he understood that the doctor could do nothing at this time, and he swallowed hard. "Thank you, Doctor. Can I go in and see her?"

"Yes. You may stay as long as you like."

"What if she asks me what you said? Have you told her she won't walk?"

"No. I've just said we're going to do more tests, and I think that's what you should tell her. Be as optimistic as you can." Smith suddenly raised his pale eyebrows. "Are you a praying man, Mr. Winslow?"

"Not as much as I should be, I guess. Why?"

"I think it might be a good time if you are a praying man to exercise that particular virtue." Dr. Smith turned without a word and walked away, and Peter followed him down the hall, through the door and down a long corridor. They made several turns and finally the doctor paused before the door, and said, "Go on in. She's awake."

"Thank you, Doctor."

Peter walked inside and saw Avis lying on a tall hospital bed, propped up by several pillows. She was wearing a white hospital gown. As he walked up to the bed, her green eyes fastened on him instantly.

"Well, I suppose you've come to view the corpse."

"Avis, don't talk like that!" Peter protested. He went over at once but did not know what to do. Awkwardly he pulled up a chair, then reached out to touch her shoulder, but she shrugged it away with an angry gesture.

"Don't touch me! I always hated it!" she said coldly. She normally had a pale complexion, but now the pallor of her skin seemed more pronounced. Dark shadows under her eyes and lines at the corner of her lips made her appear much older. She looked terrible and knew it. "My hair's a mess!" she said. "And look at this gown! How do they expect you to do anything wearing a thing like this? Look, it doesn't have any back in it." Leaning forward slightly, she plucked it with her hand, revealing the ivory contours of her back.

Peter wanted to say something encouraging, but Dr. Smith's words were ringing in his mind, and he could not think of anything to say. He felt helpless at his inability to say or do anything that could lift her from her sullen mood. Finally he said, "How do you feel? Are you in pain?"

"I wish I were." Avis bit off the words and turned to stare at him. Reaching out, she struck her upper thigh and said, "I'd give anything if I could feel pain when I do that, but I don't. Not a thing!"

"You don't feel anything at all?"

"It's like hitting a block of wood."

"It'll be all right, Avis," Peter said with more confidence than he felt. He tried to assume an encouraging look and smiled, knowing it was one of the most artificial expressions that could have come to him. "These things happen. It's some kind of nerve damage. It takes time to heal up, but you'll be all right. You'll see."

"Don't be a fool, Peter! How do you know I'll be all right? The doctors don't even know for sure. I can see it in their eyes—all of them." Avis's voice rose and there was a trace of hysteria in it. Then suddenly her hands began to tremble. She knew that Peter had seen them, and she cried, "Look at that! I'm shaking like a leaf and, Peter—I'm scared!"

Peter rose and leaned over the bed. He put his arm around her and she reached up and grabbed at him convulsively. "I'm scared, Peter! What if I never walk again? I'd rather be dead!"

"It won't be that way, Avis." Peter held her tightly and smoothed her hair with his right hand. She held to him as if she were a child, and he wished she would cry. Perhaps that would help, but she did not. Finally she pushed him away and took several deep breaths. She seemed to gain control of herself as she looked at him.

"It's like looking down a dark tunnel with no light at the end of it. I wish I had died in that wreck!"

"Don't say that!" Peter cried. "Don't ever say that!"

"Why not? It's true!" And then she uncontrollably struck out at him. "Why did you let me get in that car? Why didn't you stop me, Peter?"

Struck by the injustice of it, Peter could say nothing. He knew she was not herself and thought, *I'd probably be saying worse if I were in her condition.* She began to beat at him with her hands, and he pinioned them, saying as quietly as he could, "There, Avis, don't fight."

Slowly she stopped struggling and lowered her head, staring bitterly at her legs. "I wish I were dead, and I will be if I can never walk again," she said barely above a whisper.

Peter was frightened as he caught the implication of what Avis had just said. He did not know how to answer her, and he simply stood there for a time. Then he sat down and began to speak as encouragingly as he could. He knew what he said must have seemed foolish and inane to Avis, but at least she sat quietly, even though she was not looking at him. Finally after a time he stopped speaking, and the two simply sat there in silence.

★　★　★　★

"How is she, Peter?"

Peter was standing in the waiting room and turned to see Phil and George Camrose coming toward him, concern etching their features.

"She's paralyzed from the waist down," he said bluntly and his words hit them with a force.

"What are they doing for her?" Camrose asked.

"Nothing."

"Nothing!" Phil exclaimed. "What do you mean *nothing*?"

"I mean—nothing! The doctors say there's some kind of nerve damage, but they haven't found it yet. Until they do there's nothing to do but wait."

"How's she taking it, Peter?" Camrose asked, his eyes alert. "I mean emotionally and spiritually?"

"Not good. She's given up and doesn't have any hope of recovery left." Peter shook his head. "She's not a godly woman, Reverend Camrose." He hesitated, then looked at his two friends. "When I was with her a while ago she said that if she stayed paralyzed she would—"

When Peter broke off his words, both men instantly understood what Avis Warwick had said. "Let me go talk to her," Camrose said gently.

"You can try, but you might get insulted. She only got angry when I tried to encourage her."

"One of the first prerequisites of a preacher is to have a hide like a rhinoceros." Camrose grinned faintly, then turned and left the room. He moved down the hall and asked a nurse where Avis Warwick was and knocked on the door. When he heard a voice bidding him to come in he stepped inside and stopped. "Mrs. Warwick?"

"Yes. Who are you?"

"George Camrose. I'm pastor of the Calvary Baptist Church down on the Lower East Side."

"Didn't take you long to get here. Are you like a lawyer who chases ambulances?"

"Not exactly." Camrose sensed the hardness in Avis's tone and let nothing show in his face. "I'm a friend of Peter Winslow's."

Avis did not answer. She stared at him with a hard look in her eyes. As though something were rising in her memory, she said evenly, "I don't need any sermons."

"I didn't come to give you any," Camrose said easily. He moved over to the bed and asked, "May I sit down?"

"No. I don't remember sending for any preachers."

"I don't always wait to be sent for, although it's better that way. I won't stay, Mrs. Warwick. I just wonder if I might say a prayer for you before I go."

"Say all you want on your way out!"

"Very well," Camrose said, seeing the obvious displeasure in Avis Warwick's eyes. "But I will be praying for you."

"Lots of luck!"

Camrose left the room and turned down the hall. When he reached the waiting room, he shook his head, saying, "You were right. She doesn't want to talk to any preachers."

"She's a pretty hard woman," Peter said. "I didn't know how hard until this happened." He passed a trembling hand across his face. "It was all my fault. I never should have let her ride with me in that car!"

"Always easy to think of the right thing to do after the event," Phil Winslow said.

"Yes, it is," Camrose nodded. "The thing to do now is to be all the help we can to Mrs. Warwick, which seems to be to pray. What about her family?"

"Doesn't have any," Peter said.

"None at all?" Phil asked with surprise. "Parents not living?"

"No. She's a widow, you know. She has one sister somewhere out west, but they're not close. I asked her if she wanted me to contact her, and she said no, that she wouldn't come. Pretty sad to be that alone in the world."

The three men stood there speaking for a time, and finally Phil said, "Come on, Peter, you're falling apart. I'm taking you home." He ignored Peter's protests, and the two men walked Peter Winslow out of the hospital. "You can come back tomorrow after you've rested up. It's going to be a long pull, it looks like," Phil said. "We'll be all the help we can. Not much we can do except pray, but we'll be doing that."

Peter looked at his relative and a sense of gratitude welled up in him. "Good of you to come, both of you."

"Why, you think we'd let the devil jump on one of our own?" Phil grinned. "Come on now. Nothing's too difficult for God. You get some sleep. Tomorrow we'll talk more."

★   ★   ★   ★

As the door opened, Cara Lanier looked up quickly. When she saw Clinton enter she rose, putting down the embroidery piece she had been working on. At the sight of her brother's face, she demanded, "What's wrong, Clinton?"

"It's not good news. Avis Warwick is in pretty bad shape." Clinton shook his head, and a nervousness caused a slight tic at the corner of his lips. Cara knew him well, and she knew that tic appeared only when he was under tremendous pressure.

"How is she?" She had heard of the accident and her heart had gone out to the woman.

"Pretty bad," Clinton repeated. "She's paralyzed from the waist down, and according to what Phil says, they don't know whether she'll ever recover fully."

"You talked to Phil?"

"Yes, I did. He's been at the hospital quite a bit. He and Brother Camrose were there."

"Yes. They're very good friends. What did Phil say? Anything else?"

"He said Peter's going to pieces. Blames himself for the accident."

"That's foolishness!"

"No, it's not really," Clinton shrugged. "He never should have let her get in that car. He knows that now, but it's too late." He sat down abruptly on a Morris chair and gripped his hands tightly together. "I don't know what possessed him to do such a thing."

"Well, if what Phil's told me about Avis Warwick is true, she can be pretty persuasive."

"That's true enough. Still, a woman doesn't have any place in a race car."

Cara went over and stood beside her brother. The two were very close, and she saw that something was troubling him. "What's wrong, Clinton?"

"I ought to go try to help. I'd like to be of some encouragement to Peter."

"Why don't you go?" Cara said. "I wish you would, then come back and tell me how he is—and how Mrs. Warwick is."

Clinton had needed her words of encouragement. He rose at once and put his hands out and smiled as she came to him and took them. "You're good for me, Cara. I need a spur sometimes."

Cara reached up, pulled his head down, and kissed him on the cheek. "Yes, you do, and I'll be glad to provide it. Now go quickly, and come back and give me a report as soon as you can."

"All right. I will."

Leaving the house, Clinton went at once to the boardinghouse. When he asked the landlady for Peter, she replied, "Why, he's not here. I think he's at the hospital."

For a moment Clinton hesitated. "Is Miss Devorak here?"

"I believe she is. I'll go see, if you care to wait."

"Yes. Thank you, Mrs. Mason."

A few moments later Jolie appeared. She smiled when she saw Clinton. "You just missed Peter. He went to the hospital about thirty minutes ago."

"I guess I'll go by there—not that I can do anything, of course."

Jolie had learned to like Clinton. She knew he was unhappy, and yet powerless to break free of the bondage that his father put him under. Never having had a father to care for her, she had thought, *I'd rather have none than the one he's got.* She did not voice this, however, but said, "Let me get my coat. I'll go down with you."

"That would be great."

The two left the house, and as they walked toward the hospital, Clinton found himself enjoying Jolie's company. He thought she was an amazingly pretty girl, and now he asked, "How did you happen to meet Peter?"

"We were in a boxcar riding the rails. We were both bos."

"Bos? What's bos?"

"We were hobos!" Jolie turned and laughed up at him. "You didn't know that?"

"No, and I can't believe it."

"You'll have to, because it's true. He and Easy got on the boxcar, and I was hiding in the other end. They were nice enough to me, but I was suspicious of men. I'd had a bad experience."

Clinton turned to look at her and started to ask, but something about the look on her face stopped him. "Sorry for that," he said.

"It's all over now, but that night three rough ones got on. They started to . . . to bother me. Peter and Easy tried to stop them, and it turned out to be an awful fight. One of them had a gun and it fell." She shook her head and said quietly, "I picked it up and told them to stop. They were about to throw Peter off the train. They didn't think I'd shoot and started to push him off—so I shot one."

All this was beyond Clinton Lanier's experience. "You shot him?" he asked in shock. "Did you kill him?"

"Peter says not. He fell out the door, and Peter and Easy threw the other two out. Peter says he saw the one I shot get up, holding his shoulder. I've never been sure whether he told me that to make me feel better or not. I could have killed him."

They were walking along at a slow pace, and Clinton shook his head. "Nothing like that has ever happened to me."

"Be thankful for it."

Her terse words caught at Clinton, and he nodded. "I've had

it easy, and every wise man I've ever known said that men are made by hard things, not easy things. I guess that's why I'm not the man I ought to be."

Surprised at Clinton's words, Jolie turned. "Why, Clinton," she said, "don't say that!"

"It's true enough," he said bitterly. "My father runs every part of my life!"

"I'm sure he cares for you and wants you to do well."

"I suppose that's true. He had a hard time as a boy and a young man himself. I really think he's so afraid of poverty and hard times that he overreacts."

The two walked on talking, Clinton telling Jolie about how he had never been able to free himself from his father's domination. When they got to the hospital, Clinton suddenly stopped and said with shock, "I've never told anyone these things! I didn't mean to drop all this on you, Jolie."

"It's all right, Clinton." Jolie reached out and touched his arm, then smiled. "You've got to have faith in God."

"I think it would take God to make a better man out of me."

"That's right. It always takes God to make us better." Jolie took his arm confidently and said, "Come on. We'll talk about this later. Let's see how Peter's doing."

CHAPTER FOURTEEN

"YOU'D STRANGLE ME IN A WEEK!"

★ ★ ★ ★

Dr. Owen Smith sat behind his desk staring at the young man across from him. He was unhappy with his own performance in the case of Avis Warwick and knew that it was irrational to let his temper escape. It was also useless to blame Peter Winslow, for Smith had become well aware that young Winslow blamed himself far more than anyone else could. Smith had not been particularly interested in the racing of automobiles, which he considered a stupid risk and a senseless waste of time, but he was interested in people. Now he was concerned not only for Avis Warwick's condition, but also for young Winslow. He knew he needed to be blunt with him, but he wasn't sure how to begin.

"I can't offer you very much hope, Mr. Winslow," Smith finally said. He noticed his own nervous action in drumming the table and with some irritation pulled his hand back and interlaced his fingers. He eyed the tall young man across from him, then said abruptly, "You're not going to do yourself any good carrying on as you have been."

Peter was surprised. "What do you mean by that, Dr. Smith?"

"I mean I deal in broken bodies, but there are those doctors who deal with mental problems—and you're headed for a bad one if you don't stop blaming yourself for the accident."

"Who do you want me to blame? It *was* my fault."

"The way I understand it from Mr. Lanier and from your relative, Mr. Phil Winslow, it was the fault of that German who drove his car into yours."

"I should have avoided him."

"That's nice to believe," Smith shrugged, "but if you were thinking clearly, you would understand that you can't avoid things like this sometimes."

Peter remained silent, trying to grasp what the doctor was telling him.

"You need to pull yourself together and expend your energies now on helping your friend," Dr. Smith went on, shaking his head. "I'm very worried about Mrs. Warwick."

"She's not getting any better, is she, Doctor?"

"No, and we can't find the problem."

"Why don't you operate?"

With disgust Dr. Smith stared at him and shook his head angrily. "You mean just start cutting away, hoping to find something? That would be pretty stupid, wouldn't it?" Then he added quickly, "I'm sorry. I didn't mean to snap at you. It's just that—well, I don't like to lose, and I haven't won this case. But it's not over yet," he added.

Instantly Peter's eyes narrowed. "You think there's a chance she'll get better?"

"There's always a chance. No telling about these things. We doctors never really heal anybody. The body heals itself. Sometimes we can take a few stitches or pull something out that doesn't need to be there, but basically, when something's wrong, if it gets fixed at all it's because the body does the healing." He looked up at Peter, a curious expression in his eyes. "Or perhaps God does the healing . . . but I wouldn't know about that." He rose abruptly. "She'll be going home today. Will you take her?"

"Yes. I've already talked to her about it."

"Be as positive as you can. At this stage of the game, it's important that she doesn't get depressed."

"She's already depressed, Doctor, and you know it. And I don't blame her."

"I suppose that's so. I don't have any more answers," Smith shrugged. "I wish I did." He suddenly put his hand out and took Peter's with a surprisingly strong grip. "Try not to blame yourself,

Mr. Winslow. I'll do whatever I can to help. Come and see me from time to time."

"Thank you, Doctor."

Peter left Smith's office and went down to the room where the nurse was preparing Avis for her departure. A wheelchair stood ready, and a male orderly waited nearby to help. "I can handle this," Peter said.

The orderly lifted his eyebrows with a questioning arch. "Are you sure?"

"Yes. It'll be all right." He turned to Avis, who was sitting in the bed, her legs stretched out in front of her. She was dressed in a nightgown with a blue robe over it. "Ready to go home?" he asked as cheerfully as he could.

"I suppose so." Avis gave him an odd look, but he ignored it and moved over and picked her up easily. She automatically put her arm around his neck to steady herself, and when he put her in the wheelchair, her legs fell off to one side. He glanced at her and saw the bitterness in her lips but without comment moved her legs back onto the footrest. The nurse came forward and put a blanket over her.

"Now then. You're all ready to go. I hope you have a speedy recovery, Mrs. Warwick," she said cheerfully.

Avis looked at the nurse, her expression blank. "Thank you. I'm just sure I will." There was such bitterness in her tone that Peter flinched, and he said hurriedly, "Thank you, nurse. We appreciate all you've done." Then he pushed the wheelchair out of the room as the nurse moved ahead to open doors. "I've got a car outside."

Peter waited for her to reply, but she said nothing. He pushed the chair to the front door, and as they left the building, the bright sunlight struck Avis's face. She blinked and raised her hand quickly to shade her eyes. Peter shifted the wheelchair to a more favorable position and opened the front door. "You can sit up in the front with me." He reached down and lifted her into the car, then arranged the robe around her legs. Shutting the door, he said, "I'll go back and get the rest of your things."

"I don't have any things. Let's go," she replied briefly.

"All right then." He took the wheelchair and lifted it up with a grunt to a rack on top of the car, lashing it down with some cord he had brought. He quickly moved to the front of the car, cranked the starter, and when the engine caught, leaped in and stepped on the gas. The large car moved jerkily out into the middle of the street.

"I met your nurse, Mrs. Taylor, this morning."

"She's not a nurse. She's just my housekeeper, but she can help me do the things I can't do for myself." Avis was looking out, avoiding Peter's gaze, as the car threaded its way down the street. The April sun was rising high overhead, and the blue sky was dotted with fluffy pink clouds. The air was warm, and it ruffled Avis's hair so that she shook it and ran her hand through it.

Peter had to make all the conversation, for Avis was silent, just staring out the window. Finally he pulled up in front of a gray brick building. "It's a good thing you live on the first floor. Without an elevator we couldn't get the chair upstairs very easily."

"Yes, aren't I lucky!"

Ignoring the bitterness in her voice, Peter stepped out, untied the wheelchair, and put it down. Opening the door, he reached in and said, "Here we go." He plucked Avis out, then sat her down in the chair and carefully covered her with the blanket. As he wheeled her across the sidewalk, a man walked by and looked at Avis curiously.

"What are you staring at?" she demanded.

The man flushed, dropped his eyes, and murmured, "Sorry," and walked on away.

"Have to go up backward here," Peter said. The landing was three steps high, and carefully he lifted her up as smoothly as he could. He could not help jolting her a little bit, for he was somewhat awkward. Opening the door, he held it with his foot and backed in, and said as a woman approached, "Hello, Mrs. Taylor."

"Hello, Mr. Winslow, Mrs. Warwick. Glad to see you home." Mrs. Taylor was a tall, gaunt woman with rather forbidding features. She had served as Avis's housekeeper for some time. She was a humorless woman, Peter had quickly learned, and now she said, "I'll put you to bed if you're ready."

"No, I've had enough of bed."

"Well then, I'll go fix lunch."

When Mrs. Taylor turned and left, Peter said, "Where would you like to go, Avis?"

"In there. In the library."

"All right." Peter wheeled the chair through the foyer over polished oak floors and turned left into a large library. He had been here earlier to make sure that things were ready for Avis, but he had not been in this room. Lifting his eyes, he was almost staggered by the books that lined every wall, most of them in leather covers. "Quite a library," he said. "I didn't know you were such a reader."

"My husband was. At least he collected books. He didn't read them all, though."

She reached forward, seized the wheels, and propelled herself over to the window, then awkwardly wheeled the chair about. "Thanks for the ride. You don't have to stay around."

"Why, I thought you might invite me for lunch."

"All right, then. You're invited."

Peter, as usual, felt awkward around Avis. She had a peculiar expression in her eyes, as if she expected him to say or do something, but he could not for the life of him decide what it was. Nervously he turned and went over to one of the bookcases. He studied the titles and said, "Mostly philosophy books. Over my head."

"They were over Charles' head, too, but he hated to admit it."

Peter moved to another shelf and said, "Well, here's a pretty new book—and one I've actually read." He picked out the book and brought it back. Turning to her, he said, "*The Call of the Wild* by Jack London. Have you read it?"

"No."

"London likes to write about dogs. This one is about a big dog. He was stolen from the south land and taken to the Yukon during the Alaska gold rush. They made a sled dog out of him."

"I don't think I'd like a dog story."

"Well, actually," Peter said, "it's more than that." He came over and sat down across from Avis. The furniture, he noted, was expensive. His eyes took in the large mahogany desk, its pond lily desk lamp with a green slag and white leaded glass shade, the dark oak end table holding a Tiffany spider web lamp, and the overstuffed easy chairs with high backs and scrolled legs. He thumbed through the book he held and said, "It's really a sad book in a way. The only way Buck learns to survive in the north is to steal. There were only so many fish for the sled dogs, and he learned to steal in order to stay alive. Some other dog had to starve for that, of course. Evidently that's the way London feels about things: dog eat dog—survival of the fittest. That's what that fellow Darwin said. That we're all just some superior kind of monkey."

"Maybe he's right," Avis said tonelessly.

"No, he's not right," Peter shook his head firmly. "A man's more than a monkey. You know," he said, "when I was a boy I had a dog named Dandy, and that dog and I did everything together." A smile touched his broad lips, and he thought back to his childhood. He made a lanky shape as he sat there holding the book in his strong hands. His hazel eyes were dreamy as he spoke of that time long gone. "Dandy and I played every game you could imagine. He slept in my bed when my mother didn't catch him. We probably even ate out of the same dish. But you know something, Avis?" He looked at her and grew tremendously sober. "When I knelt down at night to say my prayers," he hesitated, then shook his head, "Dandy didn't know anything about that. There's a difference."

"You really believe that, Peter?" Avis asked. She cocked her head to one side and grasped the handles of her wheelchair so that her knuckles turned white. "You really believe that there's a God who cares what happens to us?"

"Why certainly!"

"Well I don't!" Avis clasped her hands together suddenly, squeezed her fingers, then shook her head. "I think it's all chance. Darwin's right, and London, too."

"I don't like to hear you talk like that. Of course, my parents are Christians and they gave me a good start, but I know that Jesus Christ is who He said He was—that He's the Son of God. I know that much." He rose quickly and put the book back in its place on the shelf, then turned and came to sit down beside her. "I don't mean to preach at you, but I don't see how I could go on without God in my life."

Avis did not answer. She had recovered some of her color, but still there was a stubbornness that revealed itself in the set of her lips and in the tenseness of her cheeks. She was an attractive woman, even as ill as she had been, and there was a rebelliousness that had been deeply ingrained in her. Now as she listened to Peter speak about God, she said nothing, but there was a set to her back as she held herself upright that told Peter his words were falling on deaf ears. Thinking it better not to press it, he said, "I'll tell you what. Let's pick one of these books and read it together, you and I."

"You don't have to entertain me."

"Why, I'm entertaining myself," he said. He rose and walked

around the room, perusing the shelves of books, then finally selected one. "What about this one? *Poems of Robert Browning.* I've always liked Browning. I don't understand some of his poems, but some of them are as good as anything I've read." He walked back toward Avis and said, "Some of his writing is so obscure. One time Elizabeth Browning asked what a certain line meant that he had written in one of his poems. He took it from her and looked at it, then after a while he scratched his head." A grin came to Peter's lips then. "And Browning said, 'When I wrote that only God and Robert Browning knew what it meant. Now only God knows what it means.' " He laughed and was rewarded by seeing her features relax. "Here, let's start with this one. If you don't know it, it might be fun. It's called 'My Last Duchess.' He sat back and began to read: " 'That's my last Duchess painted there looking as if she were alive. . . . ' "

★   ★   ★   ★

As the days passed Jolie grew more and more preoccupied with Peter's behavior and his almost frantic efforts to see that Avis was well cared for. She grew weary of hearing his reports, for Peter had quickly discovered that Mrs. Taylor was not a good companion at all for Avis. He had said on various occasions, "She's a cheerless, griping old woman, and Avis needs someone with her at this time who's got some joy and some hope. I'd like to throw the woman out the window!"

Jolie had sympathized with his concern. She had visited Avis twice and found Mrs. Taylor to be exactly as Peter described her. Even though Jolie was concerned about Avis's physical condition, she was even more concerned about Peter's mental and emotional state. With each passing day, she saw him becoming more and more obsessed with the tragedy that had blown up in his face. She had tried to get him involved in other things, but he seemed to have lost all interest, even in car racing. Since he had no car to work on, Jolie knew he needed to find something else to throw his energies into.

One morning when she woke up, she was vaguely aware that something had come to her during the night. She lay there in the twilight state between sleep and wakefulness, and at first she thought it was merely one of those dreams that come just when one is emerging from deep sleep. But the longer she lay there, the more clearly she remembered how she had awakened several times in the night, and always the same thought had come to her. It was almost imperceptible at first, but then it came more and more strongly. There was something almost frightening about it, and she threw the covers off, got up, and dressed, determined to put it out of her mind. She went to work, and all that afternoon, and all during the performance, she could not help but think of the dream, or whatever it was, that had come to her. Despite every attempt to put it out of her mind it did not fade, and that night when she went to bed she did not fall asleep right away. The impression came back to her, and she knew she could not ignore it. She slept only fitfully that night, and the next morning she made an early visit to Calvary Baptist Church. Since the evening she had given her heart to God, she had visited the church often and had learned to trust George Camrose's godly counsel.

George was working in his small study when Jolie arrived. He rose quickly to greet her. "Well, Jolie, it's good to see you. Come in."

Jolie smiled nervously and sat down on the chair across from Camrose's desk. "Are you open for business, Pastor?" she asked.

"Always open for business. What's on your mind?"

Jolie leaned forward. "Something's happening to me. I don't know what it is exactly, but night before last I had something I thought was a dream. It came several times, and when I woke up the next morning, I tried to put it out of my mind, but it happened again last night."

"Can you tell me about it?"

"Yes, I suppose so. It will sound foolish, though."

"Can't be as foolish as some of the dreams I've had." George Camrose smiled as he folded his hands. He saw that she was serious and even a little bit afraid. "What is it, Jolie? It stops here, you know. No one will ever hear it from me."

"Oh, it's nothing all that shameful. I have had some rotten dreams, but this time I don't think it's bad like that. It's just simply a sentence. 'I want you to help Avis Warwick.'"

"That's all?" Surprise caused Camrose to open his eyes wide. "It's probably not being overly presumptive to think that it may be the Lord speaking. Avis needs all the help she can get."

"I think it's more than that. It's as if I'm supposed to *really* help her. To devote my life to her for a while."

"I see!" Camrose stroked his chin thoughtfully, then shrugged.

"What makes you feel this is God speaking and not merely your own thought?"

"I *know* this isn't my thought!" Jolie said abruptly. "I don't like her! I never did, and I think she's been a bad influence on Peter! I think she's toyed with him! I don't think she's a good woman!"

Once again surprise showed in Camrose's eyes. "That's pretty strong," he remarked. "But at least it means that helping her isn't something you'd do out of your own natural impulses. So you really think it's of God, Jolie?"

Jolie shifted uncomfortably in her chair. "That's what I've come to ask you about. Do I just quit my job and announce that I'm there to help her? She'd probably throw me out."

"She might. She's capable of it." He grinned wryly. "She's practically thrown me out every time I tried to visit with her, but she's really a very frightened woman. She's always been able to handle everything, but now she's feeling something she can't handle. Anybody would be afraid under her circumstances. Her whole life has suddenly gone awry." He thought for a moment, then said, "Peter's afraid she'll commit suicide."

"I know."

"He told you?"

"Not in so many words, but the way he's talked about his fears, I know that's what he's thinking. Do you think it's possible?"

"I think it is, Jolie. Here's a woman who's always been able to control herself, her life, and her circumstances. She could even control people. Now she's helpless. Everything she's always wanted to do, she's done, but now all that's changed. I don't know where that could lead, but I think she feels trapped with no way out."

"That's what I've been thinking," Jolie sighed. "You think I should go to her and tell her about the dream?"

"Yes." Camrose's voice was firm. "Tell her you think it was from the Lord if you do. I know she doesn't believe in God yet, but she needs to be around people who do believe in God. She needs to see faith in someone. But she won't listen to me, so if she would let you help her, you could bear witness to the power of Jesus Christ like no one else."

"I feel terrible. I don't love her as I should."

"If you go to help her, that's love."

"Even if I don't feel anything?"

"I think so. We can't control our feelings, Jolie, but we can control what we do. Jesus said if you give a cup of cold water in His name, you won't lose your reward. It doesn't say you have to feel all thrilled or excited about it. It just says offer the water. It sounds to me like God has called you to His service just as much as He's called me and Mary Ann to Africa."

Surprise washed across Jolie's face. "Is it really like that, you think?"

"Take one step. Go to Avis. Tell her what you've told me and offer to help take care of her. See what she says. If she throws you out, then you've done what God has told you to do. But if she doesn't, you may have an opportunity to touch her spirit, or even to touch her soul."

The two talked for some time, and finally Jolie left. When she arrived at Avis's home, she stood there uncertainly for a while, then went up and knocked on the door.

Mrs. Taylor opened the door. "Yes, what is it?"

"I'd like to see Mrs. Warwick."

For a moment Jolie thought that the woman would refuse her. She was becoming more and more difficult, but then Mrs. Taylor sniffed, "You might as well come in." When the housekeeper closed the door, she said, "She's being very uncooperative today. I've given my notice. I can't put up with her any longer."

"You're leaving?" Jolie asked in surprise. She stared at the woman and saw the hard set of her features.

"Yes! I've stood all of it I'm going to! Go ahead in. She's in the library."

Jolie found Avis sitting in front of a window staring out. Hearing Jolie, she turned but said nothing.

"Are you busy, Avis?"

"What would I be busy about?" Avis asked. Discontentment marked her face. There was none of the happiness nor enthusiasm that had been in her earlier. Her voice was clipped and short, and her fingernails were bitten off.

"I'd like to talk with you."

"About what?"

"Well, it's going to take a while. Would it be all right if I sat down?"

"Suit yourself."

Taking this as an invitation, grudgingly given as it was, Jolie moved over and sat down, drawing a chair slightly closer to where Avis sat staring at her stolidly. "I understand Mrs. Taylor's leaving."

"Good riddance, the old bat! Can't stand the sight of her! Her face could curdle milk!"

Though she didn't know exactly how to respond to such a mean attack, Jolie saw the situation as an opportunity. "You'll have to get someone else."

"Whoever I get won't be any better!"

"I'm going to tell you what's been happening to me." Jolie quickly related what she had been feeling. She kept her eyes fixed on Avis's face and saw a mixture of disbelief and contempt. She ended by saying, "So, I think God is telling me to come and help you as long as you need help, Avis."

"God's telling you that! You heard His voice? It came down out of heaven, did it?"

"You know it doesn't happen like that," Jolie protested. "It's just something that came to me almost like a dream."

"And you think that's God."

"I think it is. I certainly wouldn't do it for any other reason."

Jolie's reply amused Avis, and she allowed herself to smile bitterly. "I didn't think you were so crazy about me that you came rushing over because you wanted to spend a lot of time in my company."

"We haven't been friends."

"No. You've hated me ever since I stole Peter away from you, haven't you?"

A rich color suddenly tinted Jolie's cheeks. "Yes, I have been jealous of you. I think a lot of Peter, and I . . . and I think you were bad for him. You probably already know that."

"Of course I know that! You think I'm a fool? You wanted to wring my neck!"

"Yes, I did," Jolie said suddenly. She sat up straighter and said, "I would have, too, but I didn't want to hang for it."

Abruptly Avis laughed aloud. "Well, that's honest enough. Even if you are a Christian, you're not a mealy-mouthed one." She stared at the young woman curiously. "We'd never get along," she said finally. "You'd strangle me in a week!"

Though the words were negative, Jolie heard a subtle plea running beneath the simple meaning of the words. She also saw something in the expression of the woman who sat there paralyzed and helpless. Underneath the hardness was a cry for help.

For the first time a real compassion came to Jolie, and she knew she had done the right thing. "You may want to strangle me," she said, "but I can last as long as you can. Do you want me to come?"

Avis cleared her throat and looked down for a moment. She did not speak for quite a while, then she suddenly cleared her throat and spoke. "Well, you'll be better than that old battle-ax who's been here. You'll have to quit your job. I'll pay you whatever they're paying you, plus a bonus, if you work out."

"All right. When is Mrs. Taylor leaving?"

"Send her in. I'll give her her walking papers right now. That will be one of my few pleasures since I got into that car."

"She might be a very unhappy woman. Why don't you try being a little bit more gentle?"

"You're out to reform me? Don't waste your time, Jolie!"

Jolie shook her head. "I don't know anything about her, but anybody as sour as she is, is bound to be unhappy. Why don't you just try being nice and see what happens?"

"All right, I will!"

Jolie got a lesson from that, for when Avis gave Mrs. Taylor her leave to go, Avis received an angry dressing down from the dour housekeeper. As soon as the older woman left, Avis laughed. "There, I turned the other cheek and she nearly knocked it off!"

"That's her problem," Jolie said bluntly. "You did the right thing, and God will always reward that."

"You really believe that, don't you?"

"Yes, I do."

For a moment Jolie knew that Avis was struggling with something, and she felt, perhaps, it was time to say something about her faith, but then she knew it was too soon. Something inside told her to be quiet, wait, and demonstrate her faith in God by her actions, so she just said, "I hope you like my cooking." Then she got up to leave, saying, "I'll go and get my things and move in right away."

After Jolie left, Avis sat there staring at the door. She did not move, but suddenly her lips trembled. Nervously she passed a hand across her face and pressed her lips against her fists. Her shoulders shook slightly, and then she shut her eyes and silently wept.

CHAPTER FIFTEEN

"I'M NOT DOING IT FOR YOU"

★ ★ ★ ★

Jolie remembered more than once Avis's words before she ever allowed Jolie to come to the house: *"You'd strangle me in a week!"* Now as she entered the house carrying a bag full of groceries, she dreaded facing the day. Avis had been fully as demanding and ill-tempered as Jolie had feared. Perhaps she always had been demanding, but now her illness made her even more so. As the days had gone by, it had been a monumental struggle for Jolie to bite off the bitter replies that often came when Avis screamed at her. Even as she contemplated these difficulties, she heard Avis calling, "Jolie—Jolie!" from her bedroom. "Where are you? Come in here!"

Putting the groceries down on the hall table, Jolie ran down the hall, opened the door, and found Avis sitting on the edge of her bed. "Where have you been? You've been gone two hours!"

"No I haven't. I've just been gone thirty minutes. Here, let me help you."

She moved over and began helping Avis dress for the day. From the beginning, Avis had laid down the rule that she would not lie around in a nightgown and a robe. Jolie had had no idea how difficult it would be to dress a full-grown woman whose lower limbs were helpless. She struggled, and once when she did not move fast enough, Avis screamed at her and reached out and struck her shoulder. "Be careful! Why don't you hurry up? You're so clumsy!"

"I'm sorry, Avis."

She wondered bitterly how many times she'd had to say, "I'm sorry, Avis." Once the difficult dressing was accomplished and she had helped Avis into her chair, she pushed a lock of hair back off of her brow and said, "I'll get breakfast as quickly as I can."

"Push me into the library."

"All right."

Avis was perfectly able to propel herself into the library, and Jolie knew she was doing it just to be spiteful. Nevertheless, she obeyed without question. When she had made Avis comfortable in front of the window, Jolie said, "Would you like eggs this morning?"

"No, not regular eggs. I want eggs Benedict, and don't boil the eggs too hard like you did last time."

"All right. I'll be more careful this time."

Hurrying into the kitchen, Jolie quickly began preparing the breakfast. She was only halfway through when a knock came at the door, and she scurried to open it. "Why, Peter," she said, "you're early."

"Too early?" he asked. He came almost every day, but he usually came much later than this. Now he took in the apron and said, "Let me help you cook breakfast."

"You'll have to if you want anything to eat. She's in a bad mood today. You go in and try to cheer her up. Maybe I can do breakfast myself."

Peter suddenly reached out and took Jolie's arms and held her tightly. "Maybe I haven't said thank you enough for what you're doing for Avis, Jolie. And I want to thank you for myself."

Jolie looked up, acutely conscious of Peter's grasp on her arms. "I'm not doing it for you," she said quietly. "I'm doing it because God has told me to—and I wish He hadn't."

Peter held on for a moment, then said slowly, "You know, I keep trying to see that scrawny little girl I first saw in that boxcar. I wonder where she's gone to now? All I see now is a young woman who's stronger than any woman I've ever met."

His praise brought a flush to Jolie's cheeks. "Go on in," she said. "She's waiting for you."

"All right. We'll talk later." He moved out into the hall, picked up a sack he had brought earlier, then went into the library. "Hello, Avis," he said.

"Hello. Did you come for breakfast?"

"Thought I might eat a bite. Maybe I'd better go out and help Jolie."

"She can do it. What do you have in the bag?"

"I brought you a new book to read."

He handed her the sack, and she lifted out a book and stared at it, then read the title. *In His Steps.* She looked at him and asked, "Have you read it?"

"Yes. It's a wonderful book. It came out a few years ago."

"I've never heard of it."

"It's by a man named Charles Sheldon. He tells the story of a group of Christians who decide not to do anything or make any decision without first asking, 'What would Jesus do?' "

"That sounds terribly boring," Avis replied.

"It's really very good. Especially when some of them get involved with tent meetings in the bad part of town."

Avis frowned. "Well, I don't think it sounds like something I want to read."

Peter smiled and said, "If you won't read it yourself, maybe I'll read this one to you."

Avis laughed. "All right. I'll read it, just not right now. Tell me what you've been doing."

Peter at once launched into a description of what was happening in the world of automobiles. "Well, Henry Ford is going to be the richest man in America. He's come out with this Model T, and it'll outproduce everything. It's selling for eight hundred and fifty dollars. Everybody's calling it a fliver. I went downtown to see one. It's got a wooden body on a steel frame, and you can have any color you want—as long as you want black."

"How boring! Black!"

"The real news is that Wilbur Wright had a crash. Killed a man named Lieutenant Thomas Selfridge. First man ever killed flying an airplane, but he probably won't be the last. The Wright brothers are going to get a government contract for carrying the mail. They'll probably do it, too. They flew that contraption of theirs for sixty minutes and reached a speed of forty miles an hour."

Peter talked about the news until Jolie came to say, "Breakfast is ready," and then he stepped over to wheel Avis into the dining room. He put her at the head of the table and waited. "Aren't you going to join us, Jolie?"

"No, you go ahead."

Peter stared at her, then said no more and sat down. After Jolie had brought the food, she left abruptly. "What's wrong with Jolie?"

"I didn't know anything was," Avis said coolly. "She's gotten these eggs too hard again."

"Mine are just right. You want to swap?" he offered.

"No. I'm not hungry anyway."

Peter ate slowly and became rather pensive. Noticing this, Avis said, "What's the matter? You're depressed."

"No I'm not. I'm just thinking." For the last several days, Peter had been doing some serious thinking about the direction of his life. He had wanted to be a racing driver, but with Avis seriously injured from the accident and the *Jolie Blonde* demolished, everything looked bleak. But he was reluctant to share any of this with Avis and avoided answering her questions. Finally, after breakfast, he said, "I'll wash up for Jolie."

"Let her do it. She's paid for it."

"I'd really rather help her. You want me to take you back to the library? Maybe we can play some chess later."

"I hate that game," Avis snapped. "But go ahead and take me to the library. I'll stare out the window as usual."

Peter pushed the chair into the library, then headed into the kitchen. He found Jolie washing the dishes and said, "I'll help."

"No need to," Jolie said without turning from the sink.

Jolie's voice was cool, and Peter, for some reason, felt she was upset.

"I know she's hard to get along with, but I'd be worse if I were in her shape."

Jolie turned to say, "I know, Peter. She's a little bit of a trial, but I knew she would be when I came here. This is where God has me, and I'm going to do the best I can while I'm here."

Peter smiled warmly. "You're some girl, Jolie Devorak. I miss those times together when we worked on the car."

Jolie almost said, *That was before Avis came into the picture.* Instead she merely agreed. "I do too. Do you think we'll ever do it again?"

"I doubt it. We don't have a car, and without a car I won't be able to keep on racing."

His answer surprised Jolie. She stared at Peter for a moment, then asked, "What would you do if you didn't race cars?"

"Get a job. Go to work. Do something."

He sounded so forlorn that Jolie felt a great pity for him. She knew that he had brought some of it on himself by association with Avis, and the car tragedy had complicated things even more, but it was no time to remind him of it. "Maybe we could go back to California. I liked it out there."

"Make movies again? I don't think so."

"It was fun though, wasn't it?" Jolie said. The two of them had been involved with the fledgling movie industry, Jolie as a script girl, and Peter as a stunt driver.

They stood there in the kitchen talking about those days for so long that they forgot Avis until her voice reached them.

"Peter, come here at once!" she cried out.

"My master's voice," he said. He reached out and touched Jolie's black hair. "The blackest hair I've ever seen," he said. "Pretty." Then he turned and left the room.

Jolie stared after him. A thought came into her mind and she allowed it to linger there for a moment, but then she turned away with a sigh and began planning the rest of her day.

★　★　★　★

By the time Peter left it was growing late. He had stayed most of the day and had indeed found it difficult to keep Avis entertained. Now as he walked along the streets, he felt disturbed by a sense of futility that lay just below the surface of his mind. Ever since the accident he had been so concerned with helping Avis that he had little time to think of his own personal needs. However, he was running short of money. He had thought once or twice of trying to put another car together, but he had no place to turn except to his family, and he had determined not to ask them for help. Finally he reached his boardinghouse and was surprised to see Clinton sitting on the front steps. "Hello, Clinton," he said. "You waiting for me?"

"Yes." Clinton rose at once and said, "I need to talk to you."

"All right. Come on up." The two entered the building and went to Peter's room. "Have a seat." Peter nodded toward one of the two chairs before the small table. "How's Cara?"

"Not as well as I'd like. She seems troubled these days, and she's not painting like she used to."

"What does Phil say about that?"

"Haven't talked to him the last day or two. He's worried about her, too, but I didn't come to talk about Cara. I came to talk about—well, I don't know whether it's about me or about you."

Peter turned his head to one side slightly. A quizzical look came into his eyes. He could not imagine what Clinton was thinking and finally said, "Just let it all sit on the front porch, Clinton. What's on your mind?"

Clinton fumbled restlessly with his hat, then tossed it on the floor and said in a straightforward fashion, "Are you going to race anymore, Peter?"

"Race what? The *Jolie Blonde* is torn all to pieces. I sold it for junk."

"Are you going to get another one?"

Peter stared at Clinton Lanier. "Why do you ask?"

"Well, the truth is," Clinton said rather lamely, "I've got some money put aside that I've been saving for a long time. Thought I'd take a trip someday, but what I'd really like to do is get another car for you and me and Easy and Jolie."

"Your father wouldn't care for that, would he?"

"No. As a matter of fact he wouldn't. I'd have to make sure he never found out."

Peter stared at his friend. He knew Clinton was very clever in matters of finance, but Peter was also well aware of Clinton's burning desire to do something with his hands, something with automobiles—and of his father's strong opposition to such desires. Now Peter said, "Someday, Clinton, you're going to have to decide who's going to run your life."

"I know," Clinton said and dropped his head. "Father means well, but he just can't keep his hands out of his children's affairs. He's driving Mary Ann crazy. She's in love with George Camrose and wants to go to Africa, and she knows Father would have a fit if she even mentioned it."

"She'll have to sooner or later. She can't conceal a thing like running off to Africa with a preacher."

"No, she can't. It's a real tragedy for Mary Ann."

Peter shrugged but said no more about the Lanier family. "I'd like to race, you know that, but you'd better think about it, Clinton. It's a dangerous job, and not just to the drivers. You saw what happened to the car. All that was left was junk. We lost everything we had in it."

"I know. That's part of it, but I'd like to be in on this. I'd hate to see you give up your dreams because of a lack of money, and it's something I really want to do. Even if I can't drive the car in the races, at least I can work on it with you and drive it in the trials."

Peter began to grow excited. "You know, I think we could do a really great job. We learned a lot from putting that car together, Easy and I, and now we can build on what we know, but it's expensive. How much have you got?"

"Over three thousand dollars."

"Well, that's a good start, but you and I both know it will take more than that."

The two talked for a long time, but finally the deal was made and Clinton left. Peter was more excited than he had been since the accident, and the next day he told Jolie about what Clinton had done. "He's going to have to hide his involvement from his father, though. I'm not sure I ought to lead him astray like this."

"Let him do it. He needs to break loose from his father. From what I hear, so do his brothers and sisters."

"Mr. Lanier really is a good man—he's just too strict. He had a hard time growing up, Clinton said, and now he's afraid his family won't be taken care of if he doesn't see to it himself. I can understand that."

"Well, I can't understand wanting to *own* somebody," Jolie said firmly.

Suddenly Peter smiled rashly. It made him look much younger, and he said, "You always were a bossy young woman, and you're not getting any better."

Jolie returned his smile. "It would be fun, wouldn't it, to do it again?" Then a thought came to her, "What about Avis? It might make her more depressed."

"You're right. Maybe we ought not to do it."

"No, I think you ought to go on with your life, Peter. God is going to do something in Avis's life, but you can't be a nurse for her."

"I may have to do more than that."

Instantly Jolie felt a touch of apprehension. She did not ask what he meant, for it was clear to her that he would marry Avis if she didn't get well. Aloud she said, "I believe God's going to heal her."

"I hope so." Peter's tone was glum, and his face had lost the light of excitement that had been there when he talked about the cars. "But I'll have to look after her. She doesn't have anyone else."

Jolie could sense the guilt Peter still felt over Avis's condition and wanted to say something, but she didn't know what. She finally said, "I hope you do get another car. I liked the *Jolie Blonde*."

"Maybe we can call it the *Jolie Blonde II*."

Jolie was pleased at this. "Do it, Peter. You and Easy and me—and Clinton. Who knows? We could come up with the fastest car in America!"

Peter laughed and squeezed her shoulder. "Maybe we could. It would be fun to try again." He turned and walked away, his head filled with engines and racing. For the first time he had a sense of release from the guilt that had plagued him since the accident. He still knew that sooner or later he would have to decide what to do about Avis Warwick. In his mind, she had become his responsibility, and that responsibility was not going to fade away.

CHAPTER SIXTEEN

A CALL FROM GOD

★ ★ ★ ★

"Come into my office, Clinton. I want to speak with you."

Looking up from the column of figures spread out on his desk, Clinton saw that his father's face was even sterner than usual. "Yes, sir," he said. He rose and followed his father across the large office where three clerks were busy, or at least appeared to be so while their employer made his way to the east end of the office suite.

All of them were happy with their wages, but they resented the stern policies of the Lanier firm. When the two men disappeared, Denny Kennedy leaned back in his chair. He was a short, spare young man of twenty-five with a shock of sandy hair and the burr of Scotland in his speech. "Well, the old man's out to gut someone. I've seen that look in his eye too many times."

Sitting across from Kennedy, a bulky young man wearing a gray suit and a necktie of a startling crimson design nodded. William Horton was the youngest of the clerks and fancied himself the most astute student of human nature. Now he leaned forward and put his hands flat on the desk. He had a habit of studying things like that, which really meant nothing. "I think you're right, Kennedy," he said ponderously. "I think Clinton's about to get his regular dressing down. Better him than me." He grinned at his neighbor, then slowly went back to his work.

Inside the large office that was the heart of Oliver Lanier's business transactions, a massive desk occupied the center of the room. Papers were neatly stacked, filed, and tagged. All around the room shelves rose to the ceiling, all filled to capacity with papers, files, books, packages—the monument of a lifetime of hard-fought business dealings carried on by Oliver Lanier. It was an austere office. There were no pictures on the walls, no ornaments, no trophies. Nothing but serious business took place in this room.

"Sit down, Clinton," Oliver said brusquely. He was, as usual, wearing a dark blue suit with a high celluloid collar that was too tight. His bulldog expression was augmented by a massive chin, and now as he stood by his desk, leaning on it with one fist, Clinton thought he seemed distracted.

Clinton's eyes narrowed, for his father was not usually uncertain about anything. *I wonder what he's going to jump on me about now?* he thought wearily but said nothing.

"I'm unhappy with Mary Ann, Clinton." Oliver Lanier turned suddenly and shot his thick forefinger at his oldest son, almost as if it were a loaded pistol. "She's been seeing too much of this minister, and I think it's a bad thing."

Shifting slightly in his chair, Clinton wondered how he could best defend Mary Ann without bringing his father's displeasure down on his own head. He had formed a habit of taking the easy way out, agreeing with his father outwardly when he really did not in his own mind. Now, however, he said with more assertiveness than normal, "I like George Camrose. He's a good, sound man, I think. I'm surprised that you don't like him, Father."

"It isn't a question of whether or not I like him. Mary Ann's old enough to know better. She's had all the advantages, and I didn't bring her up to see her throw her life away on some forsaken mission station in Africa." Suddenly he turned and paced the floor, his heavy tread leaving imprints on the thick carpet. He was almost like a soldier pacing his post for a time, and then he shook his head, displeasure in his eyes. "I can't think what's wrong with her. I always thought she was a sensible enough girl."

"She is sensible," Clinton said. "But she's twenty-six years old and in love."

"In love! She's been reading too many of those romances—that's what her problem is!" Lanier growled. "She always was romantic."

"Yes, she was, and still is. But I still insist that she and George have a good chance of making a strong marriage of it, Africa or not."

The window was open, and from somewhere outside came the sound of a vendor peddling ice. "Ice for sale! Ice for sale!" he bellowed in a bull-like, throaty roar.

"Why does that fellow have to shout at the top of his lungs?" Lanier snapped, irritation causing him to move over and shut the window. It did little good, for the loud cries still came through the glass itself.

"Ice for sale! Ice for sale!"

"I'm not going to put up with it, and I think you'll agree that it would be an improper match."

Knowing that it was useless to argue, Clinton asked, in as mild a tone as he could manage, "What does Mary Ann say when you talk to her about George?"

"Oh, she talks about loving him, of course, and about God calling her to go out to Africa."

"You don't think that's possible? I mean that God calls people?"

"Now, Clinton, let's not turn this into a theological discussion. It's a matter of common sense, and I'm trusting you as my oldest son to be of some help to me in this matter."

"I don't see what you could expect me to do, Father. If she won't listen to you, she certainly won't listen to me."

"She might. You two have always been very close. I'm going to talk with Cara, also, and I want you two to talk some sense into Mary Ann. I don't want to be the villain in this case." A silence fell across the room, and Oliver Lanier paused, as if the echo of his words had stirred something deep within. He was silent for a long time, and then he reached up and touched his chin with a gesture of uncertainty, a rare thing, indeed, for him. "You must understand, Clinton. I want the best for Mary Ann. It's not that I'm trying to take something away from her because I don't want her to have something that's good. I do want her to have the very best, but I think this would be a disaster for her. Those who go to Africa have to be very tough. I could have stood it. You know how I grew up, but I doubt if you could. You're too soft."

He doesn't even know he's insulting me, Clinton thought. He listened as his father went on speaking of what high hopes he had for Mary Ann, and how they would all be dashed and her life ruined if she married George.

Finally Oliver turned and said, "I can count on you, can't I, Clinton?"

"I'm afraid not, Father," Clinton responded, standing. "You and I are not of one mind about this. Mary Ann's twenty-six years old. She's in love, and she wants to get married, and I'm not the one to say that God hasn't called her. If He has called her to the mission field, she'd better go. If she's not tough enough, God will have to toughen her up, I suppose."

A scowl creased the lips of the older man, and he stared at his son. "I'd hoped for better, but I don't know why. All right, go on back to your work."

When Clinton got to the door, his father said, "That preacher, Barney Winslow, is speaking at Calvary Church again. I don't want Mary Ann to go. Don't give them any help."

Clinton stood there stock still for a moment. He almost agreed, but something rebellious came to him then, and instead of replying he clamped his lips together, turned, and moved outside, closing the door firmly behind him. He walked across the room without a glance and, stepping into his own office, shut the door. He did not return to work, however, but went to the window and stared out for a long time. The hum of the traffic two stories below filled his office, but he ignored it. He was displeased about what had just happened, and finally he jerked himself around, smacked his fist into his open palm and exclaimed, "Why didn't I tell him he's wrong! Don't I have any guts at all?" He put his hands behind him and clasped them together, hunching his shoulders forward, thinking how he might have stood up to his father, but finally he sighed and said, "I guess it's too late for anything like that."

Going back to work, he toiled steadily until almost four o'clock. Finally he heard the chiming of a church bell in the distance and pulled out his watch. As he looked at the time, his face grew intent. *Barney Winslow is speaking at Calvary Baptist Church tonight, and I'm to stop Mary Ann from going.* With a sudden angry gesture, he snapped the watch closed and replaced it in his vest pocket, then reached over and got his coat and slipped into it. He pulled the brown derby off of the rack and settled it firmly on his head. Turning to look in the mirror, he pulled the hat to a sharper angle that gave him a more dashing appearance—or so he thought. "So Mary Ann's not supposed to go hear Reverend Winslow, and I'm supposed to keep her from doing it," he murmured. He studied his image in the mirror, and as he stared at himself, something seemed to snap within him. "Well, we'll just see about that!"

Turning, he stepped outside his office door, walked by the clerks without a word, and left the building. Getting into a cab, he gave his home address and then sat back, his mind busy with the plan that seemed to form itself even as the hansom cab rolled over the cobblestones. "We'll see about that!" he murmured firmly, and an enigmatic smile pulled the corners of his lips up. "We'll just see!"

* * * *

Mary Ann was standing beside Cara, who was staring at a canvas. For nearly an hour she had just dabbed at it, not daring to make a major stroke. Ordinarily she did not mind people watching her work, but her failure to produce the portrait she had struggled with for some time made her irritable, and she turned, saying, "Mary Ann, why don't you go somewhere else? You're making me nervous."

"I never made you nervous before. What's the matter?"

"Why, I can't paint this picture. All I can come up with is some kind of a shadow of what I want." She gestured toward the canvas, which was sufficiently sketched in to reveal its main subject, a woman and her daughter, but where little progress had been made except on the background. "The background was easy enough," she said, sweeping the brush over the area behind the two figures.

"You've done very well. Why, I didn't know you'd ever been in that part of town."

"It was just once a long time ago," Cara murmured. She remembered the time and added, "James was bringing me home from the doctor. Mother was with me. There was some sort of accident and we stopped. I looked out and saw this woman and her little girl. They were poorly dressed, and they were standing in front of this old, dilapidated building with garbage cans piled in front and a mangy alley cat sunning on the stoop. You see?"

"You got all that so well. Look at that cat!" Mary Ann exclaimed. "Why, you can almost see the fleas on him!"

"Oh yes, that part's easy," Cara said wearily. She sat down in the canvas chair and tossed the brush down in a gesture of futility, which was unusual for her. "I can't get their faces, Mary Ann. I see them, but I can't make it come out on the canvas."

"You'll get it. Just keep working."

"I don't think so. All I'll ever have is a shadow portrait." She thought for a moment, then said, "Flowers are so easy. They don't have any souls, but when someone paints a portrait, the soul of that person ought somehow to come out. You saw that picture by George Luks of the laughing boy. Why, you could see so vividly what was in his heart. He had a dirty face and his right hand was all scratched up by something. An old man's coat hung on him, but the joy in him came out despite the poverty that was so obvious. How does the artist do that? I've asked Phil, but he says it has to be inside before it can get outside. He always says you can't get something out that's not in."

"I don't understand that," Mary Ann remarked.

"I do. The Bible talks about how things are perceived from out of the heart—good things and bad things. If good things are in your heart, why, you know good things will come out. And, of course, the opposite is true." She stopped speaking and stared at the portrait with great dissatisfaction. Shaking her head, she rose to get a cloth to put over it, but as she did the door burst open and Clinton stepped inside. "Why, Clinton! What's wrong?"

Moving across the room, Clinton stood before his two sisters. He ignored Cara to face Mary Ann, saying, "Did you know that Reverend Barney Winslow is speaking at Calvary Baptist Church tonight?"

"Of course I know it. George wants me to come, but I can't." A look of bitterness filled her beautiful eyes then. Though they were blue as the sky and innocent and virtuous, they were now marred by growing anger. "Father will never let me go to that church again."

"Well, I think you ought to go."

Both of the women stared at Clinton. He was holding his head in an abnormal position, and there was something different in his visage—a stubbornness they had seen previously only on a few rare occasions.

"Why, you can't mean that, Clinton!" Cara said. "She can't deliberately disobey Father."

"Mary Ann, I strongly feel that you ought to go."

Mary Ann suddenly blinked with surprise, but something of Clinton's adamant determination communicated itself. "I *would* go, but you know what Father would do."

"Don't tell him. Just go," Clinton said.

"How could we do that? Someone would be sure to report that

we were there. Why, Mary Ellen attends the services there. We can't tell her not to speak about our going," Mary Ann said. Mary Ellen was one of the family's maids and a devout Christian, but she was quite a gossip around the house. "Father would be sure to hear of it."

"Not if you do what I tell you." Clinton suddenly smiled freely for the first time. "Let the blame fall on me, but I think you ought to go. How are you going to go to Africa if you can't even go to a church service?"

"What's wrong with you, Clinton?" Cara said, stepping closer to her brother. "Why are you saying this?"

"You heard about the woman that got her children to do what she wanted by telling them not to do it? Like, 'Don't you wash the dishes,' and then they'd go wash them. Well, I feel about the same way. Father instructed me not to encourage you to go to the meeting. In fact, he asked me to do all I could to dissuade you. Therefore, I've got to do it. Here's what we're going to do if you're willing."

Mary Ann and Cara listened almost breathlessly as Clinton outlined his plan, and when he was through, he asked, "Well, will you do it, Mary Ann?"

"Yes," Mary Ann said. "I will!"

"And I will, too!" Cara said. She saw the surprise in Clinton's face and said, "You'll have to take us both, Clinton."

"All right, I will. I'll have the carriage here at six-thirty. The service starts at seven. Be ready."

After Clinton left the room, Cara said with some hesitation, "Are you sure we should do this, Mary Ann? We know we are directly disobeying Father."

"I've given up wondering about it, Cara," Mary Ann said. There was sadness in her tone, but a sudden burst of determination showed itself as she bit her lip. "I need to hear all I can about Africa. I wish that I could go with Father's blessing. But if I can't, I must go without it."

★   ★   ★   ★

As usual, Phil Winslow came in a few minutes before the service started. He had formed the habit of coming to pray with George Camrose before the service, and this time he found Camrose and Barney Winslow in the small study. They greeted him warmly, and George said, "Just time for a quick prayer."

"Right you are, and I expect to see great things happening."

"Have you ever thought God might call you to a foreign field, Phil?" Barney inquired.

"No, I never felt that way. I don't think I got the call. I believe in it, though."

Barney nodded, saying, "It's not wise to go unless God sends you." He smiled and uttered a short, rueful laugh. " 'Some got called and sent. Others just up and went.' That's what they say about the mission volunteers. A lot of them don't even make it through the first few months, but if God is in it they make it."

The three men prayed, then stepped out of the pastor's study into the large room that served as the church meeting hall. Phil always sat near the back, and now he took his seat. He was surprised to look up and see Clinton Lanier come in through the door, escorting two women wearing black veils over their faces. "What in the world is he doing?" Phil muttered. He recognized the figures of Cara and Mary Ann, though their faces were so heavily veiled he could not make out their features. He watched as they took a seat as far back as possible. Clinton turned suddenly, and caught Phil's eye and winked at him, an unexpectedly merry smile on his lips.

He looks like the cat that's eaten the canary, Phil thought. He had the impulse to go and join him, but obviously Clinton had brought the two women disguised to keep their identity a secret. It did not require a great deal of discernment for Phil to figure out that their father had forbidden them to come. He knew of Oliver Lanier's adamant stance against his daughter's serving in Africa, and something about Clinton's rebellion pleased him. "About time he broke the cord, but I hope he doesn't get caught. I'm afraid if he does, he'll pay dearly."

The service began as usual with rousing praise and singing of hymns. Phil could not concentrate as fully as he might have liked, for his eyes kept going back to Cara. *I'm not surprised about Mary Ann, but I am surprised about Cara*. He changed his seat then so that he could get a better view of her profile, but he could not see beneath the veil. He determined, however, to intercept her after the service.

The service was not long, but it was powerful. As usual, Barney spoke well, not with eloquence, but with great fervor. He was thrilled and excited to be preaching the gospel here in New York, and it showed. When he began to relate the scenes of some of the remarkable answers to prayer God had wrought in the dark continent, the audience listened breathlessly. As he told how one of the best and most effective missionaries had died in his arms, there was scarcely a dry eye in the congregation.

Finally he brought the sermon to a close and issued a call for those who felt led to give their lives on the foreign mission field to come forward.

Phil was alert, and as he expected, Clinton stepped out and escorted the two "widows" outside. They had not gone far, however, when Phil caught up with them. They were just nearing the small carriage in which Clinton had brought them. "Hello, Clinton," he said. "Great service, wasn't it?"

"Why . . . yes it was," Clinton said, looking nervously at his sisters.

"Hello, Mary Ann. Hello, Cara," Phil said in a normal voice.

"You recognized us!" Mary Ann gasped.

"Why, certainly." Phil attempted to show surprise. "Was I not supposed to?"

Cara suddenly laughed. "What a trio of idiots we are! Everybody knows you have two sisters, and we can veil our faces, but we've been here often enough that Mary Ellen would certainly know who we are, and she was here."

"I'll speak to her and see that she doesn't tell Father," Clinton said.

"And you won't tell, will you, Phil?" Cara said. She lifted her veil and smiled. There was more life in her face than usual, and she said, "It was a great service, wasn't it?"

"Yes, it was," Phil nodded. "I've never heard a preacher like Barney Winslow. He puts his whole heart in preaching the gospel. He cares for nothing else."

"I wish I could invite you home," Cara said, "but—"

"I know, but I do hear a kind heart speaking there. How's the painting going?"

Cara dropped her eyes. "Not well," she said.

"Maybe I could be of some help. Could we meet sometime and talk about painting?" He did not expect her to answer, and she did not. He could sense that she longed to escape the life of confinement she now endured and move into another realm of life, but she had not yet reached the point where she could break away from old ties.

"We'd better go," Cara said. "Good-bye, Phil. I wish—" She halted abruptly, then shook her head, and Phil helped her into the carriage. When Mary Ann and Clinton had seated themselves, Cara looked out and said, "I'm trying, but all I can do is come up with a background. I can't paint a soul yet, Phil."

"You will, Cara," Phil said reassuringly. He reached up and, to her shock, took her hand and kissed it before releasing it. She could not answer, and as the carriage moved away, she covered the spot his lips had touched. It seemed to be burning, and she did not speak on the way home.

CHAPTER SEVENTEEN

COMING OF AGE

★　★　★　★

Sunlight poured down through the skylights in solid bars, almost as tangible as yellow bands of butter. Phil Winslow narrowed his eyes and applied fine brush strokes to the painting propped before him. His shoulders ached, the fingers of his right hand were stiff, and the strokes did not please him. With an impatient snort, he shook his head, turned around and almost collided with Bill Crumpler, who had come up quietly and stood watching him. Running into Crumpler was almost like running into a brick wall, for the burly art instructor was settled firmly on his feet. Reaching out, he repelled Phil, saying, "Why don't you watch where you're going?"

"Why don't you go stand somewhere else, Crumpler?" Phil snapped back.

"Well, we have a temper today, I see." Crumpler had startling blue eyes, which always struck people as strange. He had the body of a saloon bouncer, and his short-cropped black hair made him look like a pugilist, which, as a matter of fact, he had been for a time. His features showed some of the battering he had taken, and now he pulled at his thickened left ear as he studied the painting. "What's the matter with you, Phil? You've forgotten everything I've taught you."

"I don't think so," Phil answered curtly, for he was unhappy with his efforts. He had attempted to paint a picture of children playing ball in the streets, but nothing had seemed to work. "Just one of those things that didn't come off, I guess," he said lamely.

Crumpler was studying the painting carefully. He said nothing for a time, which made Phil rather nervous. "You know what I think?" he grunted. "I think you've got woman trouble."

Phil's jaw dropped and he blinked with surprise. "What are you talking about? I do a bad job on a picture and you think I've got troubles with women! What kind of art teacher are you, anyhow?"

"I think most of the time when men fail they've got troubles with women, one way or another." He grinned abruptly and his eyes almost disappeared in a crinkling expression. "That's why I'm not a great artist. Too much woman trouble, or at least I had it when I was a young man."

"You're not old now, Bill. Still plenty of time for lots of woman trouble."

"Deliver me from that." Crumpler slumped down on a cane-bottomed chair and ignored the alarming creaking it made. "Tell me about it. Doctor Bill Crumpler, woman trouble specialist. We never close."

Phil stared at the stocky man and started to deny it, then he bit his lip and shook his head. "You know, Bill, you may be right in a way."

"I knew it. Well, tell me about it. Is she some floozy that's taken you for all you've got?"

"She wouldn't get much," Phil said. He scratched his temple with the wooden tip of the brush he was holding, then said, "No, nothing like that."

Crumpler waited for him to say more, but when Winslow remained silent, he shrugged, saying, "I sometimes think a man can't be an artist and a husband at the same time. Don't know why that is."

Phil stared at the instructor as Crumpler wandered off, and slowly began to clean his brushes. As he thought about what Crumpler said, he began to see the truth in it. Phil realized that he was disturbed about Cara Lanier. Ever since he had met Cara, he found she came into his thoughts at odd times, sometimes at night as he lay restless on the bed, sometimes as he was walking along the waterfront studying the ships that lined the harbor. When he was trying to find a new aspect for painting the bridges that spanned the East River, thoughts of her would come that were both pleasant and provoking.

With an unusual abruptness he cleaned his brushes, tossed them carelessly into a drawer, then left the institute. The sun was going down now, and a spectacular gold and pink sky was visible over the buildings to the west. He paid little attention to that, however, for he was thinking of how Cara Lanier's plight had come to plague him. He was furious with her father and wanted to knock the man down and hold him while he shouted the truth at him. He had passed beyond that to irritation with Cara for permitting herself to be manipulated; but lately he had become more compassionate, trying to understand, and succeeding in a way to see how a gentle, gracious woman who had suffered poor health could look to a strong male figure for guidance and help. Now as he walked along slowly, his eyes automatically taking in the vendors and the cab drivers, businessmen on their way home from their offices, and all the thronging multitude that inhabited the great city, he thought of Cara's face. It came before him as clearly as if it were on a canvas. To him there was something about her that no other woman possessed. Even in her weakness there was an attraction. He was totally convinced that she was stronger than she knew, and somehow he longed to see her cheeks glowing with health and her eyes bright with energy and life.

As these thoughts passed through his mind, he suddenly asked himself the question that had been flirting around the edges of his consciousness. *Am I in love with Cara Lanier?*

The question came to him with something of a shock. He had known he was interested in her as an artist whose talent was being wasted, but this was not the same thing. *If she were free from her father's tyranny and were just another young woman, I'd know what to do. But to tear her away from him now, I don't know what it would do to her. I just don't know if she's strong enough, or if she thinks she's strong enough.*

As he continued along the street a resolution formed itself, and he picked up his pace. He knew that he could not go on forever with this sort of division within his own heart and mind. It was dark now, and Phil Winslow suddenly laughed aloud. "After all, I'm going to see Cara, and if Oliver Lanier catches me, he can shoot me if he wants to!"

Usually Phil Winslow was a more deliberate sort of man, but the indecision that had come to plague him concerning Cara had gone as far as he could stand. He made his way to the Lanier house and stood looking at it for a moment. It appeared especially massive in the darkness, with its form revealed only by the soft yellow glow of the streetlights outside. The windows shone by this hour, and looking up, he saw what he knew to be Cara's window. The drapes were closed, but through them he could see the soft glow of her reading lamp.

A porte-cochere extended from the front corner of the house, and when he saw its roof connected with that of a small protective overhang in front, an idea came to him. Quickly he approached the house, scaled to the roof of the porte-cochere, and edged along the house wall toward Cara's window. Putting his ear against the glass, he listened hard but heard nothing; then he tapped with his fingernails. Still nothing. Again he tapped, this time louder, and called out, "Cara! Cara!"

A thought came to him of how ridiculous he must look, but he had ceased to care. He called again and tapped with his knuckles. "Cara, open the window!"

Suddenly the drapes opened and Cara's face appeared. He saw her eyes fly open with astonishment, and her hand covered her lips as if to seal them. Then she reached down and opened the window. "Phil, what are you doing here?"

"I've got to talk to you." Phil put his hand on the sill, lifted himself up, and swung one leg over, ignoring Cara's protests. He put both feet inside, then reached back and closed the drapes. A reckless smile was on his lips, and he said, "I'd like to be able to use the front door."

"My father would provide the reception," Cara said. Fear shone in her eyes, and the yellow lamplight reflected in them as she stared up at him. "You can't stay here!"

"Yes, I can." Phil suddenly realized how much he cared for her. He was aware of her loveliness and vulnerability in a way he had not been before.

Cara flushed as he gazed at her. Clutching her robe together at her throat, she whispered, "Phil, have you lost your mind?"

"I'm going to if I don't settle something." Reaching out, he pulled her closer. She gasped, but he gave her no opportunity to protest. Drawing her into his embrace, his hands went behind her back, and then he kissed her. He half expected her to push him away, but her lips were soft and yielding under his, and she allowed him to pull her closer. As her arms lifted and went around his neck, he knew the longings in his own heart were matched by her own. She was innocent, and yet there was a passionate crying out for something that he felt in the eagerness of her lips and the warmth of her embrace as she leaned against him.

For the moment, Cara was completely unable to think. As Phil's strong arms tightened around her, she suddenly realized that something in her had been released. It was as if a dam had broken, and she returned his caress as eagerly as he gave it. Now she knew how much this man loved her. His interest was no longer a matter of art. And for Cara Lanier there was no question but that she cared deeply for Phil Winslow.

Finally Cara gasped and put her hands against his chest. "Let me go, Phil."

Phil raised his head but did not release her. "I don't want to ever let you go, Cara," he whispered. He paused and saw the pleasure that softened her lips and was reflected in her eyes at his words. He understood she was a woman who needed to be told that she was wanted and needed, that she was beautiful and desirable. "I love you, Cara."

"Don't . . . don't say that, Phil." Cara pulled away, suddenly filled with confusion. She knew the truth of his declaration, but hearing him speak it aloud caused the reality of their situation to come to her fully.

"Why not? It's true enough. Maybe I didn't know it myself until I kissed you, but now I know."

"No, it's not that way. You don't want me."

"Why would you say a thing like that?"

"You need a strong young woman, Phil. I'm not able to give you what you need."

Phil shook his head. "That's foolishness, Cara. You've been ill, but there's strength in you. If you'll let me, I can bring it back. Why, I can already see the beginnings of something wonderful, of what we can have together."

Cara listened and her heart leaped at his words, but there was uncertainty and fear and doubt. She had been ill too long to let go of the fears that had built up slowly within her. "No, I could never do it."

"Do you love me, Cara?"

"It doesn't matter."

"Do you love me?" he insisted, and he held her tightly as she tried to pull away. "Tell me. I know you do."

He kissed her again, and this time more gently. When he lifted his lips, her heart was beating so loudly she thought she could hear it. "Let me go, Phil, and please go."

"Come away with me, Cara."

For one moment Cara thought she had misunderstood him, and then she knew she had not. "Come away with you? Why, Phil, I can't do that!"

"Come with me to England." He saw a strange expression leap into her eyes, and knew he had touched the heart of one of her deepest desires. "We won't have much money, but we'll make it. We'll have each other. We'll learn to paint. It'll be spring, and you'll see flowers such as you've never seen in this country." He spoke passionately and finally ended by saying, "Come away with me."

Cara, for one instant, knew that there was nothing in the world she desired more than to give herself into the keeping of this tall man. She had the sudden feeling that if she could just put her hands on his strong neck, the health that she felt there would flow into her. She did so now, and yet at the same time she shook her head, whispering in an agonizing whisper, "I can't, Phil. I just can't run away with you!"

"Yes you can, even if I have to kidnap you." He did not mean it seriously, but he saw alarm flicker in Cara's expression. He smiled and said, "You know I don't mean that, but I think you love me, and I know I love you. What kind of a life would we have if we didn't have each other? That's what love is, Cara. It's a man and a woman who have found each other, and whereas they were two, they become one. That's in the Bible, and it's true. I've seen it in my parents. I've seen it in a few people, and somehow I know it can be true for us."

"Phil, I can't—" Whatever it was that Cara was going to say, she never completed it. The door swung open, and with a slight cry she pulled away. When she turned to face the door she was shocked, almost as if electricity ran through her—for there stood her father, his eyes glowing with anger and his face reddened.

Phil reached out and took Cara's arm. He said, "I'm sorry I had to come like a thief, but I had to talk to Cara."

"I told you never to come into my house, Winslow! Now get out!"

"Father, please!" Cara cried. "Don't be this way!"

"You be still, Cara. You're not responsible for this. Winslow, I've tried to talk to you and that hasn't worked. We'll try something else now."

Oliver Lanier moved quickly for such a large, heavy man. He closed the distance, reached out, and grabbed Phil by the arm with his left hand and yanked him toward the door. He kept his right hand free, for he fully expected Winslow to strike him. He was sixty-one years old, but there was still a solid strength in his burly body, and he was fully prepared to fight it out with this younger and more agile man.

Phil had one impulse to strike out, but it was only a fleeting one. He knew he could not afford to strike Cara's father, no matter what happened. He tried to protest, but Lanier's hand was clamped on his arm like a vise. He felt himself being dragged to the door, and he was aware of Cara, who was weeping. When they were out in the hall, another figure appeared, and Phil heard Oliver say, "Get out of the way, Clinton!"

"Not this time, Father."

Phil suddenly heard a different strain in Clinton Lanier's voice. He felt Oliver's hand leave his arm and turned to see the older man staring with shocked astonishment at his son, who was now standing with both feet firmly planted in front of his father. He was pale, but his eyes were clear and defiant as he said, "I'm ashamed to see you act this way! Why do you have to act as if you own your children?"

The question seemed to ignite a fury in Oliver. He stepped forward and almost without thinking, shoved his son backward. "Get out of the way!" he said hoarsely. "Don't interfere!"

Clinton was staggered by the blow. He was a smaller man than his father, not over five ten and weighing less than a hundred and seventy-five pounds, whereas his father was massively built. Still, there was no fear in him. He had passed some kind of a crisis, had burned some sort of bridge, and now his voice was quiet but determined as he said, "You want to throw me out, too?"

"If you can't behave as you should, yes!" Oliver was shocked at Clinton's rebellion. It was as if an inanimate object had suddenly spoken, and now he stared at this older son of his with a strange expression in his cold blue eyes. "Get out of the way, Clinton," he said. "I'm throwing this scoundrel out of this house!"

"No you're not!" Clinton said. "Come along, Phil. I'll apologize for my father. I'd thought he was at least a gentleman. I see I was gravely mistaken."

The charge from his son's lips affected Oliver Lanier more strongly than anyone would have thought. Cara had come to stand to the side, and she saw shock and surprise and then anger all mingled in her father's contorted face. She wanted to go to him, to beg him to allow Phil to leave without a struggle, but she said nothing.

Oliver now seemed to have forgotten Phil Winslow. Some sort of enormous struggle of wills had suddenly exploded, and he stood facing Clinton, the two men both determined and rigid. Despite their respective ages and apparently disparate personalities, in this moment there was something very similar in their expressions.

"You're upset, Clinton, but just go to your room. I'll handle this, and there'll be no more said between us."

"Oh, I'm to go to my room! That's what you said to me when I was six years old. Do you still think I'm six years old, Father? That I can be sent to my room like a child?"

"You're acting like a child!"

"No, I'm acting like a man, and for the first time, I must admit. Come along, Phil."

"If you go with him, you'll be choosing against me," Oliver said. His lips grew tight, and he said, "If you leave the house with him, you needn't come back—and you needn't come to the office either!"

Instantly Clinton Lanier said, "You mean that, Father?"

For one second Oliver hesitated, but he was a proud man and could not back down. "You'll see if I mean it! Now, go to your room and let me deal with this!"

"Yes, I'm going to my room, and I'm packing a suitcase, and I won't be at the office tomorrow. Come along, Phil."

Phil turned to Cara. She was pale and her lips were trembling. "I'm sorry to have brought this into your house, Cara, but I mean what I said. I love you, and I want to marry you and take you away."

"Get out of my house!" Oliver shouted. "I won't listen to this!"

Phil saw that Cara was staring at her father, and he said quietly, "I'm sorry," then he turned and walked toward the door. He stepped outside and found that his own hands were none too steady. He waited until Clinton came out carrying a single suitcase. "Are you sure you want to do this, Clinton?"

"Yes. I should have done it a long time ago."

Phil suddenly reached out and put his arm around Clinton's shoulders. "I know it's hard to grow up." He felt a slight tremor in the younger man's frame, and then said, "I'm proud of you, Clinton. Growing up isn't always a matter of another birthday."

The words seemed to encourage Clinton. Indeed, he was frightened, but he knew now that he could never go back to his father, not on the terms he had always been given.

"Come along. You can room with me until you find something better. Or I'm sure Peter wouldn't mind you staying with him until you find something."

"I'm pretty well broke, Phil, except for what I've invested with Peter."

"Join the club, but God will take care of us."

The two walked along slowly, and Phil knew what a revolution had just taken place. Whatever Clinton Lanier did, he would never be the same young man that he was. He might go hungry and cold, but he could never go back to being the cowed young man that he had been. He looked at Clinton's face and saw the similarity to Cara's, and his heart grew cold. He wondered if Cara could ever do what Clinton did to declare his independence. The hope he had was small, but finally he prayed, "God help her to see that she's a woman and not a child."

The two men's shadows stretched out behind them, then shortened as they passed under a streetlight. Their footsteps made a slow cadence as they moved down the sidewalk, and overhead the stars burned with indifferent light as the moon reflected the borrowed glory of the sun.

PART FOUR

OPEN DOORS

★ ★ ★ ★

CHAPTER EIGHTEEN

A Mysterious Mission

★ ★ ★ ★

Yawning hugely, Peter struggled up from the bed, where for the past couple of hours he had been sleeping soundly on top of the covers. He had come in just before dark after having put in a hard day. He had spent the morning with Avis, which was beginning to be somewhat tedious, and he had been happy to meet with Easy during the afternoon. The two had traveled around the city extensively looking for a car they could afford. Clinton Lanier's money had been like manna from heaven, and late that afternoon they found exactly what they were looking for.

As Peter arched his back and relaxed his muscles, he thought about the car, which was a specially designed Ford Racer. It had been one of Henry Ford's earlier experiments, before he had tired of racing and begun his current project—developing the mass production of family cars.

Walking over to the window, Peter looked out, thinking with excitement of how he and Easy could get more speed out of the car by changing the transmission and souping up the engine. The two of them had gone over the vehicle, and not only had it taken all the money Peter had gotten from Clinton, but he had been forced to sign a note for the balance.

"If we don't win some racin' money," Easy had said, "we'll lose the whole thing."

Peter was aware of the risk, but he had fallen in love with the car and now could hardly wait to start the modifications.

As he looked out the window, he was startled to see Clinton Lanier get out of a carriage and then remove two suitcases. "What in the world is Clinton doing? It looks like he's leaving town." Peter turned and walked quickly out of the door and down the hall. "Hello, Clinton. Come in."

Grasping both suitcases, Clinton came through, set them down, and then turned to Peter with a strange look on his face. His eyes had a troubled expression and his voice was not quite steady as he said, "Hello, Peter."

"What's wrong? Somebody sick?"

"No. Not really. It's me." Clinton attempted to laugh, but it was not a very successful effort. He suddenly blurted out, "I've been kicked out of my home, Peter."

"Kicked out! What are you talking about?" Peter was shocked, and he stood there listening as Clinton related the altercation he had had with his father. When Clinton finished, Peter exclaimed, "Good for you!" He slapped Clinton on the shoulder, and said, "Nobody likes to go against his father, but you did the right thing."

"I . . . I hope so. It was the hardest thing I've ever done, but I can't help but feel it was right."

Quickly Peter took in the situation. "Well, I guess you're looking for a place to stay."

"Yes, but the trouble is, I'm broke." An embarrassed look crossed Clinton Lanier's face. It was the first time in his life this young man had lacked the money to do whatever he needed to do. Now Clinton cleared his throat and said, "I'll go out and find a job tomorrow, but could you put me up for the night?"

"Why, I'll do better than that. We'll get you a room here."

"I can't do that. I don't have—"

"Don't worry about it. Mrs. Mason is a good landlady. She'll be glad to wait for the money. Come along."

Twenty minutes later Clinton was settled in his own room, and Mrs. Mason had warmly assured him that she would be glad to wait until he found work. She had been impressed by Clinton's gentlemanly bearing, and his expensive clothes gave her even more assurance. Clinton looked around the room, which was about twelve feet square with one large window. The light blue walls were decorated with a paisley border around the top, and a simple but pretty green-and-blue rug covered most of the floor. A small iron bed, a maple chest of drawers, and a bedside table completed the furnishings. A crocheted doily, a painted globe lamp, and a brass alarm clock on the table provided a homey touch.

"Say, this is fine, Peter!" he exclaimed.

"Let me tell you what Easy and I did today," Peter said. He saw that Clinton was struggling with his feelings this evening, so he plunged into an excited description of the Ford that he and Easy had bought. Some of his excitement communicated itself to Clinton, and Peter said, "We spent all of your money. And if we don't win a race, the car may be repossessed."

"Do you think we have a chance?" Clinton asked eagerly.

"I didn't buy it to lose," Peter grinned. "Tomorrow we'll start making some changes on it, and you can help." He described some of the alterations that had to be made to the car and by the time he had finished, Clinton had managed to put the terrible scene at home out of his mind. He sat there on the bed for a time, and finally Peter said, "Well, it's getting late. You get a good night's sleep. We'll have a good breakfast in the morning, then you and Easy and I will tear into that car, and we'll make a winner out of it. Good night, Clinton. I'm glad you came."

"Thanks, Peter." Clinton stood up and shook Peter's hand warmly. "Nice to have a friend." After Peter left, he stood uncertainly in the center of the room, more alone than he had been in his entire life. Here he was in a rented room with the rent unpaid, with only a few dollars in his pocket, and no prospects. He knew he could get a job in a brokerage firm without any trouble, but as he stood there thinking, he made a sudden resolve. "I'll have to get a job sooner or later, but for a while at least, I can do what I really want to do!"

★　★　★　★

Avis Warwick sat listlessly in her wheelchair staring out the window. The spring of 1908 had been mild, and now as June was ending she knew hotter days lay ahead. The large window was open, and from where she sat she could watch as a group of sparrows scuffled in the dust for the bread crumbs that Jolie had thrown out for them. It was a furious affair, much like a small war, and Avis murmured, "If birds in their nest agree . . ."

Jolie moved around the room, casting a glance at Avis from time to time. She was aware that Avis was more depressed than usual, and finally she came over and sat down. "Would you like for me to play some of the new music that Peter brought, Avis?"

"I don't think so."

Jolie brushed her hair back where it had fallen over her forehead and tried to think of something to keep her charge amused. It was difficult, for of late Avis had been so despondent that she could not even seem to take enjoyment in abusing her. For Jolie it was a victory. She had come to Avis's house filled with jealousy and dislike, but as the days had passed, the Lord had replaced this with a compassion she knew did not come from her own spirit. Now she sat there and studied Avis, trying to read the expression on the older woman's face. In one sense it was difficult to tell that Avis had been hurt, for she sat upright in the chair and wore an attractive pearl gray dress with lace at the sleeves. Her hair was well fixed, the product of Jolie's handiwork, for Jolie had become something of an expert hairdresser, at least with Avis. But it was in the dull eyes and the tightness of the mouth that Jolie was able to read the unhappiness in Avis's heart. Jolie had prayed daily for her, and now she said, "It was a wonderful service yesterday. Reverend Barney Winslow preached at Brother Camrose's church."

She waited for Avis to cut her off as she usually did whenever Jolie tried to introduce any sort of talk of God, but Avis for once merely said, "Is that right?"

Encouraged, Jolie went on to describe the service and ended by saying, "I think George Camrose is an unusual preacher. He's very talented, you know, and I think he would have been successful at anything he had chosen to do."

"I suppose his parents are disappointed in him because he didn't become a successful businessman or professional man."

"His father isn't living, but his mother's very proud of him," Jolie said. "And, of course, Mary Ann thinks he's the only man in the world. I've never seen a young woman so in love with a man."

"From what I hear, her father will put a stop to that!"

"I'm sure he'll try," Jolie shrugged. "He's already alienated one of his sons." Jolie had been proud of Clinton Lanier for the stand he had made, and now she spoke of her admiration of him and George Camrose warmly.

"Clinton is giving up everything. And as for Reverend Camrose, I don't know much about Africa," Avis said, "but it's bound to be a dirty, hard life."

"I don't think circumstances are the most important thing in the world, Avis. I've been reading a book. It's written by a man called William Law. He was a minister back about 1720." She reached into her apron and pulled out a very small book. "It's called *A Serious Call to Holy Living*."

"Sounds terribly boring. Just the sort of thing you'd like, I suppose."

"I think you might find some of it interesting. Can I read some of it to you?"

"Go ahead. Not likely that I'm going to get into 'holy living'."

"Well, Law is talking about the things of the world, and he says, 'Another possible objection to rules for holy living is that so many things in this world are good. Created by God, they should be used; but following strict guidelines limits our enjoyment of them.'"

"I don't understand that," Avis remarked. Her interest in religious things was almost nonexistent, but she was bored and said, "Isn't he saying that God put good things in the world and we ought to enjoy them? Well, I'll agree with that."

"Yes, that's what he says, but listen to this: 'Suppose a person without knowledge of our world is placed alone with bread, wine, gold dust, iron chains, and gravel. He has no ability through his senses to use those items properly. Being thirsty he puts wine in his ear. Hungry he fills his mouth with gravel. Cold he covers himself with chain. Tired he sits on his bread. This person will vainly torment himself while he lives blinded with dust, choked with gravel, and burdened with chains.'"

Avis was an intelligent woman and the imagination of the writer had caught her attention. "I never heard of anything like that," she murmured. "What does it all mean?"

"Well, Law then says: 'Suppose some benevolent being would come and instruct him in the proper use of those materials, warning him that other uses of those materials would either be profitless or harmful. Could anyone believe that those strict guidelines would make his life miserable?'"

Jolie leaned forward and said, "What William Law is saying is that Christianity teaches us how to properly use the world. It teaches us what's right about food, drink, and clothing, and things like that. And if we learn that, we can expect no more from them than they can properly provide. But if we don't, we're like the man who stuffs himself with gravel."

Avis sat very still. For some time she had been thinking about her past life, and now that it had been taken away from her—all of those "good" things had been removed. She had, for the first time, been able to see what her life had been. Somehow the words that Jolie read went deep into her spirit.

"I see what you mean, Jolie," she said slowly. "That gold isn't either good or bad. It's what you do with it that counts."

"That's right," Jolie replied eagerly. "And that's true with many other things. Alcohol for example. It has a use medically, but if it's misused it leads to drunkenness and that's wrong. So Christianity teaches us how to use the world."

Jolie continued to speak for some time, expecting at any moment for Avis to interrupt or turn away. But this time was different. Avis was listening carefully, and finally Jolie said, "That's what Christianity is for me. It teaches me that there's going to be glory for those who don't blind themselves with gold dust, or eat gravel, or load themselves with chains. It calls us to a holy life. I know that sounds boring to those who don't really know about it, but the most happy people I've known have been those who were seeking after God and finding Him."

Avis kept her eyes fixed on the younger woman's face, and finally she murmured, "It may be so." Then she abruptly changed the subject, a habit with her. "You're in love with Peter Winslow, aren't you?"

Jolie's face reddened. "I like him a lot," she said. "He's been a good friend to me."

Avis listened but seemed not to hear the words. She said, "Tell Peter I want to see him." It was the first time she had sent for Peter, and Jolie could not imagine what was going on inside Avis's mind.

"All right," she said, getting up. "I'll go by his place tonight and tell him to come by."

★   ★   ★   ★

Jolie delivered Avis's message, and Peter came right away. He stayed with her for only a short time, and when he left he seemed preoccupied and strangely excited. He stopped long enough to say, "I'll be seeing you soon, Jolie."

"You're leaving now? Why, you hardly stayed half an hour."

"Well, I've got an errand to run." There was something mysterious about Peter's attitude. He was not good at keeping secrets, and Jolie demanded, "What are you up to, Peter?" She was afraid he would do something foolish as far as Avis was concerned, but he said nothing, just grinned and left.

The next day Jolie was in the kitchen preparing lunch when Peter suddenly burst in. She looked up from the potato she was peeling and saw that his face was suffused with excitement.

"Get your coat on, Jolie! We're going places!"

Staring at Peter, Jolie exclaimed, "What are you talking about?"

"No time for questions!" Coming up to her, he reached behind her, undid her apron, and then pulled it off as she stared at him and protested. "For once in your life try not to be stubborn," Peter said. His hazel eyes were filled with a happy excitement, and his auburn hair was wild as if he had been running his hand through it, a habit he had when he was excited. "Come on. We've got business, you and I."

Protesting all the way, Jolie could not withstand Peter's forcefulness. She soon found herself outside, where he put her into a hansom cab and then climbed in beside her. Jolie had listened but could not hear the instructions he gave to the driver. When Peter settled back, she demanded, "What are you doing, Peter? You're acting like a crazy man!"

"Well, I think I am a little bit, but a woman likes a man to be mysterious. I read that somewhere in a book."

"Well, I don't like it," Jolie frowned. "There's nothing wrong, is there, Peter? Is Easy all right?"

"Finer than frog hair," Peter said breezily. "Now, just sit back and relax. This is going to be a day you'll remember as long as you live."

Totally mystified, Jolie sat back, and the clicking of the horses' hooves beat out a staccato rhythm as they moved down the street. She kept looking out of the window, trying to get some idea of the destination, but all she saw was that they were in the downtown part of the city. Finally they turned off on Sixteenth Street, and the hansom pulled in beside a three-story red-brick building.

Peter jumped out, came around, and handed some bills up to the driver, then reached up and helped Jolie as she stepped down.

"Come along," he said. He laughed at the expression on her face. "I like being a mystery man. It gives me some kind of authority over you. You've never respected me like you should have," he said, winking at her.

"Peter, what is this place?" Jolie looked up at the signs on the wall, which mostly named lawyers and doctors. Peter did not give her the satisfaction of a reply. They walked inside, and he held firmly to her arm as they climbed to the second floor. He moved down the hall and stopped before a door that read, "Dr. Fritz Leibnez, Surgeon."

Opening the door, Peter stepped in, and keeping his hand on Jolie's arm, he smiled at the young woman who sat behind a desk. "Miss Jolie Devorak is here for her appointment with the doctor."

"Oh yes! You may go right in. You're right on time."

"Come along, Jolie."

Jolie was confused, but she stepped inside the office. A small man of some fifty years with a clipped gray beard and tense brown eyes stood up from his desk and walked around. "I'm Dr. Leibnez. This must be Mr. Winslow and Miss Devorak."

"That's right, Doctor. Here's your patient."

"Patient!" Jolie exclaimed. She turned to face Peter, and then back to face Dr. Leibnez. "I don't understand any of this."

Dr. Leibnez was somewhat startled. "Why, I assumed that you knew about our arrangements. Mr. Winslow, you didn't tell her?"

"She's a very stubborn young woman, Dr. Leibnez. You'll find that out. Now, I'm going to leave you and Jolie. I'll be right outside the door so you can't get away, Jolie. Dr. Leibnez is going to do something about that scar." He turned and left immediately, hearing Jolie's gasp. When he was outside, he shut the door firmly, then grinned at the woman. "I'll have to stand guard here. Miss Devorak is very stubborn. She might try to make her getaway."

"She's a very lovely young woman," the receptionist said. She was an older woman with silver hair and a kind face. "I think the doctor can help her a great deal with that scar."

Peter was nervous and for the next ten minutes paced the floor. He paused to look out the window, then stepped off the length of the room again, until finally the door opened and Dr. Leibnez appeared.

"Would you come in, Mr. Winslow?"

Peter quickly reentered the doctor's office. He saw Jolie sitting on a chair, her face pale and her eyes turning to him at once. Her lips were pulled tightly together as if she were trying to keep from crying. "Well, I have good news, Mr. Winslow. I think I can do a great deal to help our patient here. It will be a relatively minor operation." He shrugged his trim shoulders, saying, "I'm only surprised that it hasn't been done earlier."

"When can you do it, Doctor?"

The doctor walked over to his desk and looked briefly down at a calendar. "It would be on the twenty-sixth. Day after tomorrow."

"Right. Shall I bring her here?"

"No. Have her at Grace Hospital. Do you know where that is?"

"Sure do. Come along, Jolie."

Jolie arose and Dr. Leibnez stopped her as she wandered out like a sleepwalker. "I think you're going to be very pleased with the results, Miss Devorak. I'm very optimistic that we can do something very fine for your problem."

When they were outside, Peter put his hand on Jolie's shoulders and turned her around. "Now, that's settled," he said.

"No, it's not," Jolie said. She was frightened by it all and now looked up at him. "It's very expensive! Who's going to pay for it?"

"Avis is going to pay for it. That's what she wanted to see me about yesterday."

"Avis? Why—she can't do that!"

"You must let her do it, Jolie. You've done so much for her, and now she wants to do something for you. She's had very few generous impulses, I would guess, and this will be good for her. It's always good when somebody totally selfish breaks loose, don't you think?"

"I . . . I don't know. I can't think right now. This is all so sudden."

The trip home was a blur to Jolie, and when Peter finally let her out of the cab, she walked into the house without even saying good-bye to him, she was so stunned. She entered the house and went at once to the study, where she found Avis sitting and reading a book. "Avis," she said, "I've just come back from the doctor, but—"

"Don't tell me you're going to refuse me? I think that's pride, isn't it? Aren't you Christians supposed to be against that?"

Immediately Jolie knew exactly what she must do. She walked over to Avis and put her arms around her. She felt tears coming to her eyes, and she said, "I can never thank you enough, Avis."

Avis felt the trembling of the young woman's body. It was a new experience for her, to be a giver instead of a taker, and she found her own eyes filling with tears. She held Jolie tightly and could not say a word. Finally when Jolie drew back, both women were dabbing at their eyes, and it was Jolie who saw something in Avis Warwick she had never seen before. And she knew that whatever the surgery was going to mean to Jolie, it was, for Avis Warwick, the first time she had ever shown love and concern for another.

CHAPTER NINETEEN

A MATTER OF FAITH

★　★　★　★

The large dining room of the Lanier home was filled as, one by one, the members of the family came down to dinner. Oliver Lanier sat at the head of the table, his massive form solid and strong, and his eyes moving over the room in which he had eaten so many meals. It was a dining room fit for a wealthy family, and he saw it as a tribute to the achievements he had forged over the years. The opulence of the room pleased Oliver, and now his eyes moved around the table as the servants put the food down. Alice, at his right hand, was wearing an attractive olive-colored dress that set off her smooth brown hair. As he gazed at her, as he had done in times past, Oliver was pleased at his choice of a wife. She was completely dedicated to him, he knew, and not given to strange fancies like so many wives. At the age of fifty-one, she still had traces of the beauty that had been hers when he had first seen her at eighteen. Her mild blue eyes were clear, her complexion was good, and her figure was still trim, despite bearing six children.

On his left Benjamin Lanier sat talking to Cara. Oliver was proud of Benjamin. His rich auburn hair and startlingly blue eyes gave him a more handsome appearance than he really had. He had pleasing features and a clear voice that could fill a room with song when the occasion warranted. As he studied Benjamin, Oliver thought, *It's well enough for him to want to serve the Lord, but as for being a minister, there are plenty of others who can do that! He can go far as a lawyer. Perhaps even into politics.*

Across from Benjamin, Cara turned just now to speak to Mary Ann, who was on her right. Mary Ann always dressed well, although she did not think as much about clothes as many young women did, which pleased Oliver. He admired her slender figure, smooth blond hair, and attractive light blue eyes. She looked tired, and he wondered what could have brought that on. As she suddenly turned to look at him, he was somewhat disconcerted to see a look of fear in her eyes. Oliver knew he was a strict man, but now as he saw the expression on his daughter's face, he felt disturbed and remembered Clinton's strong words.

He did not hold her glance long but turned to look at Bess, who had on a bright blue dress that highlighted her red hair and dark blue eyes. She was an emotional child, he knew, and just now was passing from adolescence into young womanhood. Unfortunately, she was having difficulty making that transition. Oliver could not remember his other daughters having this problem, and he resolved to be more patient with her.

Bobby, sitting next to Bess, was already putting away mashed potatoes at an alarming rate. He suddenly gouged Bess with his elbow, which caused her to cry out, and then he grinned broadly at her. "Pass the potatoes, please," he said, a light dancing in his eyes.

"You shouldn't treat your sister like that, Bobby," Oliver said.

"Like what?" Bobby said. "I just asked her to pass the potatoes."

Oliver met the gaze of his youngest son, who was daring him to mention the elbow in the ribs. But Cara spoke up at that instant, saying, "You must be more gentle with ladies, Bobby."

Bobby stared at Cara. "She ain't no lady! She's my sister!"

"And don't say *ain't*!" Cara scolded him.

"I don't see what's wrong with it. You know what I'm talking about, don't you?" Bobby grinned at her broadly. "As long as you know what I'm saying, what difference does it make?"

Almost everyone had given up trying to argue with Bobby, and now it was Benjamin who said, "Don't argue with him, Cara. You won't win. He'd argue with a signpost. He ought to make a good lawyer someday."

"I'm not going to be a lawyer. I'm going to be a fireman," Bobby announced.

"You can't be a fireman. You're too little," Bess said.

"Well, I'm not through growing yet. When I get through I'll be as big as Papa, won't I, Papa?"

"I hope not quite as heavy as I am. You couldn't climb a fire ladder if you were as big around as I am, son."

"But I'll be as tall one day. I'll be as tall as you, won't I, Benji?"

"There's more to being a fireman than being tall. They lead dangerous lives," Benjamin replied. He lifted the crystal goblet and drank the iced tea thirstily, and then inadvertently, his eyes went to the empty place at the other end of the table. This had always been Clinton's chair, and his absence created a certain awkwardness for this gathering.

Cara caught Benjamin's glance and knew exactly what he was thinking. All of them were careful not to speak of Clinton in their father's presence, but now the irrepressible Bobby looked straight at his father and piped up, "When is Clinton coming home, Papa?"

"I . . . couldn't say, son."

"Why did he have to leave anyhow? Are you mad at him?"

"What makes you ask that?" Oliver said. "You're always asking questions! Now, eat your food and be quiet!"

The rebuke seemed to fall upon the entire party, and it was Cara who, as always, tried to be the peacemaker. "Tell us about things at college, Benji."

"Same old thing. Books, books, books," Benjamin said moodily. "I'll be glad when I get out of that place."

"You ought to be enjoying it," Alice spoke up. She was proud of her son who was doing so well at college, and now she smiled fondly. "I'll be glad, though, when the term's over. We miss you here at home."

"Yes, we do," Bess piped up. "Now that Clinton's gone it gets—" She stopped suddenly, realizing she had broken an unspoken rule and looked fearfully at her father.

Once again Oliver saw the apprehension in Bess's eyes. He was very fond of his youngest daughter and did not like to see her bothered any more than he did Mary Ann, who found this awkward moment very uncomfortable and hurriedly began talking about Teddy Roosevelt's affairs. Oliver had met the president on three occasions and admired him tremendously.

"I hate to think what'll happen to the country after he's gone," Mary Ann said.

"Well, I suppose Taft will be President," Benjamin remarked idly.

"Yes, and he's a nobody. We'll never have a president like Theodore Roosevelt."

"Oh, I think we might," Cara said. She was not active in politics, but she followed political affairs in the papers. "It's my guess that he'll run again after Taft has a term. He loves being President and in the thick of things."

For some time the talk centered on Roosevelt, and then Cara excused herself and went back to her room. She was very tired, for she had not been sleeping well lately. Going into her room, she took off her good dress and put on an old one. Slipping into a smock, she picked up her palette and brush and threw herself into the painting that had become so important to her. For over an hour she worked and then stood back with dissatisfaction. "I just *can't* get it right!" she exclaimed. She stood there, irritated and frustrated with herself.

For some strange reason, she also felt angry toward Phil Winslow. She thought how easy her life had been before he had entered the scene. She had painted flowers and sold them quite successfully, and had received adulation from her family for her artistic gift. Now she seemed to be caught in a miasma of disturbing emotions she could not even define. The vague unhappiness that had gripped her when Phil had first spoken of living life and painting life as it was had grown until now it occupied her mind almost constantly. She could not seem to master the brush strokes to carry out what she wanted to do, and the resulting turmoil in her heart and mind made it even worse. For years she had kept her emotions under strict control, but now she felt as though they were slipping. There were times when a sense of futility would come over her and she would cry, usually in the silence of the night.

A knock at the door startled her, and she lifted her head, saying, "Come in," and then stepped away from the painting as her father came in. She reached down to get a cloth to cover it, but before she could, he was by her side, and she saw shock run across his face as he studied the painting.

"So this is what you've been doing," he murmured.

The instant displeasure in the tone of his voice made Cara dread to enter into a conversation with him. He was tremendously proud of her gift as an artist, and she knew that he would not like her new choice of subject, as most did not like the new school of painting.

"What is this, Cara?"

"Oh, it's just a young woman and her child that I saw once when I was down on the East Side."

"Not a very attractive subject."

"Well, I haven't done well with it."

"I should think not. It's not something I would think anyone wants to remember. It reminds me," he said, "of those pictures of the slums by that fellow. What's his name—Riis? Ugly things, and I don't know why anyone pays any attention to them."

"I think Mr. Riis took the pictures because he wanted to wake up the city to some of the evils of poverty."

"That's up to the politicians," Oliver said.

"And look what the politicians have done with it. The tenement houses are horrid, squalid places to live, and diseases are mounting all over, and nobody seems to care. People shouldn't have to live like that!"

"Oh, come now, Cara! That's putting it too strongly. Many people care."

"Well, Mr. Riis doesn't think so, and his photographs have done more to get legislation passed than all of the politicians put together."

Oliver was unaccustomed to having Cara stand up to him in matters about which they disagreed. He felt uncomfortable as she stood watching him and shifted his position, saying carefully, "I think you're wasting your time on things like this. You do so well with flowers."

"There are more things than flowers in the world, Father."

Startled, Oliver looked at her and saw that there was a lift to her chin and that her back was straight. "You feel very strongly about this, but, Cara, you've done so well with your career. Of course there are more things than flowers, but I always thought it was the job of the artist to present beautiful things to make people happy."

"So did I, but I've begun to change my mind."

Instantly Oliver knew where the trouble lay. "It's that fellow Winslow, isn't it? He's put these ideas into your head!"

Cara turned away from him and moved across the room to stand beside the window. It was dark outside now, and she could see only a few stars overhead. The streetlights were on, but their light was feeble and pale in the immense darkness. She did not answer her father as he came over and stood beside her. Turning, she said, "That woman and her child are part of God's world, Father. Did you imagine that they were not?"

"Why, Cara, what a thing to say!"

"Oh, I'm sorry," Cara said and shook her head. "I don't know why I'm so snappy tonight."

"Well, I just came up to say good night." He hesitated, then said, "I don't suppose you've heard from Clinton?"

"Of course I have. He writes almost every other day."

"He never writes to me."

Cara did not miss the petulant tone in her father's voice and was amazed. "Well, Father, why would he write to you? You made it clear enough you didn't want to hear from him again."

"Oh, come now, Cara. It wasn't that bad!"

"Yes it was, Father. You told him to get out and to stay out until he was ready to do everything you said."

Oliver Lanier had grown tough in the world of business, and that toughness had carried over into his family life. He was a hard man to hurt, but Cara's strong words did. He had treated his son as he would a competitor, intending to bring him to his senses, but to hear Cara speak so frankly was more painful than anything he had endured. "I just mean well for him, Cara. You certainly know I love my own son."

Cara hesitated, then put her hand on her father's arm. "I'm sure you do, but you need to learn to show it more."

"Does love have to be demonstrated? If it's there, it's there."

"I think it does need to be demonstrated. Even God wants to see it demonstrated."

"Why, what do you mean by that?" he asked, startled again at her boldness.

"I mean, God wants us to show our love for Him. That's what praise and worship is. It's saying that we love God, that we honor Him, that we are devoted to Him. It's not enough for Him that we do love Him. He wants it *said*."

"But that's a different thing altogether."

"No, it isn't. I can't say about men, but I know that women like to be told that they're admired, that they're loved. Mother would like to be told, I'm sure."

"Are you saying I've neglected your mother?"

"Why, you've given her everything she wants as far as a house, fashionable clothes, and the things that you can put your hands on. But a woman wants more than that," Cara said. She had not intended to get into such a personal discussion with her father, but it had suddenly exploded. Now she found herself saying things she had been thinking over the years but had never had the courage to say. "Mother's like every other woman. She needs those things for her spirit as much as her body needs food. I don't know why it is—it's just the way women are made. Men are different."

Oliver stood looking down at this daughter of his. He knew that Cara had a depth of character that he lacked. There was something in her that he had never been able to put his finger on. She was far more complex than his other children, and he had always assumed that it was because she was an invalid and had time to think more. Now that he was confronted with this side of her character, he was almost dumbfounded. "I . . . I wouldn't know how to start doing a thing like that. I'm not a poet."

"Father, you don't have to be a poet to say, 'Why, Alice, how pretty that dress looks on you.' "

"But does it really mean that much?"

"Try it and see," Cara challenged him. "Just tell her that her hair looks nice. Tell her that you appreciate the way she's done something, or the way she looks. It may not be much to you, but it would mean a world of difference to Mother."

"Well—" Oliver Lanier was not accustomed to being instructed, especially by his own family. He felt uncomfortable, yet somehow he knew that what Cara was telling him was the truth. "Well, I'll say good night." Turning, he saw the glass of ale on the table and quickly said, "You haven't drunk your ale yet."

"No, and I'm not going to." It was not what Cara intended to say, but somehow the conversation had given her new courage. She looked at her father. "That ale doesn't help me physically one bit. It's an idea that you had, and I know you did it for my good. But you may as well take it with you because I've drunk the last glass of it!"

"Why, Cara, I'm surprised at you!"

Cara moved closer to her father. She knew that deep down he loved her and the rest of his family, but she was also aware of the habit of command that had been formed in his youthful years, and now she said, "Father, be a little bit more gentle. It would mean more than you can imagine." She reached up, pulled his head down, kissed him, then whispered, "Good night, Father."

"Good night, daughter."

As Oliver left the room and headed down the hall, he realized that something had happened in his own house and in his own life. He had been proud of his accomplishments, proud of his family—but Cara's words had pierced him deeply. *Maybe I've been wrong. Maybe Cara is right.* He thought of the harsh way he had treated Clinton, but his stubborn pride rose up quickly to blot out those thoughts and any remorse for his actions. "He can come home when he acts like a reasonable man and not until," he muttered and stepped inside the bedroom door. He saw his wife preparing for bed, and the memory of Cara's words came back again. Cautiously he moved over to stand beside her. She was brushing her hair, which still had not one gray hair in it. Reaching out, he touched it, stroked it gently, and thought up a speech. "You know, Alice, your hair is as beautiful tonight as it was on our wedding night."

Alice Lanier dropped the brush. It fell to the carpet as she turned, her eyes wide with astonishment. She could not speak for a moment, and Oliver was shocked to see her eyes fill with tears. "Why there. It's nothing to cry about because I tell you your hair is pretty." But she rose and put her arms around him, and he could feel her sobbing. As he held her, he was shocked. *Well, I think Cara was right about some things, anyway. . . .*

★ ★ ★ ★

Easy Devlin marched up and down the waiting room, agitation pinching his face. "What's taking so long?" he demanded, stopping to stand in front of Peter Winslow. "I could've put a whole car together in this much time."

Looking up, Peter shifted on the uncomfortable straight-backed chairs that lined the wall of the waiting room and said, "I guess it's a little bit more delicate putting a young girl's face in shape than installing a new transmission."

"Why, I don't see why!" Easy said. "It looks to me like they could have made a whole new Jolie in this time."

"It's only been two hours. That's not long at all." Actually Peter did not feel this confident. He was tense but tried to keep a relaxed atmosphere for Easy, who had had a bad dream the night before. It seemed he had dreamed of a white horse, and that was supposed to be bad luck. Easy traversed the room twice more, then stopped.

"I sure wish that would have been a bay or a chestnut instead of a white horse I dreamed about."

"Oh, don't be silly, Easy! Dreams don't have anything to do with luck!"

"For an educated man you sure are dumb, Peter," Easy snorted. He would have said more, but at that moment the door opened and Dr. Leibnez stepped into the waiting room. Peter and Easy almost ran to meet him.

"How is she, Doc?" Peter asked.

"Why, she's fine!" Leibnez said, surprise on his face. He saw the tension of both men and smiled. "After all, it wasn't a life-threatening operation."

"Is she going to be all right? I mean, is the scar going to be gone?"

"Well, I hesitate to make predictions, but I think I may say the operation was very successful." Leibnez seemed to swell with assurance. He liked to help people, and now he said, "It may take one more rather minor surgery to remove the scar completely, but I think you'd have to look close to see it. Of course it'll have to heal up, and that will take some time."

"I shore was afraid of this one, because I dreamed of a white horse last night," Easy said, shaking his head.

A blank look came across Leibnez's face. "A white horse? What does that have to do with it?"

"Never mind, Doc," Peter said. "Just tell me one more time. Jolie's going to look great, isn't she?"

"Yes, she is. She has a very good complexion and she's young. I don't know why this wasn't done a long time ago, but I'm glad she finally had it done."

"Well, it's done now," Easy grinned. "Can we go in and see her?"

"She won't be awake for a while, but you can go sit beside her."

"Thanks, Doc," Easy said. As the doctor turned and walked out of the room, the two men followed him down the hall. Stepping inside the hospital room, they saw Jolie lying very still. A sheet was pulled over her and her black hair was concealed by some sort of cap. The left side of her face was covered with bandages, and she looked pale.

"She'll have to come in several times in the next week or two for a checkup, but I'm sure you'll see to that," Leibnez said. He looked at her and shook his head, "She's a very lovely woman, and this will make her complete."

After thanking the doctor, both men sat down and began the long vigil. Neither of them said anything, but from time to time their eyes met, and once Easy grinned and said, "Well, I'll have to eat my words about that Warwick woman. This is one good thing she's done—maybe the first. . . !"

★　★　★　★

At first all was darkness, a warm darkness to be sure, but somehow it was frightening. From far away she heard the sound of voices, and sometimes she knew that whoever was speaking was someone she knew very well. Finally the voices became clearer, and as she opened her eyes just a slit, she saw nothing but a blank whiteness. But then, opening them wider and turning her head to the right, she saw a face and at once whispered, "Peter—"

"Jolie!" Peter was beside her instantly. Jolie could see the tension in his face. "Well, it's about time you woke up," he said huskily, and he reached out and touched her right cheek.

Memory came back to Jolie then, and she said, "Have I been here long?"

"Not too long. Jolie, the doctor says you're going to be fine. This other cheek, why, I'll bet it'll be as smooth as this one." His fingers were light on her cheek, and she smiled at his touch. "Easy's just gone to get some coffee. He'll be back in a minute. I bet you're glad it's over."

"Yes, I am." She felt secure lying there with Peter standing over her. He looked so big, and the touch of his fingers on her cheek was reassuring. "I'm so sleepy."

"That's all right. We'll be taking you home soon, but until then you get all the rest you can."

"Will you be here?"

"I'm not going anywhere," he said as he took her hand and sat down beside her.

Reaching up with her free hand, Jolie touched the bandages and said, "It doesn't hurt at all."

"Dr. Leibnez said there would be some pain when the medicine wore off, but they'll give you something for that. You just rest easy. You're going to be fine."

Jolie lay there quietly, contented, and tried to think what it would be like to be without a scar. For most of her life she had tried to hide it, and she could not imagine being able to turn her face fully toward someone without thinking about how ugly she looked. Now she looked over at Peter, who smiled, and she whispered, "I'd like to be pretty, so that you would like me."

"Pretty doesn't have anything to do with it," Peter said quickly. He squeezed her hand and leaned forward so that his face was close to hers. "I'd care for you no matter what you looked like, Jolie. You know that."

The words pleased Jolie. She was getting drowsier, but the world looked different, and she felt warm and comforted. Soon she dropped off to sleep again.

★ ★ ★ ★

"Well, here she is, Avis," Peter said proudly. He had walked into the drawing room where Avis was sitting reading a magazine. He had brought Jolie home from the hospital, and now she stood beside him somewhat unsteadily. "The doctor says she's going to have the smoothest skin over that scar you could ever imagine."

Jolie went forward and stopped before Avis. "I can't thank you enough for making this possible. You don't know what it means to me."

"You two can get your talking done," Peter said. "I'll go make some tea."

As soon as he was gone, Jolie said, "Why did you do this for me, Avis? I know you're in love with Peter."

"Well, as much as I'm capable of loving anyone," Avis said.

She tried to make a joke of it, but something had happened to Avis, and Jolie could see it clearly. She pulled a chair up and said, "What's wrong? You look different."

"I guess while you were gone I came to myself. Something I had to learn to handle." She was wearing an off-white dress, and her hair was not fixed as neatly as Jolie might have done it. There was a worried expression on her face, too. Sighing heavily, she shook her head and said, "Somehow, Jolie, in the back of my mind I've always thought I'd walk again, but I've had to face up to it. I'll never get out of this chair."

Jolie hesitated only for an instant, then she said, "I know you don't believe in dreams and things like that, but all the time I was in the hospital, I didn't have anything to do but wait. I couldn't do anything, so I began to pray for you, and I want to tell you something. You're going to get out of that chair and walk again, Avis!"

Jolie's statement brought Avis's eyes open wide, and then she laughed shortly. "Well, that's pie in the sky—it can never happen."

"It can if you believe."

"How can I believe? I'm not even a Christian."

"Not everyone who got healed in the Bible was saved. Why, the man that was born blind in the book of John, Jesus healed him, and when they asked him about Jesus, he said, 'I don't even know who he is.' But later on Jesus came to him and identified himself. Then the man believed. But it was after he was healed. God loves us. He wants to do good things for us. Sometimes it doesn't happen, Avis, like we want it to, but I believe that God's given me a promise, and I want you to believe with me."

"I can't do that!"

"Well, I'll just believe without you, then. But it would help if you would join me."

"I don't know about all this faith business." Avis shook her head with discouragement. She had never been a woman of any spiritual depth, and now the idea of God healing her was far beyond her imagination or hopes.

Jolie began to speak rapidly. "Sometimes we have to act on what little faith we have. Jesus said if it's only as big as a grain of mustard seed, why, that's all we need."

"I don't even have that much."

"Yes, you do. God has dealt to every man a measure of faith. You know how much a measure is? Why, it's over a quart, and all you need is as much as a mustard seed." Jolie's eyes were shining as she continued to speak. "Let me tell you what happened at church a month ago. There's a lady there whose name is Mrs. Roberts. She has a wild, wayward boy named Jim. She had been praying for Jim for years. He's forty years old now, and God gave her a promise that he was going to be saved at a meeting. Well, she told people about it, and people told Jim about it. He went to his mother and told her, 'Why are you telling this crazy story? I'm not going to get saved at that meeting!' And his mother just said, 'Yes you are. God's promised me.'"

"Kind of put the bug on Jim, didn't it?"

"I don't know what it did to Jim, but when the meeting came and started, Jim wasn't there. Everybody was waiting for him, but he didn't show up. When the service was halfway over, he came stalking in. He looked angry. Later on he said he didn't know why he came. Well, he sat there, and Brother Camrose preached a great sermon, and you could almost see Jim falling under conviction. God began dealing with him, and he got saved. He came forward at the altar call and gave his heart to Jesus Christ, and it was wonderful."

Jolie leaned forward now and said, "And here's the part I want you to hear. There was going to be a baptismal service after the regular service, and Brother Camrose said, 'Well, Jim, if you had known this was going to happen, you could have brought some clothes to be baptized in. You could have been baptized with these other converts.'

"And Mrs. Roberts suddenly seemed to dive down under the seat. She came up with a brown paper sack and said, 'I've got his clothes right here.' Everybody was so excited. You see, Avis, she believed God so strongly that even though Jim was saying no, and people were telling her not to talk as she did, she believed God. She believed it enough to bring his clothes to be baptized in."

Avis sat listening to the story, then after a moment she said in a subdued voice, "That's a wonderful story. I wish I had that kind of faith, but I just don't."

Jolie Devorak leaned over and embraced Avis. "Then you'll just have to go on my faith until you get some of your own."

CHAPTER TWENTY

AN UNGUARDED MOMENT

★　★　★　★

Mrs. Mason came to the backyard and stared with distaste at the scene she saw. A racing car painted a brilliant crimson, so red that it almost hurt her eyes, was propped up on wooden blocks. From underneath it two pair of legs jutted out, one set short, the other long. Sniffing with distaste, Mrs. Mason walked over and stared down at them and addressed them caustically. "How much longer are you going to take up all this room in the backyard with that awful machine?"

All four legs twitched and then two men wormed themselves out from under the car. Both of them were covered with grease, and their clothes were filthy. Easy Devlin winked merrily at his landlady and said, "Now, Mrs. Mason, you shouldn't be talkin' about this car like that. It's going to win every race it runs in."

Mrs. Mason shook her head. "I couldn't be saying about that, but it takes up all the room out here. How much longer will it be?"

Uncoiling his lean six foot two inches and rising up slowly, Peter Winslow pulled a rag out of his hip pocket. He started to wipe his hands but then noted that the rag was perhaps even more covered with grease than his hands. Tossing it on the ground, he shrugged his shoulders, saying, "Well, let's see. This is July fifteenth. The big race is on the twenty-fourth. How long is that?"

"Too long!" Mrs. Mason snapped. "You don't leave much

space for the children of my other tenants to play!"

Peter gave her a winning smile. "Now, Hattie," he said, "you've got to be a little bit patient. One of these days you're going to be saying, 'Why, I knew Peter Winslow and Easy Devlin when they were just poor fellows starting out in the racing game. Now look at them. They're millionaires and everyone applauds when they enter a room.'" He moved over and picked up a clean cloth and wiped his hands, then taking Mrs. Mason's hand, he lifted it, kissed it, and said, "Now, Hattie, you wouldn't want to offend a couple of future millionaires, would you?"

Hattie Mason's face flushed. She was a heavyset woman of fifty, a widow, and was actually very fond of both Easy and Peter. She knew perfectly well that Peter was getting around her, but she could not resist him. "Well, all right. You don't need to act like a movie star."

"We'll take you out to see our first race," Peter said. "You'll enjoy it."

"I hate those nasty cars. Now, you give me a nice trotting horse race—not one of those where the jockey sits down right on the horse! I don't think that's decent—but a nice trotting horse, there's nothing like it." Being from Indiana, Hattie Mason still enjoyed keeping up with the Midwest's best racer, Dan Patch.

"You'll have to come and see us win, Mrs. Mason," Easy said.

"Well, we'll see. Now, it's time to come in for lunch."

"We'll be in as soon as we get cleaned up."

The two men went over and washed off the grease with gasoline and Easy remarked, with his nose wrinkled, "Gasoline sure does stink!"

"Would you want it to smell like perfume?"

"I'd smell a whole lot better than this. Cuts the grease, though. I'm going in and change clothes before we sit down to eat."

Peter remained outside, washing the worst of the grease off his hands and thinking about the race that was to come. He and Easy and Clinton had worked for hours on the car, and it had been good for all of them. Clinton Lanier had proved to be an able partner in all respects, and there was a freedom about him now that had been lacking when he had been living under his father's roof. Right now he was out looking for parts for their new car, the *Jolie Blonde II*, and Peter was expecting him back soon. The voice he heard and made him look up, however, was that of Jolie, who had come through the house and stepped outside.

"Mrs. Mason says for you to hurry up. You're going to miss lunch."

"All right." Peter began drying his hands off. He smiled when he turned and saw Jolie. She looked very fresh and pretty, wearing a new lavender dress trimmed with white lace and little daisy-shaped buttons. His eyes lingered for a moment on the bandage on her left cheek. It was a much smaller bandage now, for she had been back twice to see Dr. Leibnez, and when Peter had asked once how it was going, she had merely said, "It's all right. Dr. Leibnez is satisfied." Peter had been disappointed, for he had wanted instant results.

"How's Avis?"

"Well, it's strange. She's not any better physically, but she's *different* somehow."

Peter frowned, and Jolie could see the guilt that had plagued him since the accident reflected in his eyes. He said nothing, though, and finally Jolie expanded on her thought. "It's strange, Peter. She was always so lively and outgoing, and now she has long periods when she doesn't say anything."

"I know. I try my best to keep her encouraged, but I just don't seem to get through to her. I worry about her all the time, Jolie."

"I know you do, but it doesn't do any good. I've changed my mind about her since I've gone there. God's given me a great love for her that I didn't have at first."

Peter had finished cleaning his hands now and looked down at his old coveralls. "I've got to go change before lunch. Mrs. Mason would never let me sit down with a mess like this on." Still, he did not go but stood for a moment staring thoughtfully off into the blue sky. Something was on his mind, and he could not quite put it into words. "I can't imagine how it's going to turn out. I can't just walk away and leave her. It's my fault she's ended up in that wheelchair."

For a moment Jolie did not answer. She could sense the struggle going on in Peter's heart. He was not a hard young man to read, for his feelings were quickly reflected on his expressive face. Finally she said, "Well, God's going to do something. I'm believing that He'll heal Avis so that she can walk again."

Hope leaped into Peter's eyes and his face lightened. "I've been praying for that, too. Have you told her?"

"Yes. She doesn't believe, of course, but I've told her she'll just have to go on my faith until she has some of her own."

The situation with Avis Warwick was unlike anything Peter had ever known. Up until now, he had not really been responsible to anyone. But suddenly this tragedy had been placed upon him. It was a heavy burden for the young man. Finally he shook his head and started up the steps, saying, "I just don't know how it's going to come out, Jolie—but I know I can't leave her."

Jolie bit her lip as she watched Peter move slowly up the back steps, as though he carried a very heavy burden. *He'll do what he thinks is right*, she thought. *He's just that kind of man.*

★　★　★　★

A few people moved about the interior of the gallery, and George Maxim looked up from time to time from the book he was reading to watch them. He had learned to judge customers very well and did not see anyone who looked like a hot prospect. His eyes kept going back to a small man, rather nondescript, and he said aloud, "That fellow likes to look—but he'll never buy anything."

Phil Winslow, who sat across from Maxim, cautiously sipping a cup of Maxim's scalding hot coffee, followed his friend's look across the cluttered room. "You mean that little fellow over there?" The object of their interest seemed incredibly average: somewhere between forty and sixty years of age; medium light brown hair; a bland, though somewhat sharp-featured, face; rather plain and utterly ordinary clothes, indicating neither riches nor poverty. "Do you know him, George?"

"He's been in several times. Never buys anything, though. Just looks. Lots of people like him. You can't stop people from looking."

Phil's brow suddenly furrowed. He slowly took a couple more sips of coffee, then shook his head. "I'm cluttering up your gallery with my junk. Nobody's ever going to buy any."

"You never know about that. Don't worry about it."

"Well, ever since the big show of The Eight, I've been expecting a rush of interest, but it hasn't come." He spoke of the show that had caught the attention of New York. "The Eight" was the Ashcan School of Artists, including George Luks and others of his persuasion. It had been widely covered by the media, not just in New York but nationwide. Most of the publicity had been unfavorable, and Phil had grown more discouraged.

"If fellows like George Luks can't sell their paintings, how can I ever hope to?"

Maxim leaned back and put his book down. He removed his steel-rimmed glasses, rubbed his eyes, and then stretched hugely. "You can't ever tell, Phil. Art is a funny business. A lot of artists don't get any recognition at all while they're alive. They have to die first."

"That's a cheerful thought!"

"But not everybody's like that. Remember that when new artists went in for realism about fifty or sixty years ago, lots of people had a fit about it, but they wound up changing the art world. Why, even when the first big impressionists started a few years later, the art establishment was pretty rejecting. But in time . . . why, if I could just get ahold of a few of old Monet's canvases, I could get rich selling them."

"Maybe I'd better start trying to paint like that."

"No, that's not your style," Maxim said quickly. He pulled at his beard and his blue eyes were thoughtful as he studied his friend. He had been concerned about Phil Winslow, for, indeed, his young friend had almost given up hope of ever making it as an artist. No painter Maxim had ever known worked harder than this young man, and he had real talent. *He's a fine painter.* Aloud he said, "Art is like a tide. Sometimes it goes out on certain kinds of painting, and then when the tide comes in, the public can't seem to get enough of it."

"Well, I'm about ready for the tide to come in." Phil suddenly sat up straighter and moved his hand across his face in a gesture of futility. "I'm about ready to give it up. I feel like a bum, George. If I don't sell something pretty quick, I'm going to go home and at least help on the ranch. I've let my family do all the work and support me, and here I am twenty-eight years old and still not making a living."

Maxim immediately said, "Don't do that! Once you quit you'll never start again. I've seen it happen before."

Phil listened appreciatively to the man's words of advice and encouragement. He was as discouraged as he had ever been in his life, but still he did not want to give up. Somewhere deep down he was sure that he could succeed as an artist, but artists had to eat, and it greatly bothered him that he was still living off his father.

The pair sat there talking quietly, Maxim trying to encourage

Phil, when suddenly a voice asked, "Who painted this?"

Phil looked up quickly and saw that the nondescript man had come to stand beside them. He was pointing at a picture, and Phil said at once, "I did."

"Indeed?" The stranger did not give his name but put a pair of mild blue eyes on Phil. "Very interesting. Have you been painting long?"

"Not as long as I should have," Phil said.

"Where have you studied?"

"I spent a few years in England, went to Spain, and to France. I've just come back recently. My name's Phil Winslow."

"My name's Smith."

"Glad to know you, Mr. Smith." Phil stood up and said, "Are you interested in the painting?"

"Tell me about it."

Rather put off by Smith's curt manner, Phil shrugged. Maxim had already told him the man looked a lot and never bought anything. Nevertheless, he had nothing else to do. The painting Smith was looking at was one he had worked hard on. It was a simple enough scene. He had been in a Chinese restaurant, and as he ate his meal, he noticed a couple who had come in to dine. They were obviously of the upper class, and the woman was ornately dressed, with a great deal of white lace on the front of her dress and an enormous plume in her black hat. A mangy calico cat had somehow wandered into the restaurant and was now seated on the parquet floor. The woman was leaning over to give him a morsel of her food. At a table beside them, two men were looking over and smiling.

It was an ordinary scene, not earthshaking by any means, but the colors of the woman's dress, the patterned wood floor, the calico cat, and the light streaming in through the two windows behind the couple had seemed extraordinary to Phil. It was mostly a dark painting with muted colors, but he was pleased with it, for he had caught the scene almost as if it were photographed—except better. Phil always thought paintings were better than photographs, and now as he explained how he had come to paint it, the man stared first at the painting and then at him.

Finally, when Phil finished, Smith said, "What about the rest of these?" He pointed quickly at Phil's other paintings, and Phil was pleased to see that he had some taste. *At least he knows which ones are mine and which ones aren't.* Rising to his feet he walked around with the small man and explained the paintings. Soon he found himself giving his life story, which surprised him. Smith was not a man he would have chosen for a confidant, but now he was telling about his days as a cowboy, about his family, and finally he shook his head and gave a half laugh. "I never talked so much in all my life, Mr. Smith. Sorry to be such a blabbermouth."

Smith had said nothing but continued to stare at the last painting. Then he turned and studied Phil carefully. Phil expected him to speak, but he only nodded curtly, turned, and left the studio.

Maxim, who had taken all this in, exploded. "Well, he not only wants to come and look for nothing, he wants a free lecture!"

"Funny sort of chap," Phil said. He was disappointed, half expecting that the man would at least make an offer on a painting, but he was accustomed to curious people who could not understand what he was attempting to do with his painting. "I don't blame him much." He looked at the painting of the woman feeding the cat, and said, "I'd trade you right now for a good suit of clothes."

"Who was it who said, 'Don't give up the ship'? Well, that's what I'm telling you, my friend. Never give up."

Phil reached over and clapped George Maxim on the shoulder. "If everybody in the world were as nice a guy as you, Max, it would be a good world," he said softly, then turned and left the studio.

Phil's shoulders, Maxim saw, were drooping, and the excitement that had always been part of his personality had gone. "Poor fellow. He's not going to make it unless something happens pretty soon."

★　★　★　★

As soon as Peter entered the library, Avis Warwick knew something was different. Usually he came in with the express purpose of cheering her up. She knew that, and more than once had said, "You don't have to entertain me, Peter." Now, however, there was a determined look in his eye, and his chin was lifted high. He had the look of a man who had decided to perform a chore, no matter how difficult it was going to be.

"Hello, Peter. Sit down." Avis waited until he was seated, then began to talk of the latest Dickens book they had been reading. She could tell that he was only waiting to tell her something, and finally she put the book aside and asked, "What's the matter? Trouble with the car?"

"No. It's not that. The car's going very well." Peter had been apprehensive when he had first told Avis that he had gotten another car and intended to race again soon. He was afraid that the mention of racing would bring back the bitterness that had overwhelmed Avis after the accident. He was fairly certain it had bothered her some when he had told her, but she handled it better than he expected, and then she had actually shown some interest. Right now, though, he could see that she was simply aware of his tension.

"Avis, I want to talk to you."

Avis waited, and then when he hesitated, she said, "Well, if it's not the car, what is it? Something's wrong with you."

"Avis, I want you to marry me."

For a moment Avis could not believe she had heard correctly. She had put thoughts of a normal life out of her mind, and now as she stared at Peter, whose face was set and fixed, she could not for the life of her come up with a suitable reply.

Finally he said, "Did you hear me, Avis? I want you to marry me. I care for you very much."

"Peter—" For a moment Avis could not frame the words, and then she said, "I could never marry you. You need a young woman who . . . one who can be a proper wife to you."

"You're a young woman," Peter said. He had made a speech up in his mind and had risen with determination. He had wrecked her life, and now he felt it was essential to do all he could to make amends. He began to speak quickly. "In the first place, I believe you're going to be healed someday. You may not believe that, but I do and Jolie does."

"I know. She's always telling me that God's promised her I'm going to be healed—but I can't quite believe that."

"Well, I believe it and she believes it."

"That's not all there is to it, Peter, even if I *were* able to walk again. If God were to do this miracle—which I can't quite make myself accept—I still couldn't be a proper wife to you. We're too different."

"I don't think that's always bad. Two people that are just alike, Avis, would make a very boring marriage." He reached over, took her hand, and said, "I know we're different. I think you need God in your life, and I think I could help you with that."

For a long time Avis struggled against Peter's request for marriage. In truth she knew he did not love her as a man should love a wife. And she did not feel that, as a paralytic, she could give him the love a husband needed. Still, he continued to plead his case ardently, until she finally said, "Peter, it would be good for me and bad for you."

He suddenly leaned over and took her in his arms. Kneeling beside the wheelchair, he kissed her and said, "We'll have a good life."

Avis was more moved than she had ever been in her life. She had been aware that Peter felt responsible for her accident. She also knew he was asking her this out of a sense of guilt, but still, with his arms around her, she felt a security she had never expected to have. She put her arms around him and held him tightly, and in her heart she was saying, *He doesn't love me and I don't love him as a woman should love a man, but I have money. He could have anything he wants. He could buy any race car he wants. I'll help him.* She pushed him back gently and said, "Is this what you truly want, Peter?"

"Yes, it's what I want."

"Then let's begin honestly. You don't really love me, and I don't think I've ever been able to love a man as a woman should, but we do have something. And I promise you this. I have more money than I could ever spend. You can go to the very top in your profession. You won't have to try to put a junk car together. You can have the very best, and I'll help you do it, Peter."

Peter knew exactly what he was doing. He had weighed all these things in the balance, and he knew what Avis said was true. They did not love each other with a grand passion. Nevertheless, the accident had made him responsible for her, and he could only fulfill that responsibility if they were married. What she said about money meant nothing to him, but he did not say this to her. It was all she had to give, and he whispered, "We'll make a great team, Avis," and he kissed her again.

★　★　★　★

"Look at all those stars, Peter. Aren't they glorious?"

Jolie waved her hand up toward the sky at the brilliance of the night's display. Against the black curtain above, millions of tiny diamond-hard points of light glittered. It was as if the sky were alive, and the stars seemed close enough to reach up and touch.

Glancing up, Peter answered, "Yes, I read the Scripture the other night that God named all the stars—or did I read that in some book?"

Peter had come to have supper with Avis, and afterward they had talked for a long time. Avis had gone to bed early, and Jolie had been surprised to find Peter still there. He had asked her out for a walk, and now, as they strolled along Seventeenth Street, the air felt pleasantly cool after the July heat that had blanketed New York all day.

Jolie noticed that Peter was more thoughtful than usual. She knew him very well, and when such silences came on him, she was sure he was trying to frame some important thought in the right words before he spoke. She did not rush him but walked quietly along beside him until he was ready.

"Jolie . . ." He hesitated, then stopped and turned her around. "I've got something to tell you."

"What is it, Peter?"

"I've asked Avis to marry me."

A shock ran through Jolie, for although she had considered this a possibility, it had been far from her mind tonight. She could only say, "Have you, Peter?"

"Yes." He began to speak quickly, telling her of how it would be, and when he was through he said almost in desperation, "I've got to do it. I owe it to her."

Jolie Devorak put away her dreams. "All right, Peter," she said, "if that's what you must do, then you must do it." The two turned and walked back, and both felt they had lost something important—something that could never be found again.

CHAPTER TWENTY-ONE

THE CHOICE

★　★　★　★

"Good afternoon, Mr. Lanier."

"Good day, Edward. I'll see you in the morning."

Oliver Lanier took his hat off of the shelf, settled it firmly on his head, then picked up his walking stick. He had been having some sort of knee trouble, which his wife called rheumatism and which he called nonsense. Nevertheless, it had grown so severe that he had bought the walking stick and now leaned on it heavily. As he left the building and waved over a passing hansom cab, he was thinking of how age crept up on a man. Giving his home address, he settled himself into the cab and gave a disdainful look at the automobiles that were beginning to replace many of the horse-drawn vehicles. He hated them, but being an astute man, he knew now that the future lay with them and not with the horse.

Something soothing in the sound of the horses' hooves as the hansom moved along the street caused him to take off his hat and place it on the seat beside him. Leaning back, he clasped his hands together and tried to put the pain of his knee out of his mind. *It's no fun growing old*, he thought. *Nothing but aches and pains, and nothing to look forward to.* Such a thought was new to Oliver Lanier, for he had been a man of such driving ambition that he had no time to think of old age. In recent months he suddenly had become aware that those days were now upon him. This realization had come to him with a rush one morning when he was shaving. He had stared at his white hair and streaked beard in the mirror, startled, yet knowing they had not grown white overnight. Since that morning he had been thinking about his life.

Now he thought of the office he had just left and felt distressed. Until Clinton had walked out, he had not realized how much he depended on him. He also had not realized how much life his son put into the business and what an integral part he played in its day-to-day operations. It was not a humorous sort of business at best, and Clinton, despite the fact that he did not care greatly for it, had brought some humor and youthful vigor into everyday affairs. Oliver had sniffed at this, but the employees had said more than once in his hearing, "The place isn't the same since Clinton left. No fun at all anymore."

The whole incident of Clinton's leaving grieved him, and as he had so often done to console himself, Oliver thought back to the days when he and Clinton had gone places together, when he had been in the first delights of his successful business career. Back then he had enjoyed taking his young children out, enjoying time together. He suddenly recalled when he had taken them to see a vaudeville performance. Clinton was no more than eight years old. The acrobats, the jugglers, and the singers had all delighted the boy. Then he thought again of the circus that Clinton had so enjoyed. "Why didn't I take him back?" Oliver murmured, then shook his head. "Too late for that now," he said gloomily.

Then he found himself thinking of Mary Ann and her determination to marry George Camrose. *Here I'm right*, he thought. *It would be terrible for her to languish away in some obscure African village.* Still, he had seen her determination. And that made him think of Cara, about whom he was most concerned. He thought he understood Cara, but now he was slowly discovering that his judgment was not as sound as he had supposed.

Lanier was startled when the carriage stopped and he looked up to see he was in front of his home. Getting out, he balanced on the cane and his good leg while he fished for the money to pay the driver. Handing it up, he nodded briefly at the driver's thanks and then moved painfully up the walk and climbed the steps. Stepping inside, he was greeted by Alice, who said with concern, "You're having more trouble with your knee, aren't you, Oliver?"

"It will pass."

"Come in and sit down. I think we ought to have Doctor McKenzie in to take a look at it."

"He can't make a new knee," Lanier said, but he followed her into the larger of the two parlors. He sank down with relief into a Morris chair, and Alice moved a hassock over and helped him to stretch his leg out. She fussed over him, bringing him a cup of tea, and insisting all the time that the doctor be called to examine his knee.

"Oliver, I've got to talk to you about something you may not like," she said finally. She pulled up a chair and sat down across from him, leaning forward and lacing her fingers together over her knees. As she took a deep breath, she looked anxious but determined. "It's about Bess's birthday party."

"I thought you had already made all the plans for that. It's tomorrow night, right?"

"Yes, but I've got to tell you one thing about the guests." She hesitated, then held herself straighter. "I'm going to insist on having Clinton—*and* George Camrose."

Shocked by her bold announcement, Oliver shook his head. "No, I don't think so. It would be bad for Mary Ann to be exposed to that young man, and as for Clinton, he knows he can come home anytime he pleases. All he has to do is agree to my terms."

Alice Lanier stared at her husband for a moment, then said quietly, "Oliver, Clinton and George are coming to the party, whatever you say. You're welcome to come, and I hope you will, but it wouldn't be fair to exclude Clinton. He's been at every birthday party Bess has ever had. You know how close they are. So, I'm sorry I have to speak to you like this, but that's the way it's going to be."

Blank astonishment filled Oliver's face, and he stared at his wife as if she had announced that she was going to move to India. "Why, Alice, I've never heard you speak like this!"

"I had hoped that I would never have to contradict you, but you're wrong about Clinton, and you're also terribly wrong about Mary Ann and George. I hope you'll change your mind, but if you don't, it will just have to be my way this time." Alice rose, gave her husband a last firm look, then turned without a word and walked out of the room. Oliver stared after her, absolutely amazed and at a loss for words.

★　★　★　★

"No point arguing about it, Clinton, you're going to the

party!" George Camrose had appeared at Mrs. Mason's boarding-house just after Clinton had returned from work. Camrose stood in the middle of the floor with a determined light in his eye. Clinton had said he did not feel free to go to his home since he and his father had had an altercation, but Camrose had stood his ground. "You can argue all you want to, Clinton, but you're going to that party. I know you and your father are upset with each other, but your mother sent word to me that I was to bring you, and I suppose you got a note, too."

"Yes, I did, but I just didn't think it would be right. After all, Father's forbidden me to come home until I agree to his terms. And I can't."

"Well, your mother hasn't forbidden you to come home. Besides, it's important for Bess, so get dressed. We're going."

Clinton tried to resist, but he finally just had to laugh. "I never knew a preacher could be so pesky. All right. Let me change and I'll go." Quickly he put on a light brown suit and slipped his feet into a pair of brown high-topped shoes and laced them up. As he did so, he noticed his fingernails. "Look at this. I couldn't get them clean no matter how hard I tried."

Camrose stared at the fingernails that were broken and had grease under them and grinned. "First time you ever got your hands dirty, but I don't think you're sorry, are you?"

"No, I'm not. Not about leaving home, at least. I'm sorry Father and I see things differently." He rose and the two left the house. They arrived just before seven. Bess was almost beside herself. When Clinton walked in, she threw herself into his arms, and he spun her around, saying, "Happy Birthday!"

"Did you bring me a present?"

"What makes you think that?"

"You always give me a nice present on my birthday. What is it, Clinton?"

"You can open it with the rest of your presents. Come along."

"All right, come on. Everybody's already in the dining room. We're going to open my presents in the parlor after dinner."

Clinton gave George a despairing look, then shrugged. Camrose came closer as they moved toward the dining room, saying, "It'll be all right. Don't worry."

When they entered the room, George immediately headed toward Mary Ann, who came to meet him halfway. "I'm so glad you brought him," Mary Ann whispered. "Mother was afraid you wouldn't be able to persuade him."

"He's a stubborn fellow, but I'm worse. You'll find out about that soon enough."

Everyone watched then as Clinton stood still, turning his glance toward his father. Oliver was seated at the table, his cane beside his chair. He had said almost nothing, and everyone was wondering exactly how he would greet Clinton. Mary Ann had said to her mother, "Father's never changed his mind that I know of. I think he'll give Clinton a hard time."

Alice had said with determination, "No, I don't think so. Not this time."

As for Oliver, he felt the weight of all eyes in the room on him. His gaze shifted to meet those of his wife, who was sitting at his right hand. She smiled at him and put her hand on his, saying nothing, but he knew what was on her heart. Looking up, he said, "Come in, Clinton, and you, too, Reverend Camrose. We've been waiting for you."

A great relief rushed through Clinton. He had half expected to be ordered out of the house, but to his surprise, he sensed something different in his father. He went forward at once and put his hand out, saying, "Thank you, Father. It's good to see you."

"Why . . . it's good to see you, too, Clinton." There was a moment's hesitation, and he said, "It's very good."

A great relief seemed to settle in the room as Clinton looked at his mother, who gave him a smile. They were soon seated and talking in a more relaxed manner than ever before. The party went on with great success. The dinner was excellent, as always, consisting of a rack of lamb with mint sauce, parslied potatoes, buttered peas, fresh baked bread, and salad. After a maid had removed the dinner dishes, a large cake with pink icing and white candles was ceremoniously carried in, along with homemade ice cream for a real birthday treat. Everyone clapped when Bess blew out every candle with one tremendous puff and then, relaxed and enjoying their Bess's special night, waited to be served their desserts.

After dinner was over, everyone moved to the parlor for the opening of presents. Bess, of course, received a great many. As everyone was finding a seat, she leaned over to her mother and whispered, "I've never seen Clinton look so well."

"No, I haven't either. I think he was very worried about what his father would say. But your father did well, didn't he?"

"Yes, he did. I'm going to tell him so later."

Clinton at first was constrained, but after the presents were opened he found himself in the parlor with his father, George Camrose, and Benjamin. The four men were very different, but it was finally Benjamin who opened the subject of Africa, and George spoke glowingly of his plans to go.

Oliver Lanier listened silently. He was, in truth, confused by what was happening in his life. He was surprised to find out how very glad he was to see Clinton, and as he listened to George, his thoughts about him began to change. Until then, he had never really listened to George speak about his missionary goals. Suddenly, a new thought came to him, as he realized how he had misjudged the young preacher. *What a fine young man he is.*

Finally George and Benjamin rose and left the room to join the others, and when Clinton stood, Oliver said with some effort, "I've got to tell you, son, how much I've missed you at the office."

"Well, that's nice of you to say, sir. I've missed you, too, but I've been very excited about the work I'm doing now."

"It means a lot to you. I didn't realize how much."

"When you were a younger man, did you want to be a stockbroker?"

"I just wanted to be a success. I didn't care what kind of work I did. I could have been as happy in something else, I suppose. Those were hard times, Clinton. I had a growing young family, I wanted to provide the best for them."

"You did a fine job, Father. You had a fine career."

It was a rare compliment from Clinton, and Oliver said, "I've been doing some serious thinking about our family lately." He hesitated, then said, "I think a lot about when all of you were younger. I was so busy I neglected you. I know that now. I wish—" He paused for a moment, then dropped his head. "I wish I had spent more time with all of you when you were younger. That was my mistake."

Clinton was astonished at his father's admission, and the wall that was between them began to crumble. *His family is breaking apart. He's having difficulty with all of us, and he doesn't know how to handle it.* Aloud he said, "It's not too late. We can still do things together."

Oliver Lanier looked up quickly. "You mean that, Clinton?"

"Why, of course. Maybe we could go take in a baseball game."

"Baseball? I don't know anything about baseball."

"I don't know much, but it's a start. How about it?"

Oliver had always ridiculed those who wasted their time at sports, but suddenly he found himself saying, "All right. I'll feel like a fool at a thing like that, but we'll try it." He saw the warm light in his son's eyes and then said, "Maybe we can find a circus to go to, like we did once before."

"I'd like that very much," Clinton replied and suddenly reached over and touched his father's shoulder. "We'll do it."

The evening was almost over and the younger children had gone to bed, when Oliver stood beside Alice as Clinton and George were leaving. He was surprised when George stopped to say, "Mr. Lanier, Mary Ann and I need to talk to you and your wife."

Instantly Oliver knew what the younger man's intentions were. He glanced at Alice, who was staring at him with a strange expression in her eyes. *She knows too*, he thought. "All right," he said. "Come back to the parlor." He hobbled back, leaning heavily on his cane, for his knee seemed to have gotten worse. When they reached the large room, he did not sit down but watched Mary Ann and George as they came to stand before him. Mary Ann's face was pale and her lips were drawn into a tight line as tension seemed to flow through her.

"I won't take long, sir," George said. "I know that what I have to say won't please you, but it must be said."

Alice stepped over and took Oliver's arm. She said nothing but squeezed it. When he looked at her he could see the pleading look in her eyes. "Go ahead, George," he said. "I think I can guess what it is."

"You probably can. I love Mary Ann and she loves me. Both of us believe that God has called us to the African field to preach the Word of God. I know this is not what you want for your daughter, but I'm asking your permission for Mary Ann to join me."

"And what if I don't give it?" Oliver said.

It was Mary Ann who spoke up quickly. "Father, I hate to be put in this position. I've always honored you and tried to obey you, but God has called me to be George's wife and to serve with him in Africa." Her lips trembled, and she whispered, "I must obey God."

Oliver stood there and knew that his life could never be the same again. He looked into the clear eyes of the two young people and thought, *Why, I've never seen such love and such dedication. They love each other, and they love God.* He felt Alice tugging at his arm and turned to her.

"Oliver, do you remember when we were young and you asked my father for permission for us to marry?"

"I do remember. I was scared stiff."

"He didn't want me to marry you, Oliver."

"I remember that, too. But your mother stood with us, didn't she? I've never forgotten that. I always loved her for it. I still do."

"This is a good thing. I hope you and I together can give George and Mary Ann our blessing. I give them mine, and I hope you will, too."

His wife's words touched Oliver greatly. He realized that at his age he might not be around much longer to make decisions for Mary Ann. And as he looked at the young man, so handsome and full of love for God and love for his daughter, he knew he had no choice.

"Be good to her, George," he said simply.

At his words Mary Ann let out a cry and ran to throw her arms around her father. His cane fell to the floor as he put his arms around her and felt her body shaking. "There, there," he said. "It's all right."

George came forward, his eyes moist, and said, "I hardly expected this, sir, but I promise you I'll always love her and take care of her the best I can."

★   ★   ★   ★

"Have you heard the news?" Jolie said, coming in as the morning sunlight streamed through the window. She came over to stand beside Avis's bed, and her eyes were filled with delight.

"It must be good news," Avis said. She struggled to an upright position and pushed futilely at her hair. "What is it?"

"A miracle, I think. You know how Mr. Lanier's been adamant against George Camrose marrying Mary Ann? Well, he gave his permission last night. I just heard the news."

"From what I've heard about Oliver Lanier, that *is* a miracle," Avis said. She sat there looking at the young woman so filled with excitement and smiled at her. "You want to hear about another miracle?"

"Yes, I'm always ready for a miracle."

"Pull your chair over and sit down beside me."

Obediently Jolie got her chair and then sat down. "What is it, Avis?"

Avis looked down at her hands for a moment, then she looked up, her eyes filled with tears. "I've always heard you talk about God speaking, and I didn't believe it. But last night I think God spoke to me."

"Oh, Avis, that's wonderful!"

"I didn't hear a voice or anything like that. I was lying there thinking about my life, and mostly thinking about what you told me about Jesus. The more I thought about Jesus, the more awake I became. And then," Avis said with a voice of wonder, "something came into my heart. It was as if a silent voice said, 'I love you, Avis, and I want you for my own.' It could only have been the Lord. I've never had anything like that happen to me."

"What did you do?" Jolie said breathlessly.

"I suddenly thought of all of the Scripture that you had read to me and one verse I've never been able to understand. It was what Jesus said, 'He that cometh to me I will in no wise cast out.' I thought about that verse a lot." Avis hesitated, then said. "I was so tired and I've been so afraid. Peter's been a great help, and you've been a gift from heaven, I think. The way I've lived my life stretched out before me. I felt so hopeless, and that verse kept coming. 'He that cometh to me I will in no wise cast out,' and then I did something I never thought I'd do. I called out aloud, 'Jesus, I need you. Please help me.' "

Jolie sat there as Avis described her experience, and finally she asked, "What happened then, Avis?"

"I don't know exactly, except that it was like a quietness coming over a noisy room. My life had been so cluttered up with so many voices, and so many things happening, and so many fears, and of course I never made any secret of my life. I've always been a sinful woman, and I began saying, 'I'm a sinful person, and I can't change myself. But I ask you, Jesus, to take me and change me. I didn't know how to pray, but I did the best I could, and Jolie—something happened.' I began to weep, and something came into my heart that I've never known. You might call it peace, but after a while I waited for the worry and the fears to come back, but they didn't!"

Jolie suddenly threw her arms around Avis and wept, saying, "I'm so glad for you, Avis."

Avis was weeping, too, but when Jolie moved back, she said, "Here's the miracle of it all. I determined I'd never make a bargain with God. Like, 'If you'll heal me I'll serve you,' and I didn't. So here's what I told the Lord last night. 'I'll love you and give you my heart whether you ever heal me or not.' "

Jolie stared at Avis and whispered, "God must be very pleased with that. He wants us to love Him for himself, not for what He does for us—but I'll tell you one thing," she added with determination, "I'm still believing that I got a promise from God, and now that you're His child, I'm going to pray even harder that one day you'll get out of that chair and walk for the glory of God!"

CHAPTER TWENTY-TWO

THREE SURPRISES

★ ★ ★ ★

"Hey, this note just came for you, Peter!"

Easy had come to Peter, who was bending over the engine of the *Jolie Blonde II*, and grinned as he handed the note over. "You've tinkered with the car enough. It's as ready as it'll ever be. Now, let me load it on the trailer. We'll either win or we won't, and I think we will. Anyhow, I got my rabbit's foot all ready." He fished into his pocket and held it up and stared at it. "Come on, baby, you got to win us that race."

Peter grinned as he opened the note. "I don't see how in the world you think the foot of a dead rabbit has anything to do with whether we win a race or not. We'll win if we've got a good car, if we've got it tuned up right, and if we drive like a winner."

Easy shook his head in disgust. "You've been too educated. Your head's full of notions. Them things are bad for a feller."

Peter ran his eyes over the note and said, "I've got to go by and see Avis. You take the car on out to the track. I'll be there in time for the start."

"If you don't, I'll drive her myself," he warned.

"Don't worry. I wouldn't miss this day, and neither would Clinton. It's okay with you about him riding with me?"

"Sure, that boy's earned it. We wouldn't have any car if it wasn't for him. Besides, he's the second best mechanic in the United States." He winked merrily and said, "You go on now. I'll try to undo any damage you've done here to the *Jolie Blonde II*."

Peter tossed his oily rag at Easy's face, who caught it deftly. Then Peter turned and walked into the house. He passed Mrs. Mason on the way in. "Well, it's the big day, Hattie. I'm going to expect you to be there to watch me win."

"I hope you will, Peter," Hattie Mason responded. "And I was only teasing you about keeping the car in the backyard. You can keep it there as long as you please."

"If we win this race, I'll have enough money to rent a garage, so don't worry about it."

Quickly he went into his room, cleaned up, and dressed, putting on the clothes he planned to wear for the race. There were no uniforms for the drivers, but he wanted to look his best and chose a pair of dark blue trousers and a snow white shirt with the words *Jolie Blonde* embroidered carefully by Jolie herself over the right front pocket. He smoothed his hair down and pulled on a soft dark blue cloth cap and then grinned at his image in the mirror. "Here we go! I'm gonna look like a winner whether I am or not."

Leaving the house, he took a cab and directed the driver to Avis's address. When he reached her house, he went in and hurried down the hall and knocked on her bedroom door.

Avis said, "Come in, Peter."

Opening the door, he pulled his cap off and asked, "How did you know it was me?"

"I saw you out the window." Avis smiled and said, "You look beautiful. Like a movie star."

"Don't tell me that." Coming over, he leaned over and kissed her on the cheek. "How do you feel?"

"Fine. How do *you* feel? Are you nervous?"

"To be truthful, I am, but don't tell anybody. I'm trying to put up a good front."

Avis smiled and gestured to a chair. "Sit down. You have a minute, don't you?"

"Oh sure," Peter assured her. "Easy and Clinton are taking the car to the track. The race doesn't start till two o'clock, so I've got plenty of time."

"It means a great deal to you to win this race, doesn't it, Peter?"

"Well, yes, it does. It's what I've been looking forward to for a long time."

Avis listened as Peter continued to talk about the race. She saw the excitement in his eyes and was glad for him. Finally she said,

"I've got something to tell you, Peter. I've really got three surprises for you."

"Well, I hope they're good ones."

"I'll let you decide."

"What are they?"

"Surprise number one," Avis said. "We're not going to get married."

Peter stared at her and blinked with surprise. "But, Avis—"

Avis held up her hand. "It was the most generous thing I ever heard of, Peter, your offering to tie yourself to a crippled woman for the rest of your life. I know what you think about marriage. It's forever—in this world, anyway."

"That's right, Avis, and I want to marry you."

"No, you don't," Avis contradicted him. As she studied him carefully, there was peace in her green eyes. Now she said quietly, "You wanted to make up for being responsible for the accident. But you weren't responsible for it, and you might as well get that out of your head. Don't argue," she said, holding up her hand as he attempted to speak. "I'm thinking some pretty deep thoughts these days, learning how to follow the Lord, and I've been reading the Bible with Jolie's help. I've been asking a lot of questions, too. Brother Camrose has been by several times, and I've asked him some hard ones. One of the things I asked him about was marriage."

"What did he say?"

"He said the Bible teaches that what God has joined together let not man put asunder. In other words, it's a lifetime proposition, and I'm not ready for that, Peter, and neither are you. Not with me, anyway."

For some time Peter argued rather vigorously, but in the end Avis simply said, "Peter, my final answer is no! This is not up for debate. You don't love me, and I don't love you. Not in the way a husband and a wife should love. Isn't that true?"

Peter flushed. He had known all the time this was going to be a marriage of convenience, and Avis had put her finger on his motive. "I do love you, Avis, and I think you care for me. But maybe you're right. It's not in the way a husband and wife should love. I've seen in my parents what it means to have a good, long-lasting marriage, but I feel so . . . so guilty!"

"Well, you can stop. Are you ready for surprise number two?" As Peter nodded, Avis said, "All right. Here it is." Throwing the blanket back, she pointed down at her right foot. She was wearing a pair of soft slippers and said, "Watch this." Mystified, Peter looked down at her foot, and suddenly he felt as if a bolt of electricity shot through him. The toe of Avis's shoe lifted once, then twice.

She laughed, saying, "Do you see that, Peter?"

"Avis, you moved your foot!" Peter stood up at once and came to stand over her, his face alight with joy. "Has the feeling come back?"

"Yes. It started three days ago in my right toe. I couldn't move it at first, but it kept getting stronger." She reached down and touched her thigh and pinched it. "I can feel here, and already the feeling's coming back into my left foot. I can twitch the toe just a little bit. You can't see it with a shoe on, but it's just like the right one."

"We'll have to get you to the doctor to see what he says."

"He's already been here, and he was so excited, Peter. He said it was a miracle from God, and science had nothing to do with it. And I couldn't agree with him more. He says it will keep getting stronger and stronger, and I'll be able to walk as good as ever."

"Avis, I'm so happy," Peter said. He suddenly reached over and picked her up out of the wheelchair and, carrying her like a child, swung her around. He let out a loud, yelping cry and danced around, yelling like a wild Indian.

"Peter, stop it!" Avis cried, but she was laughing. "Now, put me down. No, wait. Hold me up and see if I can put a little weight on that right leg."

Peter lowered Avis carefully. She held on to him, and a surprised expression crossed her face. "My legs are like rubber, but look, I'm putting my weight on this foot. I'm healed, Peter. God has healed me!"

Peter could hardly speak. He put Avis back in the chair and said, "You'll be out of that chair in a week, Avis."

"I really believe that's right. I don't understand faith, but somehow God has answered. I asked George Camrose why God didn't heal everybody. He said he had no idea, but he also said that anyone who had a need could call on God. God might say, 'Wait awhile,' or He might say, 'It's not good for you to have that right now,' but He always hears." Tears came to her eyes, and she said, "It took me a long time to find God. I'm convinced now that the accident that put me in this chair was the best thing that ever happened to me. I would never have met Jesus Christ if I hadn't been beyond my own resources."

Peter stood there staring at her. Finally he said, "I'm happy for you, Avis. Not just that you're going to be able to walk again, but that you've found the Lord."

"I'll never forget it," Avis said. "My whole life I'll be telling people how God saved me and healed me." Then she took a deep breath, brushed the tears from her eyes, and cleared her throat. "Well, are you ready for surprise number three?"

"I'm ready for anything."

"Then you wait right here. Don't leave the room."

Peter stood there as Avis wheeled herself through the door and disappeared down the hallway. He was still tremendously excited and thrilled over the healing that had come to her. The burden of guilt he had been struggling under suddenly was gone. Had she remained crippled for life, he knew full well he would never have gotten over it, but somehow he knew she would be fine now.

Movement caught his eye, and Avis wheeled herself back into the room. "Are you ready?"

"All ready. What is it?"

"Shut your eyes."

Smiling, Peter shut his eyes, and he heard movement. Then Avis said, "All right. You can open them."

Peter opened his eyes—and there stood Jolie before him. She was wearing a simple but pretty wine-colored dress, but he did not notice that. What he saw was that her left cheek was clear and smooth!

"Jolie!" Peter gasped. He reached out and touched her cheek, which was rosy and clear, and said, "I can barely see the scar! You wouldn't even notice it from a few feet away."

"Even that will get better," Avis said. "That's what the doctor said."

Peter stood there, stunned by the beauty of Jolie's face. He remembered how Jolie had always kept her face averted whenever possible, or kept her hair over the scar, but now she stood before him, her lips trembling, and tears brimming in her eyes.

"Well, don't just stand there, you idiot!" Avis called out. "Tell her she's beautiful!"

"You *are* beautiful, Jolie, but you always have been to me."

"Have I, Peter?"

"Why, of course. I'm glad for your sake," he whispered, "that the scar is gone. I know it worried you, but it never meant anything to me. It was always what was inside of you that I cared for."

"Do you care for me, Peter?"

Peter nodded, and again Avis said loudly, "Do I have to do everything? Kiss her, you dope!"

Peter shot one startled glance at Avis, who raised her hand in a sign of victory. She was smiling and whispered, "Kiss her and tell her you love her."

"I do love you, Jolie," Peter said. "I have for a long time." He bent his head and his lips touched hers. He was surprised by the sweetness and warmth of her. Her lips were soft and welcoming.

For Jolie it was like coming home. With Peter's strong arms about her, and his lips on hers, a feeling of goodness and rightness flooded her. She was where she belonged.

Then he lifted his head and said, "I love you, Jolie. I guess I always have—since the first time I saw you."

Jolie did not answer for a moment, then she whispered, "My dear . . . my dear. . . !" She laid her head on his chest and felt his arms tighten around her, and again the sensation came to her of arriving home after a long voyage.

"That's enough of that! I'll dance at your wedding," Avis said.

Both of them turned and ran over to Avis. Jolie kissed her on the cheek, and Peter raised her hand to kiss it. "I'll take you up on that."

"You always were a great dancer."

With both her hands imprisoned in those of her friends, Avis Warwick knew that her life had truly changed. She said, "We'd better get started."

"We? What do you mean we?" Peter demanded.

"You don't think I'm going to miss that race, do you? Jolie, get my going-to-the-race costume out. And figure a way to get this clumsy chair there. We're going to see Peter Winslow, the best racing driver in America, win, and I'm going to holler my lungs out!"

★　★　★　★

Oliver Lanier's right knee had grown worse. He had visited Dr. McKenzie, who had examined him carefully and then shook his head, a scowl of disapproval on his thin face. "Ach mon, you've got to get off that leg!" he exclaimed. "Look at it! It's swollen nearly twice its proper size."

Oliver had taken the medicine McKenzie had prescribed and obeyed his instruction to stay off of the leg. It was a rare thing indeed for Oliver Lanier to take a day off from the office. Alice made such a fuss over him that he finally growled, "Alice, dear, I'm not dying! It's just a rheumatic knee."

For most of the morning Oliver sat with his leg up on a hassock, staring out the window. It was a beautiful July day with a yellow sun high in the sky, throwing its beams over the street. The younger children were all at school, so the house was quiet. Occasionally Alice would come in and sit down for a while, knitting while Oliver stared out the window. Otherwise he was alone with his thoughts.

Around noon Oliver finally began to grow restless. Alice had come in saying, "I've got to go visit Mrs. Childers. She's been very ill for the past three days. Will you be all right alone?"

"I'm not a child. Of course I will be."

Alice laughed. "You're worse than a child, and you're the worst patient I ever saw. I'll be back and fix you something very special for supper tonight." She kissed him on the cheek, then left.

The house was truly silent now. Moodily, Oliver continued staring out the window, but he was taking no pleasure in the beautiful day. He was too disturbed and unhappy about his entire life. Again and again he went over the altercation he had had with Clinton, and the more he thought about it, the more he felt he had mishandled the whole thing. It was no different when he thought of Cara. He had been overly protective of her, to be sure. He thought back on the times he had kept her in the house when she had begged to go outside. Even Dr. McKenzie had told him he was keeping her too confined. Restlessly, he stirred in the chair—making his knee produce a twinge of pain. He stared at it resentfully. The look in his eye was one his employees had learned to dread. He resented anything he could not control, and now the knee had confined him to a chair and taken away his freedom.

At last boredom got the best of him, and he limped across the room and searched the bookcase. A red binder caught his eyes—the family photograph album. With a grunt he pulled it out, hobbled back, and sat down. He began going through the album, and the first picture was one of him and Alice on their honeymoon. He smiled as he saw how relatively thin he had been back then, and he mused over the youthful beauty of Alice. "We've come a long way," he muttered. "You've always been a good woman and a fine wife." He thought of how Cara had instructed him to tell Alice nice things, and he had been amazed at how it had worked a surprising transformation in their relationship. *I should have done it a long time ago, but a man doesn't think of those things.* He began turning the pages over and pausing to look at pictures of the children when they were small—first Cara when she was just a baby, so full of life and energy then. She was his first and would always be his favorite. Then little Cara holding her new baby brother Clinton. The pictures of Clinton, Oliver's first son, brought special anguish to his heart. Picture after picture showed his thin face, and then he grew up into a trim, well-built young man. Oliver had always been so proud of Clinton as a child, but what had happened to their relationship when Clinton grew into manhood? Then Mary Ann, always a beautiful child, and more so now. He traced her history and thought of what a beautiful voice she had and how in the future it would be Africans who would be hearing it instead of himself and others.

Then Benjamin. He turned to a recent picture and looked down at the photograph. Benjamin was looking straight into the camera, his pleasing features in repose, but still there was something unhappy and dissatisfied in his eyes. Here again Oliver knew he had mismanaged something in his son's life. He took great pleasure in Bess's and Bobby's more recent pictures. "I haven't gone wrong with them," he said, but then a voice whispered, *But you will. You'll try to control them just as you have your other children.*

"No!" Oliver slammed the album shut and tossed it onto the floor. He sat there a long time, and then a thought began to form in his mind. Looking up, he saw that the clock showed almost one. As the thought took clearer shape, a stubborn look came into his expression. His lips tightened, his chin began to push forward, and those who knew Oliver Lanier best would have known he had made up his mind.

Heaving himself to his feet, he hobbled to his room and exchanged his pajamas and robe for a lightweight summer suit. It pained him to bend over and tie his shoes, for whenever he flexed his right knee it was like sticking a red hot needle through it. He accomplished the task, however, and heaved himself up, picked up his cane, and headed out the door. "James!" he bellowed, poking his head into the servants' quarters.

"Yes, sir!" James came at once, saying, "What is it, Mr. Lanier?"

"Get the carriage out."

"The carriage—? You can't leave the house, sir. Not on that knee!"

"Get the carriage out, James. Do what I tell you."

James was too accustomed to obeying to question further. "Yes, sir. I'll hitch it up at once. I'll be there in five minutes."

"Don't take any longer."

Oliver stood at the front door, taking out his pocket watch more than once. Four minutes and thirty seconds later James came out of the driveway and pulled the team up in front of the house. Oliver stepped outside and Mrs. Grimshaw asked, "Sir, what will I tell your wife?"

"Tell her I've gone to the races," he said. He smiled and suddenly his face looked different. "Tell her I've gone to see my son win an automobile race."

Ignoring the astonished look on the housekeeper's face, he limped down the steps, heaved himself into the carriage. "James, do you know where those automobiles are racing today at Coney Island?"

"Why, yes, sir."

"Then take me there, and don't spare the horses. . . !"

★ ★ ★ ★

"Shall I come with you, sir?" James asked as he helped his employer out of the carriage.

"Yes, come if you want to."

"Yes, sir. Would you care to lean on me, Mr. Lanier?"

"No, I'm not that far gone. Find yourself a place, James. I don't know anything about these races, but I'm not too old to learn."

"No, sir, of course not!"

"Meet me here after the race."

Lanier hobbled off and was amazed at the crowd that had gathered. Apparently there were people from all walks of life, for he saw rich people with expensive clothing standing side by side with laboring men who seemed just to have come from work. The crowd was mostly made up of men, but there were a few women here and there. He stopped one man and asked, "Does one buy a ticket to get into this thing?"

"Why, of course. There's the ticket office right over there."

"Thank you."

Oliver purchased his ticket, paying two dollars for it, and asked, "Where is my seat?"

The ticket taker grinned. "Any seat you can find. Just hang on to that stub."

Oliver gave him an affronted look, then made his way along with the crowd. The stands were already full, he saw, as he hobbled along in front of them looking for a seat. He had about decided he would have to stand up, when all of a sudden he heard his name called. "Mr. Lanier! Mr. Lanier!"

Looking around, he saw a young woman with jet black hair standing beside a woman in a wheelchair. He recalled meeting the young woman—what was her name? Jolie Devorak, he remembered.

"Seats are about gone, but we've got one right here. Would you like to join us?"

"Very decent of you, Miss Devorak."

"This is Mrs. Avis Warwick."

"How do you do, Mrs. Warwick."

"How do you do, sir? You've come to see your son win the race?"

Lanier felt as if he were cornered. He had intended to come incognito, and now he was caught.

He did not have to answer, however, for Jolie Devorak said, "It's going to be a great race. Your son, Clinton, is right beside Peter, the driver. See? They're going to win, too."

"Come. Sit down right here. We've got a good view," Avis said. She had heard the story of Oliver Lanier and knew somehow what it had cost him to come. "You ought to be very proud of your son. To hear Peter tell it, he's the world's greatest automobile mechanic." She couldn't resist adding, "He's very nice looking, too."

At that moment the gun sounded, and Jolie yelled, "There they go!"

Oliver was startled at the roar of the engines, and suddenly all was blur and smoke and action. He could not tell what was happening, and as the car sped around the track, he tried vainly to put some meaning into it. One thing he saw immediately—this was a very dangerous occupation!

Jolie caught the look of confusion on Oliver's face. "Look, Mr. Lanier, you see that yellow car? That's the favorite. That's the one to beat. It's a Marmot and the fastest car in the race, at least in the trials. That's the one Peter and Clinton have to beat."

"And which one is Clinton in?"

"The bright red one. See?"

Oliver was somehow disappointed. "Why, they're halfway back. He can never catch up and win."

"Oh yes, they can!" Jolie exclaimed. "Some of those cars won't be in the race before long. They'll blow tires and engines will give out. All sorts of things will happen. It's a long race, and Peter's laying back. Peter and Clinton have decided just to wait and let the others wear themselves out. Then they'll catch up with that yellow bird. You'll see."

As the race continued, and Jolie pointed out what was happening, Oliver found himself fascinated. The speed of the machines amazed him, and the skill with which the drivers maneuvered around the curves and around one another was astounding. He found himself beginning to pull for the red car, and as time passed by and several cars dropped out, he exclaimed, "Look, they're not all that far behind now! Only four cars ahead of them!"

"That's right," Jolie cried, "and the *Jolie Blonde II* can beat any of them!"

"Is the car named after you, Miss Devorak?"

"Well, yes it is."

"She's engaged to the driver, Mr. Lanier," Avis said, who had overheard the conversation. "It's a brand-new engagement, too. Only part of one day old."

Oliver turned to face the young girl. He could see the slight scar on her face, but she was beautiful indeed. "My congratulations, Miss Devorak."

"Thank you, Mr. Lanier. And my congratulations to you. You're getting a fine son-in-law. I don't know a better preacher in the country than George Camrose."

Her praise of Camrose warmed Oliver and he nodded, but then somebody said, "Look, he's spinning out!" He found his heart in his throat as he expected to see the red car crashing into one of the fences, but it was another car, a blue Oldsmobile, and looking quickly, he said, "Look, Peter and Clinton are only one car back now!"

As the race drew near the finish line, Jolie found herself amused, for Oliver began to wave his cane in the air. His eyes were fixed on the cars, and suddenly he cried in a booming voice, "Come on, Clinton! Come on, Clinton! You can win, boy! You can do it!"

Jolie winked at Avis, and they both laughed. But then the end was near.

A hundred yards from the finish line the *Jolie Blonde II* was axle to axle with the yellow Marmot. Both cars hurtled ahead, and both engines were open full.

The finish came when, from somewhere, an extra surge of power came to the *Jolie Blonde II*. Peter and Clinton bent forward as it shot ahead half a length, and the checkered flag went down, and the loudspeaker boomed, "And the winner is the *Jolie Blonde II*, driven by Peter Winslow and Clinton Lanier!"

"By George, that's smashing!" Oliver shouted. He was so excited he had forgotten his bad leg.

"We're going over to watch them get the award," Jolie said.

"Well, I'm coming, too!"

"Push me along, Jolie!" Avis cried, and the three of them made their way across the track.

Jolie pushed the way clear, saying, "Open up for us!" and somehow they managed to make their way through the crowd to where Peter and Clinton were getting out of the car. Jolie ran forward and threw herself into Peter's arms.

He caught her and said, "Well, how does it feel to be engaged to a successful driver?"

"I'll tell you about that after we're married," she said. "Don't get ahead of yourself."

Clinton had come around the car, his eyes on Jolie. He grinned as she threw herself into Peter's arms, and then his eyes shifted and fell upon his father. He blinked and swallowed hard, and then his father marched right up to him and put his arm around him. "My boy, that was very exciting! I admire courage, son, and you have a lot!" He suddenly realized that he was holding his son for the first time since childhood. He started to step back with amazement but Clinton, his face black with grease and his eyes red with smoke fumes, held on to him.

"That means a lot coming from you, Father," he said with a huge smile on his face.

Oliver blinked and could not believe the feeling this simple sentence gave. He looked almost shyly at his son and said, "Maybe you and I could do some more things together."

"Anytime."

Avis watched the pair and thought, *A storybook ending. I didn't think those existed.* She lifted her right leg and took tremendous joy in seeing it move. The other leg she raised only slightly, but her thigh tingled, and she prayed, *Lord, thank you for the miracle.*

Clinton then turned to Avis. He couldn't help but notice how beautiful she looked. "Thank you for coming, Mrs. Warwick."

She smiled demurely and replied, "I loved it! You've done a wonderful job with the *Jolie Blonde II.*"

"I didn't do much really. Peter and Easy did all the real work."

"I know how much you've helped by what Jolie has told me," Avis insisted. "This victory is yours, too."

Clinton found her compliments very pleasing and suddenly seemed at a loss for words. He could only mutter, "Thank you."

Avis then said, "Do you think you could show me some of the additions you made to the *Jolie Blonde II?*"

"Why . . . why sure," Clinton said, then pushed Avis toward the automobile. As he talked excitedly about the car and all they had done to it, Avis listened attentively.

As Peter and Jolie watched the two move away, Peter whispered, "Looks like there might be another wedding in the future."

Jolie could only smile as she watched her two friends simply enjoying being together.

CHAPTER TWENTY-THREE

"I'll Go Anywhere With You...!"

★ ★ ★ ★

For nearly an hour Phil Winslow had sat on the side of his bed staring at the wall. It was not that the wallpaper was so enticing, for it merely consisted of a series of rather faded roses. He was as unaware of the faint sounds that came from Mrs. Brown's house-cleaning activities as he was of the traffic outside on the streets. He had pulled on a pair of clean brown trousers and slipped on his socks and was tying one shoe when suddenly a sense of futility swept over him. He sat holding the other shoe for a long time, staring at it blankly, as the events of his life seemed to swarm before his eyes. Finally he dropped the shoe and simply sat there staring, his eyes blank and unaware of anything in the room.

A loud screeching noise outside brought him out of his reverie with a start. Loud voices, one of them cursing, floated through the open window in the small adjoining sitting room. Then engines roared and moved on down the street. Phil picked up the shoe he had dropped, slipped his foot into it, and carefully tied the laces. Straightening up, he sat for a moment, almost paralyzed by indecision. Then he shook his head and muttered, "I've got to stop kidding myself. This is no good!"

Standing quickly, he walked over to the chest, opened a drawer, and pulled out a clean white shirt. He slipped into it, buttoned it, and stuffed it into his trousers, then pulled his suspenders up with a decisive tug. "Time to move on," he murmured. His lips drew thin, for it was a decision that had been pressing at him for days now. He had not sold a single painting yet and was as depressed as he had ever been in his life. He made a convulsive movement with his shoulders, as if shrugging off a burden, stepped over to the bed, and bent down. Pulling out his suitcase, he put it on the bed, opened it, and then began to move back and forth between the bed and the chest of drawers, packing his clothing and finally his shaving kit. By the time he finished, he had emptied the chest of drawers and the suitcase was stuffed. For a moment he stood there; then he fastened the suitcase. Picking it up, he took a last look around the room and a wave of regret swept over him. *I hate to leave here*, he thought, *but there's nothing else to do.*

Resolutely, he stepped outside and moved down the hall. He found Mrs. Brown sweeping the hallway and came over to her. "Mrs. Brown, I'll be leaving and I wanted to say good-bye."

A startled look leaped into her eyes, and she exclaimed, "Why, Phil, what brought this on?"

"Business failure." Phil made himself grin. "I've given it the best shot I had. Now it's time to go back and punch cows in Montana. I guess that's what I was supposed to do all the time." He put his arm around her and gave her a squeeze. "You've been more than a landlady. You've been like a second mother to me. I'll miss you."

Phil received her hug, then shook off her protests that it was too early to quit and left the rooming house. As he made his way down the street he calculated how much money he had left. It came to enough for a train ticket back to the ranch. *I've got to go by and tell Peter and the others good-bye, but I'll miss them something fierce*, he thought. A heaviness settled on him as he walked slowly toward Maxim's Gallery. When he entered, he found Maxim with a white apron on rearranging the paintings.

"Hello, Phil. Come to give me a hand? I'm redoing the whole thing."

"I guess so," Phil said.

Suddenly Maxim saw the suitcase in Phil's hand. "What's this?" He frowned. "You find another room?"

"I'm going back to my old room on the ranch. I'm cashing in my chips, Max." Maxim was more shocked than Phil had imagined he might be. His eyes filled with concern, and he rushed over and shook Phil's arm.

"No, you can't do that! You've got to hang on a while longer. It's just a matter of time."

"I've been through all that, Max. I've been a drain on my family long enough. I'll do what painting I can back home. What I wanted to ask you to do is to maybe keep a few of these, and I'd like to ship the rest of them. I think I've got enough money for that."

Maxim was truly grieved. For some time he stood there arguing, but it was useless, for Phil was adamant. Finally Phil said, "I'm going over and say good-bye to Peter and Easy and Jolie. I'll be back for my suitcase. The train leaves at six tonight."

Leaving the gallery, Phil went at once to his friends' rooming house, where he found Peter, Jolie, and Easy outside in the backyard, as usual, working on the *Jolie Blonde II*. They greeted him warmly, but when he told them he was returning to Montana, all of them began to argue with him. Phil listened to them, then grinned, saying, "Never was a hoss couldn't be rode. Never was a cowboy couldn't be throwed. So I guess I've been throwed this time, but I want to tell you three how much it has meant having you for friends."

"Phil, it's too soon to give up," Jolie said. "You haven't given it a fair chance."

As she looked up at him he noticed how the scar on her face was so faint now that you had to be close to see it. He shook his head, then gave her a hug. "I've said all that to myself, Jolie, but I've got to go. Good-bye." He reached over and shook hands with Peter and grinned. "I'd like to be at the wedding, but you'll have to have it without me. So long, Easy."

It was hard to say good-bye to these three. He promised to write, as did they, but as he made his way back to Maxim's, he knew such things never worked out very well. He was thinking, *Well, at least I've had a good run for my money. I've met some fine people. Some of my kin. I would never have met them if I had stayed on the ranch.*

He went by George Camrose's church long enough to bid him good-bye and promised to keep in touch when he got to Africa. "You take care of that young woman. She's a winner."

"You're making a mistake, I think, Phil." Camrose's eyes were troubled, and he said, "What about Cara?"

"Why, I wish her well. She has a great talent but a difficult way to go."

"Mary Ann says Cara is in love with you."

"Oh, there's nothing to that."

"How do *you* feel?"

Camrose's direct question troubled Phil, but he was honest. "She's like no woman I've ever met. If things were different—" He broke off and shrugged his broad shoulders. "I don't have anything to offer her, George. She's always had everything."

"That won't mean anything to her if she loves you. Go tell her."

"No, I can't do that. It would be asking too much. Good-bye, George. God bless you. I'll think of you in Africa, and you might say a prayer for me now and then."

"You can believe I'll do that!"

It was too early for the train, and for most of the day Phil simply wandered around saying good-bye to his old friends. He stopped by to bid farewell to Robert Henri and some of the other painters he had learned to admire. They were sad to see him go, and as Phil left them he felt his heart wrench, thinking, *I'll never be around fellows like this. Not out on a cattle ranch.*

As he walked the streets of the city, he came upon the Brooklyn Bridge and stopped for a moment. He remembered the times he had spent hours painting the image of the magnificent structure. "Won't be any Brooklyn Bridges out on the range," he murmured. Then weary of his own thoughts, he turned and headed back to the art gallery.

★ ★ ★ ★

"Where have you been? I've been waiting for you!"

Phil looked with surprise at George Maxim. The bearded man's blue eyes were electrified, and he grabbed Phil and almost shook him. "I could have choked you! Why did you run off so long?"

"Why, I didn't think there was any need to hurry back. My train doesn't leave until six."

"You're not catching any train! Come in here!"

Mystified, Phil allowed himself to be dragged inside. He felt Maxim's excitement, but he could not imagine what had caused it.

"Mr. Devoe, here he is. He's back."

Phil noted that there was only one customer in the shop, a small man plainly dressed, and when he turned, there was a familiar look on his face. Phil had seen him before, but he couldn't remember where, nor did he remember the name.

The man called Devoe came forward and stood before Phil, a slight smile on his plain face. He said, "I'm glad you came back, Mr. Winslow."

Phil took the hand Devoe offered, and said, "I guess you have the advantage of me, Mr. Devoe. I remember your face, but I can't seem to remember where we met."

"Right here in my shop," Maxim said. "Only he called himself Mr. Smith then."

Suddenly Phil remembered the man. He had seen him twice and remembered what Maxim had said both times. "*All he does is come and look. Never buys anything.*" Now he looked with interest at the older man and said, "Oh yes, I remember now."

"He's interested in your paintings, Phil. He wants to buy some."

Maxim's announcement caught Phil off guard. He had lost hope of ever selling his work, and now suddenly it seemed impossible that anything like this could happen. He stared at Devoe speechless, then said, "Well . . . that's good news."

"Good news!" Maxim exclaimed. "Good news? Phil, you don't understand. This is Horatio Devoe."

The name meant nothing to Phil, and he looked helplessly at Maxim, who shook his head in disgust. "I never saw such ignorance! Mr. Devoe is the owner of several railroads, but more important for you, he's a collector of paintings."

"I take more pleasure out of the paintings I purchase than I do out of my railroads, I'm afraid," Devoe said. He had a low-pitched voice and seemed not to emphasize anything. Interest, however, sparked his dark eyes as he studied Phil. "I'm not really interested in the old masters. What I like to do is find new talent."

"I should say he does. Why, he was the one who discovered Robert Monroe's work." Robert Monroe was one of the premier artists of the country, a young man whose work had taken the art world by storm.

"Well, you picked a winner in Robert Monroe. He's a fine artist. Perhaps the best," Phil said.

"Perhaps, but I keep looking for others."

Maxim could not stand still. "He got a corner on Monroe's

early paintings. He found them and bought every one of them, and now he's got them all. Every painting Robert Monroe paints now is worth thousands of dollars, but the old ones, who can say what they're worth?" He turned to Devoe, saying, "I'd love to see your collection, Mr. Devoe."

"Why, I think that could be arranged, but first let's do some trading with this young man. I'd like to buy your complete works, Mr. Winslow."

"Well, I guess you can call me Phil if you're going to buy my paintings." Phil's mind was reeling as he stared at the small man. "You mean . . . *all* of them?"

"Yes, I'm convinced that you're going to be as famous as Robert Monroe, and I want to have first call on all of your work."

Maxim suddenly gouged at Phil with his elbow. "I forgot to mention, Mr. Devoe, I'm Phil's agent."

An amused smile came to Devoe's thin lips. "I see. Rather a recent decision, I suppose?"

Phil laughed. "Not really. I know nothing about the commercial side of painting. I would appreciate it if you would deal with Max here for my work."

"Of course. Most painters prefer that," Devoe nodded. He studied the young man, then said, "I may lose money on your work. I have on several." He shook his head. "It's a gamble. I'd be better off, my wife tells me, betting on horses. It's far more stable than the world of art."

Phil laughed and suddenly the excitement began to build in him. "Let me get out of the way and you can talk to Max about money."

Phil stepped outside the shop. He did not know whether to yell or run. It all seemed like a fairy tale to him, and he couldn't quell the excitement. He took off his soft cloth hat, threw it in the air, and let out a loud yell, just as if he were on the back of a wild bronco. A uniformed policeman, who had been just behind him, came up at once and said, "Look, fella. I'm going to have to run you in. You're creating a disturbance. Are you drunk?"

Phil grinned merrily and said, "No, officer, except drunk with joy."

The policeman's broad Irish face creased with a grin. "Well, there's no law against that. Just keep it down, will you?"

"Sure," Phil agreed. He could not keep still and for over an hour he managed to stay away. When he finally went back, Devoe was gone and Maxim was sitting in a chair, a pale look on his face.

"He bought them all." Maxim was staring at a slip of paper, and he could not seem to take his eyes off of it. "Here's the check."

Phil took the small slip of paper, stared at the amount, and suddenly felt lightheaded. He could not speak for a moment, then he looked at Maxim and said in an unsteady voice, "This . . . this has to be of God, Max."

"Yes, it does. You've been faithful to Him. I know how you've always given to the church, and to those in need, and now God's going to reward you."

Phil went over and pulled the older man up and gave him a hug. "I couldn't have done it without you, Max. You really deserve all this."

"Just my usual fee. Ten percent. That's all I'll take." His eyes were misty and he wiped them with a handkerchief, saying, "It always makes me feel good to see a good person come out on top. What are you going to do with all that money?"

Phil stared at the check and said, "I'm going to invest it wisely. Come along. We're going to the bank, and I'm going to give you your percentage, and then I've got a call to make!"

★   ★   ★   ★

Cara was startled at the knock on her door. She started to respond when suddenly the door flew open—and there stood Phil Winslow. She got a brief glimpse of the maid, Ruth, who was protesting, and then Phil stepped in and shut the door. The look on his face caused her to exclaim, "Why, Phil, what is it?"

She was standing in front of the portrait she had come to call the *Shadow Portrait*. Phil walked over and took one look at it, then blinked with surprise. "It's finished!" he exclaimed.

"Yes," Cara said. She looked at the painting and asked anxiously, "Do you like it, Phil?"

Examining the portrait closely, Phil paid careful attention to the faces of the subjects—a woman and a young girl. The woman's face showed all the lines of hard living. Her eyes were shadowed and her forehead was creased. She still had traces of early beauty, but it was obvious from the expression and the lines on her face that she had endured difficult times. Now his eyes went to the young girl, where he saw the resemblance to that of the woman. She was very young and had not been scarred by time and circumstance as her mother had. There was hope in her wide open eyes, and she held her mother's hand with confidence. Her clothing was poor and ragged, but it was the expression on her face that moved Phil. She had that innocent look of one who had hope for the future, despite a miserable existence.

Phil did not take his eyes off the painting for a time, then he whispered, "You've done it, Cara! You've caught the struggle for life. Look at that woman's face. It's got everything! She's lost her youth and her beauty, but she has a child. You've got her holding on to her, and just by looking at it, you can tell she's put all of the hopes and dreams that she had for herself in the girl," he murmured. "What a beautiful child. Dirt and rags and all the rest of it, but still a beautiful soul."

Phil turned and saw tears in Cara's eyes. At once he said, "Why, there's no need to cry."

"I can't help it," Cara sobbed. "Somehow it took everything I had out of me. I've been working on it for weeks and it wouldn't come. It was only a shadow."

"Well, the shadow's gone and now we have the reality. You're a fine artist, Cara, and now I want to take back what I said. You know about life—perhaps more than I do." He stepped forward and put his hands on her shoulders. "You've had a harder blow than I ever had. I've thought about how I came in here making all sorts of proclamations about not being afraid of life." He hesitated for a moment, then said, "You're the strongest woman I know, Cara Lanier."

"Oh, Phil—!" Cara could not speak, her heart was so full, and then he pulled her forward, and she rested her face against his chest. He held her gently as she wept silently, stroking her hair and not caring if anyone came in.

Finally he took her chin and moved her face upward. Taking his handkerchief out, he wiped her tears. "Cara, I want you to come away with me."

Cara stared at Phil. She was still shaken by the scene, but now she could not seem to understand his words. "Come where, Phil?"

"Away from this house—out in the sunshine, under the trees, in the fields, in the streets." Phil did not release her but indicated the room with a quick gesture of his head. "You've got to get out of this place. It's nothing but a prison for you." He looked steadily in her eyes. "I don't know how to say this very originally, but I love you, Cara."

The words to Cara Lanier were sweet and precious beyond belief. For years she had put all thoughts of such love out of her mind, but now as she felt Phil Winslow's arms around her and looked into his eyes, she let his words of love sink down into her spirit. They were like soft rain on a parched desert, and she could not speak for a moment. All of the impossibilities of what he was asking rose before her and tried to crowd their way into her mind, but she put them all aside. Looking up at him, she whispered, "I'll go anywhere with you, Phil, anywhere in the world!"

For Phil, this was all the answer he needed, and he made no immediate reply. He had carried in his mind a picture of some woman. It had been shaped and imaged and rounded and given life by the dreaming that comes to a man in his private thoughts. Now as he looked into Cara Lanier's face, he knew there would never be another one like her for him.

As for Cara, she had imagined love as something that would come upon a woman suddenly. She had thought it would be absolutely clear and complete, with no uncertainty to it. And now she knew that was right, for she realized she loved Phil Winslow. Shyly she reached up and touched his cheek, whispering, "My dear, I do love you so much!"

And then when he bent and kissed her, her heart filled with a love so strong she knew that whatever happened in the future, they would face it together. One thought came to her, and she said, "I'm not sure what will happen if we go away."

"I'm not either. We never are sure of these things, but of one thing I'm absolutely certain," Phil said softly, his voice gentle. "I love you as a woman needs to be loved, and I'll care for you as best I can."

"That's all I ask. Just love me," Cara whispered, and then she kissed him again.

★　★　★　★

As Oliver entered the room and took one look at Alice's face, he knew something was going on. He had actually been feeling better. His knee had improved greatly since he had followed Dr. McKenzie's instructions. He had been excited by his two excursions with Clinton and had hopes that his son would return to the office, at least on a part-time basis. He himself had grown interested in auto racing and had actually gone over to watch as Clinton, Peter, and Easy worked on the car, preparing it for the next race.

Now, however, Alice's face was stiff with anxiety, and all of the buoyancy Oliver felt suddenly faded away. "What is it, Alice?" he asked. He moved across with only a slight limp and stood beside her. "What's wrong?"

"It's Cara," Alice said with difficulty. She kept her eyes fixed upon him and could not seem to go on.

Fear grabbed his heart, and he demanded, "Is she worse?"

Alice could not seem to answer the question, which seemed strange. Finally she said in a tight voice, "I don't know what you'd say to that. Physically, she's not." Taking a deep breath, Alice said, "She's gone, Oliver."

Staring at his wife with incomprehension, Oliver managed to gasp, "Gone? What do you mean—*gone?*"

"You'll have to try to understand, Oliver. She wanted to talk to you, but she was afraid that you would never understand, and I gave her my permission."

"Alice, tell me what's going on. Permission to do what?"

"All right," Alice said and seemed to grow calm. "I will tell you. She's on her way to England with Phil Winslow." Alice watched stark amazement sweep across Oliver's face and added quickly, "They're going to be married tomorrow at George's church, and they're leaving immediately afterward for England. They're going to stay there for their honeymoon until fall."

Oliver stood there stunned for a moment. He looked as if his world had fallen apart, and his lips began to tremble slightly. "But . . . but I don't understand." Then suddenly he *did* understand. He dropped his head and a wave of guilt came crashing down on him. "If I'd only been more understanding, this wouldn't have happened," he said. He felt Alice's hand on his arm, and then she put her arms around his neck.

"She loves him so much, and he loves her, too. And he's had a great success with his painting. Come let me tell you about it."

Oliver allowed himself to be led over to the couch. He sat down heavily, his mind swimming, only half hearing what Alice was telling him about Phil's good fortune in his profession. All he could think was, *Cara is gone. My little girl is gone. . . !*

★ ★ ★ ★

"Now don't be nervous, Cara," Mary Ann said. "It's only a wedding."

Cara was not wearing a proper wedding dress. There had been no time for that, but she did have on a brand-new garment she and her mother had picked out that very morning. It was a beautiful evening dress made of white silk, with teardrop pearls edging the neckline and the hem and a pattern of similar pearls adorning the skirt front. She had completed her outfit with a pair of white satin elbow-length gloves and carried a small bouquet of white and pink roses, with pink ribbons trailing down. She looked lovely, and now she smiled as she saw Mary Ann's hands tremble and heard the quaver in her sister's voice.

"If you're this shaky at *my* wedding, how will you ever make it through yours, Mary Ann?"

Laughing at herself, Mary Ann said, "That's right. Oh, I'm so excited, Cara. It's the most romantic thing I ever heard. It's like something out of a novel."

"A very bad novel," Cara said and smiled. She had spent a final night in her prison room and had lain awake for some time worrying about her father. But finally she had committed herself and Phil and her family to God, and to her surprise, she had slept better than she had in years. She had arisen early and gone with her mother to buy the dress she now wore so elegantly. As she stood in the entrance of the church, she could hear the organ filling the sanctuary with wondrous music.

George Camrose's congregation had grown so much over the last few months that they had been able to relocate to a lovely church building only a few blocks from their small storefront church. Cara looked through the glass door into the wood-paneled sanctuary. The tall stained-glass window in front, depicting Jesus in prayer, His eyes lifted toward heaven, gave Cara peace that her relationship with Phil could only have been given her by God. She stood in awe at the new life He was giving her this day.

She picked up the bouquet of flowers and quietly waited, and soon Mary Ann said, "There, that's my cue." She kissed Cara on the cheek, then hurried in, leaving her to stand there alone. In those few moments alone, Cara prayed silently for her father, and for herself, and for Phil. It all seemed like a dream to her to be leaving for England with a man she loved with all of her heart after being confined in her room for so many years. At last she'd be free to discover and enjoy a whole new realm of experiences. She had gone to Dr. McKenzie, who had been shocked more than she had imagined. He had not been able to take it all in, but finally, when he was made to understand that she was going to be married, and she was going to England, he had said finally, "Well, bless you, my dear, and I'll pray that God will give you a long, happy life." He had stared at her and added, "It grieves me to think that I may have had a part in keeping you cooped up when you should have been outside, but you've found your way at last. God be thanked for that!"

Suddenly Cara heard the familiar strains of the bridal march, and taking a deep breath, she opened the door and started down the aisle. The church was half filled, despite the suddenness of their plans. Mary Ann and her mother, and others of her friends had gotten the word out. She saw Jolie and Peter and their friend Easy Devlin. She then saw the beautiful woman that her brother Clinton seemed to be spending most of his time with lately, Avis Warwick. She smiled at these good friends of Phil and looked forward to getting to know them better. Now, however, she had no eyes for anyone except the tall man who stood beside George Camrose. Phil's eyes were fixed on her, and he smiled at her warmly as she made her way down the aisle. Beside him, her brother Clinton stood as best man, and when she reached him, with a nod from Camrose, Phil stepped up and, smiling, took her hand, squeezing it gently and whispering, "I'm glad you came."

Cara returned his smile, then the two turned to face Camrose. Both of them listened as he began, "We are gathered in the sight of God and in the face of this company to join together this man and this woman in holy matrimony. . . ." Phil's hand surrounding hers was warm and strong, and Cara felt the presence of God in that place. She knew that this marriage was right, and that God was going to bless them.

"Who gives the bride?" George Camrose said, and then his eyes suddenly widened. Cara was looking at him, and she saw that George was very startled.

"*I do!*"

The voice was loud, and every eye in the church turned to face the back. Cara and Phil both turned involuntarily, and Cara gasped when she saw her father wearing a dress suit with a flower in his lapel, standing at the entrance to the aisle. His eyes were fixed on her, and he held himself stiffly. Then he began to move, and Cara felt faint. Phil, feeling her sway, reached over and put his arm around her waist and held her steady. "Well, I'll be dipped!" he muttered. "Look at that. I reckon I've got me a mighty good father-in-law."

Cara watched as her father came down the aisle. He limped slightly, but he held himself upright and his bulky form was much like a ship plowing through heavy waters. He stopped long enough to reach down to Alice, who was sitting at the end of the front pew. He pulled her to her feet, and Cara saw her mother's face drain of color with shock. But Oliver helped her out of the pew, then advanced until he was standing only inches away from the bride and groom. "I've come to give my daughter to this man—and I'm very proud to give her to a man who loves God and clearly loves her with all of his heart."

A murmur of astonishment went over the church, and suddenly Cara stepped away from Phil and threw her arms around her father. She felt his arms close around her, and then she held on to him tightly, whispering, "Father—Father!"

Oliver Lanier held his daughter and looked over her head into Phil's eyes. He stuck out one massive hand, and when Phil took it, Oliver smiled and said, "Take good care of her, son."

"I'll do that. You can depend on it."

And then Cara stepped back and looked at her father. She knew that something was changing—that never again could she go to him as she had as a child, or as an invalid. Still, she was tremendously grateful and proud of him as well, for she knew what it had cost him, and she whispered, "Thank you, Father."

Turning, she took her place again beside Phil, and George Camrose, a twinkle in his eye, said, "If any can show just cause why these two should not be joined together—but no, I think we'll not have any of that, will we?" He waited until the laughter died down, and then he looked at the couple before him and began leading them in their vows, the familiar words about loving and honoring and obeying, about being faithful in sickness and in health. Finally George declared, "I now pronounce you man and wife. You may kiss the bride."

And then Cara felt Phil kissing her gently and tenderly, and they turned and walked back down the aisle. As soon as they were out in the foyer, Phil said, "I'm glad for you, Cara, and I admire your father."

"I'm glad, too. That makes everything perfect."

In the reception room in the basement of the church, Oliver Lanier approached the couple just before leaving. Reaching into his pocket, he pulled out an envelope and handed it to Phil. "A wedding present from a very proud father. Stay in England until it's all spent. But then please bring my little girl back."

"Thank you, sir," Phil said. "I'll see that she is safe."

Then Cara put her arms around her father and kissed him. "You made such a wonderful day for me."

"I've missed a lot of years, Cara, but I'm trying."

Cara watched as her parents left, and then she turned to Phil and said, "I'm your wife now, Phil."

"Yes, you are. Forever and ever."

He took her hand and the two left the church to begin their new life. The bells of the church began to ring, startling a flock of pigeons. They exploded from the steeple like gray smoke and fluttered their wings over the couple as they were about to step into a waiting carriage.

Cara paused to look up at the birds as they mounted on swift wings into the blue sky.

"I feel like one of those, Phil," she said. "I feel like I have wings and I could fly."

"Fly as high as you want, Cara, as long as I fly with you." Phil reached down, put his arm around her, and kissed her. Then with a swift motion he helped her into the carriage, leaped in beside her, and said, "And now, Mrs. Winslow, it's time for us to go to England. Driver, take us to England."

The driver leaned over, his weather-beaten face a study in puzzlement. "Don't reckon as how I can get that fur. This here buggy don't float, ye know!"

"Go as far as you can," Phil said. He put his arm around Cara and hugged her, and then said, "We'll go the rest of the way on our own."